Christine de Pizan

The Book of the City of Ladies

and Other Writings

Christine de Pizan

The Book of the
City of Ladies

and Other Writings

Edited, with an Introduction, by
Sophie Bourgault and Rebecca Kingston

Translated by
Ineke Hardy

Hackett Publishing Company, Inc.
Indianapolis/Cambridge

Copyright © 2018 by Hackett Publishing Company, Inc.

25 24 23 22   2 3 4 5 6 7

For further information, please address
      Hackett Publishing Company, Inc.
      P.O. Box 44937
      Indianapolis, Indiana 46244-0937

      www.hackettpublishing.com

Cover design by Listenberger Design & Associates
Interior design by Laura Clark
Composition by Aptara, Inc.

Library of Congress Cataloging-in-Publication Data

Names: Christine, de Pisan, approximately 1364–approximately 1431, author. |
    Bourgault, Sophie, editor, writer of introduction. | Kingston, Rebecca,
    editor, writer of introduction. | Hardy, Ineke, translator. | Christine,
    de Pisan, approximately 1364–approximately 1431. Livre de la cité des
    dames. English. | Christine, de Pisan, approximately 1364–approximately
    1431. Avision-Christine. Selections. English. | Christine, de Pisan,
    approximately 1364–approximately 1431. Livre du corps de policie.
    Selections. English. | Christine, de Pisan, approximately
    1364–approximately 1431. Lamentacion sur les maux de la France.
    Selections. English.
Title: The book of the city of ladies and other writings / Christine de Pizan ;
    edited, with an introduction, by Sophie Bourgault and Rebecca Kingston ;
    translated by Ineke Hardy.
Description: Indianapolis ; Cambridge : Hackett Publishing Company, Inc.,
    2018. | Includes bibliographical references and index.
Identifiers: LCCN 2018003365 | ISBN 9781624667299 (pbk.) |
    ISBN 9781624667305 (cloth)
Subjects: LCSH: Christine, de Pisan, approximately 1364–approximately
    1431—Translations into English.
Classification: LCC PQ1575 .A2 2018 | DDC 841/.2—dc23
LC record available at https://lccn.loc.gov/2018003365

The paper used in this publication meets the minimum requirements of American
National Standard for Information Sciences—Permanence of Paper for Printed
Library Materials, ANSI Z39.48–1984.

∞

ACKNOWLEDGMENTS

We would both like to thank a number of individuals. First, we would like to express our deep gratitude to Ineke Hardy, since without her expertise, this project would clearly never have been undertaken; we owe a tremendous debt to her and her hard, excellent work. We also would like to thank Alison More of the University of Toronto, who very kindly cast an eye on our Introduction in the last stages of our revisions. Any errors that remain are, naturally, ours. We thank the anonymous reviewers who all offered excellent and detailed suggestions for revision. Thanks to Taylor Putnam for helping us put together the Index. Rick Todhunter, our editor at Hackett Publishing, has been a model of reasonableness and patience. In addition, the staff in the Political Science Departments at the University of Ottawa and the University of Toronto are to be thanked for all the work that goes on behind the scenes and that makes our research work possible. We dedicate this book to our families—particularly to our mothers Ghislaine and Pauline—and to all the up-and-coming members of Christine de Pizan's "City of noble Ladies."

S.B. and R.K.

CONTENTS

INTRODUCTION

> "If all my writings are about sadness,
> it's no surprise, for a heart in mourning cannot have joyous thoughts."
> —Christine de Pizan, *One Hundred Ballads*

In 1429, when the elderly Christine de Pizan was living in a convent near Poissy, sheltered from the turmoil of the French civil war, she penned a passionate poem dedicated to Joan of Arc. It was to be her last work. In this *Ditié de Jehanne d'Arc*[1] (1429), she observed that for more than eleven years, she had not laughed, smiled, or sung once. Tears, worry, and melancholy filled her days. What ended her despair and made her pick up her quill (after a long period of almost complete silence as an author)[2] was Joan of Arc's military prowess and the coronation of Charles VII, which reestablished the claims of the Valois to the French throne. These events filled Christine[3] with hope for the future of France, whose unstable politics had deeply preoccupied her for decades. What a relief it was to see signs of more peaceful times to come. But also, she exclaimed in her *Ditié*, what an honor for women to see this sixteen-year-old accomplish what a hundred thousand men could not.[4]

While the *Ditié's* description of Christine passing long years weeping for France may seem overly dramatic for modern tastes, it is difficult to deny that she had many serious reasons to be distressed: one need only mention the popular revolts that shook France in the late thirteenth and early fourteenth centuries, the tensions associated with the Papal Schism within the

---

1. See her "Poem of Joan of Arc" in *The Writings of Christine de Pizan*, ed. Charity C. Willard (New York: Persea, 1994), 352–63.

2. She only wrote a few short pieces during these eleven years (e.g., "The Hours of Contemplation on the Passion of Our Lord").

3. Medieval writers are often referred to by distinguishing place names, which ought not to be taken as surnames as we know them. Hence, while some medieval writers are now known more popularly by their place of origin (Aquinas, Ockham), it is more common, when employing a shorter version of the name, to refer to figures by their given names (hence Giles of Rome is "Giles," Marsilius of Padua is "Marsilius," and Christine of Pizan is "Christine").

4. "Quel honneur au femenin sexe!" (*sic*) *Ditié* XXXIV, XXXV. Christine probably did not live long enough to witness Joan of Arc's burning in 1431, although the exact year of Christine's death is not known.

Catholic Church,[5] the abundant losses at the Battle of Agincourt, and the seemingly never-ending conflict between the two royal houses, the Orleanists and the Burgundians. Christine's own presentation as a "melancholic" and tearful writer ought to be noted here, for it is a self-description she used repeatedly for rhetorical and political purposes.[6] Tears and lamentations were common topoi in medieval literature, and, as we will see throughout this volume, Christine considered them to be legitimate and politically significant forms of action.[7]

As readers will discover on reading her autobiographical *Christine's Vision* (1405),[8] it was not only the older Christine who had reasons to weep. The young Christine also had many sorrows starting in 1380, when her family's fortunes began to grow sour. Things had gone fairly well since 1365, when Christine's father Thomas de Pizan accepted a prestigious post as astrologer and physician at the French court and soon moved his young family from Venice to Paris. (Born on Italian soil ca. 1364, Christine would stay in France until her death.) She describes her youth at court as joyful, financially comfortable, and untroubled, and she expresses gratitude for her early contacts with books, her exceptional education, and the erudite conversations at court to which she was privy (notwithstanding a slightly dismissive line where she notes that she only collected the "scraps" from her father's scholarly table).[9] At the age of fifteen, she would marry a young court notary, Étienne de Castel—a happy union that led to the birth of three children (two of whom survived childhood). But as we learn in her *Vision,* soon enough misfortune started compromising this highly privileged and happy life: in 1380 the death of Thomas de Pizan's patron, King Charles V, quickly led to a sharp decline in her father's financial situation and social status. Her father also seems to have become increasingly the

---

5. For some of Christine's reflections on this "terrible illness" ("abominable plaie"), see her *Book of the Deeds and Good Morals of the Wise King Charles V,* in particular III.51–62.

6. E.g., "Some people keep on asking me why I am so melancholic and why they don't see me anymore singing or laughing," she writes in her Ballad no. 18. Louise d'Arcens notes that the tears shed for her husband were particularly significant for Christine because they served to reassert her chastity and virtue as a faithful widow. See d'Arcens, "Christine de Pizan's Grieving Body Politic," in *Healing the Body Politic: The Political Thought of Christine de Pizan,* ed. Karen Green and Constant J. Mews (Turnhout: Brepols, 2005): 201–26.

7. See the examples of the Sabine women and Argia (in *The Book of the City of Ladies* II.17, 33, and in her *Lamentation on France's Ills,* in this volume).

8. See excerpts following the Introduction.

9. Christine de Pizan, *The Book of the Mutability of Fortune* 1.6.

object of virulent attacks at court from detractors of his science (something Christine herself avoids mentioning in her *Vision* [III.5]).

Less than ten years after the king's death, both Christine's father and husband would pass away, leaving her with the task of dealing with fraudulent creditors and many complicated lawsuits over her husband's estate (some of which would take more than ten years to resolve). As readers of this volume will see, the indignation Christine expresses as she recounts her legal and financial ordeals in the *Vision* is striking: she is angry at the crooks who stole her children's inheritance; she is upset with her late husband and her father, who should have had the good sense to inform their wives of their financial/legal affairs (a theme that reappears later in her works when she discusses the importance for women to have extensive knowledge of household finances). She is also infuriated by the malicious and contemptuous response she gets, as a woman, from various Parisian magistrates. Witness her indignation when she denounces, in her *Vision,* the way French princes, magistrates, judges, and knights abuse and mistreat widows: "poor widows, robbed of their possessions [...] The nobles do not take pity on them, nor do the clergy, great or small; and the princes do not bother to listen to them." Indeed, "harassed by the powerful," these widows must "travel the roads of Hell."[10] The decline in social and financial status following her father's and husband's deaths would be—notwithstanding what she would later write about the dignity of poverty[11]—a source of shame and anxiety. And yet another cause for her melancholy as a young widow in her mid-twenties was a rumor circulating to the effect that she had taken a lover (a particularly painful rumor to be the object of, when one is convinced—as were many of her contemporaries—that "chastity is women's supreme virtue").[12]

It is during those years of intense melancholy—roughly around 1393—that Christine started writing poetry both to express the grief she felt over her husband's premature death and to obtain some badly needed extra income

---

10. See the excerpts in this volume. Cf. *The Treasure of the City of Ladies* III.4.

11. E.g., *The Book of the Body Politic* III.10. Cf. *The Treasure of the City of Ladies* III.13. Naturally, there is a difference between voluntary and involuntary poverty. For a discussion of Christine's fear of poverty, see Otto G. Oexle, "Christine et les pauvres," in *The City of Scholars: New Approaches to Christine de Pizan,* ed. M. Zimmermann & D. De Rentiis (New York: Walter de Gruyter, 1994), 206–20.

12. See *The Book of the City of Ladies* II.37.

through the support of wealthy patrons at court.[13] The year 1399 represents an important turning point in her life as an author, for it was then, she tells us in her *Vision,* that she largely put aside poetry (these "pretty" and "light" works) and started devoting her attention to prose works dedicated to what she regarded as "weightier subjects."[14] (This, we should note, ought not to be taken as grounds to dismiss her poetic oeuvre: Christine's poetry is much more than simple *belles lettres.* In it one finds much that speaks to her later political commitments.) Now, her first six years dealing with more explicitly political subjects were highly productive. In addition to the important pieces she devoted to answering the misogynist defenders of the *Romance of the Rose* at court (to which we will return below), Christine also composed her first very long prose work, *The Book of the Mutability of Fortune* (a meditation on the role of Fortune in world history and in her own life), as well as a well-researched, detailed biography of Charles V commissioned by Philip, duke of Burgundy. More significantly for our purposes, it is during those years (1404–1405) that Christine also wrote *The Book of the City of Ladies,* her ideologically charged *Epistle to Isabeau of Bavaria, Queen of France,* her *Book of Man's Integrity,* and, shortly after, *The Treasure of the City of Ladies.*

The years after 1405 were equally productive. Amid growing tensions at court, Christine de Pizan composed several works that sought—indirectly or directly—to affect the course of political events and to help decrease the instability plaguing France: *The Book of the Body Politic* (ca. 1407), *The Book of Deeds of Arms and of Chivalry* (1410), and *The Book of Peace* (ca. 1412–1414). The instability and friction at court had begun roughly a decade earlier, when Charles VI had his first bout of severe mental illness. Since the king had some moments of lucidity and most nobles wanted to keep up appearances,

---

13. The oft-repeated statement that Christine was the "first female professional writer" calls for a certain interpretative caution. Like most of her male contemporaries, Christine was hardly a modern "independent writer": she was supported financially by numerous patrons (e.g., Jean, duke of Berry; Louis, duke of Orléans; Philippe, duke of Burgundy; Jean, duke of Burgundy; Queen Isabeau), and she did eventually have access to some money through her husband's estate. That said, we should note that, unlike many men with whom she debated (most notably during the quarrel over the *Romance of the Rose*), she did not have an official position at court nor at the University of Paris. It is thus unsurprising that she had to supplement her income by working as a copyist. (Recall that in Christine's days, the printing press obviously did not exist.)

14. In this volume, see *Christine's Vision* III.10. Tracy Adams (in *Christine de Pizan and the Fight for France*) challenges Christine's narrative of "rupture" and her view that her pre-1399 writings were "light" and politically insignificant. Cf. Charity C. Willard, "Christine de Pizan: From Poet to Political Commentator," in *Politics, Gender and Genre,* ed. Margaret Brabant (Boulder, Colo.: Westview, 1992), 17–32.

for a while few in court saw the urgent need to think seriously about having a clear plan of action during his breakdowns (which obviously intensified the rivalry and insecurity among the dukes). Although Philip, duke of Burgundy was able to take on princely authority alongside Queen Isabeau of Bavaria when the king was indisposed, things got more complicated and conflictual after Philip's death in 1404.[15] The Burgundians and the Orleanists (later to be referred to as the Armagnacs) became bitter enemies, leading to a serious threat of civil war.

It is in the midst of these complicated rivalries (in 1406/1407) and out of concern for France's deteriorating politics that Christine wrote her *Book of the Body Politic* (excerpts are included in this volume)—a book heavily inspired by John of Salisbury's *Policraticus* (ca. 1159).[16] Medieval scholarship generally centered around commentary on leading authorities. In this important work of medieval political thought, John of Salisbury (ca. 1120–1180)—himself commenting on a work of pseudo-Plutarch[17]—described the good political community as analogous to a healthy and well-ordered human body, with priests representing the soul, the king the head, and other subjects (counselors, peasants, etc.) representing the various limbs.[18] The body politic is

---

15. His ambitious son John the Fearless soon came to resent the fact that he did not have the same authority as his father. John begrudged the shift of power into the hands of the king's brother, Louis, duke of Orléans (whose intimate complicity with Isabeau of Bavaria John resented). Things escalated when the dauphin Louis of Guyenne was briefly "kidnapped" by John the Fearless, who was trying to foment rebellion in Paris. His greatest success in fomenting rebellion would come during the summer of 1413 during the Cabochien Revolt. Christine's *Book of Peace* would be written roughly in the midst of this bloody conflict.

16. For her stories she made ample use of Roman historian Valerius Maximus' *Memorable Deeds and Sayings*—a collection of anecdotes from ancient Greece and ancient Rome that was extremely popular in the Middle Ages. See the introduction to *Memorable Deeds and Sayings*, trans. and ed. Henry J. Walker (Indianapolis: Hackett, 2004).

17. Pseudo-Plutarch means that the text John *claimed* to be drawing from has since been demonstrated not to have been written by Plutarch despite medieval beliefs to the contrary.

18. It is not clear whether John was drawing his account of Plutarch from an apocryphal manuscript, or whether he indeed invoked Plutarch's authority for an account of the body politic that was largely his own (although inspired by classical sources). Subtitled *Of the Frivolities of Courtiers and the Footprints of Philosophers*, John's book contained, among other things, a detailed critique of court life and a treatment of the importance of wise counsel—two themes that are present in Christine's work. But if John placed the priesthood in the soul in his account of the body analogy (thereby granting the church and the pope great authority), Christine located clerks in the lower limbs (close to such groups as merchants and peasants). For a discussion of the differences between John and Christine, see Kate L. Forhan, "Polycracy, Obligation and Revolt: The Body Politic in John of Salisbury and Christine de Pizan," in Brabant, *Politics*, 33–52.

an image we still use today to talk about political community, albeit in ways distinct from John. Like the *Policraticus*, Christine's *Book of the Body Politic* falls clearly into the "mirror-for-princes" tradition of advice books dedicated to the moral cultivation of rulers offering both arguments and examples from ancient history to inspire self-examination in the ruler. While the book was officially dedicated to Charles VI, Christine chiefly had the moral education of the young dauphin in mind. But Christine in this text also cautions the quarreling French nobles about the consequences of their poor conduct and about the excessive taxation of the lower order. A good prince, Christine insists, should avoid "sucking the blood of his poor commoners" (I.10) and ensure that the rich pay their fair share (I.11). A prudent ruler must also surround himself with wise and experienced advisers (I.19–20) and try to be at once feared and loved (I.21).

By the time Christine completed *The Book of the Body Politic*, she was an accomplished and reputable writer (she was known and read both inside and outside of France),[19] and she was widely regarded as a competent political commentator. Readers should not be misled by the claims of humility one finds at the beginning of many of her works (a conventional authorial practice). Christine was convinced she had the duty and the knowledge needed to guide and advise princes and princesses competently, despite—or perhaps *because of*—her position on the margins, as an outsider, as an Italian émigrée and a female writer.[20] She emphasized her role as a capable dispenser of political wisdom most clearly in her *Vision* in 1405, but she also briefly alluded to it in 1403, in *The Long Path of Learning*. Toward the end of this very long narrative poem, the chief protagonist, Christine herself, is told that she must share her knowledge with "les grands princes français" and help serve the cause of French peace.[21] This is what she continued doing for the next decade, most passionately in her 1410 *Lamentation on France's Ills*, where Christine

19. In England, her work was known by King Richard II (whose close ally John Montagu was Christine's patron), and she later received an official invitation from his successor, Henry IV. Earlier, Christine had also received an invitation to go to the court of the duke Visconti of Milan (one she declined).

20. See in this volume *The Book of the Body Politic* III.7 for one brief appeal to her Italian origins as a means to prove her "impartiality" and good judgment about French politics.

21. For a modern French edition, see *Le Chemin de longue étude*, ed. Andrea Tarnowski (Paris: Poche, 2000).

invites hot-tempered young princes to end their destructive battles.[22] We also
see her denounce the starvation, brutalization, and plundering of peasants
by the military (a similar indictment of uncontrolled soldiers is found in her
Book of the Body Politic I.9). But the person she most directly addresses here is
the duke of Berry, brother of the late Charles V. The duke is asked (alongside
the queen) to intervene swiftly in the bloody feud between the Orleanists
and the Burgundians. Note that in general, Christine avoided taking a very
clear side in the feud between the royal houses: if some have interpreted
this as a cowardly posture or as political opportunism, others have seen it as
emblematic of her lifelong commitment to peace.

It is unlikely that Christine truly believed her *Lamentation on France's Ills*
would have an immediate impact on French peace; Tracy Adams (2014) is
probably right to suggest that the *Lamentation* was more modestly intended
to be a symbolic, ideologically charged defense of Isabeau's authority and
of the duke of Berry's as well.[23] Like other medieval writers around her, Christine wanted and expected her *Lamentation* (and, indeed, many of her works)
to be read aloud in courtly circles. And it is through such public readings
and through the circulation of different copies of her manuscripts that the
sociopolitical influence of her work could be felt.[24] Indeed, even the poetry
or letters that may appear to us to have been meant for purely private consumption were not seen that way by Christine. Take, for instance, the *Moral
Teachings* she wrote for her son when he left for the English court: it is very
probable that the didactic instructions to guide her son on the road to virtue
were intended to be circulated widely. To this extent there was an implied
pedagogy, and hence an intent of broader social and political import, in much
of her writing.

We can only speculate as to whether the *Lamentation* was widely circu-
lated/heard. But be that as it may, we know that the duke of Berry did not
succeed in "seizing the bridle firmly," as Christine urged him to do in 1410: in
the next few years, the conflict between the Burgundians and the Orleanists/
Armagnacs escalated, leading to particularly bloody episodes in the summer

---

22. Readers might see striking resonances between Christine's *Lamentation* and Erasmus' *The
Complaint for Peace* (1521).

23. See also Karen Green, "Isabeau de Bavière and the Political Philosophy of Christine de
Pizan," *Historical Reflections* 32, no. 2 (2006): 247–72.

24. For more on this convention of medieval literature, see Joyce Coleman, *Public Reading and
the Reading Public in Late Medieval England and France* (Cambridge: Cambridge University
Press, 1996).

of 1413 (when Parisian butchers, encouraged by John the Fearless, revolted) and in 1418 (when the Burgundians took Paris and executed countless individuals tied in one way or another to the Orleanists). This is when Christine decided to leave Paris, and then likely joined her daughter Marie at a Dominican convent in Poissy. In July 1429 she wrote her last known piece, her *Poem of Joan of Arc*, and it is believed that sometime shortly after she passed away at Poissy. She left us with an impressive oeuvre encompassing an incredibly vast array of genres: lyric poetry (ballades, complaints, virelais, rondeaux), rhymed and prose epistles, mirrors for princes, a treatise on chivalry and on arms, detailed biographies of kings, world histories, and so on. Despite this variety, her work is driven by a consistent and deep commitment to peaceful politics, to virtue, and to women's self-respect. Let us turn, then, to one of the works in which we find the clearest expression of this triple commitment: *The Book of the City of Ladies*.

The Book of the City of Ladies

Christine and Medieval Political Thought

The Book of the City of Ladies is not easily classified within the context of traditional approaches to the study of medieval political thought. Let us consider, for instance, the three debates singled out by medievalist Marcia Colish as most emblematic of medieval reflection on politics.[25] The first concerns the nature of the relations between the church and state. While thinkers embraced a singular Christian commonwealth and the complementary functions of church and state, the precise relationship between secular and religious authority (i.e., who had authority to do what—and particularly

---

25. Marcia Colish, *Medieval Foundations of the Western Intellectual Tradition, 400–1400* (New Haven, Conn.: Yale University Press, 1997), chap. 26. Compare with other accounts (many of which also stress the theme of princely virtue and advice), such as Antony Black, *Political Thought in Europe, 1250–1450* (Cambridge: Cambridge University Press, 1992); J. H. Burns, *Cambridge History of Medieval Political Thought* (Cambridge: Cambridge University Press, 1988); Joseph Canning, *Ideas of Power in the Late Middle Ages, 1296–1417* (Cambridge: Cambridge University Press, 2011); Cary J. Nederman and Kate Langdon Forhan, eds., *Readings in Medieval Political Theory, 1100–1400* (Indianapolis: Hackett, 2000); Ewart Lewis, *Medieval Political Ideas*, 2 vols. (London: Routledge, 1954); Walter Ullmann, *Medieval Political Thought* (New York: Penguin, 1965).

who could appoint leading church officials) was a matter of controversy.[26] A second key debate in medieval political thought according to Colish is that surrounding the structure of power *within* ecclesiastical circles. Discussions focused on the extent of the authority of the pope vis-à-vis the various councils of the Church, and their link to reflections on constitutional and institutional design as well as possible means by which corrupt or heretical church officials could be brought to account.[27] A third focus is the nature of monarchy. The feudal relation between king or suzerain and vassal was typically understood as a contractual one with reciprocal obligations and benefits. As time went on, however, principles of seigneurial consultation and consent gave way to more unambiguously monarchical attributes (including divine right and increased recourse to Roman law) that served to reinforce the preeminence of royal office. There was much debate over the nature of authority, obligation, obedience, and justice.[28]

Christine de Pizan's *Book of the Body Politic* does offer some insight into these themes (what constitutes a good monarchy, what are the reciprocal duties of rulers and ruled, etc.). Readers could also turn to Christine's biography of Charles V for reflections on the Papal Schism and the complex relations between temporal and church authorities. But things seem less evident for *The Book of the City of Ladies*. While this work mentions some contemporary rulers and events, and while its author recognizes God's role in ordering heaven and earth, this is not offered in the service of a detailed, theoretical account of the sources of authority and their respective claims. Absent too is a discussion of Roman law. Nevertheless, the work does participate in another genre of medieval thought (one that would remain central into the Renaissance—just think of Erasmus and Machiavelli): namely, advice to princes and commentary on the qualities and historical examples of effective rule. Christine also engages directly with medieval political thought by adapting the trope of the Heavenly City as developed

---

26. That is in part because rulers of regional monarchies (as well as the Holy Roman Emperor) saw their rule as sanctioned by divine right and their function as in part to oversee the welfare of their people. Augustine's *City of God* was a key source for the complementarity thesis. See Colish, *Medieval Foundations,* 336–37.

27. This pitted so-called Papalists against what have been called Conciliarists (who insisted that supreme authority within the Church was located in the ecumenical council, which could go against the pope).

28. See Ullmann, *Medieval Political Thought,* 120. In his view, "It was in the contents of justice that political ideas in the Middle Ages can be recognized, and it was the concept of justice which flavoured—and makes understandable—political ideology in the Middle Ages" (16).

by Augustine (to which we will return below). Moreover, as readers will see, the structure of authority within Christine's *Book of the City of Ladies* echoes a conventional medieval ideal, with the saints and protectors of the laws of God occupying the highest echelons of authority and helping preserve the unity and goodness of the city.[29]

But if it remains true that, on the whole, Christine does not approach her discussion in the standard terms by which political argument in the medieval era has been defined, in what sense can *The Book of the City of Ladies* be understood as a worthy contribution to traditions of political reflection? There are at least three ways to see this text as engaging with wider debates in political thought. The first relates to the idea of the "city." Her invocation of the theme of the city as a central metaphor shows that she is immersed in classical and medieval traditions of political thinking, ones that offered competing visions of the city. Christine's engagement with authors such as Aristotle, Boethius, and Saint Augustine (and through Augustine, Plato) makes *The Book of the City of Ladies* one important illustration of the medieval reception and appropriation of certain strands of classical thought. (The metaphor of the body politic making its way through Plutarch's "Life of Coriolanus" and Livy to a broad array of authors including John of Salisbury was also important for the development of Christine's political thought more broadly outside this work.[30])

Second, *The Book of the City of Ladies* contributes to philosophical debates about the nature of the virtues and their place in the well-lived life. Christine offers a portrait of human excellences, exemplified in heroes, saints, and those whose actions resulted in great benefit to humankind. In particular, the text offers an intriguing portrait of three forms of excellence—reason, rectitude, and justice—personified by the three Ladies, who are Christine's interlocutors in the text and who populate Christine's city in speech according to their respective mandates. Some insight into Christine's understanding of those qualities can be gained by studying the particular characteristics of each of the three Ladies and the women they champion.

---

29. The structure of her ideal city could be said to be in line with broad currents of what Ullmann has called "hierocratic political thought" (where the authority of rulers is said to *descend* from God—unlike in "ascending" or populist accounts of rulers' authority—for instance, that found in Marsilius of Padua). Compare Ullmann's account with Black, *Political Thought in Europe*.

30. For a brief but insightful overview of this tradition, see George Hale, *The Body Politic: A Political Metaphor in Renaissance English Literature* (The Hague: Mouton, 1971).

Third, Christine offers a corrective to many classical and medieval texts because they failed to do justice to the nature, capabilities, and aspirations of women. On a broader scale Christine was also striking against what she considered to be excessively narrow readings of history and intellectual culture. In view of the few minute examples in the early history of political thought devoted to women's relation to (and capacity for) the active and contemplative life,[31] Christine offers a uniquely focused and rich analysis. In her rehabilitation of the contributions of women throughout history, she was questioning the authority of key writers in established traditions and encouraging a more critical and creative reading of the past (and those who wrote about it), as well as challenging received opinion. In an intellectual climate that was often extremely deferential to textual authority, Christine offered a critical reconsideration of established doctrine and interpretation.

It has been argued that her work represents a kind of transitional point between the medieval and Renaissance world. Indeed, Christine's writings remind us to avoid drawing too stark a line between the Middle Ages and early modernity.[32] The fact that it is the medieval period that witnessed the first robust defense of women *written by a woman* can obviously shatter facile readings of the "darkness" of the Middle Ages. Attending more widely to Christine's work could bring new intellectual resources to contemporary efforts to think about women's struggle for voice in political and literary life.

To explore in more detail the significance of this work, the following sections will consider *The Book of the City of Ladies*' relation to the preceding quarrel over the *Romance of the Rose* and to key themes and authors in classical and medieval political thought, theology, and literature. Following this, we will discuss the text's overall structure and main arguments, then briefly conclude by considering Christine's significance for gender studies today.

---

31. We can think here of Plato's discussion of the desirability of including women in the guardian class in his *Republic*. While Aristotle is sometimes regarded as the source of a long misogynistic tradition of reflection, some commentators have proposed more nuanced readings. See, for example, Arlene Saxonhouse, "Family, Polity and Unity: Aristotle on Socrates' Community of Wives," *Polity* 15, no. 2 (Winter 1982): 202–19.

32. Walter Ullmann argues that Christine's work (especially her *Book of the Body Politic)* is particularly helpful to flag the "medieval foundations of Renaissance humanism" (the title of his well-known 1977 work). The many protofeminist texts produced by Italian women not too long after Christine's death are also powerful correctives to simplistic (and still pervasive) readings of history. Think, for instance, of the writings of Laura Cereta (1469–1499) and Lucrezia Marinella (ca. 1571–1653).

The Romance of the Rose *and Classical and Medieval Misogyny*

Christine de Pizan wrote *The Book of the City of Ladies* just after she had been involved in an extensive literary debate over the way in which women were portrayed in a popular work of medieval courtly literature, the *Romance of the Rose*. Part of this work had been written a century earlier (ca. 1230) by Guillaume de Lorris, but an important (and misogynist) addition to the work had been added by Jean de Meun in the 1270s. The quarrel essentially began in the summer of 1401, when Christine sent an indignant letter to a royal secretary in response to his short treatise praising Jean's celebrated work.[33] She was enraged at the author's portrayal of women as naturally deceptive and dishonest, a picture that for Jean justified a wide range of manipulative practices on the part of men. Soon enough, Christine would be involved in a heated exchange with two other royal secretaries, who attempted to intimidate her, demanding that she "confess her error" and "make amends" for her disrespectful reading of Jean—a faulty reading they tried to explain away by pointing to the limited faculties and overly "emotional nature" possessed by her sex (standard fare of misogynist literature). Indignant, Christine stuck to her position and insisted that being a woman was not at all a defect: "I do not in truth consider this [being a woman] at all a reproach or slander, because of the consolation arising from the noble memory and continued experience of a great abundance of noble women who have been and still are most worthy of praise and accustomed to every virtuous activity."[34] It is these numerous noble women who would soon serve as the building blocks for her City of Ladies.

From one perspective, *The Book of the City of Ladies* can be seen as Christine's more comprehensive statement in defense of women as sparked by this quarrel. She provides a detailed and robust defense going well beyond the *Romance of the Rose* to reframe and address a more generalized tradition of

---

33. In that letter to Jean de Montreuil, one can find a few of the arguments and exempla Christine uses in the *City of Ladies* (e.g., I.13). For a collection of the documents circulated during the quarrel, see David F. Hult, *Debate of the "Romance of the Rose"* (Chicago: University of Chicago Press, 2010). See also Georges Duby, *Love and Marriage in the Middle Ages* (Chicago: University of Chicago Press, 1997), chap. 5.

34. See Christine's letter in Hult, *Debate of the "Romance of the Rose,"* 97. Adding to some of her adversaries' ire, Christine decided, in February 1402, to send a copy of the letters and documents exchanged in this debate to Queen Isabeau of Bavaria.

misogyny in classical, theological, and literary sources.[35] But *The Book of the City of Ladies* rarely cites specific intellectual adversaries by name. It fixes its attention on several writers who are representative of a larger literary trend. One such writer is Matheolus, a late thirteenth-century author whose work incites the great distress of the protagonist Christine in the opening scene of the book (I.2): the work in question is *The Book of the Lamentations*, a long diatribe against marriage translated from Latin into French toward the end of the fourteenth century, which painted women as great sources of suffering for men.

Matheolus was not unique in painting women as morally depraved or inferior. Many ancient and medieval authors had depicted both women's souls and bodies as deficient. For instance, Aristotle (whose authority was immense in the Middle Ages) suggested in his *Generation of Animals* (737a26–30) that woman was to be regarded as a deformed man. Augustine had also claimed that the inferior biological features of women (regardless of a woman's actual quality of character and equality of soul) inevitably tended to corrupt men. While not making women fully responsible for corporal sin, Augustine noted that the nature of women on earth encourages corruption.[36] Misogynist authors in medieval times also liked to turn to particular biblical passages to stress the moral deficiency and inferiority of women (e.g., I Corinthians 11:3–15). Moreover, Roman writers Ovid, Horace, and Juvenal provided considerable fodder for the articulation of misogynist attitudes in medieval literature—depicting in various ways women as the masters of manipulation, temptation, and deceit. For instance, several stories contained in Ovid's *Metamorphoses* ended up in the fourteenth-century anonymous *Ovid moralisé*—a misogynist text Christine explicitly targets for the significant amount of self-hatred it can provoke in women. The existing narratives of the lives of saints

---

35. Direct or explicit references to Jean de Meun are rare (see, e.g., II.25), but readers can guess at various points of the text that he is indeed one of the targets of a particular refutation.

36. "What happened was that the women who had been depraved in morals in the earthly city, that is, in the community of the earth-born, were loved for their physical beauty by the sons of God, that is, the citizens of the other City, on pilgrimage in this world.... Hence the abandonment of a greater good, one that is confined to good people, led to a fall towards a good of little importance, one that is not confined to good people, but common to good and bad alike. Thus the sons of God were captivated by love for the daughters of men, and in order to enjoy them as wives, they abandoned the godly behaviour they had maintained in the holy community and lapsed into the morality of the earth-born society." Augustine, *City of God* 15.22 (London: Penguin, 1972). So, again, Augustine does not regard women as the sole origin of sin, but he underscores the regrettable impact that their earthly nature has on men. This may be why Augustine is insistent that women remain submissive in the household and silent and invisible in the public world.

as compiled by Vincent de Beauvais in the *Speculum Maius*, the "Great Mirror" from which Christine borrows heavily, also contained their own share of misogynist assumptions regarding female sexuality and bodies. Certainly a great deal has been documented about the slander against women in classical and medieval sources (literary, philosophical, theological, or medical). The character Christine expresses dismay at the prevalence of the view that woman is "a vessel filled with all sorts of evil and vices" (I.1).

But far from shunning classical and theological texts in light of some of their misogynist failings, Christine proposes to return to them—reinterpreting particular passages in light of the writers' moral deficiencies and underscoring overlooked ones. Indeed, her response is not to turn her back on "the canon" but to reappropriate some of its arguments and to emulate its authors' bold critical, philosophical ambitions (I.2) in order to produce a robust defense of woman.[37] This is both the basic challenge and the brilliance of the work. Let us now look briefly at a few of the most important authors and texts that informed (directly or indirectly) *The Book of the City of Ladies.*

Classical and Medieval References

The most important reference for Christine's work is Boccaccio's *De mulieribus claris* [*Famous Women* (ca. 1361–1374)], from which roughly three-quarters of Christine's stories of great women are adapted.[38] As we have noted in several editorial notes throughout the text, Christine's usage of Boccaccio is critical: she repeatedly modifies his treatment of particular examples—thereby indicating her awareness that while Boccaccio seems to praise the accomplishments of women, he does so often maligning women's nature.[39] If Christine draws from

---

37. For example, against the view that women have defective bodies and are as such "lesser beings," she will turn to scriptures to argue the contrary: woman is made from a nobler material (a rib, not dirt); woman is made in paradise (unlike man).

38. Boccaccio himself was writing within a tradition of encomium of women that can be traced as far back as Plutarch and his *Excellence of Women*. See Plutarch, "On the Bravery of Women." In *Moralia*, vol. 3, trans. F. C. Babbitt (Cambridge, Mass.: Harvard University Press, 1931). Christine will also briefly invoke Boccaccio's *Decameron,* at II.52, II.59, II.60.

39. Judith Kellogg, "Christine de Pizan and Boccaccio: Rewriting Classical Mythic Tradition," in *Comparative Literature East and West: Traditions and Trends,* vol. 1, ed. Cornelia Moore and Raymond Moody (Honolulu: College of Languages, Linguistics and Literature of the University of Hawaii, 1989), 124–31. See also Patricia A. Phillippy, "Establishing Authority: Boccaccio's *De Claris Mulieribus* and Christine de Pizan's *Le livre de la cité des dames,*" in *Romanic Review* 77 (1986): 167–93. Readers should note that if Christine's work has the term "ladies" (*dames*) in its title, Boccaccio's had "women" (*mulieres*).

Boccaccio, she often modifies his accounts (e.g., those of Semiramis [I.15], Argia [II.17], etc.).[40] Christine's revisionist work in part seeks to *reconstruct* the iconic examples publicized by Boccaccio so as to have them serve more directly the cause of women. One of the places where Christine takes the most distance from Boccaccio is in choosing to include numerous Christian, nonpagan women in her City (Part III), and in resorting to a few *contemporary* examples of great ladies. These differences inject more continuity into Christine's transhistorical narrative of women's great deeds and hence make these deeds a little closer, a little more accessible to her contemporary readers.

If it is Boccaccio's *Famous Women* that provides the great bulk of the figures employed to populate Christine's city, it is Augustine's *City of God* that gives it its dominant metaphor or trope (Christine explicitly refers to Augustine at the end of *The Book of the City of Ladies* [III.18]).[41] As with Boccaccio, she modifies the text. Her City of Ladies, like the City of God, serves as a community, determined by common qualities rather than geography and with members spanning the ages. Although the highest towers of her city are populated with saints, Christine is not offering a theory of divine justification.[42] In particular, at the start the Ladies offer women admission to the city on the basis of their moral qualities and noble deeds, and not directly through divine grace. Still, like in the City of God, the City of Ladies serves as an important focal point for serious readers. This new "virtual" community allows women to think of themselves in new ways and, for a moment, outside of household relations where their role and position was subordinate to that of men. The supplemental form of identity provided by the metaphor of the city allows women to develop a sense of themselves in solidarity with a new transhistorical community of women who have shown great qualities and who have done worthy things. This solidarity with an alternative

---

40. She also contests his perspective on the benefits of civilization (I.39). Moreover, unlike Boccaccio, who presents his exempla in a seemingly random fashion, Christine organizes hers thematically.

41. She also appeals to the authority of Saint Augustine in other works (see, e.g., *Long Path of Learning*, lines 5580–87). Like other medieval writers, Christine's conception of the city was also informed by Cicero's *Republic* (itself fed by Platonism). Like her contemporaries, she was familiar with Cicero's *Republic* largely thanks to Augustine citing long passages from it.

42. While Christine is typically discussed as a thinker of secular matters, some scholars are exploring her work as forms of theological commentary. See, for example, Renate Blumenfeld-Kosinski and Szell Timea, eds., *Images of Sainthood in Medieval Europe* (Ithaca, N.Y.: Cornell University Press, 1991); Barbara Newman, *God and the Goddesses: Vision, Poetry and Belief in the Middle Ages* (Philadelphia: University of Pennsylvania Press, 2016).

community of virtue offers women a deeper sense of their true capacities and more meaningful models of fulfillment. So Christine adopts the metaphor of the city from Augustine to motivate and encourage women who suffer from the same feelings of despondency as the character Christine at the start of *The Book of the City of Ladies*. Since women are invited to identify with this new community, they can find the support and inspiration needed to counteract further misogynist arguments in wider cultural venues—arguments that had undermined their confidence and sense of worth. In addition, and this is a crucial distinction, whereas entry into Augustine's city is in the hands of divine judgment, Christine the author places responsibility for the continued growth and maintenance of her community in the hands of women themselves. Members of the City of Ladies will remain unknown to one another unless women themselves do the work of keeping alive their reputations. In other words, their ultimate destiny as a community lies neither in divine intervention, nor in fate, but rather in the continued acts of virtue and the continued efforts of mutual recognition and remembrance. In the opening remarks of *The Treasure of the City of Ladies*, she offers a recommendation for widespread feminine vigilance to ensure that others, and especially the "wild and hard to tame," acknowledge the city and emulate virtue.[43] The building of the City of Ladies is presented to us as an *ongoing* enterprise—one that can be sustained and *strengthened* through constant additional acts of virtue and solidarity on women's part. Christine depicts her city not simply as a community but more specifically as a fortress—one that provides, all at once, deterrence against future attacks, security, healing, and consolation (II.12).[44]

Consolation is one of the chief motivations for Christine's construction of her city (and it was also an important literary genre in medieval times): think especially of the opening scene where the protagonist Christine (isolated in her small "cell" or study[45]) falls into despair and, in a dream-vision, receives the visit of three personified Virtues who seek to comfort through reasoned discussion. The imprint of Boethius' *Consolation of Philosophy* (ca. 523) is here striking, as it is in Part III of *Christine's Vision* (see excerpts in

---

43. Christine de Pizan, *The Treasure of the City of Ladies or Book of the Three Virtues*, ed. Sarah Lawson (London: Penguin, 2003), I.1.

44. In Guillaume de Lorris and Jean de Meun's *Romance of the Rose* (lines 3583–3620), chastity is locked up inside a fortress. She is to be assaulted and conquered.

45. Many commentators have noted that the original French *cele* (cell) was probably meant to evoke Boethius' prison cell.

this volume).[46] A Roman philosopher and consul who was wrongly accused of treason, Boethius (ca. 480–524) wrote his *Consolation* in prison, as he was waiting for his trial and reflecting—with the help of Lady Philosophy—on God, evil, death, and human happiness. While *The Book of the City of Ladies* does not tackle the very same questions, the imprint of Boethius' *consolatio* can certainly be felt.

Another important source and interlocutor for Christine de Pizan is Aristotle.[47] Medievalist Walter Ullmann has praised Christine for being "one of the earliest women to have made intelligent use of Aristotle's *Politics* and *Ethics.*"[48] Now, like most of her contemporaries, Christine's knowledge of Aristotle was largely (albeit not exclusively) secondhand: many of the claims and sayings she attributes to Aristotle came from her reading of authors such as Cicero, Seneca, Boethius, Valerius Maximus, Thomas Aquinas, and Giles of Rome (all important sources of inspiration for her work).[49] Christine obviously greatly admired "the Philosopher": witness the favorable invocations of his views on justice (more on this below) and political regimes.[50] But despite

---

46. For other examples of Boethius' influence on Christine, see her *Long Path of Learning* and her "Letter on the Prison of Human Life" (excerpts can be found in *The Selected Writings of Christine de Pizan,* ed. Renate Blumenfeld-Kosinski, trans. Renate Blumenfeld-Kosinski and Kevin Brownlee [New York: W. W. Norton, 1997]).

47. For a discussion of how crucial Aristotle was for medieval political thought, see C. Nederman, *Medieval Aristotelianism and Its Limits* (New York: Routledge, 1997); Black, *Political Thought in Europe.*

48. But this praise is somewhat countered by his view that "there are few, if any, original ideas" in Christine's *Book of the Body Politic* (185). The works of scholars such as C. Nederman, K. L. Forhan, and K. Green have corrected this. See our Suggestions for Further Reading section for complete references.

49. This is unsurprising given that the "revival" of Aristotle began during the late thirteenth century. The first translation of Aristotle's *Politics* into Latin appeared ca. 1260. It is likely that Christine had access to the French translations of Aristotle's *Ethics* and *Politics* produced by Nicolas Oresme, thanks to the literary enthusiasm of Charles V—whose interest in translations Christine celebrates in her biography of the king (III.12). For Giles of Rome's role as chief transmitter of Aristotle's political thought in the Middle Ages, see Joseph Canning, *A History of Medieval Political Thought, 300–1450* (London: Routledge, 1996). There is no room here to discuss the various sources of Christine's knowledge of Aristotle (and the consistency or coherence of her usage of his concepts in her work). Readers can consult K. Green's and M. Richarz's chapters in Green and Mews, *Healing the Body Politic,* and K. L. Forhan, *The Political Theory of Christine de Pizan* (Burlington, Vt.: Ashgate, 2002).

50. In this volume, see *The Book of the Body Politic,* especially I.9, I.19 and III.2. Also cf. *Book of the Deeds and Good Morals of King Charles V,* where Aristotle's authority is repeatedly invoked (e.g., III.1–3, 6-8). Like most of her contemporaries, she did not use Aristotle to discuss critically the virtues of various regimes—an issue to which we will return in our conclusion.

her respect for Aristotle, Christine also put forward many arguments in favor of the female sex that implicitly reject Aristotle's views. As one example, Christine's defense of the value of female speech could be said to counter Aristotle's famous quip in *The Politics* (1260a28) that "silence is woman's glory."[51] Christine was very likely aware of the fact that for the peripatetic philosopher, women were neither fit to speak with authority nor to rule (whether in the household or in the city). Aristotle insisted that while women's souls have a deliberative element, they lack authority (*Politics* 1260a13), which had implications for their good judgment or prudence (the crucial virtue for politics in Aristotle's view). In Part I of *The Book of the City of Ladies,* readers will see Christine challenge this Aristotelian view that good judgment is exclusively found in men (I.43–48).

If Christine engaged with "old" or venerated interlocutors such as Aristotle, Cicero, Augustine, Marsilius of Padua, and Giles of Rome, she can also be credited for having brought *new* voices to the existing conversations in France about good morals and good politics. For instance, Christine was among the first serious readers of Dante's *Divine Comedy,*[52] and it was largely thanks to her literary enthusiasm that Dante (1265–1321) became known in France. That, mixed with her familiarity and enthusiasm for Italian poet Petrarch (especially his *Remedies for Good and Bad Fortune*), has helped Christine de Pizan earn, in many literary histories, the titles of first female humanist and "French Petrarch."[53] Let us see now, more specifically, what is largely responsible for Christine earning yet another (and better-known) title: one of the first true literary defenders of the female sex.

The Organization and Rhetorical Force of The Book of the City of Ladies

We have suggested that *The Book of the City of Ladies* is a significant text in the history of political thought. But we must attend to its distinctive

---

51. The quip is actually Sophocles', but Aristotle cites it approvingly.

52. The imprint of Dante is particularly significant in her *Long Path of Learning.* For a discussion of Christine's affinities with Dante, see J. Broad and K. Green, *A History of Women's Political Thought in Europe, 1400–1700* (Cambridge: Cambridge University Press, 2009), chap. 1, and Julia S. Holderness, "Compilation, Commentary, and Conversation in Christine de Pizan," *Essays in Medieval Studies* 20 (2003): 47–55.

53. Christine's father may have known Francesco Petrarca (1304–1374) personally. Although quite familiar with some of his work, she cites him explicitly only once in *The Book of the City of Ladies* (at II.7).

approach to the subject. The first thing to note is that Christine does not begin with a conceptual inquiry into the nature of justice. Rather, the book begins with a deep and disturbing *feeling* of injustice over women not being given their due (recall that Christine understood justice—following in the footsteps of Aristotle and his heirs—as "giving each his [or *her,* in this case] due"). The character Christine, overwhelmed by how ancient and medieval authors could often demean women, expresses a deep despair. Christine uses the dramatic opening scene to underscore the manner in which this literary demeaning causes women to feel an inescapable shame for their very nature. The character Christine exemplifies how norms of cultural maligning go deep: she is denied a legitimate expression of anger and instead is left to express herself through tears and self-doubt. The degree to which the character Christine resists, at first, the message of the Three Ladies indeed demonstrates the extent to which she has internalized the cultural norms concerning women. The book represents an emotional journey from despair and self-loathing to confidence and dignity. It is a dramatic righting of a wrong, a vivid depiction of the emotional effects of an injustice being rectified.

The long dream-vision that follows her initial expression of despair will allow Christine to consider critically the reasons for widespread misogyny and to demonstrate that women are indeed capable of noble deeds and of great virtue (whether in politics, in battle, in the household, or in their spiritual lives). Christine will be helped and guided by three virtuous qualities or faculties, personified by three great ladies whose functions are rendered clear in part by the objects they carry. Lady Reason carries a mirror—offering Christine a tool to critically examine herself, history, and nature. Lady Reason will offer Christine countless examples of noble women who have either excelled in military and political affairs, or who are responsible for great inventions or sciences (deeds deemed no less political, as we shall see). The second, Lady Rectitude, armed with a ruler, promises Christine to separate right from wrong and to serve at once truth and justice during their lengthy discussion of the examples of noble wives, daughters, and mothers (Part II). Lady Justice, finally, is introduced as "God's most special daughter" (I.6) and carries a vessel of gold, intended to "mete out to each his or her rightful portion." It is Lady Justice's task to judge and provide appropriate retribution or reward.

The work proceeds by attacking the weak foundations of intellectual prejudices against women and by employing numerous exempla to show women's worth and nobility—to rehabilitate both their souls and bodies as great sites of virtue. With regard to disputation, the challenge for Christine is to draw from the intellectual resources of the medieval world and to develop an account that would contest some of the basic presuppositions of a large number of medieval authors with regard to women. The chief goal of this disputation is to clear the ground of undesirable material, making way for the stones of virtue that will serve to build the walls of the city. Let us flag here briefly four important arguments presented by the Ladies in response to Christine's enumeration of the various misogynist views she has read and heard. First, the Ladies argue that there are a number of disagreements among philosophers and that indeed some philosophers wrote with irony, suggesting the very opposite of what they intended. We are thus left here, as readers, with some degree of skepticism concerning the overwhelming consensus on the question of women's nature. Second, in response to the arguments about women's sinful nature proposed in previous literature, Lady Reason insists that many of these arguments may have been motivated by the male writers' sense of shame for their own weaknesses. Third, we are told that the souls of men and women as created by God are of equal quality, and that what are traditionally considered as women's physical disadvantages vis-à-vis men may indeed be *more* conducive to a practice of moral virtue (I.14). Fourth, readers learn that it is only a lack of proper educational opportunities that explains women's deficiencies in the present (I.27).

In addition to disputation, Christine de Pizan employs another conventional medieval literary device, the use of exempla, to advance the cause of women. A great deal of medieval (and indeed classical and Hellenistic) moral writing called on readers to copy the attributes and exploits of worthy exemplars. Christine reevaluates numerous classic examples of women, redeeming their experiences and setting them up as patterns to be imitated. For Christine, this approach also allows her to engage in dialogue with a long tradition of political thought. Like her predecessors, she uses exempla not only to foster greater virtue in her readers and to support a reasoned claim with "evidence" but also to entertain those who would hear or read sections of the book. In what follows, we will offer a brief exploration of some of the patterns that inform Christine's choice and analysis of these great exempla. As we will see, Christine's examples, in Parts I and III in particular, challenge traditional ideals of masculine courage and martial virtue, and may serve to redefine what counts as political virtue.

Part I

Part I presents the cases of many women who, through various forces of circumstance, find themselves in positions of power and who come to exercise their power successfully. Christine is arguing that while women have not traditionally held power, when they do find themselves in positions of power (when their husbands are sick or die, for instance), they are able to make the most of their circumstances and not only maintain order but also command armies and lead successful military campaigns. As commentators have noted, this discussion of the fighting and ruling skills of women was not without political significance, given an important debate that was shaking France at the time—namely, the debate over the Salic Law, which ruled out the possibility of a female heir to the throne.[54] Christine did not choose to engage in arguments of legal history and theory to address this issue; she decided instead to provide her readers with a number of cases of effective and indeed exemplary female leadership. Among the main virtues underscored in these extraordinary tales of fierce queens and fighters are courage, boldness, and good judgment. Perhaps best representative of these qualities is Amazonia, a kingdom of warrior queens said to have lasted eight hundred years, rivaling Sparta for its longevity and ancient Rome for its military excellence. She writes that one of the Amazon leaders, Queen Thamiris (I.17), defeated and killed Cyrus of Persia, and she depicts the great legislator Theseus as being matched in cunning and force with the warrior Hippolyta (I.18).[55] While we could debate whether these brave fighters and queens should be regarded

---

54. The Salic Law had been invoked recently in matters of regal accession in an attempt to invalidate any female claims to the throne (in contrast to England, where a queen as head of state remained a possibility). For more on this debate, see Craig Taylor, "The Salic Law, French Queenship, and the Defense of Women in the Late Middle Ages," *French Historical Studies* 29, no. 4 (2006): 543–64, and chap. 1 of Derval Conroy's *Ruling Women*, vol. 1, *Government, Virtue and the Female Prince in Seventeenth-Century France* (London: Palgrave Macmillan, 2016). As Conroy notes, the development of a juridical argument for the exclusion of women from holding monarchical power through invoking the Salic Law came after a number of intense political struggles in the early fourteenth century over succession. It sought to legitimate a relatively recent custom, one full of contradiction given that women were often welcomed and encouraged to rule as regents but on the condition that they would have no extended claim to office once their charge reached the age of majority. Christine's examples in Book I provide a jurisprudence of constitutional custom to demonstrate the legality of women monarchs against those jurists who denied it.

55. Cyrus and Theseus are figures of whom students of political theory today will be aware for their pride of place in Machiavelli's *Prince*, a text written more than a hundred years after Christine de Pizan's *City*.

as preeminent in the city (because they constitute the foundations) or less important (because they are on the lowest level), these examples certainly represent a challenge to the tradition—for these ruling women can be seen as transgressing conventional bounds of feminine virtue.[56]

From the exemplars of women as leaders in political life, Christine then shifts in the latter half of Part I to a presentation of a series of women learned in both the arts and sciences. Here she mixes freely historical and mythological references, and she seeks to restore the reputations of a number of intelligent women in history who were often falsely maligned and treated as witches or sorceresses. In addition, she praises women's contribution to an array of pragmatic arts, including language (Nicostrata/Carmentis, I.33), writing (Minerva, I.34), and cultivation and agricultural tools (Isis, I.36; Ceres, I.35), making the striking claim that these inventions are of greater importance to the development of human community than good political leadership. The strong praise offered by Christine for these examples and for the contribution of the practical arts in general suggests a counterpart to a standard political argument that security through force and institutional command over territory should be considered as the most important contribution to a well-functioning polity. It would appear, at least in the passages devoted to these particular women, that Christine thinks the inventors of these practical arts are *more* praiseworthy than any political leader (I.37). The significance of Part I for us as readers of the history of ideas, then, lies partially here—in Christine's acknowledgment of the importance and nobility of the more "discreet" work that women have traditionally done in history. Christine, indeed, highlights the great importance of not only cultivation and the textile arts but also caring for the sick, the poor, and the elderly (I.10; cf. numerous chapters of Part II).

This position follows an earlier argument for greater appreciation of women's characteristics as traditionally described. At I.10 Christine examines a number of characteristics for which women are often blamed. Lady Reason does not deny that some women exhibit such qualities, but she disputes the judgment placed on them. Those who describe women in this way, she says, are "vicious, diabolical people who want to turn the quality and virtue of

---

56. Later in the fifteenth century, in broader cultural trends, the versatility of women in positions of power was beginning to get wider recognition leading, among other things, to a transformation in the game of chess with the emergence of the queen as an important and indispensable piece on the board. See Marilyn Yalom, *Birth of the Chess Queen* (New York: Harper Collins, 2004).

kindness that is in the nature of women into a vice and disgrace! If women love children, it is not because they are ignorant but because of their innate gentleness." Right after this, Christine asks the Ladies about the veracity of the Latin proverb often used to disparage and deride women: "God made women to weep, talk, and weave" (I.10). Once again, Lady Reason does not deny that women are associated with these three things, but she provides a reconsideration of their value so as to portray them as virtues rather than weaknesses. She underscores, for instance, the value of tears by offering the famous example of Augustine's mother, whose tears led to her son's conversion to Christianity. And to indicate the desirability of women's speech, Lady Reason invokes Mary Magdalene's announcement of the Resurrection.[57] And finally, she celebrates the value of weaving—a craft that has, in her view, immense pragmatic benefit for society (I.10). Indeed, she insists, "without this work, the world would be in a state of chaos" (I.10). While this affirmation might strike some as hyperbolic, one could argue that the invocation of weaving is paradigmatic of a whole array of practical activities and decorative arts that she heralds as foundational of civilization (I.38). To readers immured in a tradition of thinking that stresses the fundamental importance of military security and political order for social life, Christine's reflections about what matters the most for a reasonable and humane civil life certainly offer an intriguing perspective.

Part II

The exempla of Part II presented by Lady Rectitude are sometimes deemed to be controversial by commentators today who think it is insufficiently liberating to provide such pride of place to stories celebrating women who exhibit loyalty to both husbands and parents. She notes the virtue of Xanthippe, wife of Socrates (II.21),[58] as well as the Sabines (II.33), who prevented war between the Romans and their relatives out of loyalty, it would appear, to both (for an account of the Sabines, see the explanatory notes in the text at

---

57. Note that Mary Magdalene will be placed in the highest towers of the city—at the beginning of Part III (she will come into the city right after the Virgin Mary).

58. Xanthippe has more often been associated with nagging (and with the resentful dumping of a chamber pot on her husband's head) than with unbounded love and patience. Christine's rewriting of the more traditional account of Xanthippe and Socrates' marriage aims chiefly at underscoring that there is no necessary conflict between the contemplative life and marriage. It is, as such, a direct response to various misogynist texts that have told young men to avoid the horrors of marriage.

II.33). Are these meant as the more mundane examples that offer the best practical model for her readers, as Brown-Grant has suggested?[59]

In actuality, some examples of Part II continue a celebration of great public contributions made by women—for instance, in their role as political advisers (II.29) and as peacemakers and mediators (II.34). As we noted earlier, Christine's advice to Queen Isabeau of Bavaria (and to many other female contemporaries) often stressed women's duty to work toward political stability and the reduction of violence. This certainly comes out clearest in the follow-up piece to *The Book of the City of Ladies*, *The Treasure of the City of Ladies*, where Christine stresses that one of the key responsibilities of wise princesses is "to be the means of peace and concord, to work for the avoidance of war" (I.9; cf. I.22). Moreover, many of Christine's exempla here illustrate simultaneously women's great loyalty and love and their military prowess (e.g., II.14–15).

Even apart from those explicitly public and military roles, many of the examples cited in Part II are far from mundane: take, for instance, the daughter who breastfeeds her mother on visitations in prison to save her from starvation (II.11) or the Lombard women who place raw chicken meat on their breasts as a deterrent for rapists, showing their outrage and fear at the possibility of sexual assault (II.46). We could also mention the heroic deeds of Hypsicratea (II.14) and of Queen Artemisia (II.16). These are more likely inimitable as acts, but they do offer extreme examples of qualities of loyalty and love. So it is possible to suggest that it is misleading to take Part II's emphasis on devotion to husbands and parents as a sign that the book's central message is to enjoin women to fulfill traditional roles. Rather, Part II serves to demonstrate that even women in traditional roles can ennoble their lives, not always in imitating the array of deeds offered by women in positions of civil influence and political power, but first by experiencing solidarity with them and, through that, cultivating self-respect. The inspiration provided by noble ideals can transform the spirit of otherwise routine activities. The examples provided by Lady Rectitude offer the potential for a shifting and rectification of women's sense of self. Women's good qualities and accomplishments can now be seen in a continuum that is not confined to a determined role within the household but extends to palaces and workshops.

---

59. Rosalind Brown-Grant, *Christine de Pizan and the Moral Defence of Women* (Cambridge: Cambridge University Press, 1999).

While Part II is dominated by examples of loving and virtuous daughters and of faithful, courageous wives, some readers might be struck by the relative absence of virtuous *mothers* in *The Book of the City of Ladies.*[60] Aside from the very notable case of the Virgin Mary (II.30; celebrated as queen of the City in III.1), and the stories of Queen Blanche (II.65) and of Lilia, mother of Theodoric (I.22), there are relatively few exempla[61] offered by Christine to defend the female sex via a demonstration that women can be good *mothers* (despite her ongoing emphasis on the importance of the family even for the female saints). And a few of her examples seem to serve the almost opposite aim: to argue that the most virtuous ladies will be those who are willing to put aside their maternal love for the sake of a great political or spiritual cause. In Part III, for instance, readers are presented with stories of female saints who decide, out of love for God, to "renounce [their] maternal love."[62] Now, for some contemporary scholars, the relatively small room Christine gives to a celebration of *maternal* deeds in human history indicates one of the limits of her so-called feminism.[63] Some have also been tempted to draw connections between this apparent disavowal of the significance of motherhood and the slight irritation Christine seems to have felt toward her own mother (e.g., II.36).[64]

There are obviously a number of responses one could make to these arguments. First, the fact that Christine would put the love of God above maternal

---

60. In *The Treasure of the City of Ladies*, the virtues of good mothers are given more attention. And as we see in the *Lamentation on France's Ills*, Christine is certainly willing to put to good rhetorical and political use the appeal of a loving "mother" when thinking about the relationship between the queen and her subjects.

61. See *The Book of the City of Ladies*, I.20, I.25, II.50.

62. E.g., III.11.

63. E.g., Bernard Ribémont, "Christine de Pizan et la figure de la mère," in *Christine de Pizan 2000: Studies on Christine de Pizan in Honour of Angus J. Kennedy,* ed. John Campbell and Nadia Margolis (Amsterdam: Rodopi, 2000), 149–61. Cf. Heather Arden, "Her Mother's Daughter: Empowerment and Maternity in the Works of Christine de Pizan," in *Contexts and Continuities: Proceedings of the IVth International Colloquium on Christine de Pizan,* vol. 1, ed. Angus Kennedy, Rosalind Brown-Grant, James Laidlaw, and Catherine Müller (Glasgow: University of Glasgow Press, 2002), 31–42. Naturally, much could be said to answer the implicit connection established by the likes of Ribémont between feminism and motherhood.

64. But readers should also see the highly positive things said by Christine about her mother in *The Book of the Mutability of Fortune* (I.5–9). See also Andrea Tarnowski, "Maternity and Paternity in *La Mutacion de Fortune,*" in Zimmermann and De Rentiis, *City of Scholars,* 116–26.

(or any other temporal) love is consistent with Christian piety. Indeed, she suggests in *The Treasure of the City of Ladies* (I.6) that ultimately the contemplative/religious life is more desirable than the active life—for both men and women. Despite the veneration of Mary in the Church, a devotion that transformed medieval conceptions of the role of mothers, motherhood was not yet considered the paradigmatic vocation for women at the time.[65] Second, while historians have confirmed that mothers, and parents more generally, had deep emotional attachments to their children *as children* in the medieval era, there was a broader tendency to avoid a discussion of children in public and literary documents (the more specific contours of those attachments in medieval times are still under investigation).[66] Third, that women could be good mothers was a relatively uncontroversial point (thus there may have been no need to supply numerous exempla to demonstrate this) and one with which Christine de Pizan would not have disagreed. If she chiefly emphasized women's *other* roles and neglected the issue of maternity, it was perhaps because she felt that there was more to be said about the unnoticed or poorly understood virtues and purposes of her sex. If "men tend to think that women's only useful purpose always has been and will be to carry children and spin wool" (I.37), it was time to show them otherwise.

Part III

In Part III of the book, Lady Justice turns to a different source, appealing to Christian hagiography in a long array of martyrs for the faith. Saints' lives were extremely popular during Christine's time, appealing to both female and male audiences. These accounts were meant to offer moral edification (and entertainment) to those who read or listened to them. The point of the genre was not for readers to imitate the radical acts performed by the saints but to inspire readers to aspire to the saints' *qualities*. In Christine's works, the same is obviously true: she does not invite her female readers to tear off their breasts like Amazons nor to sacrifice their children like the holy Julitta (III.11). But she does invite her readers to imitate the saints' patience, love, courage, and

---

65. According to Clarissa Atkinson, such attitudes did not become established until the next century. See *The Oldest Vocation: Christian Motherhood in the Middle Ages* (Ithaca, N.Y.: Cornell University Press, 1991), chap. 7.

66. See, for example, Albrecht Classen, "Philippe Aries and the Consequences: History of Childhood, Family Relations and Personal Emotions, Where Do We Stand Today?" in *Childhood in the Middle Ages and the Renaissance*, ed. A. Classen (Berlin: Walter de Gruyter, 2005), 1–66.

steadfastness.[67] Moreover, it might be said that Christine is using the hagiographical tradition here not solely for the sake of improving women's spiritual lives. By celebrating the great achievements of female saints who bravely challenged the authority of tyrants, Christine may also have been inviting her readers to resist all forms of unjust political rule.

On an allegorical level, these martyrs could be said to represent the long and deep suffering of all women oppressed because of their gender. At the opening of the book, and in response to Christine's lament concerning misogynist writers, Lady Reason tells her: "My dear girl, what has happened to your common sense? Have you forgotten that gold proves itself in the furnace? It does not change its quality but increases in value the more it is beaten and fashioned in various ways!" (I.2). What Lady Reason is suggesting here is that insults and violence cannot debase the nature of women. Indeed, the martyrs in this final section of the book suffer the greatest physical violence for their gender (and faith, naturally), but this does not destroy their spirit; rather, it tests their resolve and inspires greater acts of heroic virtue, making their "gold" more pure. The suggestion is that if one can approach hardship with the proper disposition, as the martyrs did, the defense of one's dignity and virtue in challenging circumstances can be an opportunity for the display and crystallization of one's excellence in action. In this context, the virginity of many of these martyrs (including the Virgin Queen who rules the city) is a symbol of their sense of relative independence from earthly attempts to define them. It helps sustain them in their struggles. While not intended to be a model for all women to follow, the status of virgin expresses in more extreme terms the broader principle uniting all women members of the City in that they no longer derive their *core* sense of identity from the household (which still remains an important locus for virtue) and from certain voices and cultural traditions that had maligned them.

We have noted that it is Lady Justice who guides Christine through the highest towers of the city, the stories of the martyrs. What might the author mean for us to understand about justice from this personification and the examples she chooses to deploy? Christine offers definitions of justice in Aristotelian terms. For instance, in works such as *The Book of the Body Politic* (I.19) and *The Book of the City of Ladies,* Christine was quite explicit:

---

67. Note that in *The Treasure of the City of Ladies* (III.5) Christine instructs young women to read, prior to getting married, the biographies of saints. So while celebrating the nobility of virginity and complete abstinence, she does write about this for women who will, she knows, have very different sexual lives.

justice is "a measure that renders to each his due," and Lady Justice's role, we learn in the *City of Ladies,* is to "judge, to divide, and to give everyone their just deserts" (I.6). Of course, giving to each her due is very broad as a rule, and readers of Aristotle will recall that the *Politics* offers a lengthy discussion of which qualities are most worthy of praise and high office in the good city—and so does Christine. What is worthy of praise and what punishment? Which qualities should be exalted and which cast down?

Part III is not without its interpretative challenges. On the surface, Lady Justice is introduced with the demeanor of a figure exercising commutative justice: "the last one seemed even more imperious than the other two. Her face had such a fierce quality that no matter how brave you were, if you looked into her eyes, you would become afraid of committing a transgression, because you instantly sensed that she posed a threat to all wrongdoers" (I.3). But the broader assumption is that she exercises distributive justice, meting out places in the city according to virtue. In contrast to the examples from Book II, which entail extraordinary deeds that are nonetheless chiefly attached to conventional feminine roles, Lady Justice's examples of the highest merit are all examples of devotion that go well beyond these. They entail a battle against tyrannical rulers for the greatest good. Why are these examples associated with Lady Justice and not with Reason or Rectitude? What do the exempla of Part III reveal precisely about Christine's conception of justice?

We should attend to the qualities these heroines exhibit. Distinct from some philosophic accounts that insist the most fulfilled soul is rational and independent, part of the suffering felt by these martyrs results from their ongoing *attachment* to certain things of the world. The martyrs are women who feel compassion (like Saint Fausta, III.7), shame (like Theodosina and Barbara, III.9), and anger (like Christine of Tyre, III.10), and they are women who weep (like Plautilla, III.18). These martyrs endure great suffering, facing it with courage. Prominent among the examples are women with a particularly effective gift of eloquence. Catherine of Alexandria (III.3) is noted to have overwhelmed fifty of the wisest philosophers known in the land of Egypt by her arguments. Similarly, Saint Lucy is deemed to have converted the evil king Aucejas (III.5), and Saint Fausta converted her executioners through her preaching (III.7), as well as Eulalia (III.8), Theodosina (III.9), Dorothy (III.9), and Christine of Tyre (III.10). These martyrs provide key examples of how tears, emotions, and the gift of speech attributed to women (as invoked in the Latin proverb in I.10) can be exercised in the service of justice.[68] Lady Justice calls on women to flee vice and cultivate virtue, guided and strengthened with the knowledge and feeling of solidarity with the community of noble women who precede them (III.19).

What Part III also reveals is the brutal nature of the struggle for justice. The various tormentors of the saints and martyrs share a set of traits. The saints are the objects of sexual desire and violence, but the lust of their tormentors is no longer portrayed as the fault of women's bodies, but as the perversion of their captors. Those who torture and torment the martyrs are all seen as suffering from an intense and often narcissistic desire for control of women's bodies, minds, and hearts. Many are driven to intense rage when confronted with the strong wills of the women who refuse to submit to them; this rage boils over into a more general hatred of women. If justice is exemplified here by the martyrs' noble resistance to tyranny, then justice, as read through the lives of the exemplars in Part III, may require not only a fear-inducing resolve involved in meting out punishment and in resistance to the unjust but also a more complex emotional engagement with the world, including compassion for the oppressed and a feeling of solidarity with the larger community of noble women. It is in these women's refusal to submit, their compassion for the downtrodden, and their steadfast adherence to truth that the martyrs earn their place in the city's highest towers.

Christine, the Canon, and Feminist Theory

One of the objectives of this new edition of *The Book of the City of Ladies* is to help readers appreciate the degree to which Christine is to be regarded as an author engaged with important strands in the history of political thought and as having made a significant and original contribution to it. We indicated above that her engagement with the tradition of political philosophy comes across quite clearly in her deployment of the metaphor of the city and in her usage of exempla to discuss the moral qualities of good rulers and subjects (two conventional subjects of ancient and medieval literature). For Christine, to think about virtues and the city was not simply an abstract theoretical exercise to be undertaken for the sake of patronage or for the joys of erudition and contemplation—as immense as those pleasures were for her.[69] She hoped that some of her writings could, somehow, influence

---

68. One can draw a parallel on the theme of weeping/tears to the work of Christine's contemporary Margery of Kempe.

69. E.g., see *Christine's Vision* III.11 (excerpts in this volume).

the course of political events in France, and it is partially for this reason that we have chosen to include in this volume her *Lamentations on France's Ills*. Indeed, that text at once captures Christine's intense personal political engagement and reiterates some of the political claims made in *The Book of the City of Ladies*. With Tracy Adams, Kate L. Forhan, Susan Dudash, Karen Green, Cary Nederman, and Stephen Rigby, we believe it is no longer possible to seriously entertain the question "Did Christine de Pizan have a political theory?"[70]

One of the distinctive contributions made by *The Book of the City of Ladies* is, as we have already noted, the healthy corrective it offered to an intellectual tradition that had attached insufficient importance to the way some very practical crafts, knowledge, and tools contributed to civilized living and thus to good politics. While Christine celebrated deeds of generals and military leaders—even, radically, suggesting an equal feminine capacity to exhibit these so-called manly virtues—she also raised up in importance virtues and crafts traditionally associated with a subpublic world, the household. We can thus read *The Book of the City of Ladies* as a highly original reassessment of what matters most for politics. The celebration of weaving, metallurgy, cultivation, agriculture, and various tools and arts whose invention she attributes to women is part and parcel of a larger effort to move certain activities and matters that have rarely been considered noble or "political" from the margins to the center of political philosophy. It is partially for this reason that we have included some excerpts from Christine's *Book of the Body Politic* Part III—for these pages also attest to Christine's genuine and pragmatic concern with the fundamental needs of the body and her efforts to give the "simple laborers of the earth" their due, for without

---

70. This is the title of a 1970s article by Claude Gauvard, "Christine de Pizan a-t-elle eu une pensée politique?" *Revue historique* 250 (1973): 417–29. Efforts to take Christine seriously as a *political* thinker are relatively recent. While there is one study that dates back to the 1830s (Raymond Thomassey's *Essai sur les écrits politiques de Christine de Pizan*), sustained discussions truly began in the 1970s. And even here, a fairly dismissive reading of Christine's importance for political thought was often proposed: Gauvard (1973) and Mombello (1971) both sum up her political reflections as mere moralism. For scholarship that has shown the interest and rigor of her political thought, see, among other works, Zimmermann and De Rentiis, *City of Scholars*; Forhan, *Political Theory of Christine de Pizan*; Green and Mews, *Healing the Body Politic*; Stephen H. Rigby, "The Body Politic in the Social and Political Thought of Christine de Pizan," *Cahiers de recherches médiévales et humanistes* (2013), http://crm.revues.org/12965; Tracy Adams, *Christine de Pizan and the Fight for France*. See also the Suggestions for Further Reading section after this Introduction.

them the "world would come to an end."[71] Christine's worries about the fate of humble peasants is not simply a standard Christian concern for the poor: it is part of a wider shift in which some of the goods of the household—the needs of bare life, treated ever since Aristotle, as mere quotidian concerns— and the half of humanity most associated with that realm are elevated to a more central place in political reflection.

Both *The Book of the Body Politic* and the *Lamentation* speak to Christine's genuine concern for the economic hardship caused by unduly heavy taxation and for the mistreatment of peasants at the hands of soldiers (her critique of soldiers' plundering and brutality is certainly sharp).[72] That Christine genuinely cared about the lot of the poor (partially in light of her organic view of the interdependence of all parts of the city) and considered the virtues or concerns of members of all social classes should not, however, make us commit the tempting historiographical sin of reading in her work a radically protodemocratic position. Certainly, we should appreciate that her City of Ladies will welcome "women of all classes" and that *The Treasure of the City of Ladies* addresses peasants, chambermaids, and prostitutes. Contra Sheila Delany,[73] Christine had no contempt for the poor or the lower estates, but on the contrary a fair amount of respect. But as readers will see for themselves when reading this volume, there is little reason to doubt that Christine was committed to monarchy, like almost all of her contemporaries (with whom she also shared the view that monarchs' authority ought to be "checked" and bettered by wise counselors). She also had substantial qualms about the people's fitness for rule.[74] Appealing to the authority of Aristotle in *The Book of*

---

71. As Christine reminds her princely readers: "Although despised and oppressed by many, [laborers] comprise the most necessary estate of all. They are the cultivators of what feeds and nourishes human beings, and without them, the world would come to an end in no time at all" (III.10).

72. See particularly Dudash's and Oexle's work on Christine's relationship to the "menu peuple." A helpful discussion of her novel take on the "third estate" can also be found in Tracy Adams, "The Political Significance of Christine de Pizan's Third Estate in the *Livre du corps de policie*," *Journal of Medieval History* 35 (2009): 385–98.

73. Sheila Delany, "'Mothers to Think Back Through': Who Are They? The Ambiguous Example of Christine de Pizan," in *Medieval Texts and Contemporary Readers,* ed. Laurie A. Finke (Ithaca, N.Y.: Cornell University Press, 1987).

74. In *The Body Politic* and in *The Book of Peace* (III.12), Christine insists that it is dangerous and "not fitting" for the common people to be given offices or authority in public affairs.

the Body Politic, for instance, she insists that the "rule of one" (monarchy) is the best political regime (III.2).[75]

The other, most obvious contribution of *The Book of the City of Ladies* lies in its powerful defense of the virtues and abilities of women. We certainly ought to take a moment to appreciate its novelty and its radical nature. While there had been previous attempts to celebrate great female figures from the past and previous texts responding to antimarriage and misogynist literature, Christine's *Book of the City of Ladies* can be regarded as the first full-length work written by a female author defending the worth of women (whether as wives, daughters, nuns, soldiers, or queens). Moreover (and perhaps most significantly), it is one of the first texts to ask in an explicit manner some crucial questions about the politics of textual interpretation. For *The Book of the City of Ladies* is not only the writing of a *woman* who thought about politics and morality, and as such warrants reading today as a corrective to the still common view that women are absent from the work of political philosophy until Mary Wollstonecraft. It is also a book that reflects on the very exercise of having a woman thinking and writing about politics. Indeed, in various exchanges between the ladies and Christine (especially in Parts I and II), one finds insightful reflections on various sociocultural and historical reasons for women's relative absence in literary circles. One also finds an inspiring invitation (at once to herself and to her readers) to embrace one of the crucial tasks of political philosophy: the questioning of received opinions. It is particularly important to stress this in light of the overwhelming presence in her work— as in that of her medieval peers—of "compilation." Christine's long series of examples drawn from classical and Christian literature is not a mere display of erudition or an appeal to the authorities from which she draws. She is engaged in a critical reevaluation and reappropriation of the textual tradition. Christine de Pizan never tackled at length the specific question of what difference it would have made if treatises about politics were written by women instead of men. But on the basis of what she affirmed about female virtue in *The Book of the City of Ladies* and elsewhere, it is possible to suggest that she thought a female perspective on what counts as desirable political deeds might be extremely salutary. Furthermore, in her earnest defense of women and her discussion of their positive contributions to sociopolitical life, she

---

75. Christine is far from the only medieval reader to treat Aristotle as a defender of the superiority of monarchy as the best regime and to use his philosophy chiefly as an idiom or way of speaking. An excellent discussion of this can be found in Black, *Political Thought in Europe*. Also see Canning, *History of Medieval Political Thought*, esp. 125–34.

offers a meaningful addition to a literary tradition that obviously remains salient today.[76]

This leads, however, to a difficult interpretive question. Christine's defense of women appears at times to take an essentialist position, suggesting that there are distinctively feminine traits that are even more praiseworthy than those qualities traditionally considered masculine. But at the same time, as we have noted above, a great many of her exempla are meant to show that the very same skills and virtues present in men can also be found in women (and the same thing applies to vices). In Part II, Lady Rectitude tells Christine explicitly that "It's beyond doubt that women are as much part of God's creatures and the human race as men. They're not a different kind of species" (II.54), and elsewhere we learn that women can certainly do everything they set their minds to (II.13). On the whole, indeed, *The Book of the City of Ladies* underscores the sameness and equality between men and women—in terms of intellectual and moral faculties. With regards to physical abilities, however, Christine underscores difference—and here she follows in the footsteps of her predecessors (most notably Augustine, who argued for the equality of women's souls but, like Aristotle, for the inferiority of female bodies). But what is significant about Christine's discussion of these so-called deficiencies (weaker strength) is that she recasts these as *advantages* women have—as an increased opportunity for virtue. Christine writes, for instance, "In terms of courage and physical strength, God and Nature have done a great deal for women by making them frail, for this pleasant defect excuses them at the very least from taking part in the dreadful cruelties, the murders, and the terrible acts of violence that have been committed by force and are still going on in the world" (I.14). And it is here—through the "back door" of their frailty in a sense—that Christine reinjects a bit of difference in her account of feminine virtue.

This apparent oscillation between sameness and difference may be evident in the tension between her championing of broad contours of female capacities and her recommendation that women should not aspire to practice law (I.11). Furthermore, it appears in the tension between, on the one hand, her celebration of women's crucial role as "means of peace" and, on the other,

---

76. See, for example, Mary Beard, *Women and Power* (New York: W. W. Norton, 2017). Beard explores how classical imagery is so often used in political campaigns to delegitimize female political leaders. Christine's project to offer evidence, arguments, and the image of the City acting as a fortress through which women's claims to dignity and respect could be advanced is clearly a product of her time. Nonetheless, the more general impulse to ensure that women's claims to dignity and respect are reflected in broader social norms and practices remains a vibrant one in the contemporary era.

her celebration of women as bold fighters and outstanding contributors to the art and techniques of war.[77] For the latter, one could cite Christine's claim that it is thanks to a woman such as Minerva (treated, we should note, as a real woman and not a goddess or a myth) that "using arms, waging war, and fighting pitched battles" (I.38) was made possible, and that all men ought to be *grateful* for this contribution. One might also mention the cases of queens such as Zenobia (I.20), celebrated by Christine for her great love of arms and her ability to inspire *fear*. *The Book of the City of Ladies* is filled with countless other examples meant to show that courage, boldness, and military prowess are not men's prerogative; in fact, some of her examples of women's military deeds are meant to indicate that women can even *outdo* men in feats of arms (e.g., the kingdom of the Amazonians). The question that students of her political thought can consider is how well all this sits with Christine's assertion, in *The Treasure of the City of Ladies*, that "women are by nature *more timid* and also of a *sweeter disposition*, and for this reason... can be the best means of pacifying men" (I.9; our emphasis).

We noted earlier that thanks to a wealth of solid scholarship in the last decades (chiefly devoted to *The Book of the Body Politic* and her *Book of Peace*), relatively few today would entirely object to the view that Christine is important for the history of political theory. Perhaps the same thing can be said about Christine's importance for the history of feminist theory—although this may presuppose some interpretive generosity on the part of first-time readers of *The Book of the City of Ladies*. Perhaps one of the most important stumbling blocks to an appreciation of Christine's work within gender and feminist studies is Part III, where she asks her readers to be patient if they are married to violent and vicious husbands and where she offers the following advice: "Keep your eyes lowered, listen rather than speak, and exercise restraint in all your actions" (III.19).[78] The same readers might also feel ill

---

77. On this, see Berenice Carroll, "On the Causes of War and the Quest for Peace: Christine de Pizan and Early Peace Theory," in *Au champ des escriptures,* ed. E. Hicks et al. (Paris: Champion, 2000), 337–58; Tracy Adams, "Moyennerresse de traictié de paix: Christine de Pizan's Mediators," in Green and Mews, *Healing the Body Politic,* 177–200.

78. These comments by Christine can perhaps be read in the context of the broader genre of women's conduct literature widespread at the time. For an introduction to this genre, see Susan Udry, "Books of Women's Conduct from France during the High and Late Middle Ages, 1200–1400," ORB: On-line Reference Book for Medieval Studies, https://www.arlima. net/the-orb/encyclop/culture/women/books4women.htm, accessed 26 November 2017. Of course, this contextual point does not solve the question of her rather uncritical adoption of the message of this literature on this point.

at ease with the passages where Christine celebrates virginity, chastity, and sexual modesty in women—after all, some may ask, hasn't the trope of "sexual modesty" been repeatedly invoked in the tradition of political theory to control female sexuality and to keep women in their place?[79]

Now, apart from reminding readers of the importance of keeping in mind the particular Christian medieval cultural context when approaching Christine de Pizan's work, we would like to briefly underscore here the fact that the virtues celebrated in *The Book of the City of Ladies* are, once again, not solely the virtues of women. For the most part, they are *Christian* and to some extent *classical* virtues that Christine tended to regard as desirable in (and equally possible for) all human beings. Indeed, most of the qualities she celebrates through her compilation of examples are also qualities she praises in men elsewhere in her oeuvre. In her biography of Charles V, for instance, Christine praises the king for his remarkable chastity (I.29) and his sobriety in speech and comportment (III.27). But if our contemporary ears might need patient retuning in order to fully appreciate a gospel of chastity and sobriety, most readers will readily appreciate the timeliness of *The Book of the City of Ladies*' simplest yet radical political message: "all things that can be done and known, whether they involve the body or the mind or any other faculty, can all be managed by women with ease" (II.13).

Through the writing of works such as *The Book of the City of Ladies*, the *Lamentation on France's Ills*, and her *Book of the Body Politic*, Christine had hoped not only to make social and literary life a little more hospitable to women but also to make political life a little less conflictual, a little more compassionate. As intimated above, Christine's celebration of peace and compassion cannot be equated with a facile pacifism or a blind attitude toward power or the importance (and necessity) of force and arms. She, after all, wrote extensively on the proper conduct and training of knights and the need for arms. If her *Lamentation* entails an exhortation to compassion and tears ("weep, therefore, weep you ladies, maidens and women of the Kingdom of France!"), let us not overlook Christine's sober advice to the duke of Berry

---

79. And should one not also feel appalled rather than inspired by her advice to women to be economical with their words, and to make sure that they laugh and speak with "moderation and modesty"? Some readers might wonder whether there is not here, in fact, another slight tension in Christine's work between her defense of the value of female speech and her celebration of women's discretion in speech. (In II.25 and 26, for instance, Christine seeks to convince misogynist detractors that women *are* capable of keeping a secret and of bridling their tongues.) Perhaps the tension disappears if we acknowledge that on words, as much as on wine and food, the ultimate Christian (and classical) counsel is to embrace moderation.

to "*firmly* seize the bridle"—an implicit acknowledgment of the necessity of force or compulsion, and the desirability of boldness.[80] As readers will be able to appreciate for themselves in the pages that follow, the "noble Ladies" praised by Christine include numerous chaste, peaceful, and patient queens, and many loving, faithful widows and daughters; they also include shrewd military strategists, brave and feared fighters, and many noble ladies who had no qualms about resorting to some coercion or even deception when the cause was right. And for the mature and tearful Christine, the cause of French peace was precisely that.

---

80. For Christine, ultimately, this was not a matter of "either-or": these apparently contradictory qualities (sternness, compassion, boldness, patience, courage, piety, etc.) could all be found within the same person, the very same soul. Christine does not shun the martial virtues but rather *rewrites* them, *pacifies* them. We noted above the fact that in her view, similar virtues can be found in both men and women. That said, Christine nevertheless tried to redefine what constituted courage, as much as what constituted a civilizing and political craft.

A NOTE ON TRANSLATING *THE BOOK OF THE CITY OF LADIES*

The prospect of translating *The Book of the City of Ladies*, a text that had already been translated into English by three others (Curnow [1975], Richards [1998], and Brown-Grant [1999]) initially seemed daunting but ultimately proved to be an intriguing challenge. Translating is a lonely profession, but this time I had company. The translations by Zimmermann (1990), Moreau and Hicks (2000), Ponfoort (1988), and Caraffi (1997) as well as those already mentioned gave me the unique opportunity of studying various problems through the eyes of my colleagues, and I am in their debt. The result is, I hope, a version that supplements rather than competes. I have strayed from the text more than Richards but stayed closer to it than Brown-Grant. I thinned the forest of adjectives and near-synonymous combinations that is so typical of Middle French to improve readability, but I also made an effort to convey the tone and flavor of the original. The book was written more than six hundred years ago, but I hope I have allowed Christine to speak to us today in her own voice.

The translation of *The Book of the City of Ladies* is based on Harley 4431, a manuscript that was commissioned by Queen Isabeau of France and presented to her in 1414. My choice was governed primarily by the assertion by Richards et al. that this manuscript "probably represents the ultimate form as intended by Christine and the possibility exists that she may have corrected it in her own hand."[1] It is also available online through the University of Edinburgh,[2] a site that offers both images and a full transcription. F.fr. 607[3] was used as a control (although the two manuscripts are very similar).

---

1. See also Charity Cannon Willard, "An Autograph Manuscript of Christine de Pizan," *Studi francesi* 9 (1965): 452–57; Gilbert Ouy and Christine Reno, "Identification des autographes de Christine de Pizan," *Scriptorium* 34 (1980): 221–38; J. C. Laidlaw, "Christine de Pizan—a Publisher's Progress," *Modern Language Review* 82, no. 1 (1987): 35–75; E. J. Richards, "Editing the *Livre de la cité des dames*: New Insights, Problems and Challenges," *Au champ des escriptures. IIIe Colloque international sur Christine de Pizan, Lausanne, 18–22 juillet 1998*, ed. Eric Hicks, Diego Gonzalez, and Philippe Simon, Études christiniennes 6 (2000): 789–816.

2. http://www.pizan.lib.ed.ac.uk

3. http://gallica.bnf.fr/ark:/12148/btv1b6000102v/f9.item

xlvi   *A Note on Translating* The Book of the City of Ladies

The translation of the excerpts from *The Book of the Body Politic* is based on the critical edition by Angus Kennedy (1998) of MS F (Chantilly, Bibliothèque et Archives du Château, 294), believed to be entirely in Christine's handwriting. MS A was used as a control.[4] I consulted the translation by Kate Langdon Forhan, also based on MS A.

The translation of the *Lamentation* is based on the critical edition by Angus Kennedy (1980) of Ms. fr. 24864.[5] I consulted the translation by Renate Blumenfeld-Kosinski and Kevin Brownlee, based on the same edition.

The translation of the excerpts from *Christine's Vision*, finally, is based on the critical edition of Christine Reno and Liliane Dulac of MS C (ex-Phillipps 128, in private hands), which is believed to have been executed under Christine's supervision. The critical edition by Mary Louis Towner of MS B served as a control. I consulted the translation by Glenda McLeod and Charity Cannon Willard, based on MS C.

The multitude of names cited has been rendered as much as possible in conformity with the spelling most frequently encountered on bona fide internet sites.

I chose not to provide notes, in the belief that my role was to supply a text, not to discuss the difficulties encountered by its translator. A comparison of the translations will occasionally show a variety of interpretations, and I consider it a bonus that critical readers will have access to many of the manuscripts and will be able to judge for themselves.

I profited immensely from the *Dictionnaire du Moyen Français* published online by ATILF;[6] the *Anglo-Norman Dictionary*, a project of Aberystwyth University and Swansea University;[7] and the *Electronic Dictionary of Chrétien de Troyes*, also published by ATILF.[8]

Finally, I would like to take this opportunity to thank my husband Hans Jager for all his support and patience throughout this project.

IH

Haulerwijk, the Netherlands,

December 2017

---

4. http://gallica.bnf.fr/ark:/12148/btv1b84497115/f98.vertical

5. http://gallica.bnf.fr/ark:/12148/btv1b8451465g/f33

6. http://www.atilf.fr/dmf/

7. http://www.anglo-norman.net/

8. http://www.atilf.fr/dect/

CHRISTINE DE PIZAN:
HER WORKS, HER TIMES

1337–1453   Hundred Years' War, pitting France against England (with shifting alliances and various periods of truce).

1361–1374   Boccaccio writes *De mulieribus claris* (*Famous Women*).

ca. 1364   Christine born in Venice. The family soon moves to Paris, where Christine's father, Thomas de Pizan, serves as doctor and astrologer at the court of Charles V.

1378–1417   Papal Schism (two Catholic popes vying for authority).

ca. 1379   At the age of fifteen, Christine de Pizan marries Étienne de Castel, notary and secretary at court; they will have three children (one will die in early childhood).

1380   Charles V dies, which triggers an important decline in Thomas de Pizan's finances. His successor is the young Charles VI, age eleven (Louis, duke of Anjou acts as regent until 1382).

ca. 1387   Thomas de Pizan dies.

1390   Death of Étienne de Castel; Christine is widowed at age twenty-five.

1392   King Charles VI is plagued by increasingly frequent bouts of insanity, which fuels the rivalries among his cousins and uncles (soon to be organized in two camps: the Orleanists—later known as the Armagnacs—and the Burgundians). Charles' wife is Isabeau of Bavaria, a powerful and controversial figure.

ca. 1393   Christine begins writing poetry.

1399–1402   Christine becomes a key figure in the battle over the *Romance of the Rose*; her *Epistre au Dieu d'amours* (*Epistle to the God of Love*, 1399) and *Le Dit de la Rose* (*The Tale of the Rose*, 1402) are both attacks on its chief misogynist author, Jean de Meun.

ca. 1400   First prose work written by Christine, the *Epistre Othea* (*Epistle of Othea*).

1403   *Le Livre de la mutacion de fortune* (*The Book of the Mutability of Fortune*), an allegorical account of Christine's life and of Fortune's role in human affairs.

1404   Christine is commissioned to write *Livre des Fais et bonnes meurs du sage roy Charles V* (*Book of the Deeds and Good Morals of the Wise King Charles V*).

1404–1405   Christine writes *The Book of the City of Ladies* and, shortly after, *The Treasure of the City of Ladies or The Book of the Three Virtues*.

1404–1407   Christine writes the *Livre du Corps de policie* (*The Book of the Body Politic*).

1405   *Epistre à Isabeau de Bavière, reine de France* (*Epistle to Isabeau of Bavaria, Queen of France*).

1405   *Le Livre de l'advision Christine* (*Christine's Vision*).

1407   Louis, duke of Orléans (brother of King Charles VI) is murdered by the faction of his cousin, John the Fearless, duke of Burgundy; conflict escalates between the houses of Orléans and Burgundy.

1410   *La Lamentacion sur les maux de la France* (*Lamentation on France's Ills*) is written, in which Christine exhorts the warring court factions to make peace and begs Jean, duke of Berry (uncle of Charles VI) to intervene. Christine also writes a treatise on warfare, *Livre des Fais d'armes et de chevalerie* (*The Book of Deeds of Arms and of Chivalry*).

1412–1414   *Le Livre de la paix* (*The Book of Peace*), dedicated to the young dauphin Louis of Guyenne (son of Charles VI).

1413   Cabochien Revolt (bloody rebellion in Paris, largely orchestrated by John the Fearless, duke of Burgundy).

1414   Christine presents a collection of her works to Queen Isabeau of Bavaria.

1415	Battle of Agincourt between the French and the English (great losses for the French side).
1415	The dauphin Louis of Guyenne dies.
1418	The Burgundians take Paris and kill countless Orleanists. The dauphin Charles, duke of Orléans, goes into exile. Shortly after having written her *Epistre de la prison de vie humaine* (*Epistle of the Prison of Human Life*) Christine leaves Paris and probably joins her daughter in a convent, in Poissy.
1419	The Armagnacs kill John the Fearless, duke of Burgundy.
1420	The Treaty of Troyes is signed.
1429	Shortly after the crowning of Charles VII by Joan of Arc, Christine writes *Le Ditié de Jehanne d'Arc* (*The Poem of Joan of Arc*), full of hope for France's future.
ca. 1430	Death of Christine de Pizan, in Poissy.

SUGGESTIONS FOR FURTHER READING

Secondary Literature

Adams, Tracy. *Christine de Pizan and the Fight for France*. University Park: Pennsylvania State University Press, 2014.

Altmann, Barbara K., and Deborah L. McGrady. *Christine de Pizan: A Casebook*. New York: Routledge, 2003.

Autrand, Françoise. *Christine de Pizan: Une femme en politique*. Paris: Fayard, 2009.

Bennett, Judith M., and Ruth Mazo Karras. *The Oxford Handbook of Women and Gender in Medieval Europe*. Oxford: Oxford University Press, 2013.

Black, Antony. *Political Thought in Europe, 1250–1450*. Cambridge: Cambridge University Press, 1992.

Blumenfeld-Kosinski, Renate, and Timea Szell, eds. *Images of Sainthood in Medieval Europe*. Ithaca, N.Y.: Cornell University Press, 1991.

Blumenfeld-Kosinski, Renate, ed. and trans., and Kevin Brownlee, trans. *The Selected Writings of Christine de Pizan*. Norton Critical Editions. New York: W.W. Norton, 1997.

Brabant, Margaret, ed. *Politics, Gender and Genre: The Political Thought of Christine de Pizan*. Boulder, Colo.: Westview, 1992.

Broad, Jacqueline, and Karen Green. *A History of Women's Political Thought in Europe, 1400–1700*. Cambridge: Cambridge University Press, 2009.

Burns, James Henderson. *The Cambridge History of Medieval Political Thought, c. 350–c. 1450*. Cambridge: Cambridge University Press, 1988.

Bynum, Carolyn. *Holy Feast and Holy Fast: The Religious Significance of Food to Medieval Women*. Berkeley: University of California Press, 1987.

Colish, Marcia. *Medieval Foundations of the Western Intellectual Tradition, 400–1400*. New Haven, Conn.: Yale University Press, 1997.

Delany, Sheila. "'Mothers to Think Back Through': Who Are They? The Ambiguous Example of Christine de Pizan." In *Medieval Texts and*

Contemporary Readers, edited by Laurie A. Finke. Ithaca, N.Y.: Cornell University Press, 1987.

Desmond, Marilynn, ed. *Christine de Pizan and the Categories of Difference.* Minneapolis: University of Minnesota Press, 1998.

Dudash, Susan J. "Christine de Pizan and the 'menu peuple.'" *Speculum* 78, no. 3 (July 2003): 788–831.

Evans, Ruth, Sara Salih, and Anke Bernau. *Medieval Virginities.* Toronto: University of Toronto Press, 2003.

Farmer, David. *The Oxford Dictionary of Saints.* 5th rev. ed. Oxford: Oxford University Press, 2011.

Forhan, Kate L. *The Political Theory of Christine de Pizan.* Burlington, Vt.: Ashgate, 2002.

Gottlieb, Beatrice. "The Problem of Feminism in the Fifteenth Century." In *Women of the Medieval World: Essays in Honor of John H. Mundy*, edited by Julius Kirshner and Susanne F. Wemple. Oxford: Blackwell, 1985.

Green, Karen, and Constant J. Mews, eds. *Healing the Body Politic: The Political Thought of Christine de Pizan.* Turnhout: Brepols, 2005.

Head, Thomas, ed. *Medieval Hagiography: An Anthology.* New York: Garland, 2000.

Hult, David F., ed. and trans. *Debate of the "Romance of the Rose."* Chicago: University of Chicago Press, 2010.

Karras, Ruth M. *Sexuality in Medieval Europe: Doing unto Others.* 2nd ed. New York: Routledge, 2012.

Kellogg, Judith. "Christine de Pizan and Boccaccio: Rewriting Classical Mythic Tradition." In *Comparative Literature East and West: Traditions and Trends,* vol. 1, edited by Cornelia Moore and Raymond Moody. Honolulu: College of Languages, Linguistics and Literature of the University of Hawaii, 1989.

Margolis, Nadia. *An Introduction to Christine de Pizan.* Gainesville: University Press of Florida, 2011.

Mayor, Adrienne. *The Amazons.* Princeton, N.J.: Princeton University Press, 2014.

Nederman, Cary J. *Lineages of European Political Thought: Explorations along the Medieval/Modern Divide from John of Salisbury to Hegel.* Washington, D.C.: Catholic University of America Press, 2009.

Nederman, Cary J., and Kate Langdon Forhan, eds. *Readings in Medieval Political Theory, 1100–1400.* Indianapolis: Hackett, 2000.

Quilligan, Maureen. *The Allegory of Female Authority: Christine de Pizan's Cité des dames.* Ithaca, N.Y.: Cornell University Press, 1991.

Reno, Christine. "Virginity as an Ideal in Christine de Pizan's *Cité des Dames.*" In *Ideals for Women in the Works of Christine de Pizan,* edited by Diane Bornstein. Detroit: Michigan Consortium for Medieval and Early Modern Studies, 1981, 69–90.

Rigby, Stephen H. "The Body Politic in the Social and Political Thought of Christine de Pizan." *Cahiers de recherches médiévales et humanistes* (2013), http://crm.revues.org/12965.

Ullmann, Walter. *Law and Politics in the Middle Ages: An Introduction to the Sources of Medieval Political Ideas.* Cambridge: Cambridge University Press, 1975.

Willard, Charity Cannon. *Christine de Pizan: Her Life and Works.* New York: Persea, 1990.

Willard, Charity Cannon, ed. *The Writings of Christine de Pizan.* Translated by Charity Cannon Willard, et al. New York: Persea, 1994.

Zimmermann, Margarete, and Dina De Rentiis, eds. *The City of Scholars: New Approaches to Christine de Pizan.* New York: Walter de Gruyter, 1994.

Christine de Pizan and Some of Her Sources

Aquinas, Thomas. *Commentary on Aristotle's* Politics. Translated by Richard J. Regan. Indianapolis: Hackett, 2007.

Augustine. *Political Writings.* Edited by Ernest L. Fortin. Translated by Douglas Kries. Indianapolis: Hackett, 1994.

Boccaccio, Giovanni. *Famous Women.* Edited and translated by Virginia Brown. Cambridge, Mass.: Harvard University Press, 2001.

Boethius, Anicius. *The Consolation of Philosophy.* Edited and translated by Joel C. Relihan. Indianapolis: Hackett, 2001.

Cicero. *On Duties.* Edited by M. T. Griffin and E. M. Atkins. Cambridge: Cambridge University Press, 1991.

Christine de Pizan. *The Book of the Body Politic.* Edited and translated by Kate L. Forhan. Cambridge: Cambridge University Press, 1994.

———. *The Book of Deeds of Arms and of Chivalry.* Translated by Sumner Willard. Edited by Charity Cannon Willard. University Park: Pennsylvania State University Press, 1999.

———. *Le Chemin de longue étude.* Translated and edited by Andrea Tarnowski. Paris: Le livre de poche, 2000.

———. *The Treasure of the City of Ladies or The Book of the Three Virtues.* Translated by Sarah Lawson. 2nd ed. London: Penguin, 2003.

———. *The Book of Peace.* Edited by Karen Green, Constant J. Mews, and Janice Pinder. University Park: Pennsylvania State University Press, 2010.

———. *Livre des faits et bonnes moeurs du sage roi Charles V.* Translated by Joël Blanchard and Michel Quereuil. Edited by Joël Blanchard. Paris: Pocket, 2013.

———. *The Book of the Mutability of Fortune.* Edited and translated by Geri L. Smith. Toronto: Iter Press; Tempe: Arizona Center for Medieval and Renaissance Studies, 2017.

Guillaume de Lorris and Jean de Meun. *The Romance of the Rose.* Translated by Frances Horgan. New York: Oxford University Press, 2008.

John of Salisbury. *Policraticus.* Edited and translated by Cary J. Nederman. Cambridge: Cambridge University Press, 1990.

Marsilius of Padua. *The Defender of the Peace.* Edited and translated by Annabel Brett. Cambridge: Cambridge University Press, 2005.

Ovid. *Metamorphoses.* Translated by A. D. Melville. New York: Oxford University Press, 2008.

Valerius Maximus. *Memorable Deeds and Sayings: One Thousand Tales from Ancient Rome.* Translated by Henry John Walker. Indianapolis: Hackett, 2004.

Christine's Vision
(excerpts from Part III)

[Le Livre de l'advision Christine]

Written in 1405 when she was already an accomplished and known author,
Le Livre de l'advision Christine *constitutes the main source of information
we have about Christine de Pizan's life and her self-understanding as a writer.[1] A dream-journey comprising three lengthy dialogues with distinct allegorical figures, the* Advision *is more than autobiography, however: it is also
a mirror-for-princes and a highly politically engaged text in which Christine
confidently underscores her importance in French literary circles and court
life. In Part I's dialogue with Lady Libera (who represents France), Christine briefly recalls key events in French history and indicates her concern for
the political instability plaguing the country (an instability fueled by King
Charles VI's insanity and the ensuing bitter rivalries between the houses of
Orléans and Burgundy).[2] Toward the end of Part I, Libera urges Christine to
counsel French princes on what they must do to build peace and avoid doom.
In Part II (largely devoted to a discussion of clerical, scholarly circles), Lady
Opinion reminds Christine of the pivotal role she played in the debate over
the* Roman de la Rose[3] *and urges her to continue her battle against falsehoods
and poor judgment. Christine then converses with Lady Philosophy in Part
III (reproduced in part below), offering us a detailed account of the numerous challenges she faced as a young widow. Here the profound influence of
Boethius'* Consolation of Philosophy *is palpable. This last part of Christine's*
Vision *is also a celebration of the contemplative life, a meditation on the role
of Fortune in human affairs, and a reply to the unflattering gossip of which
Christine de Pizan seems to have been the target. The excerpts below follow
Christine's description of her good fortune in having been born the daughter*

---

1. Other sources of biographical information include her *Livre de la Mutacion de Fortune* [*The
Book of the Mutability of Fortune*] and her poem *Le Chemin de longue étude* [*The Long Path of
Learning*]. For two readable biographies, see Charity C. Willard, *Christine de Pizan: Her Life
and Works* (New York: Persea, 1990), and Françoise Autrand, *Christine de Pizan: Une femme en
politique* (Paris: Fayard, 2009).

2. Rosalind Brown-Grant reads this text above all as a mirror for the prince in "*L'Avision
Christine*: Autobiographical Narrative or Mirror for the Prince?" in *Politics, Gender and Genre:
The Political Thought of Christine de Pizan*, ed. M. Brabant (Boulder, Colo.: Westview, 1992),
95–111. Liliane Dulac and Christine Reno show how the autobiographical and the political
dimensions are intimately linked in "*Le Livre de l'advision Christine,*" in *Christine de Pizan: A
Casebook*, ed. Barbara K. Altmann and Deborah L. McGrady (New York: Routledge, 2003),
199–214.

3. See Introduction for more details.

of Thomas de Pizan (physician and astrologer to King Charles V) and having been happily married to court notary Étienne de Castel.

Part III

Chapter 5. Christine introduces her misfortunes

This happy state of affairs lasted several years, but since Fortune was clearly envious of our blessings, she decided to block the source whence they came. Was it not truly her doing, dear mistress, that this realm suffered the grievous harm that caused such detriment to Master Thomas' household? It was then that the good, wise prince, still relatively young at the age of forty-four, failed to grow old as nature intended. He became unwell and died after a brief illness.[4] Alas! It truly often happens that good things last but a short time. His life was so necessary to this kingdom, whose government and condition today are appallingly different from those of the past. If God had seen fit to prolong his life, he would still not have been so very old even today.

Now the door to our misfortunes had opened and I entered, still very young. The death of powerful men is frequently followed by great upheaval and changes in their courts and territories, caused by a battle of wills. It is a situation that can only be remedied by great wisdom. Such was the case with the great Alexander, of whom it is written that various discords sprang up between his barons soon after his death despite the division of lands he had ordained for them. So it was that my father lost his substantial pensions. He no longer received a generous income of a hundred francs a month from his rents and gifts, and he learned that they would be much reduced. And his expectation, based on the good king's promise to settle five hundred pounds' worth of land and many other benefits on him and his heirs, did not come to pass because the good king's memory failed and he died an untimely death. It is true that the ruling princes did retain my father, but they paid him a drastically reduced salary at infrequent intervals. He was already growing old by

---

4. Here, Christine refers to the death of King Charles V (*le sage*), who brought Christine's family to the French court and whose biography *The Book of the Deeds and Good Morals of the Wise King Charles V* she wrote in 1404.

then and before long entered a long period of incapacity and illness, suffering many privations, for which he needed the money that was spent instead of saved. That is why I believe that it is proper, careful management of a man's resources while he is young that will save him in his old age.

My father remained clearheaded until the end, acknowledging his Creator as a good Catholic should, and he died at the very hour he had predicted.[5] For that reason, he remained famous among the scholars, who said that not for a hundred years had there been a man with such superb understanding of mathematical sciences and astrological interpretations. In addition, his genuine reputation for rectitude, his good deeds, loyalty, honesty, and his other virtues and lack of vices made the princes and those who knew him mourn his death and lament his passing. He had not a single reprehensible trait unless it was his extreme generosity in refusing the poor nothing he possessed, despite having a wife and children. And I do not just say this because I am partial: many of his acquaintances, including princes, still know this to be true today from their own experience. He was a man who was lamented and mourned by his peers for good reason.

Chapter 6. Still on the same subject

My husband now carried on as head of the household. He was a young man full of wisdom and virtue, well liked by the princes and everyone who visited his office, and it was thanks to his prudent judgment that the position of the family was maintained. But since Fortune had already put me on a downward spin of her wheel, intent on making me suffer by casting me from prosperity down to the very bottom, she had no intention of letting me keep this good man for long. Fortune saw to it that Death took him from me when he was flourishing, capable, prepared, and on the point of rising to high rank, as much through scholarship as through wise and prudent acquisitions and management. He was in the flower of his youth at the age of thirty-four and I, at twenty-five, was left behind with three small children and a large household.[6] No wonder I was full of bitterness, lamenting the loss of his sweet company and the joy I had known, which had lasted only ten years. Faced with the flood of trouble that came rushing at me, I longed for death more than

5. As an astrologer, his duties to the king included trying to predict the future. Thomas de Pizan died around 1387, amid criticisms and attacks against his science. Christine's husband would pass away shortly after.

6. Only two of these children (Marie and Jean) would make it to adulthood.

life. Remembering my vow and the faithful love I pledged to him, I made a conscious decision never to take another man.

So there I was, deep in the valley of tribulation, because when Fortune decides to destroy something, be it a realm, a city, an empire, or an individual, she searches far and wide for the most adverse conditions to bring the thing she has chosen in anger to the point of wretchedness, and so it happened to me. Since I was not present at the death of my husband, who died as a result of a sudden epidemic (although, by God's grace, he died as a good Catholic) in the town of Beauvais where he had gone with the king, accompanied only by some of his servants and an escort of strangers, I had no way of knowing the exact state of his finances. Married men commonly don't disclose to their wives all the details of their business affairs, and this often has bad consequences, as I have found from experience. It is certainly not a reasonable course of action for wives who are not foolish but prudent and wise managers. Consequently, I am well aware that I did not get a clear picture of everything he owned.

Now I had to set to work, and this was a task that I, who had led a life of luxury and comfort, had not learned to do. I had to pilot the vessel that was left at sea in the midst of a storm without a master, in other words, the grieving household that was far from its home and country. I was beset by all sorts of troubles and, as is the fate of widows, lawsuits and legal actions came from all directions.[7] Those who owed me money attacked me to stop me from asking them to pay. God knows it is true that one of them, pretending to be an honest man, fraudulently claimed that the evidence of my husband's financial records showed that he had paid his debt, but that claim was a lie. He was defeated and no longer dared talk to me about it and keep up his lie. Before long, an obstacle was put in my way in connection with the real estate my husband had purchased. Since it had reverted to the Crown, I had to pay the rent on it and could not enjoy the benefits. I was also in the Court of Finances, involved in a long suit with the cruel person who was and still is one of the lords and masters from whom I could not obtain justice. He wrongfully caused me the most grievous harm, which is clear to all and many people know about it. And now that he has grown old in his sinful ways, he still does not give it any thought or feel any remorse.

---

7. This in part explains the particularly passionate tone taken by Christine in *The Treasure of the City of Ladies* (e.g., III.4, I.19), when discussing the horror of widowhood, the prejudices faced by women in law courts, and the need for women to follow closely their husbands' finances.

That was not the only curse. The guardians of my little orphans placed their funds, with my consent, in the hands of a merchant reputed to be honest so that he could increase and multiply their meager assets. He did realize a reasonable return, increasing it by half in the space of a year. But he succumbed to the Devil's temptations and pretended he had been robbed of the funds. He disappeared and fled. I had to spend more money to sue and lost.

Other lawsuits sprang up in connection with the inheritance, involving demands for long-standing revenues and demands for large amounts payable in arrears, none of which was mentioned in the bill of sale of our purchase. I was advised by the most knowledgeable lawyers that I should strongly defend myself and that, since I had a strong case, I should have no doubt but that the verdict would direct me to summon those who had witnessed the sale. They had died, however, impoverished and in a foreign land, so there was no relief for me. At that point, to make my way to where Fortune was leading me, I succumbed to a long illness at the height of my misfortunes, just like Job. That caused the lawsuit to be stayed, and I lost my case through a lack of proper arbitration. This sentence of forfeiture meant that I had to cover all the costs from my meager capital. It is astounding how fiercely Fortune hounded me, because in whatever way losses can cause misfortune to a person managing her affairs guided by good advice and proper procedure, as God knows I was doing, so they afflicted me, completely contrary to what I might reasonably expect to happen to my affairs and things in general.

Oh virtue of patience! I did not always have you at hand. Instead, you were often crushed by the great bitterness I felt. I found myself having to mount a defense against lawsuits and legal actions in four Parisian courts. And I swear to you upon my soul that I was unfairly abused by malicious parties. Their quibbling, intended to make me withdraw from the suits, I perceived as utterly hateful, contrary to my peace-loving nature. I saw that if I were to have peace, I must give in to them, forfeiting my rights at great expense. And don't think that this lasted just a year or two! No, it went on for more than fourteen years, because when one misfortune ended, the next one arrived, in so many different ways that it would take forever and bore you to even relate the half of it. And so Fortune, like a leech, kept sucking away my meager possessions until she had exhausted them all and I had nothing left to lose. My lawsuits ended at that point, but not my misfortunes.

Oh sweet mistress, how many tears, sighs, moans, laments, and grievous sorrows do you think were my lot as I dwelled alone in my retreat, watching my small children and my poor relatives around me at my hearth, thinking about past times and the current misfortunes flooding over me and laying me low, making me feel powerless to find a remedy? Those troubles made me weep for my loved ones more than for myself. Someone told me one time that I had no reason to complain because, being single and alone, I did not have any obligations, and I answered him that he had not observed me very well because I was three times doubled. He said he didn't understand me, so I explained that I was responsible for five persons. Given all this, dear mistress, do you not think that my heart was troubled by the oppressive fear that people might discover the state of my affairs and by the worry that my situation might become apparent to outsiders and the neighbors? Given that the decline of this wretched state was not of my own making but inherited from my predecessors, do you not think that this ignorance made me so bitter that death would have been preferable to being ruined? Ah, what hardship and what suffering to a heart that was too anxious to survive despite Fortune's intentions! No one can believe it without having experienced it. There is no misery like it. God knows how many people have suffered and are suffering misfortunes for that reason. I assure you that my appearance and dress largely concealed the burden of my troubles from others. But beneath my gray fur cloak and the scarlet surcoat that was infrequently refurbished but still in good condition, I often trembled, and in my beautiful and well-appointed bed I spent many a bad night. Our meals were sober, as is appropriate for a widow, and one must live after all. God knows the torture in my heart when the sergeants took action against me and removed my possessions! Great harm was done to me, but I feared shame even more. But when it was necessary to ask for a loan from someone to avoid an even greater misfortune, dear Lord God, how ashamed I was and how I blushed crimson to make the request, even from a friend. Even today I am still not recovered from that affliction, which I believe did me more harm than a fever attack might have done.

Ah! When I remember how many times I wasted the morning in that palace in winter, dying of cold, searching for my counselors to review and promote my affairs! How many times during those days did I hear different conclusions that made my eyes water, and many strange responses! What troubled me above all else was the expense, which I was in no position to pay.

Following the example of Jesus Christ, who was willing to suffer torture to all parts of His body to teach us patience, Fortune wanted my heart to be tortured in various ways by all sorts of difficult and unpleasant thoughts. What greater evil and distress can befall an innocent person, what greater reason for impatience, than to hear oneself unjustly maligned, as you can read in the words of Boethius in his *Consolation of Philosophy*? Was it not said about me all over town that I had a lover? Indeed, but it should be kept in mind that it was Fortune who accomplished all this with her various blows. Reputations of that sort tend to come and go, often unjustly, as a result of being acquainted with many people who are frequently in each other's company or by conjecture and striking resemblances, but I swear upon my soul that this man did not know me and did not know who I was. No one ever saw me in public or private under the same roof or in the same place with him, because my usual route did not take me in that direction and I had no reason to go there, and may God be my witness that I speak the truth. Considering his way of life and mine, such a thing was not appropriate, nor was it reasonable for anyone to think so. I have often been astonished at where those words came from; they were carried from mouth to mouth, in the form of "I heard it said." I knew I was innocent, but when people told me about it, it sometimes troubled me. Other times, I would laugh and say: "Between God and the two of us, we know that this is not true!"

My suffering did not end there, however. I was still struggling as best I could against Fortune's battle and her campaign, and I saw my funds being drastically depleted. That was after the Court of Finance had verified and passed legal notifications about a sum of money still owed to my late husband for the income of his office, so I obtained the king's order to the governors that I be paid. Then I was forced into a tedious process that caused me great hardship, with me being tormented for several days by conflicting replies. And that this can be a long and unpleasant labor, I call to witness those who have gone through it. It is even more unpleasant now than ever before, as the old people tell us. Now you can understand how hard it was for me, a physically weak woman with a timid nature, to turn necessity into virtue, which was both difficult and costly. It involved running after them as dictated by procedure and sitting and waiting in their courts or chambers with my files and summons most days without accomplishing anything, or receiving conflicting replies and false hopes after long delays. The waiting was endless. Oh God! How many malicious words, how many foolish looks I endured, how many jokes I heard from some fat drunkard filled with wine! But being in need and worried about harming my case, I hid my feelings and didn't reply, turning away or pretending that I didn't understand, that I took it for a joke. May it please God to reform all disgraceful moral principles, because I found some very bad ones.

In the pursuit of my case I did not find any charitable person of any status anywhere, even though I asked several noblemen and important persons to speak on my behalf, in the hope that they would honor the custom obliging them to assist widows and orphans. In fact, I didn't find anything that benefited me and so, one day when I was feeling discouraged about those things, I composed this ballad, in tears:

Alas, where will they find comfort,
The poor widows, robbed of their possessions,
Because in their haven of safety in France
Where the exiles and the helpless used to flee,
Now they no longer have any friends!
The nobles do not take pity on them,
Nor do the clergy, great or small,
And the princes do not bother to listen to them.

They have no safe haven from the knights,
They do not receive good advice from the prelates,
The judges do not protect them from injustice,
The magistrates would not award them two pence.
In many cases, they are harassed by the powerful,
And before those of high office, they would never
Win half; they must proceed elsewhere.
And the princes do not bother to listen to them.

Where can they flee, since they have no refuge
In France, where they are given
False hopes and deadly advice?
They will travel the roads of Hell
If they are willing to trust the torturous paths
And the false advice that does not address their case.
There are none who are enlightened enough
To help them without doing them harm.
And the princes do not bother to listen to them.

Now you good and strong men,
Show your generosity, or the widows
Are likely to suffer many hardships.

Help them and believe my poem,
Because I do not see anyone being kind to them.
And the princes do not bother to listen to them.

The reason that prompted me to pursue this matter in person, against my wishes, was that whenever I sent my messenger there, they would not give him an audience. But when I went there myself to remind them of my status as a poor widow, on my knees before them begging for their help in the name of pity, at least I would find some measure of compassion in them.

That and other torments did not go on for just a short time! No, it continued without interruption for more than six years, in an effort to recover a fairly insubstantial sum. What was left of the money due to me after the parties dealing with these matters and petitions to the lords took their share, was paid out to me.

Chapter 7. Christine continues her lament

Do you understand, dear mistress, the sweet joy that marked the early days of my widowhood? Do you think I had reason to indulge in foolish love affairs inspired by an excessive desire for pleasure? But even though that should have satisfied her for a long time, she who was responsible for all the things that happened to me, this faithless woman about whom I have justifiably complained before, still did not feel she had done enough to me, because a painful tooth draws the tongue to it. First I will tell you, taking the matter all the way to the present, how the waves she unleashed drove me and still do.

It is true that during this time of woe I was going through, it was not wise to reveal one's affairs and adversity to others, as I've mentioned before. Why? Because charity is hard to find, and one can't surrender one's reputation to servitude that way for little profit. I found it dreadfully hard to keep my pain inside without unburdening myself, but Fortune had not yet wounded me as much as she might have done, to the point where she prevented me from being accompanied by the little muses of poetry. Although you drove them back and chased them from Boethius' company in his time of tribulation to nourish him with richer fare, my muses led me to compose sorrowful laments bewailing my dead love and the good times past, as you can see at the beginning of my first poems, at the start of my first *Cent Ballades*.[8] And in

---

8. Excerpts from Christine's *One Hundred Ballads* (ca. 1405–1410) can be found in *The Writings of Christine de Pizan,* ed. Charity Cannon Willard (New York: Persea Books, 1994), 41.

the same way, to pass the time and bring some cheer to my mournful heart, I started to compose poems about love and other sentiments, as I say in one of my virelais.[9]

Chapter 8. Christine recounts how she changed her way of life

After those things had happened and since my youth and the greater part of my activities outside the home were behind me, I returned to the kind of life that was more in my nature, that is, solitary and tranquil. Thanks to that solitude, Latin fragments, the discourses of noble sciences, and various maxims and elegant rhetoric began to come back to me. I had heard them in the past when my beloved father and husband were still alive, but I had been foolish enough to retain little of them. Although I favored these things by nature and disposition, my preoccupation with the common tasks of married women and the burden of frequent childbirth had deprived me of them. And then there was my extreme youth—that beguiling enemy of good sense that often doesn't allow children, no matter how intelligent, to apply themselves to their studies because of their desire to play, unless they are restrained by the fear of being whipped. And since I did not have that fear, the desire to play so dominated my intelligence and spirit that I was unable to properly apply myself to the task of learning.

Chapter 10. Christine relates how she embarked on her studies

At that time, when the years had brought me a certain degree of understanding as is natural, I looked back on the events of the past and ahead to the end of things, like a person who has traveled a perilous road and turns back to contemplate the journey with wonder, saying that she will not undertake it again but head for a better place instead. Given that the world is so filled with perilous traps and that there is only one way to reach one's aims (and that is the way of the truth), I turned to the direction to which my own nature and disposition inclined me, that is, my love of learning. Thus I shut my doors, meaning my senses, so they would no longer stray to extraneous matters, and took from you those beautiful books and volumes, telling myself that I would recover something from the losses of the past. I did not presume to begin with the profundities of the obscure sciences, with concepts I could

---

9. Virelais are poems set to music; they were highly popular in late medieval France.

not understand. As Cato says, "Reading without understanding is not reading at all." Instead, like a child being taught the alphabet for the first time, I started with the ancient histories of the beginning of the world: the histories of the Hebrews, the Assyrians, and the early kingdoms, proceeding from one to the next, from the Romans to the French, the Britons, and several other historians, and thereafter, to the arguments of science as far as I could understand them in the time I had to study them.

Then I turned to the books of the poets, and since my level of understanding kept increasing, I was happy to find the style that was natural to me, delighting in their subtle language, the beautiful material hidden beneath delightful, moral tales, and the lovely style of their meter and prose, accomplished by beautiful, polished rhetoric and adorned with exquisite language and unusual proverbs. Nature rejoiced in me because of this science of poetry and told me: "Daughter, be comforted by how much you have actually made the desire I am giving your own, prompting you to continue your studies every day so your understanding of the precepts will continue to grow." At that point, that was not enough to satisfy my senses and mind, but she wanted the pursuit of my studies and the things I found there to inspire me to further reading. She said: "Take the tools and hammer out on the anvil the material I will give you, making it as durable as iron: neither fire nor anything else will be able to shatter it. You will forge delightful things. At the time you were carrying your children in your womb, you experienced great pain in giving birth to them. Now I want you to give birth to new volumes that will, in times to come and in perpetuity, present your memory to the world, before the princes and throughout the world everywhere. You will give birth to them from your memory with joy and pleasure. Despite the hard work and effort, you will forget the pain of your labor when you hear the voice of your books, just as a woman who has given birth forgets her pain as soon as she hears her baby cry."

Then I began to create pretty things, initially on the light side, and then, like a workman who becomes more adept at his work the more he performs it, my mind absorbed more new things all the time, always studying different subjects. I amended my style to give it greater subtlety and put my mind to weightier subjects in 1399, when I began. I continue to do so, as is evident by my having compiled fifteen major volumes between then and today, 1405, not counting the other minor works. All these works are contained in some seventy large quires. And since great praise for this is not appropriate, since it is not very subtle to boast, God knows that I only mention it to continue the narration of my good fortune and misadventures.

Chapter 11. The enjoyment Christine derives from her studies

My way of life had changed a great deal, but my bad luck still did not improve. Rather, like a wretched intrusion into the excellence and comfort of my scholarly, solitary life, malevolence continued, directed not only at me personally but also, to my detriment, against some of those close to me, which I think is how my misfortunes grew.

It is true that word about my way of life, that is to say, my studies, had already spread even among the princes, although I would have preferred to keep that hidden. But since they had been told, I gave them presents in the form of excerpts, however small and feeble, from my books on various subjects, as if they were new texts. By their grace, since they were benevolent and most compassionate princes, they were pleased to see them and delighted to receive them, more, I think, because it was unusual for a woman to be an author (since that had not happened for a long time) than because of the merit of the texts. And so, in a short span of time, my books came to be discussed in and transported to various places and countries.

Around that time, while the daughter of the king of France was married to King Richard of England, a noble count by the name of Salisbury[10] arrived here from that country. That gracious knight loved poetry and was himself a charming poet. After he had seen some of my poems, he begged me so passionately through several important people that I agreed, albeit reluctantly, to let the eldest of my sons, a clever twelve-year-old and a talented singer, accompany him to England to be a companion to one of his own sons of the same age. The count conducted himself nobly and generously toward my son, with promises of more to come, and I believe he would not have failed to abide by them since he had the power to do so. The promises he made me certainly did not turn out to be false.

Now please note, dear mistress, how what I have said is true: how she still did not want me to have prosperity and took my good friends from me by not allowing them to live. She, that is, Misfortune, who had done me so much harm, would not tolerate my prosperity for long, and before long, as everyone knows, she brought the terrible calamity upon King Richard in England, which I mentioned before. Then the noble count was wrongfully beheaded because of his enduring loyalty to his rightful lord. And so my son's blessed introduction into the world failed to take place. Still a child at the

---

10. John Montagu, third earl of Salisbury, d. 1400. Some rumors circulated at court that he took Christine as his lover.

time of the great calamity, away from his own country, he had good reason to be terrified. But what happened? King Henry, who still rules after seizing the crown, saw the books and poetry I mentioned. Feeling anxious to please him, I had already sent several of them to the count. All this came to King Henry's attention, whereupon he delighted in taking my son to his court, keeping him close to him and in great style. In fact, he sent two of his heralds, distinguished men by the name of Lancaster and Hawk, Kings of Arms, to convey to me sincere pleas and promises of great benefits if I would consent to go there. I was not tempted in the least, considering my state of affairs, so I pretended that he could have my son, thanking him sincerely and telling him I was at his command. To make a long story short, I managed by dint of great effort and my books to obtain permission for my son to come and fetch me to take me to this country I had never seen before. And so I refused to allow that fate to befall me and him, because I could not believe that a traitor might come to a good end. I was overjoyed to see my loved one because Death had left me only one son and I had been without him for three years. My financial burden grew heavier, however, and things were not easy for me. I feared that the luxurious style he had enjoyed there might make him eager to return, since children, whose powers of observation are not very acute, are attracted by what they perceive as being more comfortable. So I looked for a great and powerful master for him who might graciously retain him. But since the child's abilities were not very apparent among the multitude of important people at his court, I had to continue to maintain his position at my own expense without drawing any benefit from his service. And so it was that Fortune cut me off from one of my good friends and one of my best hopes. But then she did even worse to me.

Chapter 15. *Philosophy answers Christine*

When I had thus finished all my arguments, I fell silent. Then the great goddess spoke. She seemed to be smiling to herself, just as a wise man does when confronted with a simple person's arguments. All the same, my ignorance did not deprive me of the comfort of her valuable words. Here is what she said:

"My friend, your words make it very clear how you are misled by a foolish bias in judging your own situation. Oh, you blind creature, attributing to ill fortune God's gifts and His own chalice from which He gives you to drink! Why are you complaining without gratitude about the blessings you have received? It is a fact that nothing is more perverted than the stomach that receives proper food and digests it to the detriment of its nourishment. Where is your sense of reason if it doesn't know what is good for you? I will prove that you are misled by giving you a simple example. Just like a medical expert who considers nature's faculties and his patient's physical characteristics before giving him a purgative and medicine based on his strength or weakness, I will prescribe for you a lean and light diet to protect the weakness of your perception's stomach, which would find it hard to digest heavy and important things such as I used to give to my beloved Boethius (as you saw in his book), so I will convert them to the sustenance you require. Since commonplace examples make it easier for the ignorant to understand the shape of things, the surest way to make you really understand, if I can, how wrong you are is based on the Holy Writ. My sweet friend, the way I take it, you are complaining bitterly and feeling unhappy about Fortune. You say that she has been averse to your prosperity for a long time now and that, when she led your parents into France along with you, it was to prepare the snare of tribulations and all the other misfortunes you say have caused you all the grief to which she wanted to lead you. I won't address these things individually, because that is not necessary—my general answer will address them all—but I will show you your extreme folly and the ignorance that leads you astray in this connection and prevents you from seeing the facts of your situation.

"Reconsider for a moment the great persecutions and fatal misfortunes that came to pass and are still happening, how there cannot be peace in the country of your birth, and think hard about whether God did not actually do you a great favor, even though you complain about it, in removing you and your relatives from the flames of those who are burning. Do you really believe that you would have escaped from there without ever suffering any grief yourself or seeing your relatives suffer? Even so, you have wept for your family there who have felt the effects. But then I smiled about your naïveté that attributes to Fortune's power the death and passing of human beings, as you recount about King Charles and other friends of yours. And when you say that Fortune robbed you of them, you seem to want to categorize as misfortune what is written in the secret of God, who disposes of all things and rules as He sees fit. It is as if Fortune had nothing else to do but occupy herself with your affairs. And do you know what prompts you to entertain such fancies? It is the excessive fondness and pity you feel for yourself and the enjoyment of pleasures that result in your attributing everything negative that befalls you to the object of your imagination. Because with respect to the death of the king and others, it is God who had ordained that they take place at that time as being to their benefit, as He does with all things. And if it had been better to leave them alive, He would have done so. And although God's judgments may seem astounding to you, it is not up to you to boldly dispute them. Being omniscient, He knows exactly what He is doing.

"As for the other adversities you complain about, you are like a spoiled child who cries out about a minor application of the rod by its father, unable to recognize the good it does. In conclusion, you certainly complain without cause, because you don't properly know what tribulations are. In this, you reveal yourself as a weak, frail, and impatient woman who cries out over minor things. And I will prove this to you with the following arguments."

Chapter 16. Philosophy's comfort

"You, who complain when minor troubles happen to you as if God were more beholden to you than to others, think about what many good, Christian people like yourself can say. People who, through a cruel misfortune, have lost not only their material goods but also their limbs, who are maimed by long illness and other misadventures, who, in some cases, are tormented in spirit and body, and who, to top it all off, live in such poverty that they don't have a place to live or anything to cover themselves with. People who do not have anything to eat unless they drag themselves around in their misery, seeking alms and often finding little compassion. What shall we say about them and others who experience various great tribulations in many forms? That they are unhappy, unfortunate, and hated by God? No, on the contrary! That goes counter to the spirit of our laws, which are the Gospels. Instead, let us say that they are blessed, just as God Himself refers to them and those who suffer: 'Blessed are the poor in spirit, for theirs is the Kingdom of Heaven. Blessed are the peacemakers, for they shall be called sons of God.' So I tell you that your judgment is faulty, for the unfortunate are not the most persecuted in terms of God's just allotments. In fact, they are the most blessed, since they come closest to the life of Jesus Christ in this world in every tribulation for your example. So I tell you that you are happy, and I will show that to you unless you want to deny the Holy Scripture, because you have nothing in common with those who suffer tribulations. You would have been happier if you had possessed more patience, because your merit would be so much greater. And if you are strong in your faith (and you would be ill-fated if that were not so), you will not doubt my words.

"Does Saint Augustine not speak on this topic in his exposition of the twenty-first psalm, when he says: 'Everyone should know that God is a physician who gives tribulations to the ailing sinner as medicine for his salvation, not as punishment for his damnation. Oh, ailing sinner, when you receive God's medicine in the form of tribulations, you grieve, you lament, you cry out to your physician. He listens to you not because you ask Him to; He listens to you for your salvation'?"

The Book of the City of Ladies

1. *Here begins* The Book of the City of Ladies. *The first chapter explains the reason why this book was written.*

It has long been my habit to devote myself to the study of literature, but as I was sitting in my study one day, amid a pile of books on all sorts of topics, my mind grew weary from trying to absorb the weighty opinions of the various authors I had been studying for so long. I looked up from my book, thinking that for once, I would put aside these complex questions and amuse myself with some lighthearted poetry instead. I looked around for some little book and, by chance, came across a curious volume that did not belong to me but had been given to me for safekeeping along with some other books. When I opened it, I saw from the title page that it was by Matheolus.[1] It made me smile even though I had never seen it before, because I had often heard it said that this particular book, unlike many others, spoke in praise of women. I thought I would leaf through it to amuse myself, but I had hardly begun when my dear mother called to say it was time to eat supper. So I put the book aside, intending to return to it the next day.

The next morning, seated in my study as usual, I remembered that I meant to have a look at this book by Matheolus, so I started to read. I kept at it for a little while but soon decided to put it aside for later study. The book's content did not seem very appealing unless you enjoy invective, and it seemed of no use whatsoever in terms of ethical and moral edification. As I leafed through it, the wording and material struck me as rather shocking, not to mention the ending. But even though the text carried very little weight, it prompted in me an extraordinary thought: why is it that so many men—clerics as well as others—have always been so ready to say and write such abominable and hateful things about women and their nature? And not just one or two of them, or even this Matheolus, who is not a respected author and makes a mockery of

---

1. Matheolus, also known as Mathieu of Boulogne, wrote his *Lamentations* ca. 1295–1300.

the subject. Generally speaking, nearly all essays by philosophers, poets, and orators too numerous to mention offer a similar view and draw identical conclusions, describing female nature as beset by vice.

As I sat thinking deeply about these things, I started to examine myself, my own moral conduct as a woman, and that of other women I have met—all these princesses and great ladies of various social ranks who have been kind enough to share with me their private and personal thoughts. Examining the question from all directions, I wondered if what so many illustrious men say about women could be true. But regardless of how long I thought about it and how much I turned the matter over in my mind, I could find no truth in their condemnation of women's nature and moral character. Yet their opinion was hard to ignore, because it would be too bizarre if so many reputable men and venerable clerics of great intelligence and vision had been telling lies on so many occasions. In fact, I could hardly find a scholarly book, regardless of its author, that did not contain some chapters or lines criticizing women. That brought me to the conclusion that my mind must be simple and ignorant and thus unable to recognize my own shortcomings and those of other women, and so I should accept the opinions of others rather than trust my own feelings and experience.

I lingered on this thought at such length that I seemed to sink into a trance, and the names of countless authors who had written on this subject trickled into my mind like drops from a bubbling fountain. Recalling them one by one, I concluded that God had created a vile creature when He fashioned woman. Indeed, I was astonished that such a worthy craftsman could have produced such an abominable creature. As the authors would have it, she is a vessel filled with all sorts of evil and vices. The idea of despising myself and the entire feminine sex as an aberration of nature made me deeply unhappy and discouraged, and in my despair, I said these words: "'Oh Lord, how can this be? Because unless I stray from my faith, I should not believe that You, in Your infinite wisdom and superiority, ever created anything lacking perfection. Did you Yourself not create woman with the utmost care and endow her with all the qualities You wanted her to have? And how could it be that You created her perfectly and yet I see so many dreadful accusations, not to mention judgments and condemnations, to her detriment? I don't understand this contradiction, but if it is true, dear Lord, that the female sex is an abomination as many would have it (and You say Yourself that one should believe the testimony of two or more witnesses), I must not doubt it. Alas, Lord, why did You not bring me into the world a male, so that I would

have the right qualities to serve You better and not go astray, and be as perfect as men claim to be? But since You, in Your benevolence, created me this
way, forgive me if I don't serve You well enough, dear Lord, and do not be
displeased, for a servant who receives fewer rewards from his master has fewer
obligations to serve him well."

Those words and many others I spoke to God, sick at heart and lamenting in my foolishness how deeply unhappy it made me that God had put me
into this world in a female body.

2. Here Christine recounts how three ladies appeared before her and how the one in front spoke to her and comforted her in her distress.

Lost in these unhappy thoughts, my head bowed as if in shame, my eyes full
of tears, my cheek resting on my hand, I sat leaning on the arm of my chair
when I suddenly saw a ray of light shine down on my lap like a beam of
sunshine. Since it was dark in my room and sunshine could not be entering
at that hour, I jumped as if I had woken from a dream, turning my head to
see where the light was coming from. Then I saw three ladies standing before
me, crowned and of noble bearing. The radiance in their faces illuminated
me and the entire room. As you can imagine, I was astonished that they had
managed to enter since I had shut the door behind me. Terrified that it was
some sort of supernatural apparition come to tempt me, I made the sign of
the cross on my forehead.

Then the lady standing in front of the other two smiled and addressed
me. "My dear daughter, do not be afraid, because we haven't come here to
harm you or upset you. We are here out of compassion, to console you in
your distress, and to shed light on the misconceptions that have so clouded
your judgment that you are rejecting what you know to be true and give
credence to things merely by force of prevailing opinion, although you know
better. You are like the fool in the joke who, while asleep in a mill, was dressed
in a woman's robe by some people wanting to play a trick on him; when he
woke up, they told him he was a woman and he believed their lies, although
he knew better. My dear girl, what has happened to your common sense?
Have you forgotten that gold proves itself in the furnace? It does not change
its quality but increases in value the more it is beaten and fashioned in various ways! Don't you know that the finest things are those that are most often

subject to heated debate? And if you want to focus on higher things, on ideas related to divine concepts, look closely at the greatest philosophers of all time whose rejection of women you quote, and see if they have never drawn the wrong conclusion. See if they don't contradict and correct each other, as you have seen for yourself in Aristotle's *Metaphysics*, where he argues and disputes their opinions, citing Plato and others. Note that Saint Augustine and other ecclesiastic authors of note have done the same, even taking issue with Aristotle on certain topics, although he is considered the prince of all philosophers, the king of natural and moral philosophy. You seem to take every word of the philosophers as an article of faith and believe them incapable of error. As for the poets to whom you refer, don't you know that they have written on various subjects in the form of fables, which you sometimes have to understand as meaning the opposite of what they appear to say. You should interpret them based on the rhetorical figure of speech called *antiphrasis* which, as you know, means that you might say that something is bad when you actually mean the opposite, and vice versa.[2] My advice to you is to turn their words to your advantage by interpreting the passages that speak ill of women the way they are meant to be understood. The book by this man named Matheolus may also have to be understood that way, for it contains many things that, if taken literally, would amount to pure heresy. As for the diatribe about the holy, worthy, God-given state of marriage that you find not only in Matheolus but also in books by other authors, notably the *Roman de la Rose* [*Romance of the Rose*], which is widely accepted because of the respect its author commands, it stands to reason that when they say that women are responsible for turning marriage into a curse, the reverse is true.[3] Because where would you ever find a husband willing to allow his wife to have such power over him that she could hurl insults and obscenities at him at will, the way these authors would

2. In drawing attention to a feature of rhetoric and style, Christine reduces the reader's sense of certainty regarding the intention and meaning of insults to women's nature in literary and philosophical traditions, as well as highlights her own knowledge of rhetoric, which will contribute to her portrayal of a much more positive assessment of women's nature.

3. For further discussion of Christine's voice in this important debate of the early fifteenth century, see David F. Hult, ed. and trans., *Debate of the "Romance of the Rose"* (Chicago: University of Chicago Press, 2010). Also, for a general overview of women's portrayal in the history of political thought, see Susan Moller Okin, *Women in Western Political Thought* (Princeton, N.J.: Princeton University Press, 1979, 2013); Jean Bethke Elshtain, *Public Man Private Woman* (Princeton, N.J.: Princeton University Press, 1982); Carole Pateman and Mary Lyndon Shanley, eds., *Feminist Interpretations and Political Theory* (University Park: Pennsylvania State University Press, 1991); Arlene Saxonhouse, *Women in the History of Political Thought: Ancient Greece to Machiavelli* (New York: Praeger, 1985).

have it? You may have read about this, but I don't believe you have ever seen it for yourself, because it is a deceitful pack of lies. Finally, my dear friend, I should tell you that it is your naïveté that has led you to form the opinion you hold right now. So do get a hold of yourself, regain your senses, and don't worry about these trivial matters. For you should know that bad things said about women do not dishonor women, only those who utter them.

3. Here Christine recounts how the lady addressing her explained her identity, function, and purpose, and announced that Christine would construct a city with the help of these same three ladies.

As I listened to these words addressed to me by this illustrious lady, I didn't know which of my senses was more absorbed by her presence: my hearing, as I took in her noble words, or my sight, as I watched her great beauty and dress, her noble bearing, and her amazing composure. The other two ladies looked the same so I didn't know which one to watch. In fact, the three of them resembled each other so closely that you could hardly tell them apart, except that the last one seemed even more imperious than the other two. Her face had such a fierce quality that no matter how brave you were, if you looked into her eyes, you would become afraid of committing a transgression, because you instantly sensed that she posed a threat to all wrongdoers. Out of respect I rose to my feet before these ladies, watching them in silence, so captivated that I could not think of anything to say. I was most curious to know who they could be, and if only I could have found the courage, I would have liked to ask them their names, where they were from, and the significance of the richly ornamented and distinct scepters each carried in her right hand. I also wanted to know why they had come, but since I did not consider myself worthy of questioning such noble ladies as these seemed to be, I did not dare speak and continued gazing at them, still frightened but also reassured by the words I had heard, which had begun to change my mind. Then the wise lady who had addressed me replied to my unspoken questions, apparently able to read my mind. She said: "My dear Daughter, you should know that God, in His wisdom, manages all things. Although we are celestial beings, He has sent us to mingle with the people of this world, to maintain order and justice for the institutions we ourselves have established for various functions according to God's command. All three of us are His daughters and born from Him. My task is to step in when men and women have lost their way and put them back on the right track. When they go astray but still know me when they see me, I go to them in spirit and preach to them, showing them how and why they failed. Then I show them the path to follow and how to avoid the pitfalls. And because it is my role to clearly and truly show all people their own strengths and weaknesses, you see me holding in my right hand this shining mirror in lieu of a scepter. You should know that whoever looks into it will see her or his true nature. Oh, my mirror has great power. It is not for nothing that it is encrusted with precious stones, as you can see, for it shows the essence, quality, proportions, and measure of all things, and nothing can be done well without it. I know you would also like to learn the roles of my sisters whom you see before you, but to make sure you perfectly understand our evidence, each of us will address you in turn and tell you her name and function.

"Now I will explain why we have come here. Be aware that since we never do anything without good reason, our appearance here has a specific purpose. Although we do not frequent all places and not everyone gets to see us, you deserved to receive a visit from us because of your great love for true knowledge, which you pursue through long and constant study. This has made you into a solitary person, withdrawn from the world, and we have come to console you in your anguish and perplexity, dear friend, and to explain the things that trouble your soul and confuse your thoughts.

"There is another, even more important reason for our visit, which we will now tell you about. You should know that we wish to prevent others from making the same mistake you have made and to ensure that from now on, ladies and all other worthy women will have a refuge and a place where they can defend themselves from all these assailants. These ladies have been defenseless for too long now, like an unfenced field, without a champion to take up their cause, while the powerful men who are legally obliged to see to their defense have allowed them to be trampled in the mud through negligence and indifference. It is no wonder that women's malevolent opponents and the villains who made women the object of vicious criticisms have won the war against them: they were defenseless. Have you ever seen a city not taken when there was no one to defend it, or an unjust case lost by someone pleading without opposition? Women, in their sweet-natured and humble way, have remained patient as commanded by God and trusting His justice. They have graciously endured the grave insults that have unjustly been meted out to them, some of them in person and many others in writing, referring to God as is their right. But now it is time to take their just cause from the pharaoh's hands and that is why you see the three of us here before you. We have come out of compassion to tell you about a certain building project in the shape of a strong, well-constructed city that you are destined to erect with our help and guidance and that will be inhabited only by illustrious, meritorious ladies.[4] For the gates of our city will be closed to those lacking virtue."

4. Here we learn how the lady, before disclosing her name, provides more details of the city Christine is to build and explains that she is charged with helping Christine construct the city's walls and enclosure.

"Thus, my dear daughter, you among all women have been given the privilege to build the City of Ladies. To lay the foundations, you will draw running water from the three of us as from a clear well, and we will provide you with building materials stronger and more durable than any marble sealed with cement. Your city will be beautiful beyond compare and it will last forever.

"Have you not read how King Tros founded the great city of Troy with the help of Apollo, Minerva, and Neptune, who were considered gods by the people of that time? And how Cadmus founded the city of Thebes at the urging of the gods? Yet in the course of time, even those cities were destroyed and fell into ruin. But I prophesy, like a true sibyl, that this city that you are going to found with our help will not be destroyed or fall into ruin but will remain prosperous until the end of time despite the envy of its malicious enemies. It will know many assaults but will never be taken or vanquished.

"A long time ago, as the history books will tell you, certain ladies of great courage who would no longer tolerate servitude founded the realm of Amazonia.[5] It lasted for a long time under the rule of several queens, illustrious

4. Note that the process through which women's contributions will be revalued and positively assessed is in part an exercise in retrieval. The traditions of misogyny in intellectual history have had the double impact of making women's traces in history more difficult to find and of devaluing those traces that still remain. This makes it particularly challenging for Christine to recover information concerning women in the lower classes even though she explicitly addresses her message to women of all classes.

5. The country of the Amazons, populated only by women and great female warriors, was long thought to have been a wholly fictional mythological construct of the ancient Greeks. A more recent scholarly study suggests that there is clear evidence of female warriors integrated in armies in ancient Scythia, a practice that most likely inspired the literary tradition. See Adrienne Mayor, *The Amazons* (Princeton, N.J.: Princeton University Press, 2014).

ladies elected by the women themselves, who governed them well and maintained their rule with great vigor. And although they were all very strong and powerful, conquering a large part of the whole Levant during their rule and though all neighboring countries feared them, including Greece (the noblest country in the whole world at that time), the power of this realm still waned over time, as is the way of all earthly monarchies. All that is left of them now is their names.

"You, however, will construct a much more powerful city. To get it started, the three of us have agreed that I should be charged with providing you with tough, indestructible cement to lay strong foundations and build the great walls that are to surround the city, tall and sturdy, with mighty towers and surrounded by moats and outer fortresses, as is appropriate for a city strong enough to be able to resist all attacks. Following our plan, you will set the foundations deep into the ground to make them last and build the walls so high that the inhabitants will fear no one. Daughter, now that I have told you why we have come and to make sure you have faith in what I tell you, I will now give you my name. Its sound alone will tell you that if you wish to follow my instructions, you will have in me a leader who will help you avoid mistakes in your work. My name is Lady Reason. Decide for yourself whether you are in good hands. That is all I have to say for now."

5. Here Christine recounts how the second lady discloses her name, explains her role, and tells Christine how she will assist her in building the City of Ladies.

When the first lady finished speaking and before I had the opportunity to respond, the second lady said: "My name is Lady Rectitude. I reside more in heaven than on earth, but I dwell among the just like a ray of light from God and a messenger of His goodness. I encourage them to do the right thing, to give each person his or her due as far as possible, to speak and uphold the truth, to defend the rights of the poor and the innocent, to refrain from stealing from others, and to uphold the reputations of those unjustly accused. I am the shield and defender of God's servants, and I curb the power of the wicked. I make sure that the industrious receive rest and the deserving are rewarded, and I am their advocate in Heaven. Through me, God reveals His secrets to those who love Him.

"This shining ruler that you see me hold in my right hand in place of a scepter is the yardstick that separates right from wrong and shows the difference between good and evil. Whoever follows it will not go astray. The just will rally to this rod of peace and draw support from it, and the wicked will be punished. What more can I tell you? This yardstick, whose powers are infinite, measures all things. Know that it will serve you, and you will need it to measure the structure you have been commissioned to erect. You will need it to build this city, to lay out its interior, to construct its tall temples and measure its palaces, houses, and dwellings, its streets and squares and everything else that is needed to populate the city. I have come to help you and that will be my role. Don't worry about the breadth and great circumference of the outer walls, because with God's help and our assistance, you will build a great city and fill it with strong, beautiful dwellings and inns, leaving no space unused."

6. Here Christine relates how the third lady described herself and her role, how she would help Christine construct the tall roof timbers of the towers and palaces, and how she would bring her a queen accompanied by a retinue of noble ladies.

Next, it was the third lady's turn to speak. She said: "My dear Christine, I am Lady Justice, God's most special daughter, for my essence flows directly from His own. I reside in Heaven, on Earth, or in Hell: in Heaven for the glory of the saints and blessed souls, on Earth to divide and allot to all their portion of good and evil as they deserve it, in Hell to punish the wicked. I am impartial because I have neither friend nor foe and I am steadfast: no one can persuade me through pity or move me through cruelty. My role is purely to judge, to divide, and to give everyone their just deserts.[6] I sustain all things; without me nothing would remain stable. I am part of God and God is part of me; we are one. Whoever follows me cannot fail, because my way is unerring. I teach all men and women of sound mind who believe in me to correct, know, and regain control of themselves above all, to do unto others as they would have them do to themselves, to distribute goods without showing favoritism, to tell the truth, to avoid and despise lies, and to reject all forms of vice. This vessel of fine gold that you see me holding in my right hand, resembling a measuring cup, was given to me by God my father. It serves to mete out to each person his rightful portion. It is engraved with the fleur-de-lis of the Holy Trinity

---

6. See also Christine's brief invocation of Aristotelian justice in *The Book of the Body Politic* I:19 (in this volume).

and always measures the right portion, so that no one can ever complain of what I allot to them. Mortal men have other measures they claim are based on mine, but they are wrong. They often claim to measure in my name but fail to measure correctly, giving too much to some and too little to others.

"I could talk at length about all the details of my function, but let me just say for now that I occupy a special place among the Virtues, because they are all connected to me. And we, the three ladies you see before you, are all one: we could not function without each other. What the first one decides, the second one puts into effect, while I, the third one, ensure that it is brought to fruition. Thus, it has been agreed among the three of us that I shall help you complete your city, and it will be my role to construct the turrets of the tall towers and the principal mansions and inns, which will all be made of fine, shining gold. Then I will populate the city for you with illustrious ladies, and I will bring you a highborn queen, who shall be honored and revered by the other ladies, even the most excellent ones. In this way, I will ensure that the city you will help build will be well fortified and sealed off with strong gates that I will search for in Heaven. And upon its completion, I will deliver the keys into your hands."

7. Here Christine recounts how she spoke to the three ladies.

These words concluded the speeches of the three ladies, to which I had listened with rapt attention. They had completely taken away the unhappiness I had been feeling before their arrival. Suddenly, I threw myself at their feet, not just on my knees but face down, moved by their splendor. Kissing the ground at their feet, revering them as exalted goddesses, I humbly addressed them with these words: "Oh, ladies of supreme dignity, radiance of the heavens and light of the earth, fountains of Paradise and joy of the blessed, how is it possible that you have seen fit to come down from your pontifical seats and shining thrones to visit this simple and ignorant student in her obscure and troubled cell? How could I possibly thank you enough for such beneficence? The raindrops and dew of your sweet words have already fallen upon me, penetrating and saturating my arid mind so that it now feels ready to germinate and send up new plants capable of bearing wholesome fruit with a delicious flavor. How can it be that I am offered such a blessing as to have been chosen to build a new city in this world, as you have explained?

"I am not Saint Thomas the Apostle who, by the grace of God, built a splendid palace in Heaven for the king of India. My poor brain doesn't know anything about craft and measures, nor has it studied the theory and practice of construction. And even if I could learn these things, where would I, as a woman, find the physical strength to accomplish such a huge task? But, honored ladies, no matter how daunted I am by the contemplation of this extraordinary task, I know well that for God, all things are possible, and I must not doubt that whatever tasks are undertaken with the guidance and help of the three of you will be brought to a good end. I therefore thank God and you, revered ladies, with all my heart for the honor of having entrusted me with such a noble task, which I accept with great joy. Behold your hand-maiden ready to do your bidding. I await your commands and I will do as you say."

8. Here Christine relates how Reason instructed and helped her excavate the ground to build the foundations.

Then Lady Reason replied and said: "Stand up, now, daughter. We must not lose any more time. Let us go to the Field of Letters. There we will found the City of Ladies, on a flat and fertile plain with all sorts of fruit and sweet rivers and the earth abounding with all good things. Take the spade of your mind and dig a deep trench along the line I have traced. I will help you carry the earth away on my own shoulders."

I immediately stood up to obey her command, feeling much stronger and lighter than before thanks to the fortitude of the three ladies. Lady Reason took the lead and I followed, and once we arrived at the field, I started excavating, digging with the spade of my thirst for knowledge along the lines she had traced. And my first task was as follows: "Lady, I clearly remember what you told me about all the men who have been attacking the ways of women, how the longer gold is in the oven, the more refined it becomes. The way I understand that is that the more women are unjustly criticized, the greater their merit and glory. But please tell me why this is so and why so many different authors have spoken out against women in their books, since I already know from you that they are wrong. Is it nature that makes them do this, or are they governed by hatred? Can you explain that?"

She replied: "Daughter, to help you understand the matter more clearly, I will carry away this first bucket of earth. You should know that their behavior is certainly not governed by nature. In fact, it is completely the opposite, because there is no greater and stronger bond in the world than that of love, which nature creates between men and women by the grace of God. The reasons why men keep slandering women are diverse, and that also applies to the authors you have read. Some have attacked women with good intentions, that is, to draw lost men away from the company of vicious and dissolute women with whom they might be besotted or to prevent them from becoming besotted. To keep men from leading a shameless and sinful life, they blamed women in their entirety to make men believe that all women are abominations."

"My lady," I replied, "please forgive me for interrupting, but since they were motivated by good intentions, did they do the right thing? It is said, after all, that men are judged by their intentions."

"You misunderstand, my dear daughter," she said, "because there is no excuse for gross ignorance. If someone killed you with good intentions but out of foolishness, could that be justified? No: those who engage in this practice, whoever they are, have acted unjustly, because injuring and harming one party in order to help another is unjust. Denouncing all female behavior is contrary to the truth, as I will show you by giving you an example. Let us suppose that it was done with the intention of curing foolish men of their foolishness: that would be tantamount to criticizing fire—a very good and necessary element—because some people burned themselves, or cursing water because someone drowned. The same can be said of all good things that can be used well or badly. One should not denounce all women because some fools seek to harm their reputations. You yourself eloquently covered this point elsewhere in your writings. But those who have made a habit of voicing these opinions, whatever their intention, have generalized merely to make their point, like someone who has an enormous robe cut from a piece of fabric just because it costs him nothing and nobody objects. In the process, he appropriates the rights of others to his advantage. But as you have rightly said elsewhere, if these writers were only trying to draw men away from foolishness and keep them from getting entangled by criticizing the life and ways of women who proved themselves vicious and dissolute, then I admit they would have produced excellent work. To tell the truth, there is no one in this world you should avoid more than an evil, sinful woman. She is like a monster deformed by nature, a fake estranged from her own character, which should be simple, tranquil, and honest. But to criticize them all when there are so many outstanding women, I promise you that I strongly disapprove and that they and everyone who shares their views are completely wrong. So cast aside these dirty, misshapen black stones; they will never be used in the building of your beautiful city.

"Other men have criticized women for other reasons: some have been motivated by their own sinful behavior, others by the deficiencies of their own bodies. Some act out of jealousy and some are guided by a natural tendency to criticize. Others like to show that they are well read and base their arguments on what they have read in books, simply repeating what others have said.

"Those who criticize women as a result of their own depravity are men who have spent their youth in debauchery and have had affairs with many different women. All those experiences have made them sly, and they have grown old without repenting their sins. They look back with regret on the follies of their past and the dissolute life they have led. But nature has grown cold in them and does not permit them to accomplish their impotent desires. They regret that what they consider the good old days are now behind them and they are confronted with younger men who seem to be leading the life they used to enjoy. The only way they know of to get rid of their nostalgia is to criticize women, in the belief that this will make them less attractive to other men. These old men often say lewd and dishonest things, as you can see in the book by Matheolus: he actually admits to being an impotent old man filled with desire. This is an excellent example to prove the truth of what I am telling you, and you can safely believe that this applies to many others.

"But these corrupt old men who are rotten like those with advanced leprosy should not be confused with the fine, upright men of old whose virtue and wisdom I have perfected, because not all old men share corrupt desires. That would be a shame! Following their hearts, these men speak exemplary words, honest and wise. They detest all misdeeds and slander, and they neither attack nor defame either men or women. They despise evil and attack it in general terms without accusing or charging anyone in particular, and they counsel the avoidance of evil, the pursuit of virtue, and following the right track.

"Those who are motivated by their own bodily infirmities are often impotent and physically deformed. They have caustic and malicious minds and the only way they know how to handle the frustration caused by their frailty is to attack those who give pleasure to other men. That way, they think they can turn others away from the pleasure they can no longer enjoy themselves.

"Those who have attacked women out of envy are often wretched men who have met women of greater intelligence and nobler ethic than they possess themselves, which pains them and makes them resentful. The envy they feel causes them to attack all women, in the belief that this will demean and diminish their merit and reputation. A good example of this is found in a book by a man whose name I have forgotten, titled *De Philoso-phia* [*On Philosophy*], in which he goes to great lengths to prove that it is inappropriate for men to honor women, whoever they may be. He says that men who make a fuss over women pervert the title of his book, trans-forming love of wisdom (philosophy) to love of folly, which you might call 'philofolly.' But I assure you that he himself turned his book into a proper work of 'philofolly' by the phony conclusions he draws from the arguments presented.

"In terms of those who are slanderous by nature, it is not surprising that they attack all women since they criticize everyone. Yet I assure you that any man who readily slanders women has a mean spirit, because he acts against reason and against nature. Against reason because he is very ungrateful and fails to recognize the great blessings women have bestowed on him—so great, in fact, that he will never be able to make up for them no matter how hard he tries, and he will always need them. Against nature because there is neither beast nor bird that does not naturally love its partner, that is, the female. Thus, it is quite unnatural for a rational man to do the opposite.

"There is no work, no matter how worthy or skillful its maker, that has not been and does not continue to be imitated by others. There are many who want to try their hand at writing, and they think they cannot go wrong copy-ing from other authors what they want to say. So they engage in slandering women, as I well know. Some of them want to join the dialogue and scribble texts that are like water without salt, one as insipid as the next. Or they produce inane ballads about the morals of women, princes, or other people, when they don't recognize and can't correct their own pathetic conduct and inclinations. But simple people, who are as ignorant as they are, claim that those works are the best in the world."

9. Here Christine tells how she dug into the ground, meaning that she asked questions of Lady Reason, and how Lady Reason replied.

"Now that I have prepared and set up your great task, you should continue digging up the earth following the line I have drawn."

To comply with her command, I struck out with my spade with all my might, saying: "Lady, why is it that Ovid, who has the reputation of being the greatest of all poets—although some people, myself included, think that

Virgil is the better of the two, correct me if I'm wrong—engaged in so much criticism of women? Take his book titled *Ars amatoria*, or *Remedia amoris* [*The Art of Love*] and others of his works."[7]

Reason replied: "Ovid was a man with superb skills in the art of poetry, and he had a great and keen understanding of everything he undertook. Yet he engaged in all sorts of frivolity and carnal pleasures and not just in one relationship: he took up with any woman he could find. He knew no restraint or loyalty and had no lasting affection for a particular woman. He led that sort of life throughout his youth as long as he could, but in the end he received his just deserts: he lost not only his reputation and possessions but even parts of his body, having been sent into exile for his lecherous nature and his encouragement of others to follow his example. And when he was eventually called back from exile thanks to some powerful young Romans, he did not stop himself from returning to the same sinful life for which he had already been punished. He was castrated and disfigured for his reprehensible acts. And this is exactly the point I was making, because when he realized he could no longer lead the life he used to enjoy, he started to attack women, using cunning arguments in an attempt to render women unattractive to others."

"Well said, my lady. But I have read a book by another Italian author by the name of Cecco d'Ascoli—I think he came from the region of Tuscany or the Marches.[8] In one of his chapters he says some really atrocious things, so bad that no one with any sense should repeat them."

Reason replied: "My daughter, you shouldn't be surprised that Cecco d'Ascoli slandered the entire female sex. He despised and hated them all, and his extraordinary malice prompted him to make sure all men despised and hated them as well. But he received his just reward, suffering an ignominious death being burned at the stake as punishment for his vicious slander."

"I read another little book, my lady, written in Latin and titled *De Secretis mulierum* [*Women's Secrets*],[9] which says many bad things about women's bodies."

---

7. Ovid is otherwise known as Publius Ovidius Naso (43 BCE–17 CE) and is known especially for his *Metamorphoses* (a key source for medieval discussions of classical mythology).

8. Cecco d'Ascoli (1257–1327) was an astrologer, mathematician, and poet from the region now known as the Abruzzo. His major work was titled *Acerba*, which was condemned by the Inquisition and led to his execution.

9. *Women's Secrets* was a popular medieval treatise discussing human reproduction and depicting women as vicious creatures—a treatise once falsely thought to have been the work of Albertus Magnus.

Reason replied: "If you look at your own body, you won't need further proof to know that this book was purposely written to deceive, because if you have read it, you know that it is full of lies. And although some say that it was written by Aristotle, it is unthinkable that a philosopher of his repute would have produced such nonsense.[10] Women will know from experience that certain things in this book are totally untrue and complete nonsense, which will permit them to conclude that the rest of the book must also be a fabrication. But don't you remember the part at the beginning that says that some pope or other excommunicated every man who read the book to his wife or gave it to her to read?"

"Yes, my lady, I remember it well."

"Do you know the malicious reason why this lie was given at the beginning of this book to convince stupid and ignorant men?"

"No, Lady, not unless you tell me."

"That was so women would not find out about this book and its contents, because its author was well aware that if women read it or had it read to them, they would know it was filled with lies, and they would contradict it and make fun of it. That was how the author wanted to trick and deceive the men who read his book."

"Lady, I remember that at the end of his detailed discussion about the inadequacy and weakness of the way the female body is formed in the mother's womb, the author says that Nature is also deeply ashamed when she sees that she has created such an imperfect body."

"Oh, my dear friend, you must see the complete madness, the irrational blindness that prompted these words! How could Nature, God's handmaiden, be more powerful than her master, the almighty God, who conceived the form of man and woman after His own image and from whom she derives her authority? It was His holy wish to fashion Adam from the clay of the field of Damascus, and when He had created him, he took him to dwell in the earthly paradise, the noblest place on this lowly earth. There, He put Adam to sleep, and created woman from one of his ribs. That means that she was meant to stand beside him and not lie at his feet like a servant, and that he should love her like his own flesh. If the Divine Craftsman was not ashamed of the creation and shape of the female body, why would Nature be? Ah, it is the height of folly to say that. Indeed, how was she formed? I don't know if

---

10. If Christine is correct to claim that Aristotle did not write *Women's Secrets*, readers should note that Aristotle did conceive of woman as a kind of deformed or deficient man (e.g., Aristotle, *Generation of Animals* 737a26–30). See also Aristotle, *Politics* 1259a37–1260a30.

you've thought of this: she was created in the image of God! How can anyone dare slander the vessel that bears such a noble imprint? But when some people hear that God created man in His image, they are foolish enough to believe that this refers to His material body. That is incorrect, however, for God had not assumed a human shape at that time. In fact, it refers to the soul, the intellectual spirit that will last to eternity in God's image. God created this soul and put equally good and noble souls in the bodies of men and women. But, to return to the creation of the body, woman was made by the Divine Craftsman. And where was she created? In the Earthly Paradise. And from what? Was it a vile material? On the contrary! It was from the noblest material ever created, the body of man, that God made woman."

"Lady, as I understand you, woman is a noble being, but Cicero said that man must never serve woman and that he who does, debases himself, for one should never serve one's inferior."[11]

Reason replied: "The superior being is he or she who is the most virtuous. People's superiority or baseness does not depend on their gender but on the perfection of their morals and virtues. And blissful is he who serves the Virgin, who is superior to all the angels."

"But my lady, one of the Catos, the one who was such a great orator, said that if there were no women in this world, we would converse with the gods."[12]

Reason replied: "Now you can see the foolishness of one who is considered wise! It is thanks to women that man reigns with God. And if anyone says that it was a woman, Lady Eve, who caused man's fall from Paradise, I would answer that man gained more through Mary than he lost through Eve, because if Eve had not sinned, humankind would never have become one with God. Thus, both men and women should be grateful for this sin that has brought them so much honor. If a creature caused human nature to take a fall, the Creator raised it that much higher. As for men conversing with the gods, if women did not exist as mentioned by this Cato, he spoke truer than he thought, because he was a pagan and among the followers of this belief, it was thought that gods resided in both Heaven and Hell, meaning that they

11. Marcus Tullius Cicero (106–43 BCE) was a famous Roman politician, orator, and scholar. His *Pro Caelio* [*For Caelius*] is known as a particularly misogynistic text.

12. Both Cato the Elder (234–139 BCE) and Cato the Younger (95–46 BCE) were regarded as accomplished orators in Rome. While the second is identified today with the name Uticensis, the first is known to have actively supported the *Lex Voconia* [the Voconian Law], which sought to restrict the financial freedom of women.

called the devils the gods of Hell. So you can see that it is no lie that if it had not been for Mary, men would indeed be conversing with those gods."

10. More discussion and answers on the same topics.

"This same Cato Uticensis also said that a woman men find attractive resembles a rose: pleasant to see but hiding a sharp thorn."

Reason replied: "Again, this Cato spoke truer than he knew, for nothing is and should be more pleasant to behold than a good, honest woman of virtue. As for the thorn, that does have a permanent place in a woman's heart in the shape of fear of committing a sin and contrition. It is what keeps her tranquil, level-headed, and respectful, and it is her salvation."

"Lady, some authors have argued that women are by nature gluttonous and obsessed with food. Is that true?"

"Daughter, you have often heard the proverb that says: 'What nature gives, no one can take away.' Thus, if women were inclined that way by nature, it would be most surprising that they are rarely or never found in places where delicacies and sweets were sold, such as in taverns and other places serving that purpose. If anyone argued that it is shame that keeps them away, I would say that this is patently untrue, that what keeps them away is their natural disposition, which is not inclined that way. But let us suppose that they were so inclined and that shame gave them the power to resist their natural inclination, then their virtue and constancy do them great honor. And on that subject, don't you remember standing at the door of your house on a feast day not long ago, talking to the honorable young lady who is your neighbor and seeing a man coming out of a tavern? He was talking to another man, saying: 'I've spent so much in the tavern that my wife won't drink any wine today.' You called him over and asked him why she would not drink any wine, and he said: 'Because, lady, she asks me every time I come from the tavern how much I have spent, and if it is more than twelve pennies, she wants to compensate what I spent by not drinking any wine herself. She says that if we both were to spend a lot of money, our earnings would not cover it.'"

"I remember that well, my lady," I said.

And Reason replied: "There are plenty of examples to show you that women are sober by nature, and those who are not, go against their own nature. There is no uglier vice in a woman than gluttony, because wherever it shows itself, this vice attracts many others. By contrast, you see large numbers of women going to church, attending sermons, and making their confession, clutching their rosaries and books of hours."

"That is all quite clear, my lady," I said, "but those men say that they go there all dressed up to show off their beauty and make men fall in love with them."

Reason replied: "That would be easy to believe, dear friend, if one only saw young and pretty women there, but if you pay attention, for every young woman you will see twenty or thirty soberly dressed elderly women frequenting these holy places. And women are not only pious; they also embrace charity, because who else visits and comforts the sick, helps the poor, visits the hospitals, buries the dead? It seems to me that this work is all done by women, and these are the noblest roads God can command us to follow."

"You put it very well, my lady, but I know another author who says that women have a weak spirit and are like children, which is why children like to talk to them and they like to talk to children."

Reason replied: "Daughter, if you closely observe children, you will see that they are naturally drawn to affection and gentleness. And what in this world is more affectionate and gentler than a well-mannered woman? Ah! The perversity of those vicious, diabolical people who want to turn the quality and virtue of kindness that is in the nature of women into a vice and disgrace![13] If women love children, it is not because they are ignorant but because of their innate gentleness, and if they are sweet like children, they are extremely well guided, for that is the word of the Gospel. When the Apostles were arguing about who was the greatest among them, didn't our Lord call over a child, put His hand upon its head, and say: 'I say unto you that whoever will be small and humble like this child shall be the most exalted, for those who humble themselves shall be raised up and those who raise themselves up shall be humbled.'"

"My lady, men have forged a strong weapon from a Latin proverb that they use to attack women. It says: 'God made women to weep, talk, and weave.'"

Reason replied: "Certainly, dear daughter, there is truth to this proverb, to the extent that whoever believes or says it does not use it to attack women. It is a wonderful thing that God instilled these qualities because many have been saved by their tears, words, and weaving. To those who attack women for their inclination to weep, I say: 'If our Lord Jesus Christ, from whom no thought is hidden and who knows and sees into every heart, had thought that women's tears spring only from weakness and simplemindedness, His sublime dignity would never have allowed His own esteemed and glorious body to

---

13. Note the significance of Christine's argumentation here.

weep tears from compassion when he saw Mary Magdalene and Martha,[14] her sister, weep over the death of their brother the leper, whom he resurrected. Oh! God bestowed such boundless favors on women when he graced them with tears! Instead of condemning Mary Magdalene's tears, He was moved by them and forgave her sins. In fact, it is thanks to those tears that she now gloriously resides in Heaven.

"Nor did He scorn the tears of the widow who wept over her only son, who had died and was being carried to his grave. Our Lord, who saw her weep and who is the wellspring of all pity, was moved to compassion by her tears.[15] He went to her and asked: 'Woman, why do you weep?' and instantly brought the child back to life. God has performed other miracles, too numerous to mention, but as you can read in the Holy Scriptures, many of them were bestowed on women because of their tears and they still are, every day. I believe that many women—and others for whom they prayed—have been saved thanks to their tears of devotion. Was Saint Augustine, the glorious Doctor of the Church, not converted to the Faith by his mother's tears?[16] That good woman wept unceasingly, praying to God to please enlighten the heart of her son who was a pagan, unable to perceive the light of the Faith. Saint Ambrose, whom this pious woman often visited to implore him to pray to God on her son's behalf, told her: 'Woman, I don't believe it is possible that so many tears could be shed in vain.' Oh, blessed Ambrose, you certainly did not believe that women's tears were frivolous! And this is how you could answer the men who take women to task for it: it is because of a woman's tears that this holy saint, the revered Saint Augustine, shines from the altar, brightening and illuminating the Holy Church. Let men say no more on this subject.

"It is also true that God gave women the power of speech. May He be praised for it! If He had not, they would be mute. In fact, the proverb you mentioned was invented by someone or other to attack women, because if woman's speech had really been so disgraceful and unreliable as some would have it, then our Lord Jesus Christ would have never seen fit to decree that so

---

14. Mary Magdalene will be given a special place in the highest towers of the city (Part III): she will be welcomed as a member of the city right after the queen, the Virgin Mary. In *The Treasure of the City of Ladies*, Christine uses the examples of Mary Magdalene and Mary Martha to discuss the respective worthiness of the contemplative and active life (while praising both, she notes that it is the contemplative life that is the "worthiest perfection" [I.6]).

15. Luke 7:11–14.

16. Saint Augustine of Hippo (354–430 CE) wrote *The City of God*. It was a significant work of late classical philosophy along with his *Confessions,* where he recounts the story of his conversion (one that attaches much significance to the impact his mother's tears had on him).

glorious a mystery as His most glorious resurrection would first be announced by a woman. He commanded the blessed Mary Magdalene, to whom He first appeared on the first day of Easter, to announce it to His Apostles and to Peter. Oh, blessed God, praise be upon You who, with the other infinite gifts and favors You bestowed upon the female sex, chose a woman to be the bearer of such exalted and precious news."

"Those jealous men should really stop saying such things if they ever thought about this, my lady," I said. "But I have to laugh at a stupid remark you hear men make, even including some foolish preachers, to the effect that God first appeared to a woman because He was well aware that she would be unable to keep quiet, so that the news of His resurrection would spread that much faster."

Reason replied: "Daughter, you have done well to call those who say that fools. Because it is not enough for them to attack women: they even impute this blasphemy to Jesus Christ, saying in effect that He decided to reveal such holy, perfect news using a human weakness. I don't understand how anyone could dare say such a thing, even in jest, because God should never be a joking matter.

"But going back to our first topic, it was fortunate that the woman from Canaan was such a voluble talker.[17] She would not stop screaming and harassing Jesus Christ, going through the streets of Jerusalem crying: 'Have mercy on me, Lord, for my daughter is sick.' And what did the blessed Lord do, He who has always been filled with compassion and to whom a single word from the heart was enough to grant mercy? He seemed to take delight in the stream of words and ceaseless prayers coming from this woman's mouth. And why would that be? It was to test her constancy, because when he had compared her to a dog—which seemed a little rude, but she belonged to a foreign faith, not that of God—she did not hesitate in giving Him a wise and intelligent answer, saying: 'Lord, that is true, but little dogs live on the crumbs from their master's table.' Oh, wise woman! Who taught you to speak that way? You won your case thanks to the wise words that sprang from the purity of your intentions. And so it proved, for our Lord, turning to His Apostles, testified in His own words, saying that He had not encountered this much faith in all of Israel, and He granted her request. Ah! Who could adequately summarize this honor to the female sex so denigrated by the envious, considering that God discovered more faith in the heart of a little heathen woman

17. Matthew 15:22–28.

than in all the bishops, princes, priests, and the entire Jewish race, who called themselves God's chosen people?

"Another notable example is that of the Samaritan woman.[18] She also pleaded her case at length when she arrived at a well to draw water and found Jesus Christ sitting there, completely exhausted. Oh! Blessed be this holy body in which God incarnated Himself! How could You see fit to open Your holy mouth and address words of salvation to this sinful little woman who was not even of Your faith? Truly, You made it abundantly clear that You did not despise the devout female sex. God, how many of today's bishops would stoop to address a lowly little woman even if her salvation was at stake?

"The woman who sat listening to Christ's sermon spoke no less wisely.[19] As they say, women can never keep quiet, and that was a good thing because she was so impassioned by His holy words that she spoke out, saying the words that have been solemnly recorded in the Gospel. Jumping up, she shouted: 'Blessed be the womb that bore You and the breasts that suckled You!'

"Now you can understand, my dear child, how God has made it clear that He has given women speech so they might serve Him better. Thus, women should not be criticized for something that is responsible for so much good and so little evil, for it is rare to see women's words cause serious harm.

"As to weaving, it is true that God wished this to be a natural occupation for women, since it is work that is necessary for divine service and for the benefit of every rational creature. Without this work, the world would be in a state of chaos. Thus, it is sheer wickedness to criticize women for something that brings them sincere gratitude, honor, and praise."

11. Christine asks Reason why women are excluded from the courts of law, and Reason's response.

"Revered and honored lady, your excellent explanations have satisfied many of my questions. But please tell me the reason why women do not plead before the courts of justice, why they aren't familiar with court cases, and why they don't hand down judgments? Men say that it is because of some woman who behaved badly in a court of law."

"Daughter, that whole inane story is a malicious invention. But if you wanted to know the causes and reasons of all things, you would never get to

18. John 4:1–26.
19. Luke 11:27.

the end of it. Even reading Aristotle would not do, despite all his explanations in his *Problemata* [*Problems*] and *Categoriae* [*The Categories*]. To answer your question, my dear friend, you might just as well ask why God did not ordain that men perform the work of women, and women the work of men. This question can be answered by saying that just as a wise, well-organized lord arranges his household by assigning certain tasks to some and other tasks to others so that no work is duplicated, God has similarly created men and women to serve Him in different functions and to help and comfort each other, each in his or her own way. To each sex He gave the nature and disposition required to perform their tasks, even if the human species often errs in what it must do. He has given men a strong, powerful body so they can move and speak decisively. It is because men have been endowed with these traits that they learn the laws so they can maintain the rule of justice in this world. In the event someone is unwilling to obey the laws that have been established by legislation, it is their duty to force that person to obey by physical means and force of arms, which women would not be able to do. God gave some women great intelligence (and there are many of them), but given their natural modesty, it would be inappropriate for them to go and boldly render judgment like men, for there are enough men to do that. What would be the point in sending three men to lift a burden when two could easily carry it?

"But if anyone claims that women are not intelligent enough to learn the laws, experience clearly proves that the opposite is true. As I will tell you later, there have been and still are many great female philosophers who have mastered fields more complex and important than laws written and laid down by men. And if anyone claimed that women don't have a natural gift for politics and government, I will give you examples of several great female rulers from the past. And to give you better appreciation of the truth of my words, I will even remind you of some women from your own time who were widowed and went on to govern their late husbands' affairs with great skill, proving that an intelligent woman can do anything."

12. Here she talks about Empress Nicaula.

"Tell me, if you can: was there ever a king who could equal the noble Empress Nicaula?[20] Do you know of any king endowed with greater knowledge of

20. Nicaula is otherwise known as the queen of Sheba (Christine will return to her example in II.4) and is thought to have been an African queen. In this first part of the work Christine is reframing examples presented by Giovanni Boccaccio in his *Famous Women*, ed. and trans.

politics, government, and sovereign justice, and a more magnificent lifestyle than she had? Although the vast and varied lands that she ruled had known many kings of great repute, called pharaohs, from whom she descended, this lady was the first to introduce laws and a political organization during her reign and to abolish the crude customs that existed in the territories she ruled. She reformed the brutal habits of the savage Ethiopians. The authors who mention Nicaula say that she is all the more to be praised because she civilized people. She was the heiress of the pharaohs I mentioned, inheriting not just a small territory but the kingdoms of Arabia, Ethiopia, and Egypt as well as the island of Meroë, which is very long and wide, extremely rich, and close to the river Nile. All this she ruled with marvelous wisdom. What more can I tell you about this lady? She was such a wise and able ruler that even the Holy Scriptures mention her vast talents. She instituted well-balanced laws to govern her people and surpassed almost all the men who ever lived in terms of sheer nobility and wealth. She had a profound knowledge of the Scriptures and sciences and was so proud that she never condescended to take a husband nor felt the need to have a man by her side."

13. Here she talks about a French queen named Fredegund and some other queens and princesses of France.

"I could tell you many stories about ladies who governed wisely in ancient times. What I am about to tell you falls under that topic. Once upon a time in France, there was a queen named Fredegund, the wife of King Chilperic.[21]

Virginia Brown (Cambridge, Mass.: Harvard University Press, 2001). For the example of Nicaula, see chap. 43 of *Famous Women*. For a compelling account of the way in which Christine subverts Boccaccio's message in the representation of some of the same examples, see Judith Kellogg, "Christine de Pizan and Boccaccio: Rewriting Classical Mythic Tradition," in *Comparative Literature East and West: Traditions and Trends*, vol. 1, ed. Cornelia Moore and Raymond Moody (Honolulu: College of Languages, Linguistics and Literature of the University of Hawaii, 1989), 124–31. Cf. Kevin Brownlee, "Christine de Pizan's Canonical Authors: The Special Case of Boccaccio," *Comparative Literature Studies* 32, no. 2 (1995): 244–61; Christine Clark-Evans, "Nicaula of Egypt and Arabia: *Exemplum* and Ambitions to Power in the *City of Ladies*," in *Contexts and Continuities: Proceedings of the IVth International Colloquium on Christine de Pizan*, vol. 1, ed. Angus Kennedy, Rosalind Brown-Grant, James Laidlaw, and Catherine Müller (Glasgow: University of Glasgow Press, 2002), 287–300. For a discussion of the various accounts of Sheba, see Nicholas Clapp, *Sheba* (New York: Mariner, 2002).

21. Queen Fredegund (ca. 550–597) achieved power as queen consort to Chilperic I, king of the Merovingian Franks.

Although this lady was unnaturally cruel for a woman, she governed the king-dom of France after her husband's death and did so with great skill. At that time, the kingdom was very unstable and in great peril, because Chilperic's sole heir was a young boy by the name of Clothar. The question of who was to rule caused great division among the barons, and a civil war had already broken out in the kingdom.[22] Fredegund called the barons into council, hold-ing her child firmly in her arms, and said: 'My lords, behold your king. Do not forget the loyalty for which the French are known, and do not scorn him because he is a child, for with God's help he will grow up, and when he comes of age, he will know who his friends are and reward them according to their merits. I counsel you, therefore, not to wrongfully disinherit him. As for me, I assure you that I will reward those who act well and loyally with such generosity that they will never want for anything.' This is how she appeased the barons, and she ruled so wisely that she kept her son out of his enemies' hands. She raised him herself until he was grown and invested him with the crown and honor of the kingdom. This never would have happened if she had not acted with such wisdom.

"The same can be said of the profoundly wise and noble Queen Blanche, mother of Saint Louis, who governed the kingdom of France during her son's minority with more dignity and wisdom than any man could ever have done.[23] And even when he was grown up, she still remained head of his coun-cil because of her experience in leadership. Nothing was ever done without her consent, and she followed her son even in battle.

"I could give you countless other examples, which I will withhold for the sake of brevity. But since we are now on the subject of the great ladies of France, we don't need to go far back in history: you yourself saw the noble Queen Jeanne when you were a child. She was the widow of King Charles IV, and if you think back, you will remember the many good deeds associated with her name, as much in terms of the notable organization of her court as her lifestyle and the way she maintained justice. No prince ever managed the rule of law and guarded his country better than this noble lady.

---

22. Note that the political instability described here closely resembles the political instability in France after the death of Charles V in 1380. In this chapter, one of Christine's aims seems to be to justify the regency of Queen Isabeau. For an insightful discussion of Christine's defense of female regency and of the historical context, see Tracy Adams, "Christine de Pizan, Isabeau of Bavaria, and Female Regency," *French Historical Studies* 32, no. 1 (2009): 1–32. See also *The Book of the City of Ladies* II.65.

23. Queen Blanche of Castile (1188–1252) acted as regent twice during her life. Christine will return to her story at II.65.

"Her noble daughter, who was married to the duke of Orléans, son of King Philip, was much like her. During her long widowhood, she ruled her country so judiciously that no one could have done better.

"Another example was Blanche, queen of France and the late wife of King John. She maintained and governed her land with the greatest observance of law and justice.

"And what about the valiant and wise duchess of Anjou, daughter of the late Saint Charles of Blois, duke of Brittany? She was the widow of the second oldest brother of the wise King Charles of France, who was then king of Sicily. This lady governed the lands and countries under her rule, including Provence, with extraordinary justice and safeguarded them for her noble children while they were still small. Oh, how much praise does this lady deserve for all her great qualities! When she was young, she was so beautiful that she surpassed all other women, and she was also perfectly chaste and very wise. In her mature years, she displayed great leadership abilities, extraordinary prudence, force, and steadfastness, as became apparent when almost the whole territory of Provence rebelled against her and her noble children after her lord died in Italy. But this great lady strove so hard and well, combining force with diplomacy, that she reestablished obedience and allegiance in the entire territory. So well did she maintain the order of law in that territory that not a single complaint of injustice was ever raised against her.

"I could tell you about other great ladies of France who governed their territories well and justly while in their widowhood. The countess of La Marche, lady and countess of Vendôme and Castres and a big landowner, who is still alive, what can one say about the way she governs? Doesn't she seek to know how justice is being maintained? She herself, good and wise as she is, takes a keen interest in that subject. What more can I tell you? I assure you that if you pay attention, it will be obvious to you that the same applies to a great many women, be they from an upper, middle, or lower class. When they became widows, they all maintained their dominions in as good a state as did their husbands while they were alive, and they are just as popular with their subjects.

"There are numerous other examples, however much that may displease men. It is true that we have our share of ignorant women, but you know that there are countless others who have a greater intelligence and a keener sense of justice than many men, don't you? And if their husbands trusted them or had the same sort of good sense, they would greatly benefit.

"Yet even though women are not commonly involved in rendering judgments or pleading cases, that should not worry them, because that means they have fewer physical and moral responsibilities. And although criminals must be punished and justice maintained for everyone, there are enough men in those functions who must wish they had never learned more about those things than their mothers, for even if they do their best to follow the right path, God knows how heavy their punishment will be if they make a mistake."

14. More exchanges and debate between Christine and Lady Reason.

"You certainly speak well, my lady, and I'm very receptive to your arguments, but leaving intelligence aside, it is a proven fact that women have weak and frail bodies, lack physical power, and are fearful by nature. In the eyes of men, these facts greatly diminish the position and authority of the female sex, because they claim that the more inferior a body, the lesser its merit and, as a result, the lesser its esteem."

Lady Reason replied: "My dear daughter, that conclusion is totally inappropriate and unjustifiable. One often sees that Nature does not give one body as much perfection as another. She makes some bodies imperfect, whether in shape or in beauty or by giving the limbs some deficiency or weakness, but then she compensates for this by giving them something even greater than what they lack. Look at what they say about the great philosopher Aristotle, for example: he is said to have had a very ugly body, with one eye lower than the other and an odd face. But if he had physical deformities, Nature made up for this in spectacular fashion by giving him a retentive mind and great intelligence, as borne out by the authority of his writings. The compensation of having received that great mind was, therefore, more valuable to him than if he had been given a handsome body or one similar to that of Absalom.[24]

"One can say the same about the great emperor Alexander, who was quite ugly, small, and sickly.[25] Nevertheless, he apparently had tremendous courage, and that applies to many others. I assure you, my sweet friend, that a robust, strong body does not guarantee a virtuous and strong spirit, because the latter springs from a natural moral strength, a gift from God that He

---

24. Son of David, king of Israel, and praised for his beauty (2 Samuel 14:25).
25. He is often referred to as Alexander the Great of Macedonia (356–323 BCE).

allows Nature to ingrain in certain rational creatures more than in others. It resides in one's mind or heart, certainly not in the strength of one's body or members. This is often quite obvious when one sees large, strong men who are spineless and cowardly while small, physically weak men act boldly and vigorously. The same holds true for other moral qualities. In terms of courage and physical strength, God and Nature have done a great deal for women by making them frail, for this pleasant defect excuses them at the very least from taking part in the dreadful cruelties, the murders, and the terrible acts of violence that have been committed by force and are still going on in the world. As a result, women will never receive the punishment such crimes impose, and it would have been and still would be better for the souls of some of the strongest men if they had made their pilgrimage in this world in a frail, female body. To return to my point, I assure you that if Nature did not give women great physical strength, she made up for that by endowing them with a virtuous disposition that prompts them to love their God and be fearful of violating His commandments. Women who behave otherwise act against their own nature.

"But keep in mind, my dear friend, that it seems as though God has wanted to prove to men that while women don't possess the great strength and physical courage usually granted to men, no one should say or believe that this is because the female sex lacks strength and physical daring. That is quite clear, because many women have displayed great courage, strength, and boldness in tackling all sorts of difficult tasks, just like the great conquerors and grandiose warriors whose feats have been written about in such detail. I will be giving you several examples of that.

"My sweet daughter and dear friend, I have now prepared a large and wide trench for you, and I have carried away all the soil in large basketfuls on my shoulders. The time has come to take some big, strong rocks and set them in place for the foundation of the walls of the City of Ladies. So take the trowel of your pen and get ready to devote yourself to your task and do some strong brickwork. Here is the first big, strong rock that I want you to lay for the foundation of your city.[26] Know that Nature herself has marked it with the astrological signs to indicate that it should be part of this work. Step back a little and I will put it in place for you."

---

26. Note that whereas Christine's first example is that of Semiramis, Boccaccio's *Famous Women* begins with the story of Eve (Semiramis comes after in his book).

15. Here she talks about Queen Semiramis.[27]

"Semiramis was a woman of exceptional strength and courage in the exercise and practice of weapons. Her skills were so outstanding that the people of that time, who were heathens, said that her great power on land and at sea showed she was a sister of the great god Jupiter and a daughter of the ancient god Saturn, whom they regarded as the gods of the earth and the sea. Semiramis was the wife of King Ninus, who named the city of Nineveh after himself. He was such a great conqueror that, with the help of his wife who rode into battle at his side fully armed, he conquered mighty Babylon, all of the great land of Assyria, and many other countries.

"It so happened that when this lady was still quite young, her husband Ninus was killed by an arrow during an assault on a city. After the funeral rites had been solemnly observed as befitted Ninus, she did not discard her weapons but went on with renewed courage and vigor to govern the kingdoms and lands that she and her husband possessed or had conquered by sword. She ruled these kingdoms and lands in remarkable fashion with exemplary military discipline. In this way, she accomplished so many remarkable deeds that no man could surpass her in vigor and strength. This lady possessed such enormous courage that she did not fear pain or danger. Braving all perils in exceptional fashion, she vanquished all her enemies, who had thought that now that she had become a widow, they could expel her from the countries she had conquered. As a result, her military might was so feared that she not only retained the lands already in her power but also marched a great army to Ethiopia. There she fought fierce battles, defeating the country and joining it to her empire.

"From there, she took a huge army to India and carried out a fierce attack on the Indians, who had never before been confronted by anyone wishing to make war on them. Having defeated them, she advanced against other countries so that, in short, she conquered and subjugated the entire Orient. In the course of her great and powerful conquests, Semiramis fortified and rebuilt the city of Babylon, which had been founded by Nimrod and the giants. Located on the plain of Shinar, this was an important,

----

27. According to tradition, Semiramis was the regent queen of the Assyrian Empire from 811 to 806 BCE. She was wife of King Nimrod and later King Ninus. The virtues of these ruling queens could be compared with Christine's depiction of a good queen and princess in *The Treasure of the City of Ladies* (1405) as well as the virtues of a good prince discussed in the first section of *The Book of the Body Politic* (ca. 1407).

exceptionally strong city surrounded by walls, but this lady strengthened the city even further with various defense measures and had deep, wide moats dug around it.

"One day, Semiramis was sitting in her chamber surrounded by her ladies who were braiding her hair, when she received news that one of her kingdoms had revolted against her. She jumped up and swore on her kingdom that the other plait, which was yet to be braided, would not be finished until she had avenged this outrage and the land was brought back under her rule. She rapidly armed a large number of her men, marched on the rebels, and brought them back under her rule with marvelous force and determination. She frightened the rebels and all her other subjects to such an extent that no one ever dared revolt against her again. For a long time, a large statue in the form of a richly gilded, copper figure on a tall pillar in Babylon bore witness to this noble and courageous act. It depicted a princess holding a sword, one side of her hair braided, the other side loose. This queen founded and rebuilt a number of cities and fortifications and accomplished so much that greater courage or more marvelous and noteworthy feats have never been recorded about any man.

"It is true that many blame her—and rightfully so, if she had been of our faith—for marrying the son she had borne to Ninus, her husband. But the reasons that prompted her to take this step were twofold: in the first place, she did not want another lady wearing a crown in her empire, which would have been the case if her son had married another woman. Second, she felt that apart from her own son, no other man was worthy of having her for a wife. That was certainly an enormous transgression, but this noble lady deserves some consideration because there were no written laws in existence as yet and the people lived by the laws of nature, which allowed everyone to do as they wished without fear of committing a sin.[28] Given her noble mind and her love of honor, there is no doubt that if she had thought she was doing something wrong or that anyone might disapprove, she would never have taken that step.

"But now the first stone has been laid in the foundation of our city and we should continue to lay stones to advance the construction of our edifice."

---

28. Note that if Christine follows quite closely Boccaccio's account of Semiramis (see *Famous Women,* chap. 2), she departs from him here in that she tries to explain or even partially justify the incest of the queen. See Julia Simms Holderness, "Feminism and the Fall: Boccaccio, Christine de Pizan and Louise Labé," *Essays in Medieval Studies* 21 (2005): 97–108.

16. About the Amazons.[29]

"There is a land called Scythia, situated beyond the far borders of Europe, along the Great Ocean that covers the entire world. It came to pass that a war robbed this country of most of its male inhabitants. When the women realized that they had all lost their husbands and brothers and male relatives and that they were left with only old men and children, they braced themselves and held a council. They resolved that henceforth, they would govern the country themselves, without male supervision, and they issued an edict banning any male from entering their country. To ensure the survival of their race, it was decided that they would visit neighboring countries at certain times of the year and then return to their own country. Any boys to whom they gave birth would be sent back to their fathers,[30] but girls would be raised by their mothers. To enforce this order, they chose two of the noblest ladies from among their ranks and crowned them both queen. Their names were Lampheto and Marpasia. Once that was done, they expelled all the remaining males from their country and took up arms. Then they went to war, women and girls together, and by fire and sword laid waste to their enemies' lands, crushing all opposition. In short, they wreaked full revenge for the deaths of their husbands.

"That is how the women of Scythia came to take up arms. They became known as the Amazons, a name that means 'those who have had a breast removed.' This is because they had adopted a custom of having a breast removed in childhood. Using a procedure known only to them, they would burn off the left breast of noble ladies' daughters so it would not hinder them when carrying a shield. Daughters of the common ladies had their right breast removed to make it easier for them to carry bows. Such delight did they take in the pursuit of arms that they significantly expanded their country and their rule through the use of force, and their fame spread far and wide.

"The two queens Lampheto and Marpasia whom I mentioned earlier each conducted military campaigns in a number of countries, leading great

---

29. As one of the foundational and iconic examples of the City of Ladies, the community of the Amazons and how it is interpreted sets much of the tone for the rest of the work. Adrienne Mayor in *The Amazons* provides an account of the community, drawing on the most recent archaeological and historical evidence. In particular, she suggests that the legends grew out of accounts of women warriors fighting alongside and on par with men, rather than separately, and she suggests that the account of breast removal is apocryphal.

30. Christine's account is thus slightly less bloody than that provided by Boccaccio (*Famous Women*, chap. 11–12), who underscores that the Amazons killed all their male babies.

armies. They were so successful that they conquered a large part of Europe and the Asian region, vanquishing numerous kingdoms and subjecting towns and cities to their rule. They also founded many cities, including Ephesus in Asia, which long enjoyed a splendid reputation.

"Of the two queens, Marpasia was the first to die, perishing in battle. To succeed her, the Amazons crowned one of her daughters, a noble and beautiful young maiden by the name of Synoppe. This young woman had such a high-minded nature that she elected never to lie with a man but remained a virgin all her life. Her sole passion was the pursuit of arms, and she never tired of conquering new territories. She avenged her mother's death in great style, putting to the sword the entire population of the country where her mother was killed and laying waste to it, adding that conquest to many others she went on to achieve."

17. About the Amazon queen Thamiris.

"As you will hear, the Amazonian state flourished for many years, ruled by a succession of brave ladies. Since it would bore the reader if I named them all, I will only tell you about the most illustrious ones.

"Among them was Queen Thamiris, who was as brave as she was wise. It was her wit, cunning, and military prowess that led to the defeat and capture of Cyrus, the great and powerful king of Persia who performed many miraculous feats, including the conquest of mighty Babylonia and much of the rest of the world. Having conquered so many countries, Cyrus decided to attack the Amazons, hoping to add yet one more territory to his rule.[31] When the wise queen learned from her spies that Cyrus was marching on her country with an army big enough to conquer the entire world, she realized that it would be impossible to defeat his troops by force, and she would have to employ a ruse. Accordingly, the wily leader allowed Cyrus to cross her borders unopposed. As soon as she learned that he had advanced well into her territory, she ordered all her ladies to take up arms and sent them off to strategic ambush positions in the mountains and forests that Cyrus would have to cross. There, hidden from view, Thamiris and her army waited for Cyrus and his troops to move into the narrow, dark passes and gullies between the rocks and dense stands of trees they had to traverse. At the crucial moment, she ordered her buglers to sound the attack, taking the unsuspecting Cyrus

31. Readers may recall that Cyrus stands as one of the heroes of Machiavelli's *Prince* (1513).

completely by surprise. The king found himself under attack from all directions by ladies pelting him with large rocks from their positions high in the mountains, crushing him and his troops. Given the difficult terrain, they could neither advance nor retreat: both in front and at the rear, they were ambushed and killed as soon as they emerged from the narrow passages in which they found themselves. Everyone was crushed and killed, except Cyrus and his barons, who were taken prisoner by order of the queen. When the massacre was over, the queen had them brought before her in a tent she had had pitched. Enraged with Cyrus over the death of one of her sons whom she had sent to his court, she was not willing to show him mercy but had all his barons beheaded in front of him. She said to Cyrus: "Because you are so cruel, you just could not get your fill of human blood. Well, now you can drink as much as you like." Then she had his head cut off and thrown into a barrel filled with the blood of his barons.

"My sweet daughter and precious friend, I am reminding you of these things even though you are quite familiar with them, because they are relevant to what I have been talking about. In fact, you recounted these tales in your *Book of the Mutability of Fortune* and even in the *Epistle of Othea*. Now I will tell you some more stories."

18. How the mighty Hercules and Theseus, his companion, came from Greece with a large fleet to attack the Amazons, and how the two young ladies, Menalippe and Hippolyta, defeated them, horses and all in one heap, and how, in the end, the two knights defeated the two young ladies despite the great force they had with them.

"What else shall I tell you about them? Those ladies from Amazonia had already accomplished so much through their physical strength that every country regarded them with fear and apprehension. The news of how these ladies kept invading and conquering lands, how they went everywhere destroying countries and regions if they did not immediately surrender, and how there was not a single force that could resist them, reached even Greece, which was far away. The Greeks were frightened, fearing that the Amazons' power might extend even to their country.

"At that time, there was a young man in Greece by the name of Hercules, marvelously strong and in the flower of his youth. In his time he performed marvels of physical strength unparalleled by any men born of women mentioned in historical accounts. He fought giants, lions, serpents, and fabulous monsters and defeated them all. In short, he was so strong that no man ever equaled him in strength except the mighty Samson. This Hercules said that it was not a good idea to wait for the Amazons to attack and that it was a much better idea to invade their country first. To accomplish this, he armed a fleet and assembled a large number of young noblemen to go on the attack. When the valiant and brave Theseus, king of Athens, received news of this, he said that Hercules should not go without him, so he joined his army to that of Hercules and off they sailed to Amazonia with a huge force.[32] When they were close to the shore, Hercules, despite his marvelous strength and boldness and the great force of valiant men he had with him, did not dare sail into port and embark in daylight, so much did he fear the great strength and bravery of the Amazons. It would be an astounding thing to say and difficult to believe if historical accounts did not testify that a man who could not be beaten by any creature alive was so afraid of these women's strength. So Hercules waited with his army until night had fallen and then, at the hour when all mortal creatures must rest and sleep, they jumped from the ships, entered the country, and started setting cities on fire everywhere and killing the women who were caught off guard and taken by surprise. Soon there were screams everywhere and the women lost no time in grabbing their arms. As fast as they could and in great numbers, they bravely started running to the beach to attack their enemies.

"At that time, the monarch ruling the Amazons was Queen Orithyia, a lady of great valor who had conquered many countries. She was the mother of the wise Queen Penthesilea, whom I will mention later on. This Orithyia had been crowned after the chivalrous Queen Antiope, who had protected the Amazons, governing them with great military discipline and showing great courage in her time. When Orithyia learned the news of how the Greeks had attacked her country at night without declaring war and how they were killing everyone they came across, you can imagine how furious that made her. She vowed that they would pay dearly for making her so angry. She immediately ordered all her battalions to take up arms, cursing the men, whom she did not fear in the least. You saw all the ladies arming themselves and assembling around their queen, who had all her troops ready by daybreak.

---

32. Theseus also figures as a hero of Machiavelli's *Prince* (1513).

"But as this assembly took place and the queen was preparing to deploy her armies and battalions, two intrepid young ladies of supreme strength and courage, brave and wise, one called Menalippe and the other Hippolyta, both close relatives of the queen, did not wait for the queen's preparations. As soon as they managed to arm themselves, lances in hand, strong ivory shields hanging from their necks, they mounted fast chargers and stormed off to the port as fast as they could. With great passion, overwhelmed by rage and chagrin, they lowered their lances and charged at the most distinguished-looking Greeks: Menalippe at Hercules and Hippolyta at Theseus. The extent of their rage was obvious, because despite the great strength, boldness, and courage of the two men, the two young women dealt such blows and attacked with such force that each struck down her knight, horse and all, in a heap. They fell from their horses as well but quickly got up and ran at the knights with their swords drawn.

"Oh! These two young women deserve such praise for having defeated the two bravest knights in the whole world! This would be almost impossible to believe if not for the written testimony of so many reputable authors. Those authors, themselves astounded by this adventure, make excuses for Hercules in particular; they say that considering his enormous strength, it could have been the fault of his horse (which might have stumbled as a result of the great blow); they believed that if Hercules had been on foot, he would not have been brought down. The two warriors, deeply ashamed at having been thrown off their horses by two young ladies, then had to defend themselves when the women attacked them with their swords. They fought a fierce, long drawn-out battle but in the end—and it was no wonder, for there had never been two men of that stature—the maidens were taken captive.

"Hercules and Theseus considered this capture such a great honor that they would not have exchanged it for the wealth of a city. They withdrew to their ship to refresh and disarm themselves, thinking that they had performed a great feat. They treated the ladies with great honor, and when they saw how beautiful and gracious they were without their weapons, they were twice as happy. Regarding them with great delight, they felt they had never captured a more pleasing prey.

"The queen was already advancing on the Greeks with her great army when she received the news that the two young ladies had been captured. This caused her great distress, and fearing that an attack against the Greeks would have dire consequences for the captured ladies, she halted her advance and sent two of her noblewomen with word that if the Greeks wanted to set a ransom for the two ladies, she would comply and send it over. Hercules and Theseus received the messengers with great honor and courteously replied that if the queen were willing to make peace with them and promise that she and her ladies would never again take up arms against the Greeks but become their allies instead, they would promise in turn to free the two maidens, asking no ransom other than their armor. This they wanted to keep in honor and perpetual memory of the victory they had won over the two ladies. The queen, anxious to have the two maidens, of whom she was very fond, returned to her, was forced to make peace with the Greeks. Following lengthy discussions, they reached an agreement, and the queen, carrying no arms and escorted by a delightful group of ladies of all ages dressed more richly than the Greeks had ever seen, rode over to joyfully celebrate and solemnize the peace.

"Theseus, however, was very displeased at having to give up Hippolyta, because he had fallen deeply in love with her. As a result, Hercules addressed the queen and pleaded so fervently on behalf of Theseus that she allowed him to marry Hippolyta and take her to his own country. The wedding was celebrated in magnificent fashion and then the Greeks departed. Theseus took Hippolyta with him, and she later bore him a son named Hippolytus, who became a magnificent knight of great fame. When the people of Greece learned that there would be peace with the Amazons, they were ecstatic, because they had never feared anyone half as much as the Amazons."

19. About Queen Penthesilea and how she came to the aid of Troy.

"Queen Orithyia lived to a ripe old age. She had kept the state of Amazonia in great prosperity and considerably expanded its power. She was very old when she died. The Amazons crowned her noble daughter, the brave Penthesilea, as her successor. More than anyone else, she distinguished herself by her intelligence, virtue, and courage, and she never tired of arming herself and fighting battles. Thanks to her, Amazonia grew more powerful than ever before, because she never rested. Her enemies feared her so much that none dared oppose her. This lady was so high-minded that she never stooped to coupling with a man and remained a virgin all her life.

"It was during her time that the great battle between the Greeks and the Trojans took place. At that time, Hector of Troy's reputation of extreme bravery and chivalry had spread throughout the world. He was one of the bravest men alive, endowed with the most superb qualities. Because everyone tends to like one's equal, Penthesilea, the most powerful woman in the world who kept hearing people say great things about the brave Hector, conceived a pure and powerful love for him and wished above all things to see him. To fulfill this wish, she left her realm accompanied by a large army and a noble company of brave, richly armed ladies of all ages and set out on the long road to Troy. But nothing seems distant or onerous to a heart full of love borne by desire.

"The noble Penthesilea arrived in Troy but she was too late: Hector had died. He had been killed in battle by Achilles in an ambush and almost the entire flower of the Trojan knighthood had perished along with him. Penthesilea was honorably received in Troy by King Priam and Queen Hecuba and all their noblemen, but she was so heartbroken at Hector's death that nothing could cheer her up. The king and queen, in constant mourning for their son Hector, told her that since they could not introduce him to her alive, they would show her his remains. They took her to the temple where his tomb had been constructed, and historical records show that it was the richest and noblest tomb ever built. There, in a rich chapel entirely made of gold and precious stones, facing the high altar of their gods, Hector's body was displayed on a throne, so well embalmed and richly dressed that it seemed as if he were still alive. With a naked sword in his hand and his face set in a proud expression, he still seemed to be threatening the Greeks. He was dressed in a long, wide garment woven entirely from pure gold and bordered with precious stones. It reached to the ground, covering his legs, which were rubbed with a fine balm that gave off a strong, delicious scent. There, by the glittering light of many candles, the Trojans worshipped the body as if he were one of their gods. The tomb was so rich that it defies description. They led Queen Penthesilea to the chapel, and she knelt down as soon as she entered and saw the body, greeting him as if he were still alive. Then she approached him, looking intently into his face, and started to cry, saying: 'Oh! You are the flower, the epitome, and pinnacle of bravery! Who will ever be able to call himself valiant or even strap on a sword now that the shiniest and most illustrious example of nobility has been extinguished? Alas! Cursed be the day that he whose arm dared commit the outrage of depriving the world of such a great treasure was born! Oh, noblest prince, why did Fortune wish me such harm as to prevent me from being by your side when the traitor who did this to you lay waiting for you in ambush? This never would have happened because I would have watched over you, and if your killer were still alive, I would know how to avenge your death and still the great sorrow and anger burning in my heart by seeing your lifeless body, unable to speak to me when that is all I desire. But since Fortune has decreed otherwise and I can do nothing to change it, I swear by all the highest gods of our faith and I solemnly promise you, my dear lord, that as long as I draw breath, I will avenge your death on the Greeks.'

"On her knees before the body, Penthesilea spoke with such force that her words reached the great crowd of barons, ladies, and knights, all weeping with compassion. She could barely drag herself away but at long last kissed the hand that held the sword and departed, saying: 'Oh! Noble and shining example of knighthood! What must you have been like while still alive, when a mere look at your dead body reveals such great nobility?'

"Then she departed, weeping softly. As soon as she could, she donned her armor and left the city in great haste with her entire army and an escort of noble retainers, advancing on the Greeks, who had laid siege to the city. To make a long story short, she and her army performed so brilliantly that if she had lived longer, no Greek would have ever again set foot in Greece. She attacked Pyrrhus, the son of Achilles and a most valiant knight in his own right, fighting him so fiercely that he was nearly killed. It was only with great difficulty that his men managed to rescue him and carry him off, half dead. The Greeks did not expect him to survive and were deeply distressed, because he had been their only hope. But if Penthesilea hated the father, she certainly made that clear to his son.

"In short, Penthesilea outdid herself in combat. She and her army fought for days, reducing the Greeks to their lowest ebb. Pyrrhus, however, had recovered from his wounds. Deeply upset and ashamed at having been struck down and injured by Penthesilea, he ordered his valiant soldiers to concentrate on Penthesilea, to surround her and separate her from her warriors. He wanted to kill her with his own hands and promised them a large reward if they succeeded. To accomplish this, Pyrrhus' men struggled for a long time before they even got within striking distance, because Penthesilea was delivering such fearsome blows that they were afraid to get too close to her. But since she was their only target, their efforts finally succeeded. Penthesilea must have been exhausted, having fought so fiercely that even Hector would have had difficulty doing as much in a single day. Pyrrhus' men surrounded her at last and separated her from her troops, cornering her women so they were unable to come to her aid. Although she defended herself with the utmost bravery, they destroyed her weapons and struck off the better part of her helmet. Pyrrhus arrived and upon seeing her head uncovered, revealing her blond hair, he struck her such a great blow that he split open her head and brain. That is how the brave Penthesilea met her end. It was a great loss to the Trojans and a profound loss to her country, which went into deep mourning. And rightly so, for the Amazons never again knew a ruler of her caliber.[33] Filled with grief, they carried her body back to her country.

"Thus began the powerful realm of the Amazons, as you have now heard. It lasted for more than eight hundred years, as you can see for yourself by checking the history books for the various periods of time that elapsed from the time the realm was founded until just after Alexander the Great conquered the world. At that time, the realm apparently still existed and the Amazons still ruled, because the history books mention that Alexander visited that nation and describe how he was received by the queen and her ladies. Alexander lived long after the destruction of Troy and more than four hundred years after the founding of Rome, which also happened a long time after the destruction of Troy. So if you take the trouble to compare the various records and calculate times and numbers, you will find that this nation ruled by women lasted a very long time. You should also note that in all the kingdoms that have ever existed in the world and lasted this long, you will not find more illustrious princes or anyone who accomplished as many extraordinary deeds as the queens and ladies of this realm."

20. Here she talks about Zenobia, queen of Palmyra.

"The Amazonians were not the only brave women in history, because Zenobia, queen of Palmyra, a lady of noble blood descended from the Ptolemies, kings of Egypt, was no less celebrated.[34] This lady's great courage and love of the military profession became apparent early in her childhood. As soon as she was strong enough, no one could keep her from leaving the walled cities and royal palaces and chambers to roam the woods and forests where, armed with her sword and spears, she avidly hunted wild game. First she went after stags and hinds, then lions, bears, and all sorts of other wild animals, which she fearlessly attacked and brought down with marvelous skill. She was not afraid of sleeping in the woods on the hard ground come rain or shine, nor did she consider that a hardship. She did not mind traveling along narrow

---

33. Note that in her semi-autobiographical *The Book of the Mutability of Fortune* (1403), Christine claims that her own mother was "more valorous than Penthesilea" (see I.5).

34. Zenobia (ca. 240–ca. 274) ruled as regent in Palmyra and led successful military campaigns against the Romans, creating an empire in Asia Minor that held important geopolitical strategic power especially over east-west trading routes.

forest paths, climbing mountains, or traversing valleys as she chased the animals. This maiden despised all carnal love and for a long time refused to
marry, determined to preserve her virginity for the rest of her life. In the end,
however, under pressure from her parents, she married the king of Palmyra.
The noble Zenobia had a perfectly beautiful body and face, but she paid no
attention to her beauty. Fortune favored her by giving her a husband who
shared her values.

"This king, an outstanding knight, decided to use military force to conquer the entire Orient and the surrounding empires. At that time, Valerian,
ruler of the Roman Empire, was captured by Sapor, king of the Persians. The
king of Palmyra assembled his great army and Zenobia, who could not be
bothered to worry about her beauty and complexion, prepared to share the
hardship of battle with her husband, don the armor, and take part with him
in all the exertions one faces in the military profession. The king, whose name
was Odaenathus, appointed Herod, a son he had sired with another woman,
to lead part of his army as an advance guard against King Sapor of Persia, who
occupied Mesopotamia at that time. Then he ordered his wife Zenobia to
take another part of his army and attack the king from one side while he himself would move in from the other side with the remaining third of his army.
Off they went, but what shall I tell you? The way it ended, as you can read in
the history books, was that Zenobia acted with such vigor and bravery, fighting so boldly, that she won several battles against this Persian king. Thanks to
her bravery, she defeated him and placed Mesopotamia under her husband's
rule. Finally she besieged Sapor in his stronghold and captured both him and
his concubines, seizing great treasures in the process.

"After this victory, her husband was killed by one of his relatives who
wanted to take over the throne. It did him little good, however, because this
noble-minded lady put a spoke in his wheel. Brave and valorous, she took
possession of the empire on behalf of her children, who were still young. She
crowned herself empress, took over the government and ruled with skill and
vigilance. To make a long story short, she governed with so much wisdom
and military discipline that neither Gallienus nor, after him, Claudius, both
Roman emperors who occupied part of the Orient on behalf of Rome, dared
move against her. The same was true of the Egyptians, the Arabs, and the
Armenians: they so feared her power and fearlessness that they were all content
to conserve the borders of their lands.

"Zenobia governed so wisely that she was honored by her princes,
obeyed and loved by her people, and feared and respected by her knights.

When she rode out at the head of her army, which happened often, she never spoke to her soldiers unless she was fully armed and wearing her helmet. She did not even have herself carried in a litter while in battle, although the kings of that time all had themselves transported that way. She always rode a war horse and sometimes, to spy on her enemies, she even went incognito ahead of her troops.

"Just as this noble Zenobia surpassed in her time all the knights in the world in the arts of war, she outshone all other ladies in her noble and upright conduct and her integrity. She led a very sober life, but often held great assemblies and feasts for her barons and guests. Those were occasions of great magnificence and royal largesse in all things, when she would generously hand out beautiful gifts, well aware of how to attract eminent people to her benevolent affection. She paid strict attention to her chastity, not only keeping herself from other men but also sleeping with her husband for the sole purpose of having children. She made that very clear by refusing to sleep with her husband when she was pregnant. And to ensure that her conduct was in harmony with her values, she made sure that lewd and morally corrupt men were banned from her court. She insisted that anyone seeking her favor be virtuous and well-bred. She honored people based on their qualities, bravery, and virtue, not on wealth or lineage, and she liked serious people and experienced knights.

"As is customary for a royal empress, she lived in lavish fashion in the Persian style, which was more sumptuous than that of any king. Her food was served in richly decorated vessels of gold adorned with precious stones. She amassed huge wealth from her revenues and her own property without extorting anything from anyone, and she gave so generously when she judged it appropriate that she surpassed all other rulers in largesse and magnificence.

"In addition to everything I've said, her prime virtue was her knowledge of literature, both that of the Egyptians and that of her own language. When she wasn't busy, she diligently devoted herself to study, and she arranged for the philosopher Longinus to teach her. He was her master and introduced her to philosophy. She knew Latin and Greek literature and used those languages to produce a painstaking summary of historical works. She also wanted her children, whom she raised very strictly, to be introduced to academic learning. So you can judge for yourself, my dear friend, if you have ever seen or read about any prince or knight more perfectly versed in every virtue."

21. About the noble Queen Artemisia.

"Could we say less about the noble and illustrious Artemisia, queen of Caria, than about the other valiant ladies?[35] She loved her husband, King Mausolus, so profoundly that his death nearly broke her heart. As I will recount to you on another occasion,[36] this lady was left with an extremely large country to rule, but she was not afraid to take this on because in addition to her strong character and wisdom, she was a very competent administrator. She was also a bold warrior and so well versed in the military arts that her many victories greatly enhanced her reputation. During her widowhood, she not only governed her land with remarkable skill but also took up arms more than once, notably on two occasions: once to protect her country and once to uphold the loyalty of friendship and a promise she had made.

"The first occasion was when her husband, King Mausolus, had died and the Rhodians, whose country bordered closely on this lady's realm, became very annoyed and indignant at seeing the kingdom of Caria being ruled by a woman. Hoping to drive her out and gain her lands, they assembled a great army and a large fleet, and headed for the city of Halicarnassus, located on an island situated on a strongly fortified hill called Icaria. This city has two ports, one of which lies inside the city, nearly hidden and tucked away behind a very narrow entrance so one could travel to and from the palace without being seen by anyone inside or outside the city. The city's other port is next to the city walls. When the valiant and wise Artemisia learned from her spies that her enemies were approaching, she summoned a large number of her people, armed them, and headed for the small port, where she ordered a boat she kept there brought over. But before she left, she gave order to the city's inhabitants and some other good and faithful people she trusted and had left behind to carry out her mission, that when she gave them a certain signal, they should make the Rhodians feel welcome and call down from the walls saying that they were ready to surrender and that the Rhodians should enter the city. She told her people to do their very best to get the Rhodians to leave their ships and head for the city's market square. Once those orders

---

35. Artemisia I was queen of the region of Caria north of ancient Lydia. She was a general for Xerxes and the Persians in the Battle of Salamis in 480 BCE, although here Christine portrays her as an enemy of Xerxes. It appears that in this account Christine is following medieval predecessors in combining (and confusing) the lives and exploits of Artemisia I and Artemisia II. The point of Christine's reference, in any case, is to highlight women's good judgment and their capacities for excellence in the military arts and in political leadership.

36. See II.16.

had been given, Artemisia left the small port at the head of her army and set sail for the high sea, taking a detour so her enemies would not notice. When she had given her signal and received the answering signal from her people in the city indicating that the enemy had entered, she immediately returned via the large port, seized their fleet, and entered the city. Then she had ambushes laid all over the city while she and her army launched a full-blown attack on the Rhodians. In this way, she defeated and killed them all and secured the victory.

"But Artemisia did an even braver thing by boarding her enemies' ships and sailing to Rhodes with her entire army. Then she had the flag of victory raised as if the Rhodians were returning victorious. When the inhabitants spotted this sign, they assumed they were seeing their own people and rejoiced, leaving their port open. Artemisia entered, ordered some of her men to seize and guard the port, and went straight to the palace. There she captured and killed all the members of the royal family. The unsuspecting Rhodians were also captured, and Artemisia took possession of the city. Soon after, the entire island of Rhodes surrendered to her. After she had placed it all under her control and ordered its people to pay her tribute, she put reliable guards in charge and took her leave. But before she departed, she had two brass statues erected in the city, one depicting Artemisia herself as conqueror and the other the conquered city of Rhodes.

"One of Artemisia's other notable deeds took place when Xerxes, king of Persia, had marched on the Lacedaemonians. The country was already filled with his cavalry and foot soldiers and his big army, and the coast completely occupied by his ships and vessels, giving every indication that he intended to destroy all of Greece. The Greeks, who had a friendship treaty with Queen Artemisia, sent for her help, but the queen, that brave warrior, did not just send troops: she went there in person with an enormous army. She did an outstanding job and, to make a long story short, immediately engaged in battle with Xerxes and defeated him. Once she had defeated him on land, she returned to her ships, sailed toward his fleet, and engaged in battle near the city of Salamis. As the battle raged, the valiant Artemisia stood among her senior barons and captains, steadying and encouraging them by her own courage, saying: 'Onward, my good brothers and knights, do the best you can so the honor will be ours. You will earn praise and glory, and I will not be frugal with my treasures.'

"In summary, she acted with such skill that, just as she had on land, she defeated Xerxes at sea. He fled in shame even though he had countless troops, because several historians attest that he had such a huge army that wherever it passed, wells and rivers dried up. And so this valiant lady won a noble victory and triumphantly returned to her own country, adorned with the crown of honor."

22. Here she speaks of Lilia, mother of the brave knight Theodoric.

"Although the noble lady Lilia was not personally present on the battlefield, she deserves great praise for her bravery in admonishing her son Theodoric, a most valiant knight, to return to the battle, as you will hear. In his time, Theodoric was one of the most important princes in the palace of the emperor of Constantinople. He was very handsome and had proven his value as a knight, and thanks to the way his mother had raised him, he was also very virtuous and impeccably behaved.

"One day, a prince by the name of Odoacer marched on the Romans, hoping to destroy them and all of Italy. When the Romans went to seek help from the emperor of Constantinople, he sent them Theodoric, his most outstanding knight, accompanied by a large army. As he was fighting this Odoacer in a pitched battle, the fortune of war turned against him, and his fear caused him to flee toward the city of Ravenna. When his brave and wise mother, who had carefully watched the battle, saw her son flee, she was deeply saddened, thinking that there can be no greater shame to a knight than to have fled a battle. But her noble character made her forget all maternal compassion, and she decided that she would prefer seeing her son killed honorably rather than have him incur such shame. She immediately rushed over to him, begging him not to dishonor himself by fleeing but to reassemble his troops and return to battle. But when he paid little attention to her words, she was overcome by rage. Lifting up the front of her dress, she told him: 'Truly, dear son, there is only one place you can flee to and that is the womb from which you came.' Theodoric was so ashamed at this that he stopped his flight, reassembled his troops, and returned to the battlefield. Spurred on by the shame brought on by his mother's words, he fought so valiantly that he defeated his enemies and killed Odoacer. In this way, all of Italy, which was in danger of perishing, was saved by this lady's good sense. I think that the honor of this victory should be attributed more to the mother than the son."

23. *Here she talks once again about Queen Fredegund.*

"Queen Fredegund of France, whom I have mentioned to you before, also displayed exceptional bravery in battle.[37] As I told you, she had become widowed by her husband King Chilperic, when she still had her son Clothar at her breast. When the kingdom was attacked, she told the barons: 'My lords, do not be afraid of the huge number of enemies that have marched on us, because I have devised a ruse that will allow us to defeat them. But you must trust me. I will abandon all female fear and arm my heart with male boldness in order to raise your courage and that of our army for the love of your young prince. I will walk ahead with him in my arms and you will follow me. You will do exactly as I have ordered our commander in chief to do.' The barons answered that they were hers to command and that they would willingly obey her in all things.

"She formed up the entire army in battle order and rode out at its head, her son in her arms, with the barons behind her, followed by the battalions of knights. Thus they rode off toward their enemies until nightfall, when they entered a forest. The commander in chief cut off a tall branch from a tree and all the others did likewise. They covered all their horses with hawthorn leaves and hung little bells on some of them as is customary for horses going out to pasture. Then, in close formation, they rode on toward their enemies' tent camp, hawthorn branches in their hands. The queen courageously rode at their head with the little king in her arms, exhorting them with promises and kind words of encouragement. The barons behind her were all moved to compassion for the little one and felt all the more anxious to protect his rights. When they decided they had come close enough, they halted and kept very quiet.

"When the dawn began to break, the enemy sentries saw them and said to each other: 'Look at this amazing spectacle! Last night there was neither wood nor forest around us, and now there is a huge and very dense forest!' The others who saw this said the wood had to have been there already because there was no other explanation: they must have been stupid enough not to notice it. It must be a forest, they said, given the sound of the bells of the horses and other animals grazing there. And then, as they were busy discussing this, never suspecting a ruse, the queen's men suddenly threw down their branches. What their enemies had taken as a forest turned out to be armed

37. See I.13.

knights, who surged toward them so suddenly that they had no time to arm themselves, because most of them were still in bed. The queen's army stormed the camp, going from tent to tent and killing or capturing them all. That is how they won their victory, thanks to Fredegund's astuteness."

23. Here she talks about the virgin Camilla.

"I could tell you a great deal more about brave and valiant women, such as the virgin Camilla, who was no less intrepid than those I have already mentioned.[38] This Camilla was the daughter of Metabus, an ancient king of the Volscians. Her mother died at her birth, and soon after, her father was dethroned by his own people who rebelled against him and forced him to flee to save his life. He did not have a chance to take anything with him except his daughter Camilla, whom he loved deeply. When he came to a big river he had to cross, he was in a quandary because he could not think of a way to bring his little daughter across. After pondering the problem at length, he tore off great patches of bark from the trees and fashioned a bowl that resembled a small boat. He put the child inside and tied the little boat to his arm with strong ivy vines. Then he got into the river and started swimming, pulling the little boat behind him. That is how he and his little daughter crossed the river. The king took refuge in the forest because he dared not go anywhere else for fear of enemy ambushes. He fed his daughter milk from wild does until she got stronger and bigger, and dressed himself and the little girl in the hides of the wild animals that he killed. They also served as the only bed and covers they had.

"When she was old enough, she started to hunt the wild animals and kill them with slingshots and stones, chasing after them with such speed that no greyhound could have caught her. So it went until she reached adulthood, when she had become very brave and able to move with amazing speed. Well acquainted by her father with the wrong that had been done to him by his subjects, she left the forest, feeling strong and brave. She armed herself and, to make a long story short, she put up such a fight with the help of some relatives that she reconquered her country, personally taking part in the fierce battles. She continued to perform acts of bravery in battle and gained a tremendous reputation. But she was so proud that she did not stoop to taking

---

38. Camilla is a Roman mythological character discussed, as are most of these examples, in Boccaccio's *Famous Women* (chap. 39).

a husband or lie with any man. This Camilla was the virgin who went to the aid of Turnus against Aeneas when he was attacking Italy, as the history books mention."

25. Here she talks about Queen Berenice of Cappadocia.

"There was a queen by the name of Berenice who lived in Cappadocia. As the daughter of the great King Mithridates, who ruled a large part of the Orient, she was of noble blood and spirit. She was the wife of King Ariarathes of Cappadocia, and when she was widowed, one of her late husband's brothers made war on her to disown her and her children. In the course of this war, the uncle happened to kill two of his nephews, that is, that lady's sons. She was so overcome with grief that she became enraged and lost all the fear that is natural to a woman. She took up arms herself and marched on her brother-in-law at the head of a great army, fighting so fiercely that she wound up killing him with her own hands. She crushed him under her chariot and emerged victorious."

26. Here she talks about the bravery of Cloelia.

"The noble Cloelia was a brave and wise lady from Rome, even though she never took part in wars or battles.[39] One day, the Romans agreed to guarantee various treaties conducted between them and a king who had been their adversary, by sending the noble young lady Cloelia and other high-ranking Roman virgins as hostages. When Cloelia had been held hostage for some time, she thought to herself that it was a great blot on the honor of Rome to have so many noble virgins kept prisoner by a foreign king. So Cloelia armed her spirit with all the boldness she possessed and with sweet words and promises managed to deceive the guards, allowing her to make off during the night along with her companions. They traveled on until they reached the river Tiber. Cloelia found a horse grazing in a meadow nearby, and although she had never ridden a horse before, she mounted, put one of her companions behind her, and crossed the river without any fear of the depth of the water.

---

39. Cloelia (as told by the Roman historians Livy and Valerius Maximus) is said to have been taken hostage with a number of other Roman women as part of the peace treaty to end the war with Clusium in 508 BCE. Valerius Maximus' *Books of Memorable Deeds and Sayings* (a detailed compilation of anecdotes and stories from Roman and Greek history) was a widely used source in medieval scholarship. Christine made abundant usage of the French translation of the work—most notably in *The Book of the Body Politic* and *Book of the Deeds and Good Morals of the Wise King Charles V.* See also Boccaccio, *Famous Women*, chap. 52.

Then she went back to get her next companion and continued this until they were all across, safe and sound. She led them all the way back to Rome and returned them to their parents.

"The bravery of this virgin was highly praised by the Romans, and even the king who had kept her hostage respected her for it. In fact, he was amused by it. In permanent memory of this deed, the Romans erected a statue of Cloelia in the form of a young lady mounted on a horse.[40] They put this statue in a prominent place along the road leading to the temple, where it remained for a long time.

"But now the foundations of our city are complete and we must proceed to erect the high walls that are to surround it."

27. Christine asks Lady Reason whether God has ever wished to ennoble the mind of any woman with the noblest sciences, and Lady Reason's reply.

Having listened to all these things, I replied to the lady who had been talking to me with so much truth, saying: "God has truly revealed amazing strength in the women you have been telling me about. But please tell me again whether it has ever pleased God, who has bestowed so many gifts on women, to honor the female sex by granting some of them the gift of keen intelligence and great learning. Do they even have the talent for this? I would love to know, because men claim that women have only a limited intelligence."

Lady Reason replied: "My daughter, given what I have told you before, you should be well aware that the reverse of what they claim is true. To make that even more obvious to you, I will prove this by example. I tell you again, and don't doubt my words: if it were customary to send little girls to school and have them study the sciences as is customary for boys, they would learn and understand the subtleties of all the arts and sciences just as well as boys. There actually happen to be such women because, as I briefly mentioned before, just as women have more delicate bodies than men, just as they are weaker and less able to do certain things, so their minds are more open and more keenly directed at whatever they apply themselves to."

"Lady, what are you saying? With all due respect, please explain this further. Men would certainly never acknowledge this view if it was not explained

---

40. An equestrian statue is an honor that the Romans usually only gave to men.

more clearly, because they would say that it is obvious that men know more than women do."

Lady Reason replied: "Do you know why women know less?"

"Not unless you tell me, lady."

"Without a doubt, that is because women do not get involved in as many different things. They stay at home and content themselves with running the household. There is nothing more instructive to a rational creature than practice and concrete experience of many different things."

"My lady, since women have as much intelligence to comprehend and learn as men, why do they not learn more?"

Lady Reason replied: "Because, my daughter, society does not consider it necessary for them to get involved in things that are left to men. As I have told you before, it is enough for them to do the ordinary things that are expected of them. And it is based on that experience, which seems to show that women are usually less knowledgeable than men, that one arrives at the conclusion that they have less intelligence. But look at the farmers in the countryside or those who dwell in the mountains or many other regions. You will find that they are so simpleminded that they resemble animals. And yet, there is no doubt whatsoever that Nature has provided them with the same physical and intellectual qualities that you find in the wisest and most learned men living in cities and towns. All this stems from a failure to learn, although, as I have told you, some men and women have better minds than others. To illustrate what I have said about women's intelligence being similar to men's, I will tell you about some extremely erudite and intelligent women."

28. Reason starts to talk about women who were enlightened by great learning, beginning with a noble young lady by the name of Cornificia.

"The parents of Cornificia, a noble young lady, sent her to school at a young age as a joke, along with her brother Cornificius.[41] But this young girl, endowed with a prodigious intelligence, studied so hard that she acquired the sweet taste of learning. It would not have been easy to deprive her of this joyful activity

---

41. Cornificia (ca. 85 BCE–40 BCE) was a well-known poet in Rome, but her work has been lost. It is of interest to compare Boccaccio's praise of Cornificia in *Famous Women* (chap. 86) and that of Christine. Boccaccio suggests that through her skill and labor Cornificia was able to rise "above her sex," whereas Christine underscores here that many women by nature are capable of great achievements if given the appropriate opportunities.

on which she spent more and more time, neglecting all female activities. She worked so long and so hard that she soon became an outstanding poet. Not only did she flourish and become an expert in the art of poetry, but she also seemed to have been nourished with the very milk and teaching of philosophy, and she wanted to learn about every field of knowledge. She succeeded so well that she surpassed her brother, who was also a great poet, in all manner of learning.

"Knowledge alone was not enough for her unless she could put her mind to work, pen in hand. In fact, she compiled several very important works. These books and her poems were much appreciated in the time of Saint Gregory, who mentions them himself. Even the Italian Boccaccio, who was a great poet himself, mentions this woman in his book, praising her in these words: 'Oh, what a great honor for you, a woman who abandoned all female activities and applied and devoted her mind to the study of the greatest scholars!' Boccaccio also supports what I told you about the minds of women who lack confidence in themselves and their own intelligence. As though born in the mountains, ignorant of virtue and honor, these women become discouraged and say that they are good and useful only for embracing men, having babies, and raising them. God has given them a good mind so that if they wish, they can apply themselves to all domains dominated by glorious and excellent men. If they wish to study, that is neither more nor less appropriate than it is for men, and if they make an honest effort, they can acquire perpetual fame, just as distinguished men like to do. My dear daughter, you can see how this author Boccaccio confirms what I have said and how he praises and supports learning in women."

29. Here she talks about Proba of Rome.

"Proba, a lady from Rome and the wife of Adelphus, was also a lady of great brilliance.[42] She was a Christian and had such keen intelligence and so loved to study that she completely mastered the seven liberal arts and became an outstanding poet. She studied the works of the poets, particularly Virgil's poems, so intently that she knew them by heart. One day, when she was reading them with intense concentration and all her considerable intelligence, she reflected on their significance and conceived the idea of rewriting the Scriptures and the stories of the Old and New Testaments in the style of those works, in pleasing and meaningful verse. 'Which,' remarked Boccaccio,

---

42. Faltonia Betitia Proba (ca. 306 CE–ca. 353 CE) was one of the most influential Latin poets of her age.

'is admirable: to see such an important idea arise in a woman's brain.' But it was even more admirable, he said, that she was able to put that idea into action. Because this woman, anxious to carry out her plan, set to work, rapidly perusing first Virgil's *Bucolica*, then his *Georgics*, and then his *Aeneid*. She leafed and read, sometimes borrowing entire verses, other times only small sections. The marvelous skill and ingenuity she possessed allowed her to compose entire lines of well-constructed verse, ordering and joining the small sections while respecting the rules of poetry, meter, and feet patterns without ever making a mistake. She arranged her verses in such masterful fashion that no man could have done better. She started with the creation of the world, followed by all the stories of the Old and New Testaments and ending with the Outpouring of the Holy Spirit on the Apostles, harmonizing everything so well with Virgil's works that unless you knew of her composition, you would have thought that Virgil was both a prophet and an evangelist.

"That is why Boccaccio himself says that this woman deserves great recognition and praise, because it is clear that she possessed a true and exhaustive knowledge of the sacred books and volumes of the Holy Scripture. That is something you rarely encounter, even among the many great scholars and theologians of our time. This noble lady wanted the work she had drawn up to be called the *Cento*. And although the great effort that went into this enormous work would have been enough for one man's lifetime, she did not content herself with it but wrote several other excellent and most laudable books. Among them was another book called *Cento*, because it contained a hundred lines of verse. For this one, she used the writings and poems of Homer, which leads one to conclude that she not only knew Latin but also Greek literature to perfection. Boccaccio observes that it must be a great pleasure for women to hear about this lady and her accomplishments."

30. Here she talks about Sappho, a poetess and philosopher of great genius.

"The learned Sappho, a young lady from the city of Mytilene, was no less erudite than Proba.[43] This Sappho had a most beautiful body and face, and her manner, bearing, and speech were also extremely pleasant. But of all the

---

43. Sappho (ca. 630/612 BCE–ca. 570 BCE) was a Greek lyric poet from the island of Lesbos. Most of her poetry is lost, though some papyrus fragments remain, including one at the Bodleian Library of Oxford University. She is particularly celebrated for her evocation of *eros* between women.

gifts she was blessed with, one surpassed all the others and that was her keen intelligence. She was very skilled and an expert in many arts and sciences and did not limit herself to the works and writings composed by others: she created many new things herself and wrote several books and poems. The poet Boccaccio says this about her, in the sweetness of his poetic language: 'Sappho, who was criticized by primitive, ignorant men for her lively wit and burning desire for constant study, frequented the heights of Mount Parnassus, that is, the pinnacle of learning. Endowed with courage and boldness, she kept company with the Muses, in other words, the arts and sciences, without being turned away. She entered the forest of laurel trees, filled with hawthorns, greenery, flowers of different colors, soft fragrances, and many herbs, where Grammar, Logic, high Rhetoric, Geometry, and Arithmetic rest and dwell. She went on until she came upon the deep cavern of Apollo, God of knowledge, and found the bubbling waters of the fountain of Castalia. There she took up the harp's plectrum and played wonderful melodies on its strings while the nymphs led a dance, that is, in accordance with the rules of harmony and musical accord.

"What Boccaccio says about her should be understood as referring to her profound intellect, and the ancient writers say that her books are so erudite that they can only be understood by men of great intelligence and learning. Her remarkable books and writings have survived to this day and serve as an illuminating example of perfect poetry and composition to those who have come after her. She invented several forms of songs and poetry: *lais*, tearful laments, and strange lamentations about love and other sentiments. They were so well written in such perfect prosody that they were named 'Sapphic stanzas' after her. Horace refers to her poems, saying that after the death of Plato, the great philosopher and Aristotle's teacher, Sappho's poems were found under his pillow.

"In short, this lady was such a distinguished scholar that a bronze statue was dedicated to her in her native city. Made after her likeness, it was erected in a prominent place, so that she would be honored by all and forever remembered. Thus, Sappho was counted among the greatest and most famous poets, and as Boccaccio put it, the prestige of royal diadems and crowns and bishops' miters is no greater than that of the poets, nor that of the victors' crowns, laurel wreaths, and palm leaves.

"I could give you many other examples of women of great learning. Leontium, a woman from Greece, was also a very distinguished philosopher, so much so that in her desire to seek the truth, she had the audacity to criticize and oppose the philosopher Theophrastus, who was very famous in his time."

31. Here she talks about the virgin Manto.

"If women are qualified and able to master literature and sciences, you should know that art is also a subject they are allowed to study, as you will hear. Long ago, following ancient pagan law, people used divination to predict the future in the form of a flight of birds, the flames of a fire, or the entrails of dead animals. This was a distinct art or science that was held in great respect. One who had perfectly mastered this art was the young daughter of Tiresias, the high priest of the city of Thebes (although we would refer to him as a bishop today because under the laws of that time, priests were allowed to marry).

"This young woman by the name of Manto flourished in the time of Oedipus, king of Thebes. She was endowed with such a clear and brilliant intellect that she mastered the art of pyromancy, that is, prophesy by fire. This was an art invented and used in ancient times by the Chaldeans, although others say it was invented by the giant Nimrod. Thus, there was not a single man in her time who knew more about the movement of the flames of a fire, its color, and the sound it produces, just as she knew exactly how to read the veins and entrails of animals and the throat of bulls. People believed that she was often able to use her gift to make spirits speak and answer her questions. During this lady's lifetime, Thebes was destroyed by the conflict between the sons of King Oedipus, so she went to live in Asia and built a temple there to the god Apollo, which became quite famous over time. She died in Italy, and to celebrate her importance, a city was named after her in that country. It still exists and is named Mantua, the birthplace of Virgil."

32. Here she talks about Medea and another queen named Circe.

"Medea, who is mentioned in many history books, was no less learned in the arts and sciences than Manto.[44] She was the daughter of Aeëtes, king of Colchis, and his wife Persa. Medea had a beautiful body, tall and straight, and a lovely face, but in knowledge she surpassed all other women. She knew the properties of every herb and every possible spell, and she knew something

---

44. Medea and Circe are both important figures in Greek mythology, and they have been depicted in a number of competing ways. Christine's account here sidesteps the tradition of demonization that often accompanies references to these two figures. Her narrative may shed light on and seek to counteract a long-standing historical tendency to ascribe evil intentions to learned and highly intelligent women.

about every art known to man. Using a song she knew, she could make the air turn cloudy and dark, draw the wind from the earth's pits and caverns, start windstorms, cause rivers to stop flowing, mix potions, spontaneously start a fire to burn whatever item she chose, and all sorts of other things of that kind. It was thanks to this lady and her magic that Jason won the Golden Fleece.[45]

"Circe was also a queen. Her country bordered the sea and was located on the coast of Italy. This lady knew so much about the art of magic that there was nothing she could not do if she so wished, using the power of magic. She could prepare a potion that had the power to change the bodies of men into wild animals and birds. This is borne out by the story of Ulysses, which recounts that when he was returning after the destruction of Troy, intending to go back to his own country in Greece, Fortune and numerous storms tossed his ships here and there, so that he wound up in the port of Queen Circe's city. But since the wise Ulysses had no desire to land without leave and permission from that country's queen, he sent over his knights to find out if she was willing to give him permission to land. Circe, however, immediately took them for her enemies, and gave the knights one of her potions, which instantly changed them into pigs. Ulysses rushed over to see her and managed to have them changed back to their original form.

"Some people say the same thing happened to Diomedes, another Greek prince, claiming that when he arrived in Circe's port, she transformed his knights into birds, which they still are to this day. These birds are quite large and have a different shape from other birds. They are quite savage, and the people in that region call them 'Diomedes birds.'"

33. Christine asks Lady Reason if there was ever a woman who acquired previously unknown knowledge.

Upon hearing these things from Lady Reason, I, Christine, answered her as follows: "My lady, it is clear that you can name numerous women who are well versed in the arts and sciences. But I would like to ask you if you know of any women who, thanks to their intuition and ingenuity of mind and

---

45. Jason, in order to gain his rightful place on the throne of Thessaly from his half brother who had usurped power, was sent on a quest for the Golden Fleece. He assembled a crew who became known as the Argonauts and made his way to Colchis where he was able to claim the Golden Fleece with the help of Medea. See also Christine's discussion of Medea and Jason in II.56.

comprehension, have invented important, useful arts and sciences that had not yet been discovered or were previously unknown. I say this because following and learning a field of study that has already been discovered is not as great a feat as discovering something new and unknown yourself."

Reason replied: "Rest assured, my dear friend, that many noteworthy and great arts and sciences have been discovered through the intellect and ingenuity of women. That applies to both theoretical research, which is set down in writing, and the technical domain, given form by handicraft and physical labor. I will give you several examples.

"First, I will tell you about the noble Nicostrata, whom the Italians called Carmentis. This lady, the daughter of a king of Arcadia by the name of Pallas, had a marvelous intellect and had been endowed by God with special gifts of knowledge. She was a great scholar in Greek literature, and her use of language was so lovely and astute and so admirably eloquent that the poets of that time claimed that she was the lover of the god Mercury. They said that a son she had with her husband and who was also very learned in his time was actually the son of Mercury.

"Following certain upheavals that took place in the land where she lived, she left her country on board a large fleet of ships and headed for Italy, accompanied by her son and a great many followers. She sailed up the river Tiber, landed there, and proceeded to climb a high hill, which she named Mount Palatine, after her father. That is where the city of Rome was founded. This lady and her son and those who had followed her built a fortress there, and when she discovered that the local men were very primitive, she drew up some laws that urged them to observe the rules of law and reason and in accordance with justice. She was the first to establish laws in this country that subsequently became so famous and was the cradle of all laws.

"Among all her other talents, this noble lady had a special gift for divination and prophecy, and she knew that this country would one day gain such excellence and fame that it would rise above all other countries in this world. Thus it seemed to her that with the dawning of the grandeur of the Roman Empire, which was destined to rule the entire world, it would be improper to use a strange and inferior, foreign alphabet. And so that her wisdom and keen intelligence would be evident to the generations to come, she set to work and invented her own letters, which were entirely different from those of other countries. In other words, she invented the Latin alphabet and syntax, how to form words, the difference between vowels and consonants, and a complete introduction to the field of grammar. She delivered this alphabet and linguistic system to the people and taught them, hoping that they would become widely known. This was certainly no small or insignificant field of knowledge this woman invented, nor one for which should she receive only minor praise. Taking into account the ingenuity of this branch of knowledge and the great good and benefit that the world has derived from it ever since, one can say that a more worthwhile invention had never been created in the world.[46]

"The Italians have not been ungrateful for this blessing, and rightly so, because they thought this invention such a marvelous thing that they not only considered this woman superior to any man but also saw her as a goddess. That is why they honored her even during her lifetime by paying her divine homage. When she died, they built a temple dedicated to her name, situated at the foot of the hill where she had lived. To ensure perpetual remembrance, they started using various terms from the system she had invented and gave her name to many other things. The people of that country even called themselves Latins in honor of the subject of Latin this lady had developed. And because *ita*, which means *oui* in French, is the most categorical affirmation in Latin, it was not enough to call their country the 'Latin land': they wanted the whole country beyond the mountains, encompassing a very large area with many different regions and kingdoms, to be called *Italy*. Poems were called *carmen* in Latin after this lady Carmentis, and even the Romans, who came a long time after she died, called one of the gates of the city of Rome the *Porta Carmentalis*. Regardless of the prosperity the Romans enjoyed and the power of some of their emperors, they never changed these names. As you know, they still survive.

"What more do you want, sweet daughter? Can one say anything more grandiose about any man born of woman? Do not think, however, that this lady was the only woman in the world to have many different fields of learning."

---

46. In this acknowledgment of the centrality of language and eloquence for civilization and human community, Christine shows her intellectual affinities with humanism. On Christine's debts to early humanists such as Petrarch and Dante, see Lori Walters, "Translating Petrarch," in *Christine de Pizan 2000*, ed. Angus J. Kennedy (Amsterdam, 2000), 283–97; Thelma Fenster, "'Perdre son latin': Christine de Pizan and Vernacular Humanism," in *Christine de Pizan and the Categories of Difference*, ed. Marilynn Desmond (Minneapolis: University of Minnesota Press, 1998), 91–107; Julia Simms Holderness, "Compilation, Commentary, and Conversation in Christine de Pizan," *Essays in Medieval Studies* 20 (2003): 47–55.

34. Here she talks about Minerva, who invented countless technologies, including the technique of forging armor from iron and steel.

"As you have written elsewhere yourself,[47] Minerva, also known as Pallas, was a young lady from Greece. This young lady was so marvelously intelligent that the ignorant people of that time said that she was a goddess descended from heaven, because the identity of her parents was unknown and they saw her do things that had never been done before. As Boccaccio says, the fact that they knew little about her ancestry made them all the more astounded at her great knowledge, which was superior to that of any other woman of her time. She was very astute, and her wide knowledge was not limited to one particular field, but extended to all subjects. Aided by a fertile mind, she invented various Greek letters called characters, which can be used to compress a long narrative in a short text with far fewer letters. It was a great invention, demanding a sharp mind, and the script is still used by the Greeks today. She also invented numbers and a method of counting, and a way of doing quick additions. In short, her mind was so enlightened with knowledge that she developed a number of skills and techniques that had not been known before, such as the art of making wool and cloth. She was the first ever to think of shearing sheep and then picking, combing, and carding the wool with various tools, cleaning it, softening it with metal brushes, and spinning it with a distaff. Then she invented the tools to turn it into cloth and the technique of weaving.

"Likewise, she discovered how to make oil from fruits of the earth by pressing olives and other fruit and extracting their liquid.

"Likewise, she discovered how to make wagons and carts to easily transport things from one place to another.

"This lady did something else as well, and that is truly astounding because it is foreign to a woman's nature to conceive of such things. In fact, she developed the technique of using iron and steel to forge harnesses and armor, which are used by knights and soldiers in battle to protect their bodies. She first conveyed this technique to the people of Athens and taught them how to deploy their armies and battalions, and how to fight a pitched battle.

---

47. Minerva is discussed in other works by Christine, most notably *Epistle of Othea* and *The Book of Deeds of Arms and of Chivalry*. In *The Book of the City of Ladies*, see also I.38 and 39.

"Likewise, she was the first to invent flutes and pipes, trumpets, and other wind instruments.

"This highly intelligent lady remained a virgin all her life. Her exemplary chastity led the poets to recount in their fables that Vulcan, the god of fire, wrestled with her for a long time until she finally triumphed and defeated him, meaning that she overcame the passion and desires of the flesh that assail the body in one's youth.

"The Athenians held this lady in such high esteem that they worshipped her as a goddess and called her the goddess of arms and warfare because she was the first to develop these arts. They also called her the goddess of knowledge because of the great intelligence she possessed.

"After her death, they dedicated a new temple to her in Athens and erected a statue of her there in the form of a young woman representing wisdom and the art of war. This statue had terrifying and ferocious eyes because it is a knight's duty to impose rigorous justice. It also symbolized that one can but rarely fathom what goes on in a wise person's mind. She wore a helmet on her head, meaning that a knight must be strong, tough, and ever courageous on the battlefield, with the symbolic meaning that a wise person's plans are hidden and secret. She wore a coat of mail, symbolizing the power of the estate of knighthood as well as the fact that a wise person is always armed against the vicissitudes of Fortune. She held a long spear or lance, meaning that a knight must be the lance of justice, and that a wise person launches his or her arrows from a great distance. Round her neck she wore a crystal shield, meaning that a knight must always be alert and ready to see to the defense of his country and its people; it also symbolized that to a wise person, all things are clear and manifest. In the center of this shield was an image of the head of the serpent named Gorgon, which meant that a knight, like a snake, must always be farsighted and vigilant toward his enemies. It also symbolized that a wise person is always aware of any malice that might harm him or her. Next to this statue, as if to guard it, they put a night bird known as an owl, signifying that a knight must be ready day and night to defend society when called upon, and that a wise person always strives to do the right thing.

"This lady was highly revered for a long time, and her fame spread so far that temples were built and dedicated to her in numerous locations. Even long after the Romans had reached the pinnacle of their power, they still included her in their pantheon."

35. Here she talks about Queen Ceres, who invented the art of cultivating the earth and many other techniques.

"Ceres, who was queen of the kingdom of Sicily in ancient times, had a very keen mind. She had the privilege of being the first to discover how to cultivate the earth and to invent the required tools. She taught her subjects to subdue and tame cattle and train them to accept the yoke. She also invented the plow, showing her subjects how to break up the soil with a tool made from iron and all the other skills one needed. Next, she taught them how to scatter seed on the ground and cover it, and once the seed had sprouted and flourished, she showed them how to scythe the grain and separate the wheat from the chaff by threshing it with a flail. Then she taught them how to grind the grain between two heavy stones and how to construct mills. And finally, she showed them how to prepare the flour and use it to bake bread. Thus, this lady taught men who had been accustomed to live like animals off acorns, wild grasses, apples, and hawthorn berries to eat more appropriate food.

"Ceres did not stop there. She gathered together the people of that time, who were accustomed to leading a nomadic life, scattered across the wild forests and roaming like wild animals, and taught them to form communities and build towns and cities where they could live together. Thus, this lady brought them from their primitive state to a more civilized, rational life.

"The poets wrote a fable about Ceres that tells how her daughter was abducted by Pluto, the god of the underworld. Thanks to her vast knowledge and the great good she had brought to the world, the people of that time worshipped her, calling her the goddess of grain."

36. Here she talks about Isis, who invented the art of building gardens and growing plants.

"Isis is another case in point.[48] She had such a vast knowledge of working the soil that she was not only named queen of Egypt but also revered by the Egyptians as a very special goddess. The fable tells of how Jupiter loved Isis and turned her into a cow, and how she regained her original form. All

---

48. Isis is a central figure of ancient Egyptian religion and mythology. While often celebrated for her strongly maternal qualities, we see here how Christine emphasizes her technical knowledge and the practical benefits of agriculture and writing that she brought to the Egyptian people.

this testifies to her great knowledge as you yourself have pointed out in your *Epistre Othea* [*Epistle of Othea*]. She invented a system of characters that she taught the Egyptians, providing them with the means to compress their excessively lengthy script.

"Isis was the daughter of Inachos, king of the Greeks, and the sister of Phoroneus, who was a very wise man. As it happened, she moved from Greece to Egypt, accompanied by her brother. There she taught the Egyptians many things, such as how to garden, grow plants, and do grafts with various stocks. She introduced a number of good, just laws and taught the people of Egypt, who had been living in a primitive state without justice or law and order, to live according to the rule of law. In short, she accomplished so much there that she was greatly revered both before and after her death. Her fame spread far and wide, and temples and oratories were consecrated to her all over the world. Even at the pinnacle of their power, the Romans had a temple built in Rome in her name where they held sacrifices and solemn rites in the same style as the Egyptians used to observe.

"This noble lady's husband was called Apis. The pagans mistakenly believed him to be the son of the god Jupiter and of Niobe, daughter of Phoroneus, who is frequently mentioned in ancient history and the works of the poets."

37. About the great blessings these ladies brought the world.

"My lady, I greatly admire what you have told me, that so many blessings have been bestowed on this world thanks to women's intelligence. Men usually say that female knowledge is negligible, and they have an offensive habit of saying 'That's women's talk!' when someone says something foolish. In short, men tend to think that women's only useful purpose always has been and will be to carry children and spin wool."

Reason's reply: "Now you can understand the enormous ingratitude of those who say that! They are like people who live off the generosity of others without knowing who they are or rendering thanks to anyone. It should also be clear to you how God, who does nothing without a purpose, has wanted to show men that He doesn't disdain either the female sex or their own, since it has pleased Him to endow women's brains with the ability not only to learn and assimilate the sciences but also to discover new ones themselves—sciences, in fact, that are so useful and profitable to the world that they have been more necessary than anything else. A good example of this is Carmentis, whom I mentioned to you just now[49] and who invented the Latin alphabet so favored by God that He spread the system she invented to the point where it even effaced some of the glory of Hebrew and Greek. Almost all of Europe, which represents a large part of the world, uses this alphabet. Innumerable books and volumes of all sorts have been written and composed in this alphabet, providing a permanent record of the deeds of humankind, the noble and magnificent glories of God, and the arts and sciences. And let no one say that my words are biased: they are Boccaccio's own words, and his authority is well known and beyond doubt.

"Thus you can conclude that this woman's blessings are infinite, because even if people may not realize it, it is thanks to her that they have emerged from ignorance and become civilized. It is thanks to her that they have a way to send their innermost thoughts and ideas as far as they wish and announce and publicize whatever they wish wherever they wish. At the same time, they have a means of knowing the events of the past and the present and even some of the future. In addition, this woman's system allows people to reach agreements and become friends with people who are far away and get to know each other through the answers they give each other without ever having met. In short, it is impossible to describe all the blessings that the alphabet has brought about, because it allows us to describe God and make Him understood and known, and the same applies to celestial things, the sea, the earth, all people, and all things. I ask you: has there ever been a man to whom we owe more?"

38. More on the same topic.

"In the same vein, was there ever a man from whom the world derived more good than it did from the noble Queen Ceres whom I just mentioned to you? Who could ever gain a greater reputation than one who convinced nomadic, primitive men living in the forests like wild animals without the rule of law to live in towns and cities, taught them to be ruled by the law, and provided them with more nourishing food than acorns and wild apples, that is, wheat and grain? Thanks to this food, men's bodies are more handsome, their complexions clearer, and their limbs stronger and more flexible, because this food is more beneficial and better adapted to human beings. A land overgrown

---

49. See I.33 and II.5. Carmentis is also known as Nicostrata and in Roman mythology was a goddess of prophecy and childbirth.

with thistles, thorns, neglected shrubs, and wild trees: what greater merit is there than to have taught people to work this land, tidy and clear it, and sow seed, so that this cultivation transformed it from wilderness to farms and it became profitable to everyone? Thanks to this lady, humanity was blessed with the transformation of a harsh, savage world into a cultured society. She transformed the minds of nomadic and lazy men rooted in ignorance, encouraging them to exercise their minds and engage in suitable activities. By designating certain men to work in the fields, she saw to it that towns and cities became populated and able to feed those residents who perform other tasks that are necessary to survive.

"The same applies to Isis and her gardening. Who could express the immense benefits she brought the world by developing a way of growing trees that produced so much rich fruit and cultivating all sorts of nice herbs that are so nourishing for human beings?

"And then there is Minerva, who used her ingenuity to provide humanity with so many necessary items, including woolen clothing for people who depended on animal skins. She relieved them of the necessity of carrying their goods from one place to another in their arms by inventing the art of making wagons and carts to help them. And for the noblemen and knights, she devised a way of making harnesses to cover their bodies for greater protection in battle. That armor, Christine, was better looking, stronger, and more suitable than what they had before, which consisted of animal hides."

Then I said to her: "Oh, my lady, now I understand even better what you say about the immense ingratitude and ignorance of these men who say so many bad things about women. It seems to me that they have enough reason not to criticize them, since every man's mother is a woman, and it is quite obvious how many good things women do for men. Now, however, I see even more clearly the innumerable and enormous benefits men have received and continue to receive from women. Let them be silent![50] Let them be silent from now on, those writers who malign women, all those who have criticized women and who talk about them in their books and poems. Let them be silent, all their accomplices and supporters! They should lower their eyes in shame for having dared to express criticism in the face of the truth, which contradicts their words. They only have to look at this lady Carmentis, who

---

50. Note that for the first time here the character Christine is no longer the mouthpiece for the critics of women and their nature. She is finally able to overcome the depth of skepticism concerning women's nature that had been ingrained in her through the force of tradition.

used her powerful mind to teach them as if she had been their schoolmistress, because they certainly cannot deny that it is the knowledge she taught them that is making them feel so superior and highly respected. In other words: the Latin alphabet.

"But what do the noblemen and knights say, all those who make a habit of maligning women without just cause? Let them keep their mouths shut from now on and remember that using arms, waging war, and fighting pitched battles—skills they take such pride in and consider so worthy—were given to them by a woman. And in general, would men who live from bread and lead a civil life in the city and those who cultivate the fields have any reason to criticize women and express their disapproval, as many do, if they considered these great blessings? Certainly not! It is from women such as Minerva, Ceres, and Isis that they have received all these great boons that allow them to lead honorable lives and make a living. Do these things not count? They certainly do, my lady. It seems to me that neither Aristotle's philosophy, which has been immensely useful to the human mind and is justifiably held in such high esteem, nor all the other philosophers who have ever lived, have given the world any blessings that are comparable to the benefits accrued from the ingenuity of these ladies."

And she said to me: "They were not the only ones. There were many others and I will tell you about them."

39. Here she talks about young Arachne, who invented the art of dyeing wool and making fabrics called high-warp tapestries and who also discovered the art of cultivating flax and making linen.

"In fact, it was not only through these ladies that God chose to provide the world with many useful and necessary things. There were many others, such as Arachne, a young girl from the land of Asia. A daughter of Idmonius of Colophon, she possessed an amazingly keen mind and great ingenuity. After racking her brains at length, she invented the art of dyeing wool in different colors and weaving cloth the way painters do, following a technique we would call today the high-warp method. She was highly skilled in all aspects of weaving, and there is even a fable that says she was changed into a spider because she had dared challenge Pallas.

"This woman discovered another, even more indispensable technique: she was the first to discover how to cultivate flax and hemp and to prepare, ret, thresh, hackle, and spin it, using a distaff, and so produce linen. To my mind, this technique has been a great boon to humankind, although many men have criticized women for practicing it.

"Arachne also discovered how to make nets, snares, and traps for catching birds and fish; she invented the art of fishing and of using snares and nets to catch ferocious wild animals as well as rabbits, hares, and birds. These were all techniques that were unknown before her time. Thus it seems to me that this woman performed no small service to the world, which has derived great comfort and benefit from her inventions.

"Some authors, however, including the poet Boccaccio who discusses these things, have said that this world was better off when people only had berries and acorns to eat and dressed in animal skins than it is now that they have been taught to live a more refined life. But with all due respect to him and all those who claim that these things invented to comfort and nourish the human body are harmful to the world, I say that the more blessings, favors, and great gifts human beings receive from God, the more beholden they are to serve Him. And if they make poor use of the blessings their Creator has granted both men and women to use properly and well, that is because of the wickedness and perversity of those who misuse them and not because these things are not inherently excellent and profitable when used appropriately. Jesus Christ Himself showed us this by using His own body as example: He used bread, wine, fish, colored robes, linens, and all sorts of indispensable things, which He would not have done if He had thought it more appropriate to live off berries and acorns. He paid great honor to Ceres' inventions, that is, bread-making, when He chose to give men and women His own glorious body in the form of bread to eat at Communion."

40. Here she talks about Pamphile, who invented the art of harvesting silk from worms and how to dye the thread and make it into cloth.

"Among all the good, useful, and profitable techniques invented by women, we should not forget the one invented by the noble Pamphile, who lived in the land of Greece.[51] This lady was highly skilled in various crafts and took such pleasure from investigating and researching curious phenomena that she

---

51. Pamphile is the subject of a legend related by Roman philosopher Pliny the Elder. See Boccaccio's account of Pamphile in chap. 44 of *Famous Women*.

was the first to discover the art of making silk. Blessed with an inquisitive mind and a vivid imagination, she noticed the silkworms on the branches of the trees in the country where she lived. She thought the cocoons these worms had made were very pretty, so she took a few of them and removed the thread to twine it. Then she experimented to see whether these threads could be dyed in various pretty colors, and when she had tried all these things, she saw that the results were excellent and started weaving silk fabrics. The ingenuity of this woman has brought great beauty and profit to the world, and her invention spread throughout the world, because God is honored and served in many silk vestments. After all, the noble robes and vestments of prelates used for the divine service are made of silk, as are the garments of emperors, kings, and princes. In some countries, people even wear nothing but silk because they have no wool but an abundance of silkworms."

41. Here she talks about Thamaris, who was supremely talented in the art of painting, and about another woman by the name of Irene and about Marcia, a woman from Rome.

"What else should I tell you to convince you that women are by nature gifted and quick to learn theoretical sciences and invent new sciences and techniques? I assure you that women are also very well-equipped and skilled at implementing them and putting them to ingenious use once they have learned them. A good example of this you'll find in what is written about a woman by the name of Thamaris.[52] She was so gifted in the art and science of painting that, during her lifetime, she was the best and most talented painter known. Boccaccio says that she was the daughter of the painter Mycon and lived during the ninetieth Olympiad. The Olympiad was a day of great solemnity, so called because it was dedicated to various games. The winner was granted whatever he asked for, within reason. This festival and the games were held in honor of the god Jupiter and were celebrated every six years, with a four-year interval between the last and first games. Hercules was the first to organize this festival, and from its inception, the date was set the same way the Christians do, based on the birth of Jesus Christ.

---

52. Thamaris (or Thamyris)—not to be confused with the Amazonian queen Thamiris—was a painter in fifth-century BCE Greece discussed by Pliny the Elder.

"This Thamaris, having put aside all the usual activities of women, put her great talents to use learning her father's art. She had such a tremendous reputation while Archelaos ruled the Macedonians that the Ephesians, who worshipped the goddess Diana, commissioned her to put all her skills into painting the image of their goddess. This painting, on a tablet, was highly revered for a long time afterward as the greatest and most excellent work of art, and it was only shown during the feast days dedicated to this goddess. The painting survived for many years, bearing witness to this woman's talent, and her genius is still mentioned even today.

"Another woman, by the name of Irene, also from Greece, was equally gifted in the art of painting. In fact, she surpassed everyone else in the world at that time. She was a student of a painter by the name of Cratinus, who was a masterful artist. But she had so much talent and learned the techniques so well that she outdid and surpassed her master. This seemed such an astonishing accomplishment to her contemporaries that they had a statue sculpted of this young woman as she sat painting. To honor her, they placed it among the statues of the greatest artists of outstanding works that had preceded hers. This was a custom of the ancients, to honor all those who excelled and surpassed others in any domain, be it knowledge, strength, beauty, or some other quality. And in order to perpetuate their memory, they erected their statues in prominent and honorable places.

"The Roman virgin Marcia was another lady of great virtue and noble moral principles. She, too, was gifted in the art of painting, practicing this art with such skill and mastery that she surpassed all men, even Dionysius and Sopolis, who were considered the best painters in the world. In short, as the masters would have it, she outdid herself and reached the very pinnacle of all that can be known in this field. In addition to all her other famous works, Marcia painted a masterful portrait of herself looking into a mirror, in an effort to ensure that the memory of her talents would live on. It was such a good likeness that anyone who saw it would swear that it was alive. This portrait was carefully conserved for a long time and shown to other artists as a priceless treasure."

Then I said to her: "My lady, these examples show that long ago, the wise were honored more than they are now and the sciences were held in greater esteem. But regarding your words about women who are expert in the art of painting, I know a woman right now by the name of Anastasia who is so talented and skilled in painting decorative borders on manuscripts and landscape backgrounds that one cannot find an artisan to equal her in the whole city of Paris,[53] where the best in the world are found. She so excels at painting flower motifs in the most exquisite detail and is so highly esteemed that she is entrusted with the richest and most valuable manuscripts. I know this from my own experience, because she has done work for me that is considered exceptional among the decorations created by other great artisans."

Lady Reason replied: "I can well believe it, my dear daughter. Those willing to search would find many supremely talented women in the world. I will give you another example involving a woman from Rome."

42. Here she talks about Sempronia, a lady from Rome.

"Sempronia of Rome was a woman of great beauty, but although her body and face were more exquisite than those of any other woman of her time, it was the great brilliance of her mind that outshone all others. She was so exceptionally intelligent that there was nothing she heard or read, no matter how complex, that she could not immediately recall in detail without ever making a mistake. She controlled her faculties so well that she could repeat anything she had ever heard, no matter how lengthy the story. She had mastered Latin and Greek and wrote so well in both languages that everyone was amazed.

"Likewise, her speech, eloquence, and conduct were so lovely and gracious that she could use her words and manners to win over anyone she chose. If she decided to have people amuse themselves, there was no one so sad that she could not rouse him and make him feel pleasure and joy or, if she so chose, anger or tears or sadness. Similarly, she could make any man perform acts of bravery or physical strength or have him do anything else, and if she wanted to, she could make anyone who listened to her agree with her. In addition, the way she spoke and held her body were so courteous and sweet that people never tired of watching her and listening to her. She was an accomplished singer, had mastered all string instruments, and always won every game. In short, she was extremely proficient and resourceful in all things the human mind is capable of."

---

53. Christine's reference to Anastasia here is the only known literary reference to this illuminator of manuscripts in the School of Paris of the fifteenth century, though by this reference Anastasia is also honored in Judy Chicago's well-known work of art *The Dinner Party* celebrating famous women.

43. Christine asks Lady Reason if nature has endowed women with the ability to judge, and Lady Reason's reply.

Then I, Christine, said to her: "My lady, I do understand that it is true that God, may He be praised for it, has given women a mind that is more than capable of understanding, knowing, and retaining all domains of knowledge. But you see many people with such keen and perceptive minds that they understand everything they are shown and who are so ingenious and quick to grasp everything that there is not a science they cannot master, so all they have to do to acquire great erudition is to devote themselves to study. Yet I am amazed to see that many of them, even the most accomplished scholars, sometimes exhibit so little wisdom in their moral and public behavior, because there can be no doubt that science imparts and teaches morals.[54] That is why I would like to learn from you, lady, if you would be kind enough to tell me, whether the female mind, which, based on your examples and my own experience, seems sharp enough to understand and retain complex issues both in science and in other domains, is also acute and capable enough to deal with matters falling under the heading of wisdom. In other words, are women able to judge between good and bad and learn from the lessons of the past, growing more experienced from the examples they encounter, increasing their ability to conduct today's affairs, and gaining wisdom to deal with the future? That, I believe, is the essence of judgment."

Lady Reason replied: "You are right, my daughter, but you should know that Nature bestows this judgment you are talking about on both men and

54. Christine here addresses the question of the relationship between good practical knowledge (also called the virtue of prudence and exercised in judgment) and theoretical knowledge (traditionally linked to the virtue of wisdom). This is a question raised throughout classical philosophy and ethics, most notably by Aristotle and by later philosophers such as Cicero and Boethius. Some philosophers (including Aristotle) have been interpreted as holding that while women have a capacity for rational deliberation, in many cases their judgment was faulty or ineffective (often because their reason was overtaken in the final instance by nonrational parts of the soul). Christine is raising the question here, in light of her evidence that women can excel in the realm of theoretical wisdom, whether it is not also the case that they can apply their knowledge and reason effectively, thereby demonstrating a good capacity for judgment or prudence. Capacity for prudence, of course, was also considered as a preeminent qualification for exercising political power effectively. For two competing interpretations of Christine's concept of prudence, see Kate L. Forhan, *The Political Theory of Christine de Pizan* (Burlington, Vt.: Ashgate, 2002); and Karen Green, "On Translating Christine as a Philosopher," in *Healing the Body Politic: The Political Thought of Christine de Pizan*, ed. K. Green and C. Mews (Turnhout: Brepols, 2005).

women, on some more than others. But it certainly does not come from knowledge, although that can aid those with a natural gift for judgment. Because you should know that two forces joined together are more powerful and resistant than each force by itself. That is why I said that a person who has both a natural gift of judgment (called common sense) and an acquired knowledge deserves praise for great excellence. As you have said yourself, however, some have one but not the other, because one is a natural gift from God and the other is acquired through lengthy studies. Both are good, however.

"Yet some would prefer natural common sense without acquired knowledge instead of vast knowledge and little common sense. That proposition can give rise to many opinions and poses many questions, because you could say that more good is achieved by choosing what is most valuable for the benefit of the common good. That is why one person's knowledge of various domains is of more benefit to all (because it is passed on) than all the common sense he or she might possess. Common sense can only last as long as a person lives, and when he or she dies, the common sense dies with that person. Acquired knowledge, on the other hand, lasts forever for those who possess it in terms of their fame, and many people profit by it since it can be taught to others and is recorded in books for future generations. Thus, their knowledge does not die with them, as I can demonstrate through the example of Aristotle and others who transmitted their knowledge to the world. The knowledge they acquired is of more benefit to the world than all the judgment without knowledge of any person, past and present, although many kingdoms and empires have been well governed and directed thanks to good judgment. But all these things are transient and pass with time, whereas knowledge lasts forever.

"But I will leave these questions unanswered and for others to decide, because they are not relevant to the construction of our City. Instead, I will return to the question you posed, namely, whether women possess a natural ability to make judgments. My answer is yes. And you should know this already from what I said to you before, just as you can observe this in general from the way women manage the duties they have been assigned. If you care to pay attention, you will see that all, or at least most, women are so assiduous, careful, and diligent in running their households and providing all things to the best of their ability that it sometimes irritates certain lazy husbands: they think their wives push them too much and prod them to do what they should be doing in the first place. They say their wives want to run the show

and be smarter than they are, and so they turn into malice what many women
say with the best of intentions. Prudent women like that are discussed in the
Epistle of Solomon, and that is what I will summarize next, because it fits in
with our theme."

44. *The Epistle of Solomon, or the* Book of Proverbs.[55]

"A husband who can find a strong, in other words, a clever woman, will
never lack for anything. Her excellent reputation is known everywhere, and
her husband trusts her because she brings him good things and prosperity at
all times. She seeks out and purchases woolens, that is, she provides work to
keep her household occupied in profitable activity. She decorates her house
and she herself lends a hand to the work to be done. She is like the merchant's
ship that brings all sorts of goods and supplies bread. She bestows these gifts
on those who merit them: her family and servants. She stocks her house with
plenty of food, even for her servants. She considers the value of a dwelling
before she buys it and uses her common sense to plant the vineyard that
provides for the household. She has girded her loins with the strength to provide constant solicitude, and her arms grow strong from the continuous good
work she does. And yet the light shed by her work is never extinguished no
matter how dark it is. She even handles heavy chores but does not shun feminine tasks, in which she actively participates. She reaches out to the poor and
those who suffer and lends a hand. She sees to it that the house is protected
against the cold and snow and her servants are dressed in padded robes. She
makes herself clothing of silk and other rich fabrics, in honor and respect,
and her husband is honored when he is seated as one of the first among the
country's elders. She makes cotton and linen fabrics that she sells, and wraps
herself in strength and glory. For all these reasons, her joy shall be eternal. She
always speaks words of wisdom and her tongue is ruled by the law of kindness. She keeps careful track of her household's provisions and does not eat
the bread of idleness. Her children's behavior shows that she is their mother
and their actions show that they are happy. The way her husband is turned
out does her credit. She supervises her daughters in all things even when they
are grown. She despises false glory and vain beauty. Such a woman fears our
Lord. She shall be praised, and He shall give her the fruit of her works, which
will sing her praise far and wide."

---

55. See the Old Testament, *Book of Proverbs* 31.

45. Here she talks about Gaia Cyrilla.

"With regard to what Solomon's Epistle says about judicious women, we should remember the noble queen Gaia Cyrilla.[56] This lady was either from Rome or from Tuscany and the wife of the Roman king Tarquin. She was virtuous, showed excellent judgment, and possessed a natural sense of loyalty and goodness, so that she was esteemed above all women for being a brilliant housewife with an amazing capacity for planning ahead. Although she was the queen and did not need to work with her hands, this lady always took delight in being profitably engaged and hated being idle, so she was always engaged in some activity and made the ladies and young girls who attended her do likewise. She found a way of sorting wool and making fine fabrics of all sorts, passing her days in what was at that time considered a very honorable fashion. Thus, she was praised, honored, and esteemed by everyone. Because of her fame and to preserve her memory, the Romans, who grew even more powerful after her lifetime, established and long maintained the following habit at their daughters' weddings: when the bride first entered the house of her bridegroom, she was asked what her name should be, to which she would reply 'Gaia.' That signified the bride's desire to follow this lady's example in her actions and deeds."

46. Here she talks about the judgment and intelligence of Queen Dido.

"As you have said yourself, judgment is the faculty of reflecting carefully, of pondering the things one wants to do and how one can bring them to a good end. I will give you some examples of how women are capable of careful reflection, even when it comes to important issues. First among these powerful women is Dido, who originally was called Elissa.[57] Her actions clearly revealed her excellent good sense, as I will tell you. She founded and built a city called Carthage in the land of Africa and was its first queen and ruler. The way she founded and acquired the territory and held on to it showed her strong perseverance, courage, and virtue—qualities that are essential components of prudence.

---

56. She is also known as Tanaquil. Most accounts suggest she was the wife of the fifth Tarquin king in Rome, Tarquinius Priscus.

57. Dido is most famously celebrated in Virgil's *Aeneid*; there is also some speculation that she was an actual historical figure.

"Dido was descended from the Phoenicians, who had come from distant parts of Egypt and settled in the land of Syria. There they built and founded many noble towns and cities. Among these people was a king by the name of Agenor, who was a direct ancestor of Dido's father, whose name was Belus. He was king of Phoenicia and conquered the kingdom of Cyprus. He had only two children: his son Pygmalion and his daughter Dido, who was also named Elissa. On his deathbed, he ordered his barons to be loyal to his two children and to hold them in affection. To ensure their compliance, he made them swear a solemn oath. When the king had died, they crowned his son Pygmalion and married Elissa, who was very beautiful, to a duke who was the most powerful man after the king of that country. His name was Acerbas Sychaea or Sychaeus. He was the high priest of the temple dedicated to Hercules, according to their religion, and extremely wealthy. They loved each other very much and led a happy life, but King Pygmalion was an evil man, cruel and excessively greedy. No matter how much he had, he always coveted more. His sister Elissa, who was well aware of his greed, knew that her husband was very rich and that his wealth was legendary. She advised him to be wary of the king and to put his treasure in a safe place to prevent the king from taking it. Sychaeus took this advice to heart but failed to adequately protect himself against the king's ambushes as she had counseled him to do. And so it came to pass that the king had Sychaeus killed, to enable him to seize his treasures. Elissa was so distressed at his death that she almost died herself of grief. She cried and lamented for a long time, piteously mourning her beloved husband while cursing her cruel brother who had caused his death. The treacherous king, feeling tricked because he had found little or nothing of Sychaeus' treasure, believed his sister had hidden the treasure and bore her a deep grudge. Realizing that her own life was in danger, Elissa had the good sense to decide to leave her native country and settle elsewhere. Having considered her situation, she resolutely gathered her courage, asked herself what she should do, and armed herself with strength and tenacity to carry out her plans. She was well aware that the king was quite unpopular with the barons and the people because of his cruelty and the acts of violence he committed, so she summoned several princes and some citizens and peasants. After she had sworn them to secrecy, she outlined her plans to them so convincingly that they agreed to go with her and swore an oath of fidelity and obedience.

"Elissa had her ship made ready in great haste and in the utmost secrecy, and set sail during the night, taking her great treasure and a considerable number of people with her. Having ordered her sailors to make great haste, she implemented an even greater ruse: knowing that her brother would have her chased as soon as he found out that she had left, she secretly gave orders to collect great chests, coffers, and large bags and fill them with heavy, worthless objects, making them look as if they were her treasures. That way, she could turn those chests and bags over to her brother's envoys so they would let her go and allow her to continue her journey. And so it came to pass. They had not covered a great distance when a large number of the king's men came chasing after her to stop her. The lady addressed them in prudent tones, telling them that she was merely going on a pilgrimage and that they should not stand in her way. But when she saw that this strategy had no effect, she said that she was well aware that her brother the king was not after her personally but that it was her treasure he wanted, and if there was no other way, that she was prepared to turn it over to him. The king's men, knowing that this was precisely what the king was after, told her she should indeed turn the treasure over to them, because that would allow them to satisfy the king and effect a reconciliation. Then the lady, looking crestfallen as if she were most reluctant, had all the chests and coffers turned over to them and loaded on their ships. The king's men, thinking they had done well and had good news for the king, left at once.

"Elissa, showing no outward signs, had only one thought: to continue her journey at full speed. They sailed on, day and night, and finally arrived at the island of Cyprus. There they made a brief stop to stock up on fresh provisions. After the lady had made sacrifices to the gods, she returned to her ship, taking with her the priest of the temple of Jupiter and his household. This priest had predicted that a lady from the land of the Phoenicians would arrive one day and that he would leave his country to accompany her. Thus they set sail, leaving the island of Crete behind them, and went on, passing the island of Sicily to the right. They sailed along the coast of Massylia for some time until, at length, they arrived in Africa.

"When they landed, the local people immediately came out to see the ship and the people it carried. When they saw the lady and realized that she and her people had come in peace, they brought them abundant provisions. Elissa addressed them in a very friendly fashion and told them that the reason they had come was because they had heard so many good things about their country, and that they would like to stay there if the people were agreeable. They replied that they were happy to let them stay. The lady, pretending that she did not want to establish a large settlement in a foreign land, asked them to sell her an area of land along the beach the size of a cowhide, to allow her to construct a dwelling for her and her people. That request was granted and the terms of the sale were agreed upon and sworn to. Then it became clear that this lady had brains and acumen: she had a cowhide brought over and cut into the thinnest possible strips, which were then tied together to form a long belt. This she laid down on the ground by the shore, encircling an amazingly large piece of land. The sellers were astonished by this and impressed by this woman's clever move and her intelligence, but they had no choice but to abide by the agreement.

"That is how this lady acquired land in Africa. Then a horse's head was discovered on her property. Using this head and the flight and cries of the birds as prophetic signs, they concluded that the city they would found there would be inhabited by extremely skilled warriors. Thereupon, Dido immediately ordered her people to start looking everywhere for workers and opened her treasure. She financed and oversaw the construction of a marvelously beautiful city, big and strong, that she called Carthage. The tower and keep she called 'Byrsa,' which means 'cowhide.'

"Just as she was beginning to construct her city, she received news that her brother was threatening to attack her and all those who had accompanied her because she had made a fool of him and tricked him out of her treasure. But she told his envoys that the treasure had been quite intact when she had turned it over to have it taken to her brother and that those who were transporting it might have stolen it and replaced it with worthless objects. It was also possible, she said, that because of the sin the king had committed in having her husband killed, the gods had not wanted him to enjoy her husband's treasure and had transformed it. As to his threats, she believed she was well able to defend herself with the help of the gods. Then she summoned all those she had brought with her and told them she did not wish them to stay with her against their will, or suffer any harm on her account. For those reasons, if any or even all of them wished to return, she would compensate them for their labor and let them go. They all replied with one voice that they would live and die with her and never leave her for even a single day.

"The messengers departed and the lady hurried to complete her city as fast as she could. When it was finished, she established laws and rules for the people so they could live according to law and justice. She conducted herself with such distinction and wisdom that her fame spread throughout the world, and everyone talked about her.

"Thanks not only to her great merit but also her courage, the bold project she had undertaken, and her wise rule, they changed her name to Dido, which equates to *virago* in Latin and means 'she who has the virtue and strength of a man.' She lived a long, glorious life, which would have been even longer had not Fortune, often jealous of those who are successful, decided to do her harm. In the end, Fortune prepared her a bitter drink, which I will tell you about in due course."

47. Here she talks about Ops, queen of Crete.

"In ancient times, Oppis or Ops, who was considered a goddess and mother of the gods, was famous for her judgment. Ancient records state that thanks to her good judgment and constancy, she was always able to handle both the prosperity and adversity she encountered in her time. She was the daughter of Uranus, a very powerful man in Greece, and his wife Vesta. The world was still quite primitive and ignorant at that time, so her husband Saturn, the king of Crete, was also her brother. This king of Crete dreamt that his wife would bear a son who would kill him, so to escape that fate, he ordered that all male children the queen would bear should be killed. This lady was smart enough, however, to take careful precautions, and she managed to save three sons: Jupiter, Neptune, and Pluto. She was greatly honored and praised for her good sense, and her intelligence and the reputation of her sons gained her such fame and honor in the world that people foolishly called her a goddess and the mother of all gods. That is because her sons were already regarded as gods during their lifetime, being so much more knowledgeable about many things than other men, who were like animals. As a result, the people dedicated a temple to Ops and made sacrifices to her. They stuck to their foolish beliefs for a long time, and even in Rome, in the heyday of the Roman Empire, this folly endured, and she was still revered as a goddess."

48. About Lavinia, daughter of King Latinus.

"Lavinia, queen of the Laurentines, was also famous for her prudence. This noble lady also descended from Saturn, the king of Crete, of whom we spoke just now. She was the daughter of King Latinus and eventually married Aeneas. Prior to this marriage, Turnus, king of the Rutulians, had wanted to marry her, but her father, who had learned from an oracle that she should be married to a Trojan nobleman, kept postponing the wedding despite heavy pressure from his wife, the queen, to make it happen.

"When Aeneas arrived in Italy, he sent for permission from this King Latinus to land in his country. The king not only gave him permission but also immediately offered him the hand of his daughter Lavinia. That caused Turnus to declare war on Aeneas. Many people were killed in the ensuing hostilities, including Turnus himself. Aeneas won the war and married Lavinia, who bore him a son, but Aeneas was killed before the child was born. When her time was near, she became very afraid that a man by the name of Ascanius, a son of Aeneas by another woman, would kill the child she was about to deliver, because he wanted to take over the throne. In her fear, she fled to a forest to give birth, and she named the boy Julius Silvius. She vowed never to marry again, and conducted herself in her widowhood with exemplary prudence, keeping the kingdom intact thanks to her great insight. She managed to gain her stepson's affection, so he harbored no ill feelings toward her or his brother. After he had founded the city of Alba, he left and took up residence there. Lavinia ruled with great wisdom until her son came of age. From this son descended Remus and Romulus, who founded Rome, and the great princes who followed.

"What more can I tell you, my dear daughter? It seems to me that I have provided enough evidence to prove my point, namely, to show you through reason and by concrete example that God has never condemned, nor does He now condemn, either the female or the male sex, as should be obvious to you by now. The testimony of my two sisters here will prove the case even more strongly. It seems to me that I have done my share, having built for you the walls enclosing the City of Ladies. They are all finished and covered with plaster, so let my other sisters come forward, and may you complete the City's construction with their assistance and advice."

Here ends the first part of The Book of the City of Ladies.

Here begins the second part of this book, which relates how and by whom the dwellings of the City of Ladies were constructed, laid out, and populated.

1. The first chapter talks about the ten sibyls.

After Reason, the first lady, had spoken, the second lady, called Rectitude, turned to me and said: "My dear friend, I must not stand back now that it is time for the two of us to commence the construction and layout inside the enclosure walls already built for the City of Ladies by my sister Reason. So take your tools and come with me. Go ahead: mix the mortar in your inkpot and wet your pen to begin the building work, because I will supply you with plenty of material. Before long and with the grace of God, we will have constructed the majestic palaces and noble mansions for the eminent, illustrious ladies who will inhabit this city and dwell there in perpetuity."

Having listened to the words of this honored lady, I, Christine, replied as follows: "Most excellent lady, I stand before you ready to take your orders, eager to do your bidding."

And she replied as follows: "My friend, look at the beautiful shining stones, more precious than any others, that I have assembled and prepared so they can be placed in the stonework. Have I stood idly by while you and Reason were toiling away? Come, arrange the stones along the line I have traced here, in the order that I will specify.[1]

---

1. The order of the pantheon of ladies is clearly significant, but there are some questions in Christine scholarship surrounding the relative importance of the examples of Parts I, II, and III. Are the ladies of Part I *most* important due to their foundational purpose? Or are the ladies of Part II seen as particularly worthy of emulation due to their greater resemblances to Christine's actual medieval audience? Adding to the complexity of the question, Christine will note, later on in the book, that the lessons taught by the lives of the saints and martyrs in Part III are "more edifying to all other women than anything else" (III.3).

"First among the worthiest ladies are the wise sibyls, whose wisdom is legendary. Based on what the most credible authors note in their writings, there were ten of them, although some maintain there were only nine. My dear friend, pay close attention: is there any prophet, regardless of who he was and how beloved of God, upon whom God ever conferred a greater gift of divine revelation than upon these eminent ladies I am talking about? Did He not endow them with the divine spirit of prophecy that allowed them to see so far into the future that their words did not seem to be prophecies of the future at all but chronicles of past events? And what they said and wrote was amazingly clear and intelligible. They even spoke about the coming of Jesus Christ, which happened a long time after they lived, with more clarity and in more detail than all the prophets. These ladies remained virgins their whole lives and despised carnal desires. They were all called sibyl, but that should not be understood as a proper name: the word 'sibyl' means 'one who knows the thoughts of God.' They were given this name because they foretold such miraculous things that they had to have come straight from God. The term 'sibyl' is thus a descriptive title and not a proper name. They were born in various countries in the world and not all at the same time. They all made a great many prophecies, including the coming of Jesus Christ, which they announced in the clearest of terms, as I told you. Yet they were all pagans and did not subscribe to the faith of the Jews.

"The first sibyl came from the land of Persia and is thus called Persia. The second was from Libya and so was named Libica. The third one was from Delphi, born in the temple of Apollo; for that reason, she was called Delphica. She foretold the destruction of Troy long before it happened, and Ovid dedicated several lines to her in one of his works. The fourth one came from Italy and was named Cimeria. The fifth one was born in Babylon and was named Herophile. When the Greeks came to consult her, she told them that they would destroy both Troy and the stronghold of Ilium and that Homer would produce a false account of these events. She was called Erythrea after the island where she lived, and that is where her books were found. The sixth one was from the island of Samos and so was called Samia. The seventh was called Cumana because she was born in Italy in the city of Cumae, in the land of Campania. The eight was known as Hellespontina, born in Hellespont on the plains of Troy; she flourished in the time of Cyrus and the famous author Solon. The ninth came from Phrygia and was called Phrygica; she had much to say about the decline of many kingdoms and also foretold in vivid detail the coming of the false prophet Antichrist. The tenth was called Tiburtina or Albunia; her writings were greatly revered because she wrote about Jesus Christ in very clear language. And although these sibyls were all descended from pagans, they rejected the pagan faith and opposed polytheism, saying that there was only one god and that idols were false."

2. Here she talks about the sibyl Erythrea.

"It should be noted that of all the sibyls, Erythrea was the most gifted. Her talent was so exceptional, thanks to a special gift from God, that she described and foretold many future events in such clear terms that her words resembled gospel more than prophesy. At a request from the Greeks, she wrote such an explicit description of their exploits and battles and the destruction of Troy that these events were as clear before the fact as they were afterward. She also wrote a concise and true account of the Roman Empire and its reign and various exploits long before they happened and in such a fashion that it read more like a brief history of past events than a prophecy.

"She performed an even more miraculous feat by predicting and fully revealing the secret of God's powers, in other words, the mystery of the Holy Spirit and the incarnation of the Son of God in the womb of the Virgin. This secret had not yet been revealed by the prophets except metaphorically and in obscure terms. In her book she wrote: *Jhesus Crytos Ceuy Yos Sother*, meaning 'Jesus Christ, son of God our Savior.' She also predicted his life and work, the betrayal, the capture, the humiliation and His death, the resurrection, the victory and the Ascension, the descent of the Holy Spirit on the Apostles, and His coming on the Day of Judgment. She wrote it as though giving a brief description of the mysteries of the Christian faith instead of foretelling the future.

"Here is what she wrote about the Day of Judgment: 'On that fearsome day, the earth shall sweat blood as a sign of judgment. The King who will judge all humankind shall descend from the heavens and the good and evil alike shall behold Him. Every soul shall rejoin its body, and every person shall be judged according to his or her merits. There shall be no more riches and false idols. There shall be fire and everything living thing shall perish. There will be tears and grief, and people will gnash their teeth in distress. The sun, moon, and stars shall lose their glow, mountains and valleys shall be leveled, and the sea and land and all things here below shall be made equal. Heaven's trumpet shall call the human race to judgment. There shall be great terror and all people shall lament their folly. And then the earth shall be created anew.

Kings, princes, and everyone else shall appear before the Judge, who will reward or punish them all according to their merits. And the sulphurous fire shall descend from the heavens and fall upon Hell.' Erythrea described these events in twenty-seven lines.

"Boccaccio says (and all the other learned authors who have written about her share his view) that she must have been very beloved by God, and except for the holy Christian women of Paradise, she deserves more honor than any other woman.[2] She remained a virgin all her life and presumably led a life of complete purity, because so much knowledge of things to come could never illuminate a heart tainted with vice."

3. Here she talks about the sibyl Almathea.

"The sibyl Almathea, as mentioned, was born in the land of Campania, situated near Rome. This lady, too, was blessed with a very special gift of prophecy. Some historians say that she was born at the time of the destruction of Troy and lived until the time of Tarquin the Proud.[3] Some called her Deiphebe. Although she lived to an amazingly old age, she remained a virgin all her life. Because of her great wisdom, some poets claim that she was beloved by Phoebus, whom they called the god of wisdom, and that her great knowledge and long life were the result of a gift from him. This should be taken to mean that God, the sun of wisdom, loved her for her virginity and purity and granted her the light of prophecy that enabled her to foretell and write many things about the future. It is also written that as she was standing on the shore of Lake Avernus near Baiae, she received a miraculous message and divine revelation that has been recorded and preserved in her name, written in rhymed verse. And although this happened in ancient times, anyone who reads it and thinks about it still feels admiration for this woman's grandeur and brilliance. Some tales claim that she led Aeneas to Hell and brought him back out again.

"This lady came to Rome and brought nine books with her, which she offered for sale to King Tarquin. But since he refused to meet her asking price,

2. Boccaccio indeed acknowledges the high honor that God bestowed on Erythrea and, like Christine, notes that she should be revered above all women in antiquity. But Christine de Pizan's account differs from Boccaccio's here in emphasizing that the "holy Christian women of Paradise" deserve *greater* reverence. See *Famous Women*, chap. 21.

3. According to tradition, Lucius Tarquinius Superbus (Tarquin the Proud) was the last king before the advent of the Roman Republic (his reign lasted from 534 to 509 BCE). In II.44, Christine attributes the father's name to his son Sextus Tarquinius—the man responsible for the rape of Lucretia.

she burnt three of them in his presence. The next day she asked him the same price for the six remaining books as she had asked for all nine and announced that if he did not pay her this price, she would at once burn three more books, and the remaining three on the following day. King Tarquin then paid her the original asking price. The books were carefully preserved, for it was discovered that they contained the entire future history of the Romans. All major events that would come to pass in the Roman Empire were found to be predicted in these books, which were carefully guarded in the emperors' treasury so one could consult them just as one would a divine oracle.

"So take note, my sweet friend, and consider how God bestowed such a great favor on a single woman, allowing her to counsel not only one emperor in her own lifetime but also all the future Roman emperors, and to predict all the empire's major events. Tell me, if you can: was there ever a man who did anything as exceptional as this?[4] And you, like a fool, considered yourself unlucky to belong to the same sex as these remarkable beings, thinking that God held your sex in contempt!

"This sibyl is mentioned in one of Virgil's books. She ended her days in Sicily, where her tomb was kept on display for a long time."

4. About several female prophets.

"Those ten ladies, however, were not the only ones in the world to be favored by God with the ability to predict the future. In fact, there have been many, belonging to various religions. If you look at the Jewish faith, for example, you will find someone like Deborah, who was a prophetess in the time of the Judges of Israel. It was thanks to Deborah and her acumen that the chosen people were delivered from servitude from the hands of the king of Canaan, who had kept them enslaved for twenty years.

"Another example is the blessed Elizabeth, Our Lady's cousin. When the glorious Virgin went to see her, she said: 'How is it that the Mother of God has come to see me?' Weren't her words prophetic? She could not have known that Mary had conceived of the Holy Spirit except through her gift of prophecy, just like the prophet Simeon to whom Our Lady presented Jesus Christ at the altar of the temple on Candlemas day. The holy prophet, aware that

---

4. Boccaccio's version of the story of Almathea in *Famous Women* (chap. 26) includes the following observation: "if women are able to achieve so much through their keenness of intellect and the gift of prophecy, what ought wretched men to think who have greater aptitude for everything?"

this was the Savior of the world, took him in his arms and said: *Nunc dimittis.*
And when the good lady Anna, walking through the temple to perform her
duties, saw the Virgin enter holding her infant, she knew intuitively that this
was the Savior. She fell to her knees to worship Him, exclaiming that this
child had come to save humankind.

"You'll find many other women prophets in the Jewish faith if you look
for them, and there are countless others in the Christian faith, many of whom
are saints. But let us leave these ladies aside, because you might say that God
granted them special favors. Let us talk about some pagan women.

"The Holy Scriptures mention the queen of Sheba,[5] stating that she was
supremely intelligent. When she heard people talk about the wisdom of Solomon, whose fame had spread far and wide, she decided to go and see him.
So she left her country in the East and rode from a far corner of the remotest
part of the world through Ethiopia and Egypt along the shores of the Red
Sea, crossing the great deserts of Arabia. Accompanied by a distinguished
entourage of richly dressed princes, lords, knights, and noble ladies and carrying a rich treasure, she arrived in the city of Jerusalem to visit the wise King
Solomon and to see for herself if what was being said about him all over the
world was true.

"Solomon received her with great honor, as befitted her rank, and she
spent a long time with him, testing his wisdom in many fields. She asked him
numerous questions and set him many obscure and cryptic riddles, which he
solved so easily that she declared that Solomon's wisdom was not the fruit of
human intelligence but a gift from God. She gave him many valuable presents,
including some small trees that produced sap and balm. The king had them
planted near a lake by the name of Asphaltites and gave orders for them to be
carefully tended and cultivated. In turn, he gave the lady many precious jewels.

"This woman's wisdom and prophecies are mentioned in several books,
which recount that while she was in Jerusalem and Solomon took her to see
the grandeur of the temple he had ordered built, she saw a long plank lying
across a muddy puddle, serving as a footbridge to cross that boggy area. The
lady stopped, looking at the plank, and revered it, saying: 'This plank, which
people see as a repulsive object right now and are treading with their feet, shall
be honored beyond all trees in the world in days to come. It shall be adorned
with precious stones from royal treasures, and the man who will destroy the
Jewish faith shall die upon the wood of this plank.' The Jews did not take

5. See I.12.

these words in jest but removed the plank and buried it in a spot where they thought no one would ever find it. But what God chooses to keep is kept well, because the Jews did not succeed in hiding it well enough to prevent it from being found at the time of the Passion of Our Lord Jesus Christ. It is said that the cross on which Our Savior suffered His death and passion was made from this plank. Thus, this lady's prophecy was vindicated."

5. More about Nicostrata, Cassandra, and Queen Basine.

"Nicostrata, whom we discussed earlier,[6] was also a prophetess. As soon as she had crossed the river Tiber and climbed Mount Palatine with her son Evander, who is often mentioned in history books, she prophesied that the most famous city of all time would be built upon this hill and that it would rule all earthly kingdoms. Wanting to lay the founding stone, she had a fortified castle built there, as I told you before, and that is where Rome was founded and built.

"Then there was the noble Trojan maiden Cassandra, daughter of King Priam of Troy and sister of the valiant Hector.[7] She was such a great scholar that she knew all the arts. She did not wish to take a husband, no matter how great a prince he might be, because she knew in her heart what would happen to the Trojans, and her sadness knew no bounds. Was she not also a prophetess? During the period leading up to the war between the Trojans and the Greeks, she watched Troy grow more prosperous and glorious, and the more it flourished, the more she cried and lamented. Seeing the city's splendor and richness and the fame of her handsome brothers, especially the valiant, highly esteemed Hector, she was unable to keep quiet about the great misfortune that was to befall him. When she saw the war break out, her grief intensified. She could not stop crying and wailing and kept urging her father and brothers to make peace with the Greeks for the love of God, warning them they would be destroyed by this war. But her words went unheeded. They did not believe her, and since she continued to lament the great loss and destruction

---

6. See I.37.

7. There are competing versions of the story of Cassandra in mythology, but the name often conjures up the idea of someone predicting the worst. Note that we see here another clear example of the potential benefit of tears (to be understood within the context of the trilogy of weeping, talking, and weaving discussed in I.10). If Cassandra's family had taken her tears seriously, tragedy could have been avoided. The power and significance of weeping is a theme common in other medieval literature. See especially *The Book of Margery Kempe*.

and understandably refused to keep silent, she suffered many beatings by her father and brothers, who said she was crazy. But she never let up; she would not keep quiet to save her soul, and she kept telling them what would happen. Finally, they decided that the only way they could have peace was to lock her up in a distant location to block her constant cries from their ears. But they would have done better to believe her, because everything she had foretold came to pass. In the end, they regretted not having listened to her, but by then it was too late.

"And then there was Queen Basine's prophecy. Was it not just as magnificent? She had been married to the king of Thuringia, and the chronicles recount that she then wed Childeric, the fourth king of France. The history books say that she told King Childeric on their wedding night that if he kept himself chaste that night, he would receive a marvelous vision. She told him to get up, go to the bedroom door, and take note of what he saw. The king did as he was told, and he thought he saw great beasts known as unicorns, as well as leopards and lions wandering through the palace. He drew back in utter terror and asked the queen what this meant. She replied that she would tell him in the morning and that he should not be afraid but turn back to the door. He did, and this time he thought he was seeing large bears and wolves trying to attack each other. The queen sent him back to the door a third time, and he then thought he was seeing dogs and small animals tearing each other to pieces. Seeing the king utterly terrified and dumbfounded by what he had seen, the queen explained that the animals he had seen in his vision represented their descendants: the various generations of princes who would rule France. The nature and diversity of the beasts and animals he had seen, she said, symbolized their moral values and their conduct. So it should be quite clear to you, my sweet friend, that Our Lord has often revealed his secrets to the world through the intermediary of women. In fact, He still does."

6. About Antonia, who became empress.

"It was no small secret that God revealed through a woman's vision to Justinian, who later became emperor of Constantinople. This Justinian was in charge of guarding Emperor Justin's treasures and coffers. One day, Justinian went off to entertain himself in the fields, taking with him a woman he loved by the name of Antonia. At noon, Justinian wanted to take a rest so he lay down under a tree to have a nap, putting his head in his girlfriend's lap.

When he had fallen asleep, Antonia saw a large eagle approach and fly over their heads, taking pains to spread its wings to shade Justinian's face from the sun. Antonia, in her wisdom, understood its significance, and when Justinian awoke, she gently said to him: 'My sweet friend, I have always loved you and I still do. You know that you are the master of my body and my soul. Since there is no reason why a lover who is cherished by his lady should refuse her anything, I want to ask you a favor in exchange for my virginity and my love. It will seem like a small thing to you but it is very important to me.' Justinian replied that she should feel free to ask and that he would grant her anything within his power. Then Antonia said: 'The favor I ask of you is that once you become emperor, you will not reject your humble mistress Antonia but you will honor her and make her your empress through a legal marriage. Please promise me that you will.' When Justinian heard these words, he burst out laughing, thinking that she was speaking in jest. Convinced that he could not possibly ever become emperor, he promised her that he would marry her if he ever became emperor. In fact, he swore an oath by all his gods and Antonia thanked him for it. She made them exchange rings as a token of this promise. Then she said: 'Justinian, believe me when I tell you that you will most certainly become emperor and you will not have to wait long.' On that note, they parted.

"Not long afterward, when Emperor Justin had assembled his army to march on the Persians, he took ill and died. The barons and princes gathered to elect a new emperor, but since they were unable to reach a consensus, they elected Justinian emperor out of spite for each other. Justinian did not waste time but immediately gathered a large army and launched a fierce attack on the Persians. He won the battle and took the king of Persia prisoner, gaining great honor and bringing back considerable spoils of war.

"When he had returned to his palace, his mistress Antonia did not stay away but used her wiles to gain entrance to where he sat on his throne, surrounded by his princes. And there, on her knees before him, she pled her case, telling him she was a maiden who had come to ask him for justice regarding a young man who had betrothed her and had given her his ring, taking hers in exchange. The emperor, who had completely forgotten her, replied that if someone had, in fact, betrothed her, it was appropriate that he take her as his wife and that he, the emperor, would gladly see to it that justice be done, provided she prove her case. Then Antonia pulled the ring from her finger and handed it to him with these words: 'Noble emperor, I can prove it with this ring. Take a look and see if you recognize it.' Realizing that he had become trapped by his own words, the emperor decided to keep his promise. He had her taken at once to his chambers and dressed in elegant clothing, and went on to marry her."

7. Christine talks to Lady Reason.

"My lady, your words make it very clear that the accusations against women are completely unfounded, and I realize more than ever that they do them an enormous injustice. Yet I can't help bringing up a tradition that is quite common among men and even some women: when women become pregnant and give birth to girls, their husbands are upset. Many of them complain because their wives have not presented them with a son. And their foolish wives, instead of being ecstatic that God has granted them a safe delivery and feeling profoundly grateful, are unhappy as well because they see their husbands upset. Why is it, my lady, that they become so distressed? Are daughters a greater burden to their parents than sons or less affectionate and more indifferent toward them than boys?"

"My dear friend," replied Lady Reason, "since you ask me the reason why this happens, I can assure you that it is because those who become distressed by this are extremely foolish and ignorant. The main reason why they are upset, however, is that they are thinking about the money they will have to pay from their own pockets to marry their daughters off. Others are distressed because they fear that a young, ignorant girl could be led astray by a smooth-talking male. But none of these reasons stands up to close scrutiny. As regards their fear that their daughters might dishonor themselves, their parents only need to raise them in a sensible manner and make sure the mothers set a good example through their own integrity and propriety, because if a mother leads a dissolute life, she sets a bad example for her daughter. Also, daughters[8] should be kept from bad company, raised by strict rules, and taught to fear God, because discipline prepares children and adolescents to lead exemplary lives.

"As far as the expense is concerned, I think that if the parents took a close look at what their sons cost them, whatever their station in life, in terms of their education or vocational training, their upkeep, and even extra expenses

8. Readers should note that Christine advises similar things when she discusses the education of young boys and princes elsewhere. See, for instance, *The Book of the Deeds and Good Morals of the Wise King Charles V* (e.g., part 1, chap. 7–13), penned roughly at the same time as the *City of Ladies*; see also *The Book of the Body Politic*, esp. part I.

when they keep bad company and play all sorts of pranks, I think they would find that there is hardly any financial advantage to having sons instead of daughters. And if you consider the vexation and worry that many sons cause their parents (which happens all too often) by getting involved in nasty fights and ugly brawls or leading a dissolute life, all to the distress and at the expense of their parents, I think those things far outweigh the worries they might have on account of their daughters.

"Tell me how many sons you can find who look after their parents in their old age with kindness and respect, as is their duty. I am convinced they are few and far between because it rarely happens. There certainly have been and are some who do, but they are rare. But when fathers and mothers raise their sons like gods and they grow up and become rich and affluent thanks to their fathers' efforts to have them educated to learn a trade or through good luck, and then their old father has the misfortune of losing his money and faces ruin, the sons despise him and are embarrassed and ashamed when they encounter him. And if the father is rich, they cannot wait for him to die so they can inherit his wealth. Oh! God knows how many sons of great lords and rich men desire their parents' death to obtain their lands and wealth! Petrarch was right when he said: 'Oh, foolish man, you want to have children, but you could not wish for more deadly enemies, for if you are poor, they will consider you a burden and they will wish for your death to be rid of you, and if you are rich, they will want to see you dead just as much so they can have your wealth.'[9] I don't mean to say that they are all that way but many are, and if they are married, God knows how terribly greedy they can be, always wanting something from their father and mother. They don't care if those miserable old people died of hunger, as long as they have what they want. Oh, what scoundrels! Or if their mothers are widowed—those same mothers who cherished them and lovingly raised and pampered them—they are handed a bitter reward instead of being comforted and supported in their old age. Because their wayward offspring think that everything should be theirs, and if the mothers don't give

---

9. Italian poet Petrarch (1304–1374) is generally considered (along with Dante) to be the scholar who gave rise to the broader movement of Renaissance humanism. He was based in Avignon at the papal court for much of his life. Christine was probably familiar with Petrarch's *Remedies for Good and Bad Fortune* [*De remediis utriusque fortunae*], which is the likely source here. On Christine's use and knowledge of Petrarch, see Lori Walters, "Chivalry and the (En) Gendered Poetic Self: Petrarchan Models in the 'Cent Balades,'" in *The City of Scholars: New Approaches to Christine de Pizan*, ed. Margarete Zimmermann and Dina De Rentiis (New York: Walter de Gruyter, 1994), 43–66.

their sons everything they ask for, the sons do not hesitate to make their displeasure abundantly clear. God knows how little respect is shown on those occasions. And there is worse: some won't scruple to take their mothers to court and bring lawsuits against them. That is how many of them are rewarded for having spent their whole life devoted to bettering the lives of their children. There are many such sons and there may well be daughters who behave like that, but I think you'll find that if you look closely, there are more disgraceful sons than there are daughters.

"Even if we assume that all sons are good, then you will still see that daughters tend to keep their parents company more often than sons, visiting them more frequently, and looking after them in sickness and old age. The reason is that sons are more prone to go out into the world and travel, while the daughters don't move about as much and stay close to home, as you can see by your own example. Even though your brothers were very kind and loving sons, they still went out into the world, leaving you behind, alone, to keep your dear mother company, which is a tremendous comfort in her old age.[10] That leads one to conclude that those who are worried and upset about the birth of a daughter are extremely foolish. And since you have introduced this topic, I want to tell you about several women mentioned in some history books who were kind and loving daughters."

8. Here, she starts giving examples of daughters who loved their parents. First, Drypetina.

"Drypetina, queen of Laodicea, loved her father dearly. She was the daughter of the great King Mithridates and loved him so much that she followed him into all his battles. She was quite unattractive because she had a double row of teeth that made her look very deformed. But she adored her father so much that she never left his side, be it in prosperity or adversity. Although she was queen and first lady of a great kingdom and could have lived in peace and comfort in her own country, she shared all the trials and tribulations her father had to endure in his many campaigns. Even when he was defeated by the great Pompey, she never abandoned him but looked after him with the utmost care and attention."

---

10. After the death of their father, Thomas de Pizan, Christine's two brothers decided to move to Italy, leaving behind their mother and one daughter.

9. Here she talks about Hypsipyle.

"Hypsipyle put herself in mortal danger to save her father. His name was Thoas and he was king of Lemnos. When his country rebelled against him and the people were storming the palace to kill him, his daughter Hypsipyle immediately hid him in one of her trunks and went out to appease the people. She did not succeed, however, and after the mob conducted a thorough search for the king and could not find him, they pointed their swords at Hypsipyle and threatened to kill her if she did not reveal the king's whereabouts. They promised her that if she did, they would crown her queen and swear fealty to her. This good and caring daughter, however, preferred saving her father's life rather than becoming queen. She did not bow to the fear of death but replied with great courage that he must have fled long since. Unable to find him and impressed by her assurances that he had fled, they believed her and crowned her queen. She ruled them peacefully for some time, but since she had now kept her father hidden for an extended period of time, she feared she might at some point be denounced by someone who envied her. So she freed him from his hiding place one night and sent him to safety by sea, provided with great wealth. Eventually, however, her disloyal subjects found out and expelled their queen Hypsipyle. They would even have killed her if some of the people had not been moved to compassion by her loyalty."

10. About the virgin Claudine.

"Oh! What profound evidence of deep-seated love for a father did the virgin Claudine provide on his victorious return to Rome after performing many heroic deeds and winning tremendous victories. The Romans received him with supreme honor in a ritual they called 'triumph.' This was an exceptional distinction accorded to princes who returned from war after winning great victories, such as Claudine's father, who was a very brave Roman prince. As he was receiving this honor, he was attacked by another Roman lord who hated him. His daughter Claudine had been consecrated to the goddess Vesta (this would equate today to being a nun in a convent) and was on her way to meet her father in a procession with some other ladies from her order, as was the custom. When she heard the noise and learned that her father was being attacked by his enemies, the great love she had for her father made her completely disregard the simple and demure conduct appropriate to a virginal nun. She cast aside all fear and jumped out of the cart in which she had been riding with her companions, ran through the crowd, and boldly planted herself between her father and the swords and lances aimed at him. Grabbing the nearest assailant by the throat, she defended her father with all her might. A great commotion ensued but was soon brought under control. Since the valiant Romans used to pay tribute to anyone who performed a deed they admired, they greatly esteemed this virgin and accorded her high praise for what she had done."

11. Here she talks about a woman who breastfed her mother in prison.

"The history books mention another Roman woman who adored her mother. That lady, having committed some crime, was condemned to die in prison and no one was permitted to give her anything to drink or eat. Her daughter, moved by her great love for her mother and saddened by this sentence, asked the prison guards for a special favor, requesting that she be allowed to visit her mother every day as long as she was alive so she could encourage her to suffer her punishment with patience. In short, she cried and begged so vehemently that the prison guards took pity on her and gave her permission to visit her mother every day. But before she was allowed to see her mother, they searched her carefully to make sure she was not carrying any food. The visits went on for so many days that it seemed impossible to the jailers that their prisoner could still be alive without anything to eat. But she was still alive, and although she was visited by her daughter, she was closely searched each time she came and the guards were astounded. One day, they were watching the mother and her daughter together and saw the poor girl, who had recently given birth, giving her breast to her mother so that she could drink her fill from the milk. That is how the daughter gave her mother in her old age what she had taken from her in her infancy. The sight of such devotion and so much love from a daughter for her mother moved the jailers to great pity, and when they reported the matter to the judges, they, too, were filled with compassion. They freed the mother and returned her to her daughter.

"On the same subject of filial love, one could mention the virtuous, wise Griselda and the love she had for her father. She eventually became marchioness of Saluzzo; I will tell you more about her great virtue, firmness, and constancy later on. Oh! The profound love inspired by her loyal character that prompted her to look after her poor, ailing father Giannucolo with so much care, humility, and obedience! She, in the flower of her youth, pure and innocent, nursed her poor father, elderly and ailing, and did her utmost to earn a meager living for the two of them by toiling away at manual labor. How fortunate it is that so many kind and loving daughters are born to parents! Even though they are only doing their duty, their souls reap great rewards. They deserve high praise, as do similarly minded sons.

"What more do you want me to tell you? I could give you any number of similar examples, but this will do for now."

12. Here, Lady Rectitude announces that the construction of the city is finished and that it is time to look for inhabitants.

"It seems to me, my dear friend, that our construction work is now well advanced. Tall buildings and strong royal palaces are lining the wide streets of the City of Ladies. The donjons and fortified towers, straight and tall, can be seen from far away. It is time, therefore, to begin the search for inhabitants to reside in this proud city, so it does not sit desolate or empty but is filled with illustrious ladies, for they are the only ones who are welcome. Oh, how happy the residents of our city will be! They have no need to be afraid of being thrown out of their homes by foreign intruders, because the nature of our project is such that owners can never be expelled. A new Realm of Women has now come into being, much more perfect than the previous one because the ladies residing here do not need to leave their land in order to conceive and give birth to new daughters to maintain their realm from generation to generation throughout the ages. The ladies we will invite into our city will stay here forever.

"Once we have seen to it that the city is filled with noble citizens, Lady Justice, my sister, will come and bring the queen, that most excellent of all women, accompanied by princesses of great nobility. They will reside in the finest dwellings and the highest towers. It is appropriate that when the queen arrives, she will find her city already inhabited and occupied by noble ladies who will receive her with honor and acknowledge her as their ruler, the empress of their sex. But what sort of citizens shall we invite? Shall they be dissolute women of ill repute? Certainly not! They shall all be valiant women of great beauty and prestige, because there can be no better people or a greater asset for our city than good and virtuous women. So get ready, Christine, let us set to work and go in search of these ladies."

13. Christine asks Lady Rectitude if it is true what books and men say: that the reason married life is so hard to bear is the miserable failings of women. In her reply, Lady Rectitude starts recalling women who showed their husbands devoted love.

As we started searching for these ladies as instructed by Lady Rectitude, I said to her: "My lady, you and Lady Reason have truly answered and solved all the questions and problems that I could not address myself, and I now consider myself well informed about the things I wanted to know. I have learned so much from the two of you! I understand that all things that can be done and known, whether they involve the body or the mind or any other faculty, can all be managed by women with ease. But could you please explain and confirm for me something that really troubles my mind: is it true what men claim and many authors say, that married life is filled with hardship because of women's impetuosity and their constant nagging? As many authors assert and many men claim, women have so little love for their husbands and their company that nothing irritates them more. To avoid such misery, several authors have said that if men are wise, they should not marry at all, claiming that few, if any, women are faithful to their husbands.[11]

"Even Valerius in his letter to Rufinus and Theophrastus' book on marriage say that wise men should not take a wife, because women cause too much worry, lack affection, and do nothing but gossip.[12] If a man wants to marry in order to have someone to serve him and look after him when he is sick, he would do better to hire a loyal servant who would faithfully tend to him and cost him a good deal less. And if a wife falls ill, her husband will be anxious and afraid to move from her side. There is a great deal more on this subject, but it would take too long to go into detail. So I say to you, my dear lady: if these things are true, women's shortcomings are so vile that they completely cancel out all other merits and virtues they might have."

---

11. Many of the medieval arguments against marriage can be traced to Saint Jerome's *Against Jovinianus* (393 CE), which brings together a number of classical arguments on this topic and was used as an authoritative source by such thinkers as John of Salisbury (in his *Policraticus* ca. 1159) as well as Chaucer. See Katharina Wilson and Elizabeth Makowski, *Wykked Wyves and the Woes of Marriage: Misogamous Literature from Juvenal to Chaucer* (Albany: State University of New York Press, 1990).

12. Christine is referring here to the short tract *Advice of Valerius to Rufinus the Philosopher Not to Marry*, whose authorship is uncertain, and to pseudo-Theophrastus' *Golden Book on Marriage*. There is no evidence that Theophrastus (ca. 371–287 BCE) himself wrote this antifeminist text.

Lady Rectitude replied: "My dear friend, as you yourself have already said on this topic, anyone who goes to court without an opponent has no trouble pleading his case. I promise you that the books stating these things have not been written by women. I have no doubt that if you wanted to research marital disputes in order to write a new book, this time based on the truth, you would come up with some very different stories. Oh, my dear friend! You know yourself how many women lead a miserable existence under the yoke of marriage because of their husbands' cruelty, suffering more than if they had been slaves under the Saracens. My God! Think of how many good, upright women are viciously beaten without cause, suffer abuse, live in servitude, and are subjected to insults, indignities, and outrage! And none of them cry out for help! Not to mention those who starve and suffer with a house full of children while their husbands dawdle in sinful places or entertain themselves in every tavern in town. And even so, these poor women are beaten when their husbands return, and *that* is their supper! Tell me: do I lie? Have you never seen any of your neighbors suffer that fate?"

I said: "Certainly, my lady; I have seen many, and I really pitied them."

"I can well believe you. And to say that husbands are so upset when their wives fall ill! I ask you, my dear friend, where are they? Without saying more about this, it is easy to see that all this nonsense said and written about women always has been and still is nothing but an invention that flies in the face of the truth. Men control their wives and not the other way around, so they would never allow themselves to be dominated that way. I assure you, however, that not all marriages are conducted in this style. Some couples lead a peaceful life characterized by mutual affection and loyalty, because both partners are kindhearted, understanding, and reasonable. And although there are bad husbands, there are others who are good, honorable, and wise, and the women who meet them are born under a lucky star because God brought them together and granted them glory in this world. You should know this yourself because you could not have wished for a better husband: one who, in your opinion, surpassed all other men in terms of kindness, serenity, loyalty, and sincere love. That is why you will never be able to stop grieving for what death took from you. But while it is true that many good wives are mistreated by their bad-tempered husbands, it should be said that some wives are petulant and unreasonable, because if I told you that they were all good, I could easily be proven wrong. But they are in the minority, and I would rather not discuss them because such women are aberrations of nature.

"But let us talk about good wives and your quote from Theophrastus, that a man will be looked after as faithfully and carefully by a servant as by a wife when he is sick or hurt. Ah! There are numerous women who nurse their husbands in sickness and in health as devotedly as if they were tending to gods. I don't think you would ever find a servant of that caliber. And since we are now on this subject, I will give you several examples of the devoted and faithful love women have shown their husbands.

"And now, thank God, we are back at our City, in the fine company of magnificent, upright women to whom we will offer a home here. To begin with, there is the noble Queen Hypsicratea, once married to the mighty King Mithridates. Because she lived in ancient times and her stature is so outstanding, she will be the first we will welcome in the magnificent palace that has been prepared for her."

14. Here she talks about Queen Hypsicratea.

"How could anyone show greater love to another human being than the beautiful, kind, and faithful Hypsicratea showed her husband? She certainly proved it. She was the wife of the great King Mithridates, who ruled over countries where twenty-four different languages were spoken. Although this king was supremely powerful, the Romans waged a merciless war on him. Yet in all the time he spent on the battlefields, making heroic efforts, his wife never left his side wherever he went. This king had several concubines as was customary with the pagans, but this magnificent woman always loved him so fiercely that she would not let him go anywhere without her. She often accompanied him in great battles when he risked losing his kingdom as he braved death fighting the Romans. Whether he went to unknown regions or distant countries, whether he crossed the sea or perilous deserts, he never went anywhere without her at his side as his faithful companion. Her love for him was so all-encompassing that she thought no man could serve his lord as perfectly and faithfully as she served her husband.

"Contrary to what Theophrastus says on this subject, this woman knew that kings and princes often have servants who can't be trusted and serve them badly. She, on the other hand, loved him faithfully and was always able to provide her lord with exactly what he needed. Even if it caused her great hardship, she wanted to be with him at all times. Women's clothing was impractical in those circumstances, however, and it was also inappropriate for a woman to be seen in battle at the side of such a great king and magnificent warrior, so she cut her long, golden-blond hair, women's finest attribute, to disguise herself as a man. Indifferent to her lovely complexion, she also wore a helmet, so her face often grew dirty with sweat and dust. She covered her lovely, tender body in armor and a coat of chain mail. She took off her precious rings and rich jewelry and used her hands to carry heavy axes, lances, and bows and arrows. Instead of an ornate girdle, she wore a sword around her waist. And so this magnificent lady, driven by her great and faithful love, transformed a lovely, young body that was meant to be soft and delicate into that of a powerful and vigorous armed knight.

"'Oh,' says Boccaccio, who recounts this story,[13] 'the things love can achieve! Here we see a woman used to a life of refinement such as sleeping in a soft bed and enjoying every comfort and luxury, driven by her own strong will to cross mountains and valleys by day and by night as if she were a tough, strong man, sleeping in deserts and forests, often in fear of the enemy, surrounded by wild animals and snakes!' But none of that seemed a burden to her as long as she could spend all her time at her husband's side to comfort and counsel him and see to his every need.

"After she had endured many great hardships, her husband was cruelly defeated by Pompey, commander of the Roman army, and forced to flee. Although all his men had deserted and he found himself alone, his faithful wife did not abandon him but fled with him, crossing mountains and valleys and dismal, inhospitable places. She followed him everywhere, and her husband, who had been abandoned by all his friends and had lost all hope, was comforted by his good wife, who gently encouraged him to hope for better times. The more desolate the situation, the more she took pains to console him, cheering him up with gentle words and inventing amusing and entertaining games to make him forget his despair. All this, combined with her infinite gentleness, gave him so much comfort that regardless of how much misery and suffering he had to endure, no matter how great his tribulations, she made him forget his troubles. This often prompted him to remark that he did not feel in the least as if he was living in exile but rather as if he were enjoying himself in his palace with his faithful wife."

---

13. Christine largely follows Boccaccio's account of the story (chap. 78) but skips the end, where Boccaccio mentions that Hypsicratea was poisoned to death by her husband.

15. About Empress Triaria.

"The noble Empress Triaria, wife of the Roman emperor Lucius Vitellius, strongly resembled Queen Hypsicratea both in terms of her circumstances and her faithful love for her husband. She loved him so much that she followed him everywhere and bravely rode by his side on all the battlefields, armed like a knight and fighting with great courage. One day, when this emperor was fighting a war against Vaspanianus for control of the empire, he happened to be attacking a city of the Volscians and managed to enter the city by night. Finding the inhabitants asleep, he launched a ferocious attack. The magnificent lady Triaria, who had followed her husband throughout the night, was nearby, fully armed and wearing a sword. Anxious for him to win victory, she fought fiercely at his side, now here, now there, in the dark of the night. She felt no fear or repulsion whatsoever but fought so relentlessly that when the battle was over, she had outdone everyone and performed extraordinary deeds. Boccaccio comments on the great love she bore her husband, expressing approval of the marriage bond so strongly criticized by others."

16. More about Queen Artemisia.

"Among all the ladies who showed their husbands tremendous love and demonstrated this by their actions, I should mention the noble Artemisia, queen of Caria, of whom we have spoken before.[14] As mentioned, she followed King Mausolus into many battles, and when he was killed, she was so stricken by grief that it was almost unbearable. She had given ample proof of her love for him while he was alive, and she did no less at his death. After completing all the solemn rites that were customary for a king at the time, she held a funeral ceremony in the company of princes and barons to cremate his body. Then she collected the ashes, washing them with her tears, and put them in an urn made of gold. It seemed wrong to her that the ashes of the man she had loved so deeply should have any other grave but her heart and body, where her great love had taken root, so she proceeded to mix the ashes with a little liquid and drank them, little by little, until she had swallowed them all.

"She also wanted to erect a sepulchre that would stand in perpetual memory of her husband and spared no expense, sending for certain craftsmen skilled in designing and building marvelous monuments. Their names were Scopas,

---

14. See I.21.

Bryaxis, Timotheus, and Leochares, all brilliant artisans. The queen explained to them that she wanted a sepulchre built for King Mausolus, her lord, and that it should be the most splendid tomb ever built for any king or prince in the world because she wanted her husband's name to last for all time through this marvelous monument. The men told her they would gladly do as she asked, so the queen ordered a large quantity of marble and jasper in various colors and everything else they asked for. Thus the artisans erected a magnificent, marble monument in front of the city of Halicarnassus, Caria's capital. It was brilliantly carved, in the form of a square. Each side was 64 feet long and 140 feet tall. And what was even more spectacular, this enormous structure rested on thirty heavy marble columns. Each of the four artisans tried to outdo the others in carving one of the structure's sides, and their work was so superb that it not only commemorated the man for whom the tomb had been built but also attested to the builders' genius. A fifth artisan, whose name was Ytheron, came to complete the work. He built the tomb's pyramid, peaking forty steps above what the others had built. Then came the sixth artisan, named Pythius, who carved a chariot out of marble and put it on top of the entire structure.

"This monument was so extraordinary that it was considered one of the Seven Wonders of the World. Built for King Mausolus, it was named after him and called 'mausoleum.' Boccaccio says that since it was the most famous tomb ever built for king or prince, all other tombs erected for kings or princes have been called mausoleums ever since. That is how Artemisia, through her actions and their symbolism, expressed her lifelong love for her faithful husband."

17. Here she talks about Argia, daughter of King Adrastus.

"Who would dare say that women have little love for their husbands considering the example set by Argia, daughter of Adrastus, the king of Argos, who loved her husband Polynices beyond measure? This Polynices was involved in a struggle with his brother Eteocles for control of the kingdom of Thebes, which belonged to Polynices under the terms of certain agreements conducted between them. But since Eteocles wanted to appropriate the entire kingdom, his brother Polynices declared war on him. King Adrastus, his father-in-law, came to his aid with a great army. Fortune turned against Polynices, however, when he and his brother ended up killing each other on the battlefield. King Adrastus, the third party in the battle, was the only survivor.

"When Argia learned of her husband's death on the battlefield, she left her royal residence behind and departed at once, taking with her all the ladies of the city of Argos. Boccaccio describes her actions as follows: 'The noble lady Argia heard that the dead body of Polynices, her husband, was lying unburied among the other bodies and rotting corpses of the foot soldiers who had been killed along with him. Filled with grief, she took off her royal robes and finery and abandoned the comfort and luxury of her ornate chambers. Her burning desire and profound love made her conquer her feminine weakness and sensitivity, and she traveled for several days until she came to the battle site, undaunted by the ambushes of enemies lying in wait and feeling no fatigue in spite of the length of the journey and the heat.' When she arrived at the battlefield, she did not fear the savage animals and huge birds attracted by the cadavers, nor the evil spirits that hover around men's corpses, as some foolish people would have it. What is even more amazing, says Boccaccio, is that she ignored the edict and prohibition issued by King Creon, who had publicly announced that no one was to visit or bury the bodies on pain of death, no matter who they were. But Argia had not traveled all that way to obey this edict. Arriving at nightfall, she was undaunted by the terrible stench that rose from the unburied corpses. Driven by her burning grief, she immediately began to examine the bodies, one by one, searching everywhere for the one she loved. Carrying a small torch, she kept up her search until she found her beloved husband. 'Oh,' says Boccaccio, 'what marvelous love, what ardent devotion and love this woman showed!' Even though her husband's face was half eaten away by the rust of his armor and although it was terribly decayed, covered with dried blood and stained with dirt, so pale and livid that it was already barely recognizable, this woman who loved him so deeply knew him at once. Neither the foul smell of the body nor the filth covering his face could stop her from kissing him and tightly holding him in her arms. King Creon's edict and prohibition did not stop her from crying out: 'Alas! Alas! I have found the man I loved!' Then she dissolved into tears and checked for a sign of life by covering his mouth with kisses. She washed his decomposing flesh with her tears, calling his name over and over again as she sobbed and lamented. Finally she performed the last rites, saddest of all, committing his body to a funeral pyre amid cries of despair. Afterward, she tenderly gathered his ashes and placed them in a vessel of gold.[15] When all this was done, she

---

15. Christine's source here, Boccaccio, proposes an unusual account of Polynices' postmortem fate—one partially borrowed from Hyginus' *Fabulae*. (The more standard story of Polynices' burial is that found in Sophocles' *Antigone*, where it is Antigone who buries her brother, not Argia.) But note that Christine adds something to Boccaccio's version, namely, the vengeful attack Argia orchestrates against Thebes.

vowed that she was ready to risk her life to avenge her husband's death. To show her resolve, she attacked the city, aided by the many ladies who had come with her. They fought so fiercely that they breached the walls, captured the city, and put all the inhabitants to death."

18. About the noble lady Agrippina.

"Another excellent and faithful lady who deserves to be ranked among all the magnificent women who were deeply devoted to their husbands is Agrippina, daughter of Marcus Agrippa and Julia, the daughter of Emperor Octavian, who ruled the entire world.[16] This noble lady had been given in marriage to Germanicus, a well-educated, wise Roman prince who was devoted to the public good. The emperor in power at that time was Tiberius,[17] who was an immoral man. He heard people talk about the wonderful things Germanicus was doing and how everyone loved him, and became so jealous of Agrippina's husband that he had him ambushed and killed. Agrippina was so distraught by her husband's death that she longed to be killed as well. She did all she could to make this happen by constantly insulting Tiberius, who had her beaten, cruelly tortured, and thrown in jail. But Agrippina, who could not forget her grief over her husband's death, would rather be dead than alive, so she decided to refuse all food and drink. When this decision came to the attention of the tyrannical Tiberius, he was determined to prolong her torment by forcing her to eat, but that did not work. Thereupon he tried to have her force-fed, but she made it very clear that although he had the power to put people to death, he could not keep them alive against their will, and she died as she had wished."

19. Christine addresses Lady Rectitude, who replies with several examples and talks about the noble Julia, daughter of Julius Caesar and wife of Pompey.

After Lady Rectitude had told me these things, I answered as follows: "My lady, it certainly seems to be a great honor to the female sex to hear the stories of so many outstanding ladies. Everyone should be very pleased to know

16. Also known as Agrippina the Elder. Not to be confused with Agrippina the Younger, mother of Nero (the Roman emperor discussed by Christine in II.48).

17. Also known as Augustus, the emperor Octavian (63BCE–14CE) was the adopted son of Julius Caesar. Christine also mentions him at II.49.

that such profound love can reside in a married woman's heart, in addition to all the other virtues women possess. Let them go back to sleep and keep quiet, Matheolus and all the other malicious slanderers who have told so many lies about women. But, my lady, I also remember that the philosopher Theophrastus, whom I have mentioned before, said that women hate their husbands when they get old and that they don't like scholars or clerks. The reason for that, he says, is that the energy required to deal with women and the effort of devoting oneself to academic study are mutually incompatible."

Lady Rectitude replied: "Oh, my dear friend, don't say such things. It will take me no time at all to find examples that completely contradict and disprove these statements.

"Julia was the daughter of Julius Caesar, who later became emperor, and Cornelia, his wife, both descended from Aeneas and Venus of Troy. She was the noblest of the Roman ladies in her time and married to Pompey, the great conqueror. Boccaccio says that Pompey was already old and frail at the pinnacle of his glory, having defeated kings and deposed them in favor of others, subjugated nations, and wiped out pirates. He won the respect of Rome and kings all over the world and acquired various territories on land and on the sea, all thanks to his marvelous victories. His young wife, the noble Julia, loved him so deeply and faithfully in spite of her youth that she wound up paying with her life for an unfortunate event. One day, Pompey felt the urge to praise the gods for all the magnificent victories he had won. As was the custom at the time, he wanted to make a sacrifice. When the sacrificial animal was on the altar, the pious Pompey held it on one side, but his robe became smeared with blood from the animal's wound, so he removed his robe and had one of his servants take it to his residence to fetch a clean one. Unfortunately, the servants carrying the soiled robe came across Pompey's wife Julia. Seeing her husband's bloodstained robe and aware that prominent people in Rome were often attacked and occasionally killed out of envy, she was overwhelmed by the sight that met her eyes and became convinced that her husband had become the victim of such an event. She was so overcome by grief that she felt she could not go on living. Pregnant at the time, she fainted and lost all color, her eyes turning up in her head, and she passed away before anyone could tend to her or allay her fear.

"Her death must have been a devastating loss not only to her husband and the Romans but to the whole world, because if she and her child had lived, the epic war between Julius Caesar and Pompey, so disastrous for all countries of the world, would never have happened."

20. About the noble lady Tertia Aemilia.

"The beautiful and virtuous lady Tertia Aemilia, wife of Scipio Africanus the Elder, was another one who certainly did not hate her husband for being old. This virtuous lady was still young and both attractive and wise, yet her husband, in his old age, slept with one of her servants, who served her as a chambermaid. This happened so often that his wife found out. Although this caused her acute grief, she used the strength of her great wisdom rather than surrender to the passion of her jealousy. She hid her knowledge so well that neither her husband nor anyone else ever heard her mention it. She did not want to bring it up with him because she felt it was shameful to criticize as great a man as he was, and even worse to mention it to anyone else, because that would undermine and belittle the reputation of such a venerable man and tarnish the honor of one who had conquered kingdoms and empires.[18] Thus this noble lady continued to serve him faithfully and love and honor him, and when he died, she freed the servant and married her to a free man."

I, Christine, answered as follows: "Indeed, my lady. What you were saying reminds me of seeing other such women who knew that their husbands were not faithful to them yet still continued to love them and treat them well. They even supported and comforted the women with whom their husbands had children. I heard the same thing about a lady from Brittany, the viscountess of Coëmon, who died quite recently. She was in the flower of youth and more beautiful than all the other ladies, and she did the same, prompted by her exemplary loyalty and kindness."

21. Here she talks about Xanthippe, wife of the philosopher Socrates.

"The noble Xanthippe, a kind lady of great wisdom, was the wife of the great philosopher Socrates. Although he was already quite old and more interested in doing research and studying books than in buying his wife pretty and fancy things, the good lady never stopped loving him. Instead, the excellence of his knowledge, his great virtue, and his steadfastness led her to love and revere him.[19] When this noble lady learned that her husband had been

---

18. A similar message is emphasized by Boccaccio in *Famous Women*, chap. 74. Scipio was the famous Roman republican general who defeated the Carthaginian forces led by Hannibal.

19. In this chapter and the next, Christine obviously seeks to refute the common old charge that contemplative pursuits and marriage are incompatible.

condemned to death by the Athenians because he had criticized them for worshipping idols and told them that there was but one god they should worship and serve, she could not bear it and ran to the palace, all disheveled, filled with grief, crying and beating her breast. There she found her husband, amid the treacherous judges who had already given him the poison that was to end his life. Arriving at the very moment Socrates was about to raise the cup to his mouth to drink the poison, she rushed toward him and angrily tore the cup from his hands, pouring its contents on the floor. Socrates scolded her for this, telling her to be patient, and he comforted her. Because she could not prevent his death, she was filled with sorrow and cried out: 'Oh! What a terrible shame and a tremendous loss to wrongfully put to death such a just man!' Socrates continued to comfort her,[20] telling her that it was better to fall victim to injustice than to be put to death for cause, and so his life ended. But the grief in the heart of the woman he loved lasted for the rest of her life."

22. About Pompeia Paulina, Seneca's wife.

"Seneca, the wise philosopher, was already quite old and devoted all his efforts to study, but he was still deeply loved by his beautiful young wife by the name of Pompeia Paulina. This lady's only thought was of serving him and making sure he could work in peace, because she loved him faithfully and dearly. When she learned that the tyrannical emperor Nero, who had been his pupil, had condemned him to bleed to death in a bath, she almost went mad with anguish. Wanting to die with her husband, she went and screamed terrible insults at the tyrant Nero so that he would visit his cruelty on her as well. Since that did not work, she mourned her husband's death so intensely that she died soon after."

I, Christine, replied: "Truly, honored lady, your words remind me of many other beautiful young women who adored their husbands even though they were ugly and old. Even in my time I have seen many a woman adore her lord and bear him faithful love for as long as he lived. I remember a noble lady, the daughter of one of the great barons of Brittany, who was given in marriage to the valiant constable of France, Lord Bertrand du Guesclin.

---

20. Notwithstanding Plato's well-known critique of wailing, the behavior of Xanthippe would have been considered perfectly customary and legitimate by an average Athenian at the time. Compare Christine de Pizan's portrait of the patient, loving Socrates and of the non-nagging Xanthippe with Xenophon's *Symposium* 2.10. See also Plato's *Phaedo* 60a.

Although he was very unattractive and old, this noble lady, in the flower of her youth, set greater store by his virtues than his physical appearance, and loved him so deeply that she mourned his death all her life. I could mention many others like her, but that would take too long."

Lady Rectitude: "I believe you. In fact, I'll tell you about other ladies who were devoted to their husbands."

23. About the noble Sulpicia.

"Sulpicia was the wife of Lentulus Cruscellio, a noble man from Rome whom she adored with evident devotion. Her husband, accused of certain crimes, was sentenced by the judges of Rome to spend his life in exile in miserable poverty. The noble Sulpicia, who possessed great wealth in Rome, could have remained there leading a comfortable life of luxury, but she preferred to follow her husband into poverty and exile rather than remain behind to live in opulence, so she renounced her entire inheritance, her goods, and her country. She was closely guarded by her mother and other relatives for that very reason, and it took considerable effort to steal away, but she managed to escape by wearing a disguise and went to join her husband."

I said: "Indeed, my lady, what you say reminds me of certain women I have known in my time whose circumstances were similar. I have known some whose husbands became afflicted by leprosy so that they had to be separated from society and sent to a leper colony. Their loyal wives, however, refused to leave them. They preferred to go with them to look after them in their sickness and honor their marriage vow to be faithful rather than stay behind in a comfortable house without their husbands. I think I know one such woman right now, a young, respectable, and pretty lady, whose husband is suspected of having this illness. But although her parents keep urging her to leave him and come to live with them, she tells them that she will never leave him even for a day. She says that if he is examined and found to be suffering from this disease, he would be forced to go into isolation, and she has every intention of going with him in that case. With that in mind, her parents are not putting pressure on her to have him examined.

"Likewise, I know other women (whom I will not name because that might displease them) whose husbands are so perverse and lead such degenerate lives that the wife's parents wish them dead and make every effort to persuade their daughters to come to live with them and leave their evil husbands. But these women prefer being beaten and ill-fed and living in poverty and enslavement with their husbands rather than leaving them. They tell their family: 'You gave him to me, so I will live and die with him.' These are things one sees every day, but no one pays attention to them."

24. Here she talks about several ladies who acted together to save their husbands' lives.

"I want to tell you about some other women who were as devoted to their husbands as the ones I have mentioned before. It so happened that after Jason had been in Colchis to win the Golden Fleece, some of the knights he had brought with him who hailed from a Greek city called Orchomenos left their native country and moved to another Greek city called Lacedaemonia.[21] They were made very welcome and received with honor, as much for their ancient lineage as their wealth. They married highborn ladies from the city, becoming so rich and gaining so much influence that they grew arrogant enough to mount a conspiracy against the city's rulers to seize power for themselves. Their plot was discovered, however, and they were all thrown into jail and sentenced to death. Their wives were horrified and gathered together as if to share their grief, but they actually wanted to discuss whether they could find a way to save their husbands. Their discussion led them to formulate a plan whereby they would all dress up one night in old clothes and cover their heads with their cloaks so that they would not be recognized. Dressed like that, they went to the prison and tearfully pleaded with the guards, making them promises and offering them gifts until they received permission to visit their husbands. When the women were inside, they dressed their husbands in their robes and dressed themselves in their husbands' clothes. Then they sent them outside, and the guards mistook them for the wives returning home. On the day the prisoners were to be put to death, the executioners arrived to lead them to the place where they would be put to death, but when it was discovered that they were the prisoners' wives, everyone admired their clever trick and praised them for it. The citizens took pity on their daughters and all were spared. That is how these brave women saved their husbands' lives."

---

21. On Jason, see note above for I.32.

25. Christine talks to Lady Rectitude about how some men claim that women cannot keep a secret, and Lady Rectitude replies by giving the example of Portia, daughter of Cato.

"My lady, I am now certain of what I already suspected: many women have shown their husbands great love and loyalty, and they still do. That is why I am so baffled by an opinion that is shared by many men, including Master Jean de Meun, who emphasizes it in his *Romance of the Rose*, along with many other authors. What they say is that men should not tell their wives anything they want to keep secret because women cannot keep anything to themselves."

"My dear friend, you must know that not all women are wise, and neither are all men. If a man has any sense, he must assure himself that his wife is sensible and trustworthy enough before he tells her anything he wants kept confidential, because if she doesn't, he may be courting trouble. But when a man feels that his wife is wise and discreet, there is no one in the world he can trust more and who can lend him greater support than his wife.

"As to the view expressed by some that women are indiscreet and to continue the topic of how much women love their husbands, that opinion was not shared by the noble Roman Brutus, husband of Portia. That noble lady was the daughter of Cato the Younger, the nephew of Cato the Elder. Portia's husband, who believed she was very smart, discreet, and virtuous, told her that he and Cassius, another Roman nobleman, intended to kill Julius Caesar in the Senate. Foreseeing the terrible consequences of that deed, Portia had the sense to try to dissuade him and did her best to talk him out of it. She was so upset by her husband's plan that she was unable to sleep all night. When morning came and Brutus left his room to go and carry out his plan, Portia was desperate to stop him. She grabbed a barber's razor as if to cut her nails, dropped it, pretended to pick it up, and deliberately dug it into her hand. Her ladies, seeing her injured, screamed so loudly that Brutus came back. When he saw her injury, he chided her, saying that it was a barber's job to use a razor, not hers. She replied that her action was not as foolish as he thought: she had done it on purpose to find out how she could kill herself if his plan failed. He refused to be convinced, however, and left. He and Cassius killed Julius Caesar shortly thereafter. They were sent into exile for what they had done, and even though he had fled Rome, Brutus was subsequently killed. When Portia, his good wife, learned of his death, she was so overcome by grief that she lost the will to live. Since all knives and sharp objects she could have used to kill herself had been taken away from her because everyone knew what she wanted to do, she went to the fireplace, took some burning coals, and swallowed them.[22] And so the noble Portia killed herself by burning her internal organs. She truly died the strangest death of all."

26. On the same topic: the noble lady Curia.

"I will provide you with even more evidence to contradict those who claim that women cannot keep a secret, still on the topic of how devoted many women are to their husbands.

"Curia, a noble lady from Rome, was tremendously loyal, steadfast, wise, and loving toward her husband, Quintus Lucretius. Her husband and several other men had been condemned to death for a certain crime of which they had been accused. When they became aware that they were being sought to undergo their sentence, they fortunately had enough time to flee. Frightened by the thought of being found, they hid in caves among wild animals but did not have the courage to build a proper shelter for themselves. Lucretius, however, had paid attention to his wife's sensible advice and did not leave his room. When those searching for him arrived, she wrapped her husband in her arms in the bed, hiding him so well that they did not notice him at all. Then she hid him so cunningly between the walls of her room that no one in her household or anyone else knew he was there. She took extra precautions to keep his presence secret by dressing in rags and running through the streets in and out of temples and churches, disheveled and crying, wringing her hands as if she had lost her mind, asking everywhere if anyone had seen her husband or knew his whereabouts. Wherever he was, she cried, she wanted to join him in exile and share his misfortune. She managed to put on such a convincing performance that no one had the slightest suspicions. That is how she rescued her husband and comforted him in his panic. In short, she managed to save him from exile and death."

---

22. Maureen Quilligan suggests that it is significant that Christine decided to invoke the story of Portia's suicide (a burning of one's throat and internal organs—a self-silencing) to make a particular claim about women's ability to bridle their tongues. See Maureen Quilligan, *The Allegory of Female Authority: Christine de Pizan's* Cité des dames (Ithaca, N.Y.: Cornell University Press, 1991), 151. The motivation of Portia here is also of interest to consider. Were the consequences she foresaw merely that of her husband's own security, or the broader fate of the Roman commonwealth? It would appear to be both from the remarks in II.28.

27. More on the same topic.

"Since we are providing examples to refute those who claim that women cannot keep a secret, I could give you any number of them, but I will limit myself to one.

"During the time the tyrannical emperor Nero ruled Rome, there were some men who believed that it would be a great service to society to take his life for all the evil and cruelty he committed. Accordingly, they entered into a conspiracy against him to plan his death. They met in a house owned by a woman whom they trusted so implicitly that they did not hesitate to discuss the conspiracy in front of her. On the eve of the day they had decided to put their plan into effect, they dined with this woman and were not careful enough to refrain from discussing the matter. Unfortunately, they were overheard by someone who was anxious to please the emperor and win his favor, so he wasted no time in rushing over to tell him what he had heard. As a result, the conspirators had no sooner left the woman's house than the emperor's guard arrived at her door. When they failed to find the men, they brought the woman before the emperor, who interrogated her at length. But he could not convince this woman to tell him the identity of those men, whether by offering her gifts and promises or applying severe torture. He could not even persuade her to admit that she knew anything at all. Thus, she proved herself extremely steadfast and discreet."

28. Refutations of the claim by some that a man who trusts his wife's advice or lends it credence is stupid. Christine asks some questions and Lady Rectitude replies.

"My lady, given what you have told me and having seen for myself how sensible and kind women are, I am astounded at the oft-heard claim that men who believe and trust their wife's advice are stupid."

Lady Rectitude replied: "I have already told you that not all women are smart, but men who do have reliable and prudent wives would be fools not to put their faith in them. A good example of this is what I told you earlier about Brutus, because if he had believed his wife Portia when she told him not to kill Julius Caesar, he would not have been killed himself and all the misfortune that resulted from that deed would not have come to pass. Since we are on this subject, I will give you some more examples about other men who failed to believe their wives and suffered dire consequences as a result. Then I will tell you about men who greatly benefited from taking their wives' advice.

"If Julius Caesar, whom we have discussed before, had believed his clever and dependable wife, he would never have been assassinated. She had seen several omens foretelling her husband's death and had a horrible dream the night before, so she did her best to prevent him from going to the Senate that day.

"The same applies to Pompey, who had married Julia, daughter of Julius Caesar, as I told you before. Then he took another very noble lady by the name of Cornelia as his second wife. Going back to our earlier theme, Cornelia loved him so deeply that she did not ever want to leave him, no matter what misfortune might befall him. Even when he was forced to flee by ship after he had been defeated in battle by Julius Caesar, this good lady stayed with him and accompanied him on his perilous journey. When he arrived in the kingdom of Egypt, its king, the treacherous Ptolemy, pretended to be pleased to see him and sent his people out to meet him as if to welcome him. In fact, they were supposed to kill him. They invited him on board their ship and told him to leave his people behind so that they could take him into port more easily because their ship was lighter. But as he was about to board, his clever and loyal wife Cornelia advised him not to go and not to leave his people behind under any circumstances. When she saw that he refused to heed her and knowing in her heart that nothing good would come of it, she made a desperate effort to launch herself in the boat with him, but her husband wanted no part of it, and she had to be forcibly restrained. At that moment, the brave woman was beset by a grief that would last the rest of her life because, keeping her eyes riveted on her husband, she saw him murdered by those traitors on their ship before he had gone very far. She was so distraught that she would have thrown herself into the sea had she not been restrained.

"A similar misfortune befell the brave Hector of Troy. The night before he was killed, his wife Andromache had a most extraordinary dream that told her that if Hector went into battle the next morning, he would inevitably be killed. The lady, terrified by what was no dream at all but a true prophecy, knelt before him and begged him with folded hands not to join the battle that day, even bringing him their two beautiful children in her arms. But he paid no attention to her words, thinking that he would forever be dishonored by refusing to go into battle based on the advice of a woman. She even asked his father and mother to help her with her pleas, but he still would not listen.

And so her prediction came true, because he was killed by Achilles. It would have been so much better if he had believed her.

"I could give you countless other examples of men who ended up badly one way or another by not bothering to believe the advice of their good, smart wives. In any case, those who suffer because they ignored their wives' advice do not deserve sympathy."

29. Lady Rectitude gives examples of men who benefited from taking their wives' advice.[23]

"I will now tell you about some men who profited from following their wives' advice. The examples I will give you should be proof enough, although I could cite so many cases that we would never finish. What I told you before on this subject about the numerous smart, reliable women also applies here.

"Emperor Justinian, whom I have mentioned before, had a companion whom he loved as he loved himself. He was a baron by the name of Belisarius, and since he was a very brave knight, the emperor had appointed him commander of his cavalry and had him sit at his table where he enjoyed the same service as Justinian himself. In short, he showed his affection for Belisarius so openly that the other barons became jealous and told the emperor that Belisarius intended to assassinate him and seize the empire for himself. The emperor chose to believe them without further ado. Looking for a surreptitious way to kill Belisarius, he ordered him to go and fight the Vandals, a people so fierce that there was no way he could defeat them. When Belisarius received this command, he clearly understood that the emperor would never have charged him with this mission unless he had completely fallen out of favor. He was so upset by this realization that all he could do was return to his house.

"When his wife Antonia, the emperor's sister, saw her husband lying on his bed, pale and pensive, his eyes full of tears, she was filled with compassion and would not rest until he had told her, in great distress, the reason for his misery. When this wise lady had heard him out, she pretended to be overjoyed and consoled him, telling him: 'What? Is that all that's bothering you? There is no reason to be so upset!'

---

23. Just as Christine has earlier in Part II given examples of where women's tears could have been effective if taken seriously, here she demonstrates the effectiveness of women's speech or verbal advice, as linked to her earlier trilogy of weeping, talking, and weaving (I.10).

"It should be kept in mind that in those days, the faith of Jesus Christ was still quite recent, and because Antonia was a Christian, she told him: 'Have faith in Jesus Christ, who has been crucified. With His help, you will prevail, and if those who envy you try to harm you by telling lies, you will expose them as liars through your good deeds and cause them to come to grief as a result of their own intrigues. You must trust me and pay attention to my words, and if you put all your hope in the Living God, I promise you that you will be victorious. Be careful not to give the impression that this matter bothers you or that you are upset: you should seem happy and content. I recommend that you assemble your army as quickly as possible, and take care that no one knows which way you are headed. Also, make sure you have enough ships at your disposal. Then divide your army in two, march one half to Africa as rapidly and secretly as you can, and attack the enemy at once. I will have the other half of your troops with me, and we will make our way by sea, arriving at the port from the other side. With the enemy intent on doing battle with you, we will come from the other side into the towns and cities and put everyone to death and everything to the torch, achieving total destruction.'

"Belisarius showed his wisdom by trusting his wife's advice. He organized his campaign exactly as she had said, no more and no less. He did so well that he defeated his enemies and subjected them to his rule. He captured the king of the Vandals, and thanks to his wife's advice, insight, and bravery, won such a noble victory that the emperor loved him more than ever.

"Belisarius fell from the emperor's grace a second time, again as a result of lies told by the jealous barons. It was so bad that he was summarily dismissed from the knighthood. His wife again comforted him and gave him hope. The emperor himself was eventually deposed by the same barons, but Belisarius took his wife's advice and assembled the knights who had remained loyal. Even though the emperor had treated him very badly, he managed to restore the empire to its ruler. That is how the emperor found out just how loyal his knight truly was and how he had been betrayed by the others, all thanks to the excellent advice of Belisarius' clever wife.

"A similar case was that of King Alexander, who also heeded the words and the advice of his wife the queen. She was the daughter of Darius, king of Persia.[24] One day, Alexander was in so much pain that he wanted to throw himself in the river to end his suffering by taking his own life. He realized

---

24. Her name was Stateira (a.k.a. Barsine); she would eventually be killed by Alexander the Great's first wife, Roxana.

that he had been poisoned by his disloyal servants. He ran into his wife and although she was terribly distraught, she comforted him and told him to go home and lie down on his bed. There he should speak to his barons and issue orders as befitted an emperor of his stature, because his reputation would greatly suffer if it were to be said of him after his death that he had allowed himself to be ruled by a lack of self-control. He heeded his wife's advice and issued his orders, exactly as she had counseled him.

30. Christine talks about the great good that women have always brought to the world and still do.

"My lady, it is clear to me that women have brought infinite good to this world and yet, some men claim that they bring nothing but evil."

Lady Rectitude replied: "My dear friend, you can see from what I have already told you that the opposite of what they say is true. There is not a man who can sum up the enormous good women have done and continue to do every day. I already proved this to you by giving you examples of the marvelous ladies who gave the world arts and sciences. But if what I have told you about the material benefits they have brought is not enough, let me tell you about their spiritual benefits. Oh, how can a man be so ungrateful as to forget that it was a woman who opened the gates of paradise for him! It was the Virgin Mary, of course, and men can't ask for a greater blessing! As I have told you, it was through her that God assumed a human form. And who could forget how devoted mothers are to their sons and wives to their husbands? At the very least, men should not forget women's gifts on the spiritual level. Let us take a look at the ancient faith of the Jews: if you read the story of Moses, to whom God gave the written laws for the Jews, you'll find that it was a woman who saved him from death, this prophet who went on to do so much good. I will tell you the story.

"In the days when the Jews lived in captivity under the kings of Egypt, it was foretold that a man would be born into the Hebrew tribe who would free the people of Israel from servitude. So it happened that the noble leader Moses was born. His mother was afraid to raise him and had no option but to put him in a small basket and send him floating downriver. Since God will save those whom He wants to save, He saw to it that Thermutis, the pharaoh's daughter, was walking along the river bank at the very moment the basket came floating by. She immediately had it pulled from the water to see what was inside. When she saw that it was an infant, the most beautiful baby you could imagine, she was overjoyed. She had him nursed and said that he was hers, and since he miraculously refused to be nursed by a woman from a different faith, she had him brought to a Hebrew wet nurse who nursed and fostered him. When Moses, chosen by God, had grown up, Our Lord gave him the Law, and he delivered the Jews from the hands of the Egyptians, crossing the Red Sea and leading the children of Israel. As you can see, it was thanks to the woman who saved Moses that the Jews were blessed with such great good fortune."

31. About Judith, the noble widow who saved her people.

"The noble widow Judith saved the people of Israel from destruction at the time when Nebuchadnezzar II, having conquered the land of Egypt, sent the leader of his cavalry to march on the Jews.[25] This general, by the name of Holophernes, laid siege to the Jews with a strong force, having already inflicted so much damage on them that they could not hold out much longer. The city was cut off from its water supply, and the food supplies were nearly exhausted. Their situation had become hopeless and they were on the point of being captured by Holophernes. They were deeply distressed and kept praying to God to have pity on His people and deliver them from the hands of their enemies. God heard their prayers and just as He would later send a woman to save the human race, he chose to save the Jews through a woman.

"In that city lived a noble, valiant lady by the name of Judith. She was still young and very pretty, but she distinguished herself even more through her chastity and virtue. She deeply pitied the people in their anguish and prayed to Our Lord day and night to save them. Inspired by God, in whom she had placed her trust, she devised a daring plan. One night, commending herself to Our Lord's care, she left the city accompanied only by her servant, and walked until she reached Holophernes' camp. When the guards saw her great beauty in the moonlight, they took her straight to Holophernes who, struck by her beauty, received her with delight. He had her seated beside him and was deeply impressed by her knowledge, beauty, and bearing. The more he watched her, the more he burned with desire for her. But she had other ideas and kept praying to God in her mind, asking Him to help her carry out her plan. She continued to distract Holophernes with pretty words until she

---

25. See the Book of Judith in the Catholic Old Testament. Associations between Judith, political bravery, and radical gestures of self-sacrifice were extremely popular in Christine's days. Judith was also important for Christine de Pizan's *Tale of Joan of Arc* (1429).

judged the time was right. On the third night, Holophernes had invited his barons to share the evening meal, and he did some heavy drinking. Inflamed with wine and food, he could no longer wait to sleep with this Hebrew woman. He sent for her and when she came, he told her what he wanted. She didn't refuse his invitation but asked him to send all his men from the tent for the sake of propriety. He should go to bed first, she said, and she would come to him without fail around midnight, when everyone was asleep. He agreed and the good lady went off to pray, begging God to give her fearful woman's heart the boldness and strength to deliver her people from this cruel tyrant.

"When Judith judged Holophernes must be asleep, she and her servant woman crept over to his tent and stopped to listen at the entrance. Hearing him sound asleep, she said: 'Let us be brave and go ahead, for God is with us.' She entered the tent, fearlessly took the sword she spotted at the head of the bed, unsheathed it, lifted it, and with all her might, cut off Holophernes' head without making a sound to alert anyone. She wrapped the head in her skirts and fled toward the city as quickly as she could, arriving at the gates without incident. There she cried: 'Come on! Come and open the gate, for God is with us!' When she had been admitted, the joy prompted by her actions was indescribable. In the morning, they impaled the head on a stake on top of the walls. Then they took up their weapons and boldly flung themselves at their enemies, who were still asleep in their beds, not expecting anything. When Holophernes' men arrived at their leader's tent to wake him up and stir him into action, they were thrown into panic, utterly distraught to find him dead. The Jews killed or captured them all. And so the people of God were delivered from the hands of Holophernes thanks to Judith, that brave woman, who will forever be praised in the Holy Scriptures."

32. Here she talks about Queen Esther, who saved her people.

"Another woman chosen by God for that purpose was the magnificent, wise Queen Esther.[26] She delivered His people from the slavery imposed by King Ahasuerus. King Ahasuerus was more powerful than any other king and ruled many kingdoms. He was a pagan and kept the Jews enslaved. One day, he ordered a search in all his kingdoms for the noblest, most beautiful and well-educated maidens so he could choose among them the one who pleased him

---

26. As with the previous chapter, Christine is here invoking the authority of the Old Testament to celebrate the virtue of this queen (see the Book of Esther).

most and take her as his wife. One of the maidens brought to him was Esther, a noble, sensible, and beautiful Hebrew girl, well loved by God. The king liked her best of all and fell so deeply in love with her that he could not refuse her anything she asked for.

"Some time later, a treacherous sycophant by the name of Haman managed to set the king against the Jews to the point where he ordered them captured and killed wherever they could be found. Queen Esther knew nothing about this; had she known, she would have been horrified to see her people treated with such cruelty. But her uncle Mordecai, leader of the Jews, told her about it and begged her to intervene as quickly as she could, since there was little time left before the king's order was due to be carried out. The queen was sick at heart at this news. She dressed in the most elegant clothes and finery she possessed and went out with her women as though to amuse herself in a garden she knew the king could see from his window. On her return, she passed by the king's window as if by chance and saw him there. She immediately fell to her knees and greeted him, prostrate on the ground. The king, pleased with her humility and enchanted by her radiant beauty, called her over, telling her that whatever she wanted would be hers. The lady replied that all she wanted was to have him dine with her in her chambers, bringing Haman with him. He happily agreed.

"After he had dined with her three days in a row, enjoying the hospitality, respect, and the virtue and beauty of his lady, he urged her once again to express a desire. Esther threw herself at his feet, burst into tears, and beseeched him to have mercy on her people. She reminded him that he had elevated her to the highest rank and begged him not to dishonor her by cruelly destroying her lineage and her people. Enraged, the king replied: 'My lady, who dares do such a thing?' She replied: "Sire, it is Haman, your provost, who is standing here before you.'

"To make a long story short, the king repealed his order and Haman, who had made up the whole thing out of envy, was thrown in prison and hanged for his crimes. Mordecai, the queen's uncle, was appointed in his place, and the Jews were freed and granted the highest privileges and greatest honor among all the other peoples. And so, as in the case of Judith, God again chose a woman to save His people. But don't think that these two ladies are the only ones mentioned in the Holy Scriptures as having been chosen by God to deliver His people. There are many others, but time does not permit me to mention them all. I have already mentioned Deborah, who also freed her people from bondage, and many other women followed her example."

33. About the Sabine women, who made peace among their loved ones.

"I could also tell you many things about ladies of the ancient pagan faith who were responsible for saving countries, towns, and cities, but I will give you just two famous examples that will serve as proof for all.

"When Remus and Romulus had founded the city of Rome and Romulus had populated the city, filling it with all the knights and soldiers he had managed to find and assemble after winning many victories, he was anxious to find them wives so they could have progeny who would hold and rule the city in perpetuity. But he was not sure of how to go about finding wives for himself and all his companions, because the country's kings and princes and other inhabitants did not want to give them their daughters. They considered them irresponsible and had no desire for familial ties with these wild and fickle people, so Romulus concocted a ploy. He had announcements made throughout the land that a tournament and joust would be held, inviting the princes and kings and everyone else to bring their ladies and daughters to watch the entertainment offered by the foreign knights. On the day of the festival, a huge crowd had gathered on both sides, including a large number of ladies and maidens who had come to watch the games. Among them was the beautiful, gracious daughter of the king of the Sabines, along with all the country's ladies and maidens who had accompanied her. The jousts were held outside the city on a plain at the foot of a hill, with the ladies seated in rows near the top. The knights strove to outdo each other in bravery and perform feats of great daring, because the sight of all these pretty ladies boosted their strength and courage.

"To make a long story short,[27] when the tournament had gone on for some time and Romulus decided it was time to carry out his plan, he took a great, ivory horn and sounded a loud call. The knights, hearing this sound, at once understood it as their prearranged signal. They stopped their jousting and galloped toward the ladies. Romulus took the king's daughter, with

---

27. A well-known account of the theft and rape of the Sabine women can be found in Livy (I.9), for whom the rape was regarded as a necessary part of founding. Plutarch in the "Life of Romulus" suggests this was ordered by Romulus to strengthen communal bonds within Rome. Christine does not enter here into a discussion of rape (as she does in II.44); she rather stresses, like the standard and most famous account, the peacemaking abilities of women. In the follow-up to this book (*The Treasure of the City of Ladies*), she will insist that one of the key duties of queens and princesses is "to be the means of peace and concord, to work for the avoidance of war" (I.9).

whom he had already fallen in love, and the others followed his example, each taking the one he wanted. They forced the women up on their horses and rode toward the city at a furious speed, closing the gates behind them when they were safely inside. Outside the walls, there was a tremendous outcry of anger and grief from the fathers and relatives. More screams came from the ladies who had been abducted by force, but their tears were in vain. Romulus married the lady of his choice with great pomp and ceremony, and the others did likewise.

"This incident caused a great war, because the king of the Sabines assembled a large army as soon as he could and marched on the Romans. But the Romans were a brave people so it was no easy task to defeat them. The war had already lasted five years when, one day, the two sides assembled on a field with all their might. It was obvious that there would be enormous casualties and an appalling bloodbath. The Romans had already left for the battlefield in great numbers when the queen called all the ladies of the city together in a temple to discuss the matter. The wise, beautiful queen addressed them, saying: 'Honored Sabine ladies, my dear sisters and companions, you know how we were abducted by our husbands and how this has caused our fathers and relatives to wage war on our husbands, and our husbands on them. There is no way whatsoever that this deadly conflict can be brought to an end or continue without it being to our detriment, no matter who wins. We rightly love our husbands as we have already borne them children, and if they are defeated, we will be devastated and grief-stricken to see our young children turned into orphans. If, on the other hand, our husbands win the war and our fathers and kinsmen are killed and destroyed, we will also be filled with grief to think that this disaster happened because of us. What is done is done and cannot be undone. That is why I think it would be a very good idea if we could find a way to end this war and reestablish peace. If you are willing to trust my advice, follow me, and do as I do, I am convinced that we can bring this matter to a good end.' The ladies all replied that her wish was their command and that they would be happy to obey.

"Then the queen loosened her hair and took off her shoes, as did all the other ladies. Those who had children carried them in their arms and took them along, so there was a great crowd of children and pregnant women. The queen took the lead, and the piteous procession arrived on the battlefield precisely at the hour when the two armies were due to join battle. They positioned themselves between the two opponents so that they were unable to attack each other without running into the women and children. The queen knelt down, followed by all the other women, and shouted: 'Beloved fathers and kinsmen, beloved husbands, for God's sake make peace! If not, we are prepared to die under the hoofs of your horses.' The husbands, who saw their wives and children before them in tears, were shocked and certainly most unwilling to run at them. The fathers were equally moved by seeing their daughters in tears. Touched by the women's humble plea, the two sides looked at each other and their rage faded, replaced by the filial piety sons feel for their fathers. Both sides felt compelled to throw down their weapons, embrace each other, and make peace. Romulus led the king of the Sabines, his father-in-law, into the city and welcomed him and all his company with great honor. That is how the good sense and moral courage of the queen and her ladies saved the Romans and the Sabines from destruction."

34. About the noble Veturia, who convinced her son to make peace when he wanted to destroy Rome.

"Veturia was a noble lady from Rome and the mother of a very distinguished Roman citizen by the name of Gnaeus Marcius, a man of great virtue and wisdom, ingenious and perceptive, gallant and brave.[28] The Romans sent this noble knight, Veturia's son, to fight the Corolians with a great army. Having defeated them and captured the fortress of the Volscians, he was given the name Coriolanus to acknowledge his victory over the Corolians. He received so much honor for this feat that before long, he gained control of most of the government of Rome. But it is a very tricky thing to govern a people and try to please them all, so the Romans eventually became angry with him, sentenced him to be exiled, and banished him from Rome. He managed to avenge himself, however, by appealing to those he had previously defeated and convincing them to rebel against the Romans. They appointed him their leader and marched on the city of Rome with a huge army, wreaking enormous destruction everywhere they went. Seeing the danger they were in, the Romans were terrified and sent several messengers to sue for peace, but Marcius did not bother to receive them. They sent more messengers but to no avail. Marcius continued to wreak destruction, so the Romans dispatched their bishops and priests in all their vestments to humbly beg for peace, again without result. The Romans, at their wits' end, sent the city's noble ladies to see Lady Veturia, Marcius' mother, to ask her if she would try her best to

---

28. See Boccaccio, *Famous Women*, chap. 55.

convince her son to make peace with them. The kindhearted Lady Veturia agreed and left the city at the head of a procession of all the other ladies to go see her son. Marcius, who was a considerate and humane person, dismounted as soon as he caught sight of her and went to meet her, receiving her with the sort of deference that any son should show his mother. When she begged him to make peace, he replied that a mother should not have to beg her son: she should command him. Thereupon he accompanied the noble lady back to Rome, and thanks to Veturia, the Romans were spared from destruction on that occasion. She alone accomplished what the top-ranking Roman functionaries had not been able to do.

35. Here she talks about Clotilde, queen of France, who converted her husband King Clovis to the holy faith.

"Another woman I told you about, one of those to whom we owe great spiritual blessings, was Clotilde, daughter of the king of Burgundy and wife of the powerful Clovis, king of France. Was she not the one who first introduced and spread the faith of Jesus Christ to the kings and princes of France? What greater blessing could anyone ask for than that? When she became enlightened by the faith like the good Christian and saintly lady she was, she never tired of urging and begging her lord to receive the holy faith and be baptized. But he was not willing to comply, so Clotilde spent her days weeping and fasting and doing devotions, praying to God to enlighten the king's heart. She prayed so fervently that our Lord finally took pity on her anguish and enlightened the king when he had gone into battle one day against the king of the Alemanni. Finding himself threatened by defeat, he lifted his eyes toward Heaven as God had wished, and passionately cried out: 'Almighty God in whom my wife, the queen, believes and whom she worships, please help me with this battle and I vow that I will accept your holy faith.' He had no sooner made this vow than the battle turned in his favor and he won a complete victory. He gave thanks to God and when he returned home, to the joy and relief of both himself and his wife, he was baptized along with his barons and all his people. Thanks to the prayers of the good and saintly Queen Clotilde, God so generously granted his mercy that from that moment on, the faith has never been defeated in France, nor was there ever a heretic king, thank God. The same cannot be said about kings and emperors of other countries, so the French kings deserve high praise. That is the reason why they are called 'most Christian kings.'

"If I wanted to tell you about all the great blessings bestowed on us by women, this book would never be finished. But I will say this about spirituality: how many holy martyrs (about whom I will tell you later) were not comforted, lodged, and fed by young girls, widows, and good and honest women? If you read the martyrs' stories, you will find that it pleased God to see all or most of them comforted in their adversity and martyrdom by women. What am I saying? Not only martyrs but also the Apostles, Saint Paul and the others, even Jesus Christ, were fed and cared for by women.

"And the French, who are so devoted to the body of the blessed Saint Denis (and for good reason, because he first brought the faith to France), is it not thanks to a woman that they possess his body and those of his holy companions Saint Rusticus and Saint Eleutherius? When the tyrant who had them beheaded ordered their bodies thrown into the Seine, those who were to carry out his order put them into a sack to carry them there. En route, they lodged with a righteous widow by the name of Catulla, who got them drunk and replaced the holy bodies in the sack with dead pigs. Then she buried the blessed martyrs in her house with as much honor as she could contrive and placed an inscription on top of the grave so that it would be known in the future. A long time afterward, it was again a woman (my lady Saint Genevieve) who erected the first chapel on this spot, until the good King Dagobert of France founded the church that still stands there today."

36. Against those who claim that women should not be educated.

I, Christine, replied as follows: "Lady, it is quite clear to me that women have contributed many good things. Even if a few corrupt women have done some wicked things, I think that the blessings we owe to virtuous women far outweigh them. This applies in particular to those who are smart and well educated in literature and the sciences, as mentioned above. That is why I am amazed by the opinion of some men who say that they would completely oppose the idea of their daughters or wives or other female relatives receiving an education, claiming that this would corrupt their morals."

Lady Rectitude replied: "That proves to you that not all opinions held by men are based on reason, because these men are wrong. The presumption that moral standards are corrupted by studying ethics, which actually teaches virtue, is not based on reason.[29] In fact, there is not the slightest doubt that it actually improves and ennobles them. How could anyone think that teaching women good lessons and principles can possibly harm them? That idea is inconceivable and untenable. I am not saying that it would be a good thing for men or women to devote themselves to the study of witchcraft or forbidden areas of study, because it is not for nothing that the holy church has forbidden their practice. But it is nonsense to say that women are corrupted by knowledge of what is right and proper.

"Quintus Hortensius, a great Roman rhetorician and accomplished orator, did not share that opinion. He had a daughter named Hortensia of whom he was particularly fond for her keen intellect. He had her educated in literature and study rhetoric, which she mastered so thoroughly that according to Boccaccio, she not only equaled her father Hortensius in wit, excellence of memory, and eloquence, but also in elocution and the art of oratory. In fact, he did not surpass her in anything. With respect to what we said before about the blessings we owe women, the contributions by this woman and her knowledge were remarkable among all others. You should know that Rome was governed by the triumvirate at that time. Hortensia took up the cause of women and did something all men were afraid to undertake. It was a time of economic shortage in Rome, and it was proposed that taxes should be levied on women and their jewelry. Hortensia spoke so eloquently that she was listened to as readily as her father, and so she won her case.[30]

"To give you a similar, more recent example, without going back to ancient history, there is the case of the famous jurist Giovanni Andrea. He taught at Bologna not quite sixty years ago. He, too, did not share the opinion that education would corrupt women, so he had his lovely and cherished daughter Novella educated in literature and law. When he was busy with other tasks and unable to lecture his students, he would send Novella in his

29. The question of the relation between virtue as a practice and ethics as an object of study is a complex one. In Aristotelian terms, habit is seen as the foundation for the development of virtue, and ethics as a study is regarded as particularly valuable to those already attuned to virtue as a practice, to deepen understanding of the principles by which they already intuitively or habitually act. Christine is suggesting here that the Aristotelian account should be seen as gender neutral and that both men and women who are well disposed to virtuous principles can only benefit from an education in ethics.

30. Immortalized in Appian's *Roman History*, the speech Hortensia gave in front of Octavian, Mark Antony, and Lepidus (the triumvirate) in 42 BCE is indeed said to have led to a partial repeal of this unpopular tax on wealthy women. See also Boccaccio's account of Hortensia's deed, in *Famous Women*, chap. 84.

place to present the lecture. In order to ensure that her beauty did not distract her audience, she lectured from behind a small curtain. In that way, she complemented her father and sometimes lightened his load. He loved her so much that he wanted to commemorate her name, so he authored an important legal treatise and named it after his daughter Novella.

"So you see that not all men, particularly not the most educated men, share the opinion that women should not be educated. It is true that many ignorant men say so, because they don't like the idea of women knowing more than they do. Your father, who was a famous scientist and philosopher, was certainly not of the opinion that education is harmful to women. On the contrary: he was delighted to see your passion for study, as you know. What prevented you from delving more deeply into the sciences during your childhood was the female prejudice of your mother, who wanted to keep you engaged in the customary female activities of spinning and weaving.[31] But you know the saying I have quoted before: 'What Nature gives you, no one can take away.' That is why your mother was not able to smother your natural passion for learning to the point where you did not at least taste some droplets. I'm sure you don't respect yourself any less as a result. On the contrary: I think you consider it a great boon, and rightly so."

And I, Christine, replied: "Indeed, my lady, what you say is as true as the Lord's Prayer."

37. Here Christine talks to Lady Rectitude, who refutes the opinion of those who claim that few women are chaste and gives the example of Susanna.

"From what you tell me, my lady, all good and virtuous things can be found in women. So why do some men say that few women are chaste? If that were so, all their other virtues would be worth nothing, since chastity is women's supreme virtue.[32] But from what I have heard you say, the truth is the complete opposite of what they claim."

---

31. But see the positive account of her mother Christine offers in 1403 in *The Book of the Mutability of Fortune* (I.5). There she claims that her mother *surpassed* her father in knowledge, strength, and virtue.

32. A defense of this claim is provided by Christine in Part III. Readers should note that for Christine, chastity is also a virtue to be embraced by men (and by all good rulers): see, e.g., *The Book of the Deeds and Good Morals of the Wise King Charles V* (I.29) and *The Long Path of Learning* (line 5524). The importance of chastity as a virtue was of course central to medieval

Lady Rectitude replied: "From what I have already told you and from what you know about it yourself, it should be quite obvious to you that the reverse is true. I could tell you more about this and repeat it until the end of time. Oh! How many valiant and chaste ladies are mentioned in the Holy Scriptures who chose death rather than violating the chastity and purity of their bodies and minds? Take the lovely and virtuous Susanna, wife of Joachim, who was very wealthy and one of the most influential men of Jewish descent. One day, when the valiant Susanna was alone in her garden, relaxing, two old men pretending to be priests appeared before her and made indecent proposals. She vigorously repulsed them, and when they saw that sweet words accomplished nothing, they threatened to denounce her to the authorities, claiming that they had found her in the company of a young man. Hearing their threats and aware that according to the custom of the time, women were stoned in cases like that, she said: 'I am lost whatever I do. If I don't do what these men want of me, I risk physical death, and if I give in to their demands, I will be committing a sin in front of my Creator. I think it is far preferable to choose physical death and die innocent than to incur the wrath of my God by committing a sin.' So she started to scream and the servants came running out of the house.

"To make a long story short, the would-be priests succeeded in getting her condemned to death with their false testimony. But God, who never abandons those He holds dear, caused the prophet Daniel to speak. He was still a small boy in the arms of his mother but when he saw Susanna being led to her execution in a great procession of weeping people, he cried out that Susanna was innocent and had been wrongly condemned. Thereupon she was led back, and the false priests were questioned more closely and subsequently found guilty by their own confessions. The innocent Susanna was freed and the men were put to death instead."

38. Here she talks about Sarah.

"The chastity and virtue of Sarah are discussed in the Bible, I think in the twentieth chapter of Genesis. Sarah was the wife of Abraham, the great

---

thought and discussed in some of her key sources (e.g., Augustine's *City of God* and *Confessions*; John of Salisbury's *Policraticus* [e.g., Book IV, chap. 5 and 6]). Christine's contemporary and friend, Jean Gerson (chancellor of the University of Paris), also had a lot to say on chastity. See excerpts from his work in David F. Hult, ed. and trans., *Debate of the "Romance of the Rose"* (Chicago: University of Chicago Press, 2010).

patriarch. The Holy Scriptures say many good things about this lady, which I will omit here for the sake of brevity. But her chastity should be mentioned in the context of what we have been talking about, to show that many beautiful women are chaste. Sarah was so exceptionally beautiful that she surpassed all the women of her time and many princes desired her. But she was so faithful that she rejected them all. One of those who desired her was the pharaoh, king of Egypt. He wanted her so badly that he took her from her husband by force, but thanks to her great virtue, which surpassed even her beauty, she was granted the grace of Our Lord, who cherished her so much that He protected her from all evil. He struck the pharaoh and his household with such terrible diseases of body and soul and various visions that he never touched Sarah and was forced to give her back."

39. Here she talks about Rebecca.

"The good, honest Rebecca was no less virtuous and beautiful than Sarah. Rebecca was the wife of Isaac the patriarch, father of Jacob. The Holy Scriptures give her exceptional praise for many things. The 24th chapter of Genesis relates that she was such a wise, virtuous, honest woman that she exemplified chastity for all women who encountered her. She behaved with such marvelous humility toward her husband that she did not seem like a noblewoman at all. Her husband Isaac, a man of integrity, honored her for these qualities and loved her passionately. But Rebecca obtained a much greater reward for her chastity and virtue than her husband's love: the grace and love of God. In fact, He cherished her so much that even though she was already quite old and barren, He gave her two children to carry in her womb: Jacob and Esau, from whom descend the tribes of Israel."

40. Here she talks about Ruth.

"I could tell you many stories about virtuous, chaste ladies who are mentioned in the Holy Scriptures, but I will leave them aside for brevity's sake. Ruth was another noble lady, from whose line descended the prophet David. This lady was very chaste in her marriage as well as in her widowhood. She clearly adored her husband because after his death, she left her native country to spend her life with the Jews from whom her husband descended, wishing to live with his mother. To make a long story short, this noble lady was so good and so chaste that a book was written about her and her life, recounting this story."

41. About Penelope, wife of Ulysses.

"You will also find many stories written about pagan ladies who were chaste, honorable women. One such example is Penelope, the wife of Ulysses, who was a most virtuous lady. Among her many fine qualities, she was much praised for the virtue of chastity and she is mentioned in detail in several books because of her judicious conduct during her husband's ten-year siege of Troy. Even though she was courted by a number of kings and princes on account of her great beauty, she refused to listen or pay attention to any of them. She was wise, sensible, and devoted to the gods, eager to lead a virtuous life. After the destruction of Troy, she waited for her husband for another ten years. He was believed to have perished at sea, where he had faced many calamities. When at last he returned, he found her under siege by a king who was so impressed by her chastity and virtue that he was trying to force her into marriage. Ulysses arrived disguised as a pilgrim and made inquiries about her. He was overjoyed at the good reports he received and to find his son Telemachus, whom he had left as a small boy, all grown up."

I, Christine, then said: "My lady, from what you say, it is clear that these ladies did not find beauty an obstacle to being chaste. Yet many men say that it is hard to find a woman who is both beautiful and chaste."

She replied: "Those who say that fail to mention that there always have been and will be many women who are both beautiful and chaste."

42. Here she refutes those who claim that beautiful women are rarely chaste, citing the example of Mariamne.

"Mariamne, a Hebrew woman, was the daughter of King Aristobulus. She was so beautiful that her contemporaries believed not only that her beauty surpassed that of all other women but also that she was a divine or celestial apparition rather than a mortal woman. A portrait was painted of her and sent to King Mark Antony of Egypt. Struck by her exceptional beauty, he judged her to be the daughter of Jupiter, because he could not believe that she could have been sired by a mere mortal. Numerous great princes and kings, struck by her great beauty, courted and tempted her, but she resisted them all, armed with her virtue and moral strength. This garnered her more praise and enhanced her already splendid reputation. The fact that her marriage to Herod Antipater, king of the Jews, was very unhappy further raised her prestige. He was a very cruel man, who did not even hesitate to have her brother killed. She hated him for that and many other brutalities he had made her suffer, yet she continued to behave as a virtuous and chaste wife even after discovering that he had issued orders that if he were to die before her, she would immediately be put to death so that no other man would ever have a chance to enjoy her great beauty."

43. More on the same topic, citing the example of Antonia, wife of Drusus Tiberius.

"It is widely considered to be as difficult for a beautiful woman to resist seduction in the company of young men and courtiers eager for love as it is to stand in a fire without being burned. But the beautiful, virtuous Antonia, wife of Drusus Tiberius, Emperor Nero's brother, certainly knew how to protect herself. Extraordinarily beautiful, she was widowed while still in the bloom of her youth when her husband Tiberius was poisoned by his own brother. She was brokenhearted and vowed that she would never remarry but live out her widowhood in chastity. She kept her vow so well throughout her life that no other pagan lady ever earned greater praise for keeping her chastity. And what makes her chastity even more commendable, says Boccaccio, is that she resided in a court filled with well-dressed and elegant young men eager for love, living in idleness. She spent her life there without ever giving rise to criticism for even the slightest lapse. Boccaccio says that such behavior is worthy of the highest praise, since she was a beautiful young woman and the daughter of Mark Antony, who himself led a life of debauchery and dissolution. But the bad example he set her did not stop her from staying pure among the flames of lust. She preserved her chastity throughout her life until she died of old age.

"I could find you many other examples of beautiful women living a life of chastity among sensuous men and even at court, surrounded by young charmers. Even today there are many who do, I assure you, and you should keep that in mind regardless of malicious claims to the contrary. I don't believe there have been as many malicious tongues in all the times gone by as there are today, nor as many men ready to target women with baseless slander. I have no doubt that if the good and beautiful ladies I described to you were living today, they, too, would be slandered by envious tongues instead of basking in the praise the Ancients bestowed on them.[33]

"But to return to our topic of good, chaste ladies leading honorable lives among sensuous men, I refer you to what Valerius Maximus[34] said about the noble Sulpitia, a woman who was very beautiful yet reputed to be the most chaste of all the ladies in Rome."

44. Lady Rectitude refutes men who claim that women like to be raped. She gives several examples, starting with Lucretia.

Then I, Christine, said: "My lady, I truly believe what you say and I'm certain that there are many beautiful women who are good and chaste and know how to protect themselves from the traps laid by men intent on seducing them. Yet I am saddened and troubled by men who say that women want to be raped and that it doesn't displease them at all despite the protests they may utter. I have difficulty believing that such an abomination could possibly please them."[35]

Rectitude replied: "My dear friend, don't believe for a minute that chaste, respectable women take any pleasure whatsoever in being raped. Indeed, it is an ordeal that is worse than anything else, and some women have demonstrated this by their own example. Take Lucretia, for example, a high-born woman from Rome who was more faithful to her husband than anyone else. She was married to a nobleman by the name of Tarquinius Collatinus. Then Tarquin the Proud, son of King Tarquinius, fell deeply in love with the noble Lucretia and was afraid to tell her, because he knew how chaste she was. Entertaining little hope of achieving his goal by offering gifts or making entreaties, he thought of a ruse to bend her to his will. He pretended to be a close friend of her husband's, thus assuring himself of access to her house at all times.

---

33. Associating life at court with gossip, slander, and moral corruption was common in classical and medieval literature, and it certainly would remain an important issue discussed in Renaissance mirror-for-princes. Christine has more to say on this issue in her other works, e.g., *The Book of the Body Politic* and *The Long Path of Learning*.

34. Roman historian Valerius Maximus is the author of *Memorable Deeds and Sayings*—a well-known collection of anecdotes from which Christine de Pizan draws countless exempla throughout her oeuvre.

35. On Christine's treatment of rape, see Diane Wolfthal, "'Douleur sur toutes autres': Revisualizing the Rape Script in the *Epistre Othea* and the *Cité des dames*," in *Christine de Pizan: Texts/Intertexts/Contexts*, ed. Marilynn Desmond (Minneapolis: University of Minnesota Press, 1998), 41–70.

One day, he went to the house knowing that Lucretia's husband was away. She received him with all the respect appropriate for someone she considered a close friend of her husband's. Tarquinius, however, had other things on his mind. He managed to enter her bedroom at night, scaring her half to death. To make a long story short, after he spent a long time trying to convince her to give in to his desire, making grand promises and offering gifts, he saw that his entreaties were getting him nowhere, so he drew his sword and threatened to kill her if she made a sound and did not submit to his will. She replied that he might as well go ahead and kill her because she would rather die than consent. This proved to Tarquin that all his efforts were fruitless, so he had another heinous idea, telling her that he would publicly announce that he had found her with one of his servants. To make a long story short, the thought that people would believe his words so appalled her that she finally submitted to him.

"Lucretia, however, did not have the fortitude to endure this great shame, so when morning came, she sent for her husband, her father, and her closest relatives, who were among the most powerful people in Rome, and confessed to them what had happened to her, weeping and wailing. Seeing her so distraught, her husband and relatives tried to comfort her, but she pulled out a knife that she had kept hidden under her robe and said: 'Even if I absolve myself from my sin and show my innocence, I still cannot free myself from my torment or escape my punishment, and no other woman will ever be shamed and dishonored by following Lucretia's example.' Having said these words, she plunged the knife into her breast and collapsed, fatally injured, in front of her husband and friends. Enraged, they all rushed at Tarquin. The event caused turmoil in all of Rome: they chased out the king and would have killed his son if they could have found him. There would never again be a king ruling Rome. And some claim that because of Lucretia's rape, a law was enacted stipulating that if a man committed rape, he would be executed. That is an appropriate, just, and holy law."[36]

45. More on the same topic, presenting the case of the queen of the Galatians.

"The story of the noble queen of the Galatians, wife of King Ortiagon, is another example that is pertinent to our discussion. At the time the Romans

---

36. The rape and subsequent suicide of Lucretia, as most famously discussed by Livy, is of central importance to the history of Rome, as noted by Christine. Lucretia is also highly celebrated by Boccaccio, in chap. 48 of *Famous Women*.

were making their great conquests in foreign lands, it so happened that they captured both the king of the Galatians and his wife in battle. During their internment, one of the Roman army commanders who had captured the king and queen became enamored of the noble queen, who was very beautiful, innocent, chaste, and virtuous. He pleaded with her to submit to his will by offering great gifts, but when he saw that his entreaties did not produce any results, he took her by force. The lady was outraged by this heinous act and became obsessed with the thought of revenge, but she bided her time, hiding her thoughts until she saw her chance. When the ransom was delivered to free her husband and herself, the lady asked that the money be handed over in her presence to the commander who was keeping them captive. She told him to weigh the gold to make sure it was the right amount and he was not being cheated. When she saw that he was getting ready to weigh the gold and that none of his men were there, she drew a knife and stabbed him in the neck, killing him. Then she took his head and carried it to her husband without the slightest reserve, telling him the whole story and how she had taken revenge."[37]

46. Still more on the same topic: the story of the Sicambrians and those of several virgins.

"I can give you many more examples of married women who found the anguish of being raped unbearable, but I will show you that this applies just as much to widows and virgins.

"Hippo was a Greek lady who was captured and kidnapped by sailors and pirates who were enemies of her country. Since she was a very beautiful woman, her captors lusted after her, and when she saw that she could not escape being raped, she was so horrified and disgusted that she decided she would rather die, so she threw herself into the sea and drowned.

"Likewise, the Sicambrians (now called the French) launched another attack one day on the city of Rome, bringing a great army and many people. Expecting to destroy the city, they had brought their women and children along. But the tide of war turned against them, and when the women saw this, they took counsel among themselves and decided they would rather die defending their chastity than suffer dishonor. They knew that the rules of war

---

37. The story of the Galatian queen Chiomara is told by Polybius in his *Histories*, XXI.38, as well as by Livy (38.24). Whereas some traditional accounts suggest that Chiomara instructed one of her men to commit the murder, in Christine's version it is the queen herself who is responsible for the vengeful deed.

dictated that they would all be raped. Accordingly, they barricaded themselves with their wagons and chariots and took up arms against the Romans. They defended themselves as best they could and killed many Romans, but in the end almost all the women were killed, and those who remained pleaded with folded hands to be spared from being violated and be allowed to spend the rest of their lives serving in the temple of virgins dedicated to the goddess Vesta. But their pleas were refused, and they decided they would rather kill themselves than be raped.

"There are similar examples featuring virgins, such as that of Virginia, a noble young woman from Rome. When the perfidious judge Claudius realized that pleas would not work, he thought he could take her by ruse and by force. But despite her youth, she preferred death to rape.

"Likewise, a city in Lombardy was conquered by the enemy who killed the seigneur. His daughters, who were very beautiful, believed the enemy would rape them and conceived of an unusual strategy, for which they deserve great praise: they covered their breasts with raw chicken meat. This soon started to rot in the heat so that when the enemy wanted to approach them, they caught the horrible smell and left them alone at once, exclaiming: 'My god, these Lombard women stink to high heaven!' But that stink produced the sweet scent of honor."

47. A refutation of the claim that women are inconstant. Christine speaks first and Lady Rectitude replies, talking about the inconstancy and weakness of several emperors.

"My lady, you have given me great examples of the marvelous constancy, strength, and virtue of women. Could anyone say more about the strongest men who ever lived? Yet beyond all the vices women are accused of by men, particularly in writing, is one they unanimously proclaim, that is, that the female sex is fickle and inconstant. Women are unpredictable and flighty, they say, women are weak-hearted, they vacillate like children, and they are unsteady. Are the men who accuse women of unpredictability and inconstancy themselves so steadfast that they see indecision as something completely foreign or highly unusual? Really, if they are not steadfast themselves, it is truly shameful to accuse others of the same vice or to demand a virtue they themselves are unable to demonstrate."

Lady Rectitude replies: "My sweet young friend, have you not always heard people say that a fool can clearly see the splinter in his neighbor's face

but is unable to perceive the beam in his own? I will show you the great inconsistency in what men say about the volatility and inconstancy of women. They
all generally claim that women are weak, and in light of that accusation, it
must be assumed that they consider themselves strong-minded, or at least,
that they see women as less strong-willed than they are. The fact is that they
demand greater constancy from women than they are capable of themselves.
Those who claim to be strong and noble can't prevent themselves from committing many mistakes and sins, not only out of ignorance but through pure
malice, well aware that they are doing the wrong thing. They offer the excuse
that to err is human, but if a woman commits the slightest lapse (for which
men are themselves to blame through their perpetual scheming), they are
immediately ready to accuse her of weakness and inconstancy. It seems logi-
cal to conclude that since they consider women weak, they should be more
tolerant of their weakness and not treat as a great crime what they consider a
minor fault in men. There is no law or book stipulating that only men have
the right to sin or that their misdeeds are more excusable. In fact, they give
themselves that right, unwilling to let women get away with anything, and
they continue to offend and hurt women in word and deed. Nor are they
willing to acknowledge women's strength and constancy for enduring men's
outrages. So you see, men always claim they are right and enjoy the best of
both worlds. You have discussed this yourself in detail in your *Epistre au Dieu
d'Amours*.[38]

"You have asked me whether men are so strong and steadfast that they are
justified in accusing others of inconstancy. I say to you that if you examine
history from antiquity until today and take into account those books, your
own observations in life, and what you can still see yourself every day with
your own eyes, you can decide for yourself how much perfection, strength,
and constancy you can really find in men, not just the simple and lowborn
ones but also those from the upper classes. That applies to the vast majority
of them, although there are indeed some men who are wise, steadfast, and
strong. They are sorely needed!

"If you want me to provide you with examples from the past or the present of men who consistently accuse women of these weaknesses as if they
themselves are never inconstant or indecisive, consider the lives of the most
powerful princes and the most eminent men, even emperors, in whom such

---

38. Christine is here pointing to her *Epistle to the God of Love,* a long poem she wrote in 1399.
This epistle is her first contribution to the debate over *The Romance of the Rose.*

weaknesses are even more inappropriate.[39] I ask you: what woman's heart was ever as frail, as fearful, and as inconstant as that of Emperor Claudius? He was so capricious that he would issue orders and countermand them an hour later. It was impossible to rely on what he said, and he agreed with everyone's advice. Gripped by madness and cruelty, he had his wife killed yet that same evening asked why she had not come to bed. He ordered the servants he had beheaded to come and play with him. He was so fearful that he was always trembling and trusted no one. What else can I tell you about him? This wretched emperor was the epitome of moral debauchery and mental deficiency. But why am I telling you only about him? Was he the only feeble ruler to govern an empire? Was Emperor Tiberius any better? Did he not display more inconstancy, capriciousness, and lewdness than has ever been seen in any woman?"

48. Here she talks about Nero.

"Since we are discussing the deeds of emperors, what about Nero?[40] His extreme weakness and capriciousness were abundantly obvious. He started out quite respectable, striving to please everyone, but as time passed, his lechery, greed, and cruelty knew no bounds. To give full rein to these vices, he often went out at night with his fellow profligates, carrying arms, to visit orgies and places of ill repute, cavorting and fooling in the streets and committing all sorts of misdeeds. Looking for a pretext to provoke a brawl, he would jostle passers-by, and if they protested, he would attack and kill them. He broke into taverns and whorehouses where he raped women, and one time he was almost killed by the husband of a woman he had raped. He organized bath orgies and ate all night. He ordered one thing and then something else altogether, depending on where his madness directed him. He indulged in every sort of lechery, excess, and violence, and spent huge sums of money. He liked evil men and persecuted good people. He consented to the killing of his father and later had his own mother killed. After she died, he had her body cut open so he could see the place where he was conceived. When he had seen it, he said that she had been a beautiful woman. He killed Octavia, his wife, who was a good lady, and took another woman, whom he initially

---

39. The following two chapters stand out as rare instances where Christine engages in finger-pointing at the other sex more than in a critical, positive exposé of virtuous *female* examples.

40. Above all remembered for his extreme cruelty, Nero reigned as emperor from 54 to 68 CE.

cherished but subsequently killed as well. He had Claudia, his predecessor's daughter, put to death because she refused to marry him. He had his stepson, who was not even seven years old, put to death because the child was being carried out to play as if he were a general's son. He had Seneca, the noble philosopher who was his teacher, put to death because he could not help feeling ashamed of his actions in Seneca's presence. He poisoned his steward by pretending to give him a cure for his toothache. He put poison in the food and drink of the noble princes and the most respected, experienced barons who yielded great power. He had his aunt killed and confiscated her possessions. He had the most highly born Roman noblemen killed or exiled and their children massacred. He had a cruel Egyptian taught to eat raw human flesh so he could have his victims eaten alive.

"What more can I say? It is impossible to list all his cruel and evil deeds. To crown it all, he had fires started throughout the entire city of Rome. They raged for six days and six nights and many people perished in this calamity, but Nero stood on top of his tower and watched the flames and destruction, taking such delight in the beauty of the flames that it made him sing. He had Saint Peter and Saint Paul and many other martyrs beheaded at his dinner table. When his cruel reign had lasted fourteen long years, the Romans had suffered enough and revolted against him. Nero was overcome by despair and killed himself."

49. About Emperor Galba and other emperors.

"The shocking story I have told you about Nero's depravity and inconstancy may strike you as an extreme case, but I assure you that the emperor who succeeded him, by the name of Galba, would hardly have been any better if he had lived long enough. His cruelty knew no bounds, and in addition to his other vices, he was so capricious that he was never steadfast or consistent, now cruel and profligate, now feeble and powerless. Careless, jealous, and suspicious, he had little respect for his princes and knights. He was weak, cowardly, and incredibly greedy. He reigned only six months until he was assassinated to put an end to his cruel reign.

"As for Otho, who succeeded him, was he any better? Well, it is said that women are obsessed with themselves, but Otho was so coquettish and pampered his body to such an extent that he was more effeminate than anyone else. Fainthearted, he sought only to please himself. He was a shameless thief, a complete fool, an unabashed glutton, a weak, lecherous, backstabbing traitor full of contempt, always ready to indulge in any sort of debauchery. He eventually committed suicide after ruling for three months, after his enemies defeated him.

"Vitellius, who succeeded Otho, was no better. He was a depraved man. I don't know what more I can tell you about this, but I assure you that I am not exaggerating. Read the stories of the emperors and the accounts of their lives, and you will find that there were very few good, just, and stable rulers among them at any given time. Among the latter were the emperors Julius Caesar, Octavian, Trajan, and Titus. But take it from me: for every one of those good emperors, you will find ten bad ones.

"I could tell you similar stories about the popes and servants of the Holy Church, who should be more perfect and holier than anyone else. In early Christianity they certainly were, but ever since Constantine endowed the church with great revenues and riches, the corruption that resulted has been shocking. You only need to read their histories and chronicles. If you tell me that those things happened long ago and people are virtuous nowadays, look around you and tell me if the world today is improving and the behavior and decisions of princes show great firmness and constancy either in the secular or the spiritual domain. The answer is clear enough, I need say no more. So I really don't know why men talk about the inconstancy and capriciousness of women and why they don't scruple to say so when it should be clear to them that it is their own actions, not those of women, that show the inconstancy and capriciousness of a child. Let them take a look at the quality of the resolutions and accords they reach in council!

"Essentially, what is inconstancy and capriciousness other than a violation of the dictates of Reason, which urges every reasonable creature to do what is right? When a man or a woman allows Reason to fall victim to sensuality, weakness and inconstancy are the result. And the more often one falls into error or sin, the weaker one becomes, being no longer enlightened by Reason. According to what history tells us (and I believe experience does not contradict this), the truth is that regardless of what the philosophers and other authors say about women's capriciousness, you will never find a woman as thoroughly perverse as many men.

"The most depraved women you will encounter in any books were Athalis and Jezebel, her mother, queens of Jerusalem, who persecuted the people of Israel; Brunhilde, queen of France; and a few others. But think about the perfidy of Judas who so cruelly betrayed his noble master whom he served as an apostle and who had done so much for him. Consider the pitilessness and cruelty of the Jews and the people of Israel, who not only killed Jesus Christ, driven by envy, but also many other holy prophets who preceded Him. They beheaded some, others they beat to death or killed them in another way. Take Julian the Apostate, who is considered by some to have been one of the Antichrists because of his extreme perversity, or Denis, the treacherous tyrant of Sicily, who was so despicable that merely reading his biography makes one ashamed. And think of all the evil kings in various countries, the traitorous emperors, heretical popes and other faithless, greedy prelates, the antichrists yet to come! You will see that men should really keep their mouths shut and women should bless and praise God, who placed their precious souls in a feminine vessel. I will say no more about this, but to refute what men say about the weakness of women, I will give some examples of several women who were endowed with great strength. Their stories are interesting and serve as examples to others."

50. Here she talks about the strength and virtue of Griselda, the marquise of Saluces.

"The books make mention of a man called Gualtieri, marquis of Saluces, who did not have a wife. He was handsome and brave, but very eccentric. His barons often pleaded with him, urging him to marry in order to continue his lineage. He refused for a long time but finally told them that if they promised to accept the woman he chose, whoever she might be, he would agree to marry. His barons accepted this and ratified it with an oath.

"The marquis liked to hunt and hawk. There was a small country village near his fortress, and among the poor laborers was a frail, impoverished old man called Giannucolo, who had been a good, honest man all his life. This man had an eighteen-year-old-daughter called Griselda, who lovingly looked after him and supported him with her spinning. The marquis, who often passed through the village, had noticed the girl's good manners and sincerity and had been struck by her lovely face and body. It so happened that the marquis, having agreed to take a wife, told his barons to assemble for his wedding on a certain day, adding that he wished all the ladies to be present. He ordered elaborate preparations to be made, and when the day came and everyone was assembled before him, he had everyone mount on horseback to accompany him as he went to fetch his wife. He rode straight to Giannucolo's house, where he encountered Griselda returning from the well, carrying a jug of water on her head. He asked her where her father was and Griselda knelt before him, telling him her father was at home. 'Go fetch him,' he said, and when Giannucolo appeared, the marquis told him that he wanted to marry his daughter. Giannucolo replied that he should do as he wished. Then the ladies entered the little cottage, carrying the rich robes and jewels the marquis had made ready, and dressed and adorned the bride as befits the rank of a marquis. The marquis took his bride to his palace and married her, and to make a long story short, this lady behaved so kindly toward everyone that all members of the nobility, regardless of their rank, and all the people adored her. She was so at ease with everyone that they were all delighted, and she served and cherished her lord as was her duty.

"That same year, the marquise gave birth to a daughter, who was welcomed with joy. When she was old enough to be weaned, however, the marquis decided to test his wife's constancy and patience, so he told her that the barons were unhappy with the idea of being ruled by someone of her lineage and that he therefore wanted the child killed. This would have been distressing to any mother, but Griselda replied that the girl was his daughter and that he should do as he wished. She handed the child to one of his squires who pretended he had come to fetch the child to have it killed. Instead, he secretly took it to Bologna to the marquis' sister, the countess of Panico, who kept the child and looked after it. Griselda showed no sign of distress whatsoever, even though she believed her daughter had been killed. A year later, the marquise found herself pregnant again and gave birth to a handsome son, who was welcomed with joy. Once again, the marquis wanted to test his wife, so he told her that the boy would also have to be killed to satisfy his barons and men. Griselda replied that if the death of her son was not enough, she was ready to die herself if he so wished. She handed her son to the squire as she had done with her daughter without showing any signs of distress or saying anything except to beg the squire that when he had the child killed, to please have it buried so wild beasts and birds would not eat its tender flesh.

Despite this shattering hardship, Griselda did not appear to show any emotion, yet the marquis was still not satisfied. He wanted to test his wife once more, even though they had been together for twelve years and her conduct had always been so flawless that the marquis should have been satisfied by now. One day, he summoned her to his chamber and told her that his subjects were unhappy with him because of her and that he was at risk of losing his domain, because the people hated the idea of having Giannucolo's daughter as their first lady and mistress. In order to appease them, she would have to return to her father's house where she had come from and he would have to marry another woman of a nobler lineage. This proposal must have been extremely upsetting and difficult for Griselda, yet she replied: 'My lord, I have always been acutely aware of the gulf between your aristocratic roots and magnificence and my poverty, and I have never claimed to be worthy enough to be your wife or even your servant. I am ready to return to my father's house right now, where I will live out my life. As to the dowry you have commanded me to take back with me, you remember that when you met me at the door of my father's house, you had me stripped naked and dressed in the robes I wore when I came with you. I did not bring you any dowry except faith, wisdom, love, respect, and poverty. It is appropriate that I return your property to you. Here is your robe, which I will take off, and here is your ring with which you married me, and I will also return all the other jewelry, rings, clothes, and ornaments that I was given in my wedding chamber. I came from my father's house completely naked and I will return there completely naked, although it seems inappropriate to me that this body that carried the children you sired should be exposed to the eyes of the people. So I would beg you to please allow me to wear a simple shift, in compensation for the virginity I brought to your palace and cannot take back with me. That simple garment will cover the nudity of your former wife, the marquise.' Listening to these words, the marquis could hardly keep himself from weeping with compassion, but he controlled his feelings and left his chamber to issue orders for a shift to be fetched.

"Then, in the company of all his knights and their ladies, Griselda undressed, removing her shoes and all her ornaments until she wore nothing but a shift. The rumor that the marquis intended to divorce his wife had already spread far and wide, and everyone had come to the palace, upset by the news. Griselda, naked except for her shift, bareheaded and barefoot, mounted a horse and rode off, accompanied by the barons, knights, and their ladies, who all wept and cursed the marquis for breaking up with such a virtuous lady. Griselda, however, never shed a tear. She was taken to the house of her father, that old man who had always had his doubts, convinced that his lord would grow tired one day of such a misalliance. When he heard the noise, he went out to meet his daughter, carrying the old, worn tunic he had kept. He dressed her in it without showing any emotion. Griselda remained with her father for some time, living a humble life of poverty and looking after him as she had done before, showing no evidence of grief or regret whatsoever. In fact, she comforted her father in his sadness at seeing his daughter fallen from such a great height to such complete poverty.

"When the marquis decided that he had tested his loyal wife enough, he sent for his sister, telling her that she should come with an escort of lords and ladies and bring his two children, without telling anyone that they were his. He informed his barons and subjects that he wanted to marry a new wife, a noble young woman who had been raised by his sister. He called for a magnificent company of knights, ladies, and noblemen to assemble in his palace on the day his sister was due to arrive, and made preparations for a great celebration. He summoned Griselda and told her: 'Griselda, the girl I want to marry will be here tomorrow, and because I want my sister and her noble company received in great style, I would like you to be in charge. You know how I like to receive guests and where to put them so that everyone is treated according to their rank, especially my fiancée, who will be with them. All the servants will do your bidding. Just see to it that everything is well organized.' Griselda replied that she would be happy to do so. When the company arrived the next day, there was a magnificent celebration, and Griselda, in spite of the poor dress she was wearing, warmly welcomed the young girl she believed her husband was about to marry. She humbly curtseyed and told her: 'Welcome, my lady.' She greeted the boy and all members of the company the same way, warmly welcoming them all as befitted their rank. Although she was poorly dressed, it was obvious from her bearing that she was a woman of great distinction and wisdom, and all the visitors wondered at the contrast between such eloquence and dignity and such poor garments. Griselda had organized the festivities so well that everything went smoothly, but she felt such a strong attraction to the girl and the boy that she could not leave their company and kept staring at them, struck by their beauty.

"The marquis had arranged everything as if to prepare for his wedding. When it was time to celebrate Mass, he came forward, called Griselda over in front of everyone, and said to her: 'Griselda, what do you think of my new bride? Is she not beautiful and virtuous?' Griselda replied: 'Indeed, my lord. I never saw anyone more beautiful or virtuous. But I would ask you just one thing: don't inflict upon her the torments and hardships you inflicted upon your first wife, because she is much younger and has been raised more delicately. She would not be able to endure as much as your first wife could.' The marquis, hearing Griselda's words and seeing her great steadiness, strength, and constancy, deeply admired her virtue. He was filled with sorrow for having made her suffer so much and for so long without deserving it. Thereupon, in front of everyone, he said: 'Griselda, you have more than proven your constancy, true loyalty, abiding love, and humility. I don't think there is anyone under the heavens who has received as much proof of the strength of the love between a man and a wife as I have from you.' Then the marquis went over to her, wrapped her in his arms, and kissed her, saying: 'You are the only wife I want. I want no other and I will never have another. This girl who you think is to become my wife is actually our daughter, and the boy is your son. All those gathered here should know that what I have done was for the sake of proving my wife's loyalty and not to condemn her. I did not have my children killed: I had them raised by my sister in Bologna. Behold them: here they are.' The marchioness, hearing her lord's words, fainted from joy. When she regained her senses, she took her children in her arms and shed tears of happiness. You can be sure that her heart was filled with elation. Those present all wept as well, filled with joy and compassion. Griselda was now more respected than ever before. She was dressed in rich garments and adorned with jewels, and the celebration that followed was magnificent and joyful. Everyone outdid each other heaping praise on Griselda. She and her husband lived together for another twenty years in peace and harmony. The marquis had thus far ignored his wife's father Giannucolo, but now he summoned him to the palace and treated him with great respect. He arranged splendid marriages for his children, and following his death, he was succeeded by his son, with the barons' full endorsement."

51. Here she talks about Florence of Rome.

"If Griselda, the marquise of Saluces, was a model of strength and constancy, the noble Florence, empress of Rome, was her match. She endured great adversity with tremendous patience, as you will read in the *Miracles de Nostre Dame*.[41] This lady was a great beauty, but her chastity and virtue were even more remarkable. It so happened that her husband had to make a long voyage to a distant war, so he left his empire and his wife in the care of one of his brothers. When the emperor had departed, this brother succumbed to the devil's temptations and fell madly in love with his sister-in-law Florence. To make a long story short, he put so much pressure on her to submit to his desire that the lady had him imprisoned in a tower, fearing that when he realized his pleas were having no effect, he would resort to force. There he stayed, until the emperor returned. When the news came that the emperor was on

---

41. The author of this collection of poems devoted to the Virgin Mary is Gautier de Coinci (1177–1236).

his way, Florence set her brother-in-law free to allow him to go out to meet the emperor, having no idea that he would tell lies about her. She just wanted to make sure that the emperor did not find out about his brother's treachery. But when he met with the emperor, he accused her of all possible sorts of evil deed, telling the emperor she had imprisoned him so she could indulge in her vices at her leisure. The emperor believed him and sent for his men, ordering them to go ahead of him and discreetly kill her, because he did not want to ever lay eyes on her again or even find her alive. Florence was horrified to learn this news. She pleaded so piteously with the men charged with killing her that she eventually convinced them to let her escape in disguise.

"She traveled far and wide and one day, through a strange twist of fate, she was put in charge of the child of a great prince. Then the prince's brother fell in love with her, and when she ignored his entreaties, he killed the child lying next to her as she slept, driven by spite and consumed by a rage to destroy her. The noble lady endured this great adversity with endless patience and unwavering courage. When she was being led to the place where she was to be executed for murdering the child, the lord and lady were moved to pity, given the exemplary lifestyle and great virtue they had observed in her, prompting them to send her into exile instead of having her killed. There she led a life of great poverty, which she bore with patience, devoting herself to God and his blessed mother. One day, she fell asleep in an orchard after saying her prayers. There she had a vision of the Virgin, who told her to pick a certain herb on which her head was resting and that this would allow her to earn a living, curing people of any disease.

"Florence went on to cure so many illnesses with this herb that her fame spread far and wide. Then God decided that the prince's brother who had killed the child should fall victim to a terrible disease, and Florence was summoned to cure him. When she arrived in his presence, she told him that it should be obvious to him that God was chastising him with His scourge and that if he wanted to be healed, he should publicly confess his horrible crimes. That, she said, was the only way she could cure him. He was overcome with contrition and confessed his terrible crimes, explaining how he himself had killed the child and then blamed the good lady who was looking after it. The prince was enraged and wanted nothing more than to see his brother in court, but the noble lady intervened and managed to placate him. Then she cured his brother, repaying evil with good in accordance with God's commandment.

"Not long afterward, the emperor's brother who had been instrumental in getting Florence sent into exile fell victim to such an advanced case of leprosy that his body turned putrid. Since it was common knowledge by then that there was a woman who could cure every sickness, the emperor had her sent for but failed to recognize her, in the belief that his wife had died long ago. When she came face to face with his brother, she told him that she would be unable to cure him unless he publicly confessed. He refused for a long time but finally confessed all the details of the loathsome deed he had inflicted upon the empress without any reason whatsoever. It was for this sin, he knew, that God was punishing him. When the emperor heard this story, he was enraged at the thought that he had been responsible for the death of his faithful, beloved wife. He wanted to kill his brother, but the good lady identified herself and made peace between the emperor and his brother. In that way, thanks to her infinite patience, Florence regained her standing and happiness, to the great joy of the emperor and all his people."

52. About the wife of Bernabo of Genoa.

"While we're on the topic of wise, steady women, I should mention another story, told by Boccaccio in his *Decameron*.[42] One day, several merchants from Lombardy and Italy happened to have dinner together in Paris. They talked about many things, including their wives, and a Genovan among them by the name of Bernabo started praising his wife for her beauty and wit, and especially her chastity. The group included a hothead called Ambrogiuolo, who said that it was foolish to praise one's wife like that, especially for her chastity, since there wasn't a woman alive who was strong enough to resist being seduced by a man who plied her with enough gifts, promises, and sweet words. A heated debate ensued between the two men that went so far that they each wagered the sum of five thousand florins. Bernabo bet Ambrogiuolo that he would never succeed in sleeping with his wife regardless of all his talents. In his turn, Ambrogiuolo bet that he could and that he would bring Bernabo such irrefutable evidence that he would be convinced. The others did their best to put an end to this dispute but to no avail.

"Ambrogiuolo left at once and traveled to Genoa. Upon his arrival, he thoroughly acquainted himself with the lifestyle and habits of Bernabo's wife, but he heard so many good things about her that he lost all hope of ever winning his bet. Deeply worried, he regretted being such a fool, but the thought

---

42. See Boccaccio, *Decameron* II.9. This most famous work by Boccaccio, much like Chaucer's *Canterbury Tales*, involves a series of tales within a larger one and offers us a glimpse into various facets of medieval life.

of losing five thousand florins was no less upsetting, so he devised a nasty plot. He talked to an old, impoverished woman who lived in the lady's house and bribed her with enough money and promises to convince her to hide him in a chest that was subsequently carried into the lady's bedchamber. The old woman gave the lady to understand that the chest was filled with precious objects entrusted to her care. Since there had already been an attempt by some thieves to steal it, she asked the lady for permission to keep the chest in her chamber for a short period until the objects' owners returned. The lady was happy to oblige. Inside the chest, Ambrogiuolo spied on the lady until he saw her completely naked at night. He slipped out of the chest and took a small purse and a belt she had richly embroidered, then slid back into the chest so quietly that the lady and a small girl lying next to her never heard a thing. He stayed in the chest for three days, until the old woman arrived to remove the chest.

"Proud of his stratagem and elated at his success, Ambrogiuolo reported back to her husband before the whole group, telling him that he had indeed spent a leisurely night in bed with Bernabo's wife. He first described the chamber's layout and the paintings on the wall and then showed him the purse and the belt, which Bernabo instantly recognized. Ambrogiuolo told him that she had given him these things as a present, and went on to describe the lady's naked body, noting that she had a beauty spot in the shape of a small red mole under her left breast. Based on this evidence, the husband was completely convinced by Ambrogiuolo's account, and anyone can guess how much distress this caused him. Nevertheless, he paid Ambrogiuolo the five thousand florins he owed him. Then he rushed off to Genoa, but before he arrived there, he formally ordered one of his retainers, who managed his property and enjoyed his full confidence, to kill his wife, detailing how he wanted it done but not why. In accordance with his instructions, the retainer asked the lady to mount a horse, claiming that he was taking her to see her husband. The lady readily believed him and was delighted to go with him. When they arrived in a forest, however, he told her that her husband had ordered him to kill her. To make a long story short, this noble, virtuous lady managed to convince him to let her go, on condition that she left the country.

"After her escape she went to live in a small town where she persuaded a kind woman to sell her some men's clothing. She cut her hair short and disguised herself as a young man. Eventually, she obtained a position in the service of a rich man from Catalonia called Señor Ferant [*sic*], who had just disembarked from his ship to refresh himself. She served him so well that he was amazed, saying he had never had such an outstanding servant. The lady was now calling herself Sicurano da Finale. Señor Ferant returned to his ship with Sicurano and sailed for Alexandria, where he bought some splendid falcons and horses. Then he went on to see the sultan of Babylon, who was a very good friend of his. After he had spent some time there, the sultan noticed Sicurano serving his master with great diligence. The sultan thought him so handsome and gracious that he asked Señor Ferant whether he could have Sicurano as his own servant, assuring him he would be an excellent master. Ferant reluctantly agreed to the request. To make a long story short, Sicurano served the sultan so well that he became his sole confidant and gained so much influence that he gained control of all his affairs.

"One day, a large fair was due to be held in one of the sultan's cities, drawing merchants from far and wide. The sultan ordered Sicurano to make his way to that city to supervise the fair and protect the sultan's rights. As God willed it, one of the Italians who had come there to sell jewelry turned out to be the traitorous Ambrogiuolo, greatly enriched by Bernabo's money. Sicurano, in his capacity as the sultan's deputy in the city, enjoyed considerable respect, and since he held a very important and influential position, the merchants offered to sell him all sorts of unusual jewelry. Among them was Ambrogiuolo, who opened a small case to show Sicurano the jewels inside. Among the precious objects in the case were the little purse and the belt mentioned above. Sicurano instantly recognized them. He picked them up and closely examined them, wondering aloud how they could have wound up there. Sicurano, who had not thought about the affair for a long time, smiled broadly. Noting his merriment, Sicurano said: 'My friend, I think you are laughing at my amusement over this little purse, which is a woman's thing. But it is very pretty.' Ambrogiuolo replied: 'My lord, it is yours if you wish it. I only smiled because I remembered how I acquired it.' 'May God reward you if you tell me how you obtained it,' said Sicurano. 'Well,' said Ambrogiuolo, 'I got it from a beautiful woman with whom I slept one night. She gave it to me, and it brought me five thousand florins thanks to a bet I made with her fool of a husband. His name was Bernabo and he had the audacity to bet that I would never succeed in sleeping with her. The unfortunate fellow killed his wife for it, but he deserved punishment more than she did, because every man should know that women are weak, easily seduced, and not to be trusted.'

"The lady finally understood the reason for her husband's anger, which she had not known before. Prudent and steadfast as she was, she wisely hid the knowledge until the right time and place. She pretended to be vastly amused by the story and told Ambrogiuolo he was a fine fellow. She would like to be friends with him, she said, and wanted him to stay in the country to engage in trading for their mutual benefit. She would see to it that he would be richly rewarded. Ambrogiuolo was delighted with this proposal, and Sicurano actually even had a house built for him. To strengthen the deception, she gave him a considerable sum of money and showed him so much affection that he spent every day in Sicurano's company. She had him recount his funny story in front of the sultan, pretending she wanted to make him laugh.

"To make a long story short, the way it ended is that Sicurano learned that Bernabo had fallen into poverty, partly as a result of the large bet he had lost and partly because of his grief. Then she asked some Genoans who were in the country to tell Bernabo that the sultan wished to see him. When he presented himself before the sultan, Sicurano immediately sent for Ambrogiuolo. She had told the sultan earlier that Ambrogiuolo was lying when he boasted of having slept with the lady. She had also asked him that when the truth emerged, he should punish Ambrogiuolo as he deserved. The sultan had agreed.

"When Bernabo and Ambrogiuolo stood before the sultan, Sicurano said: 'Ambrogiuolo, it would please our lord the sultan here before you to hear your prank again in all its detail: how you won a five-thousand-florin bet from Bernabo, who is standing beside you, and how you slept with his wife.' Hearing this, Ambrogiuolo's face changed color as if he could hardly believe that the truth might triumph over his faithless treachery. The matter had arisen so suddenly that it had caught him off guard. But he regained his composure to some extent and replied: 'My lord, there is little point in telling the story. Bernabo knows all about it, and I am ashamed on account of his shame.' Bernabo, overcome with sadness and shame, begged to be spared from hearing the story repeated and asked permission to leave. Sicurano, however, smiled and replied that Bernabo should stay and listen to the story. Ambrogiuolo, realizing he could no longer avoid it, started to tell the story with a trembling voice, exactly as he had originally told it to Bernabo. When he had finished, Sicurano asked Bernabo if the tale Ambrogiuolo had told was true, and Bernabo said that it was indeed true. 'And how,' asked Sicurano, 'could you be sure that this man actually slept with your wife, even if he brought back some meager evidence? Are you such a fool that you don't know he could have used fraudulent means to obtain a description of your wife's body without having slept with her? Is that why you had her killed? You deserve to die yourself because you didn't have sufficient proof!' Ambrogiuolo was terrified and Sicurano, who felt that the right time had come to speak out, said to Ambrogiuolo: 'You double-dealing, lying traitor! Tell the truth! Tell the truth before I get it out of you by torture! You have no choice, because there is proof that you have been lying through your teeth! I want you to know that the woman you have been boasting about is not dead. No, and she is quite close by to disprove your treacherous lies. You never touched her and that is a fact.' The assembly, made up of many of the sultan's barons and a large number of Lombards, were astonished to hear these words. In short, Ambrogiuolo was under so much pressure that he confessed the whole fraud in front of the sultan and the entire audience, telling them how he had used an abominable trick to win the five thousand florins. Bernabo almost went out of his mind when he heard this, thinking his wife had been killed unjustly, but the good lady approached him and told him: 'What would you give, Bernabo, to the person who would give you back your wife, alive and well and untouched?' Bernabo said he would give everything he possessed. Then she said: 'Bernabo, my beloved, my friend, don't you recognize me?' He was so stunned that he thought he was dreaming, so she unbuttoned her tunic and told him: 'Look, Bernabo, I am the faithful companion you condemned to death without cause.' Then they fell into each other's arms, overcome with joy. The sultan and his people were completely amazed and praised the lady's virtue. She received many wonderful gifts, and all Ambrogiuolo's assets were turned over to Bernabo. He and his wife returned home, and the sultan had Ambrogiuolo executed in great agony.

53. Following Lady Rectitude's discourse on the steadfastness of women, Christine asks her why all the worthy ladies of the past have never refuted the books and men who maligned them, and Lady Rectitude answers her question.

After Lady Rectitude had told me all these things, she told me many more stories that I will omit for the sake of brevity. But I will mention the one about Leaena, a Greek woman. Despite all the torture they made her endure, she refused to denounce two male acquaintances. Instead, she used her teeth to bite off her own tongue before the judge so he could no longer make her talk through torture. Rectitude told me about many other women who were so steadfast that they preferred to drink poison rather than turn against justice and truth. Finally I said: "My lady, you have clearly demonstrated that women possess immense fortitude of mind and many other virtues. So many, in fact, that you could not say the same about a single man. That is why I am surprised that so many meritorious ladies who possessed great wisdom and a thorough education, ladies who composed beautiful books and poems, kept enduring the devastating criticisms leveled against them by various men without contradicting them, when they were well aware that those criticisms were completely unwarranted."

Answer: "My dear friend, that question is quite easy to answer. Based on what I have told you before, it will be clear to you that the ladies whose outstanding virtues I have described all used their intellectual capacities in different fields, without ever devoting themselves to the same subject. The writing of this book has been reserved for you and not for them, because they gained great respect from intelligent and discerning people without the need to write more books about their accomplishments. As to the length of time that has passed without them contradicting their accusers and slanderers, let me tell you that in the eternal scheme of things, there is a time and a place for all things to come to a good end. How else could God have tolerated for so long the heresies against His holy faith? They were very difficult to eradicate and would still exist today if they had not been challenged. So it is with many other things that were tolerated for a long time before they were contested and refuted."

Then I, Christine, said to her: "My lady, you put it very well, but I am convinced that the critics will malign this work. They will say that even if it is true that there are and have been some virtuous women, that doesn't apply to all of them or even the majority."

She answered: "It's just not true that the majority of women lack virtue. This is amply proven by what I have told you before about the everyday experience of women's piety, their acts of charity, and their other virtues, no less than by the fact that the terrible things and the evil that keeps occurring in this world are not committed by women. But the statement that not *all* women are virtuous is hardly surprising. In all of Nineveh, a big and densely populated city, not a single good man could be found when our Lord ordered the prophet Jonah to go there and destroy it unless it turned away from evil. It was even worse in the city of Sodom, as evidenced by the fact that it was destroyed by fire sent down from heaven after Lot's departure. You should also note that the company of Jesus Christ, which numbered only twelve men, still included one evil member. To think that men have the nerve to say that all women must be good and that those who aren't should be stoned! I would ask them to first look to themselves and let he who is without sin cast the first stone. In other words, they should first examine their own conduct. I tell you, when men become perfect, women will follow their example."

54. Christine asks Lady Rectitude whether it is true that few women are faithful in love as some men claim, and Rectitude's reply.

Continuing the discussion, I, Christine, said: "My lady, let us move on to other topics and go a little beyond the issues we have been addressing up to now. I would like to ask you some questions if I could be sure that this would not trouble you, because the subject I want to discuss goes a little beyond Reason's usual scope, although it is based on natural laws."

She replied: "My dear friend, ask me anything you like, because a teacher should not rebuke an eager student for asking all sorts of questions."

"My lady, there is a natural law in this world that applies to the behavior of men toward women and that of women toward men. It is not a man-made law but one that springs from a carnal impulse that arouses in them strong feelings of lust and causes them to love each other passionately. They don't know why this passion takes possession of them, but the feeling is common and known as people's love life. Men tend to claim that regardless of the promises women make, they are rarely faithful to one man, lack a real capacity for affection, and are amazingly deceitful. All this, they say, stems from women's frivolous nature. One of the many authors leveling this criticism is Ovid, who makes strong allegations in his book *Ars amatoria* [The Art of Love]. After attacking women for their frivolity, Ovid and his fellow authors say that the reason why they express their views on women and their deceitful ways and malice is to serve the common good, to warn men about female wiles so they will be better prepared to avoid them, like snakes hiding in the grass. My dear lady, can you please tell me the truth of this matter?"

She replied: "My dear friend, regarding this accusation that women are deceitful, I don't know what more I can say to you. You have addressed the subject in detail yourself, refuting both Ovid and others in your *Epistre au Dieu d'Amours* [Epistle to the God of Love] and *Epistres sur le Roman de la Rose* [Epistles on the Romance of the Rose]. As to the point you raised that men claim they level their criticisms for the common good, I will show you that this is not their true reason. Here is why: the only things in a city, country, or any community that qualify as being for the common or public good are benefits in which both women and men participate and which they share equally. Something done to benefit some and not others is called private welfare, not public. The act of taking from some and giving to others qualifies even less: it should not even be defined as public or private good but as pure extortion, a wrong done to one party to benefit another.[43] These authors don't address women to warn them to beware of traps laid by men, yet they certainly deceive women on many occasions with their tricks and lies. It is beyond doubt that women are as much part of God's creatures and the human race as men. They are not a different kind of species or breed that might justify their exclusion from moral teachings. I can only conclude that if these authors were acting for the common good, meaning both sides, they would have also warned women to beware of the traps laid by men, the same way they warned men to beware of women.

"But let us leave these issues and move on to another topic, namely, that women do have loving hearts and are much more faithful than those men claim. All I need to do to prove it is to give you some examples of women who were faithful until death. First, I will tell you about the noble Dido, queen of Carthage. I already told you about her great merit and you have discussed her yourself in your own writings."

55. About Dido, queen of Carthage, and women's faithfulness in love.

"As I told you, Dido, the queen of Carthage, was a brilliant ruler who governed her city in happiness and peace.[44] As fate would have it, the Trojan leader Aeneas arrived there one day at the head of a host of Trojans, having fled his city after its destruction. With his ships scattered and destroyed by a thousand storms, his provisions depleted, and many of his men lost, he

---

43. Note this important discussion of the nature of the common/public good as distinct from the private. (Quite significantly, for Christine, the notions of "public good" and "common good" seem to be interchangeable.) Here Christine de Pizan provides a defense of women not only on the grounds of their personal merits but also because of the stakes they have in the public good, defined as benefits in which men and women participate and "share equally." This argument might be considered an extension in terms of gender of a similar sort of logic found in John of Salisbury and other authors regarding class, namely, the idea that all classes are included in a conception of the general welfare.
44. See I.46.

was in need of rest and tired of drifting across the sea. Penniless but needing shelter, he arrived in the port of Carthage. To avoid giving offense by going ashore without permission, he sent a messenger to the queen to ask permission to bring his ships into harbor at her pleasure. The noble queen, an honorable and courageous lady who was well aware that the Trojans enjoyed a better reputation than any other nation at that time and that Aeneas was a member of the royal family, not only gave him permission to land but went out to meet him on shore accompanied by an illustrious company of barons, ladies, and damsels. She received him and his entire company with great honor, led him into her city, and treated him with great ceremony. A feast was held in his honor, and he was made comfortable. Why make a long story of it? Aeneas' visit was so pleasant and restful that he barely remembered the torments he had suffered. He spent so much time with Dido that Love, who knows how to steal hearts with great finesse, made them fall in love with each other.

"What followed, however, showed that Dido's love of Aeneas was much deeper than his love for her. He had given her his word that he would never marry another woman and that he would be hers forever, but he left her after she had restored him to health, provided him with money and all the necessities of life, rigged and repaired his ships, and loaded them with treasure and goods, sparing no expense for the man who had captured her heart. He slipped away at night without taking his leave, fleeing in secret like a traitor, without her knowledge. That is how he repaid her for her hospitality. His departure caused poor Dido, who adored him, so much heartache that she wanted to renounce joy and even life. In fact, after long laments, she threw herself onto a great pyre she had ordered lit. Some say that she killed herself with Aeneas' own sword. And that is how tragically the noble queen Dido met her end, she who had enjoyed greater respect than any other woman of her time."

56. About Medea in love.

"Medea, the daughter of the king of Colchis, possessed immense knowledge.[45] She was deeply in love with Jason, a Greek knight and a highly skilled warrior. He had heard of a marvelous, golden sheep guarded by various spells on the island of Colchis, where Medea's father was king. It seemed that its fleece was impossible to capture, although it was prophesied that it would one day be

---

45. Christine also speaks of Medea and Jason in I.32.

taken by a knight. When Jason, always eager to increase his fame, heard this story, he set out for Greece with a large company to take up this challenge. Upon his arrival in Colchis, the country's king told him that it would be impossible to capture the Golden Fleece by either force of arms or bravery because it was protected by a spell. Many knights had already perished in the attempt, said the king, so he should not risk his life this way. To make a long story short, Jason told him that now that he had undertaken the quest, the thought of losing his life would not stop him.

"Medea, the king's daughter, noted Jason's good looks. Aware of his royal lineage and his fame, she concluded that he would make a good husband and was worthier of her love than any other man. The thought of seeing this knight perish filled her with sadness, so she decided to save his life. She talked to him freely and at length, revealing all the charms and spells she knew and teaching him in detail how to conquer the Golden Fleece. In return, Jason promised her that he would take her as his wife and never marry another woman, vowing that he would love her faithfully for the rest of his life. But after he had reached his goal, he broke his promise and abandoned her for another woman. Medea, who would rather have let herself be torn to pieces than cheat him like that, became so despondent that from that moment onward, her heart never again knew happiness or joy."

57. About Thisbe.

"As you know, Ovid, in his *Metamorphoses*, tells the story of two rich, noble men living in the city of Babylon. They were such close neighbors that the palaces in which they resided had a common wall. They had two extraordinarily good-looking children: a son named Pyramus and a daughter called Thisbe. These two children, still quite innocent as children are at the age of seven, already loved each other so much that they could not do without each other. Every morning they were in a hurry to get up and have breakfast in their respective homes so they could go out to play with the other children and meet up with each other. You always saw the two of them playing together. This went on until they became adolescents. As they matured, the flame of love grew in their hearts, so much so that people noticed how much time they were spending together and rumors began to circulate. They reached the ears of Thisbe's mother, who locked her daughter in her rooms, saying angrily that she would see to it that Pyramus stopped stalking her. This imprisonment caused the two children so much grief that their pleas and tears were heartbreaking. The separation was just too hard for them to bear. Their distress went on for a long time but never weakened the intensity of their love. On the contrary, even though they did not see each other, their love grew as the years went by, until they reached the age of fifteen.

"One day Thisbe, still obsessed with Pyramus, was sitting alone in her room crying when Fortune decreed that her eyes should turn toward the wall that joined the two palaces. In her grief, she cried out: 'Oh, you tough wall of stone that separates me from my loved one, if you had any compassion at all you would crack so that I could see the one I so desire.' As she said these words, she noticed a crack in the corner of the wall through which she could see daylight. She rushed over to the crack and scratched at the opening with her belt buckle, the only tool she had. She succeeded in enlarging the opening enough to stick the buckle all the way through, so Pyramus could see it. And he did. It served the two lovers as a sign to meet each other by the hole, which they did many times, talking together and bemoaning their pitiful fate. In the end, their love proved so overwhelming that they devised a plan to steal away from their parents at night and meet up outside the city near a spring under a white mulberry tree, where they had often played as children. Thisbe, whose love was the stronger, was the first to arrive at the spring. As she stood waiting for the one she loved, she heard a lion roar on its way to drink from the spring. Frightened, she fled and hid in a nearby copse. In her haste, she dropped the white scarf she was wearing. The lion found it and vomited the entrails of the animals it had devoured all over it. Pyramus arrived before Thisbe had found the courage to move away from the copse. Seeing the scarf by the light of the moon, covered with entrails, he became convinced that his love had been devoured. His grief was so overwhelming that he threw himself on his sword. As he lay dying, Thisbe emerged and found him. Seeing him clutch the scarf to his breast, she instantly understood the reason for this catastrophe and was so overcome by grief that she had no wish to go on living. When she saw her lover's soul leave his body, she uttered heartbreaking cries and killed herself with the same sword."

58. Here she talks about Hero.

"The noble damsel Hero loved Leander no less than Thisbe loved Pyramus. To protect Hero's honor, Leander was ready to run grave risks to keep their love a secret rather than visit her openly where everyone could see him. To that purpose, he had developed a routine that involved sneaking from his bed at night without anyone seeing him and then making his way, alone, to a wide inlet called the Hellespont. There he would remove all his clothes and swim across the inlet toward a castle by the name of Abydos, situated on the opposite shore. That is where Hero awaited him, watching from a window. In winter, when the nights were long and dark, she would hold up a torch at her window to show him the way.

"The two lovers used this routine for several years until Fortune grew envious of their pleasurable life and decided to deprive them of it. It so happened that winter that a storm battered the sea, lashing the waves and creating a very dangerous situation. The storm lasted so many days without letup that the long wait to see each other began to stress the two lovers. They complained bitterly about the wind and the bad weather that were going on for so long. One night, Leander noticed that Hero was showing the torch at the window. Inspired by his passionate desire, he thought she was signaling him and felt he would be seen as a coward if he did not brave the danger and go to her. Alas! The unfortunate damsel was terrified, and if she could have stopped him from putting himself in so much danger, she readily would have. She was merely holding up the torch to direct him in case he decided to make his way over. As it happened, Fortune did not smile upon Leander but decreed that he should lose his struggle against the waves, which carried him so far off course that he drowned. Poor Hero, who knew in her heart what had happened, could not stop crying. At dawn, unable to sleep or rest, she went back to the window where she had been all night. When she saw her lover's body float by on the waves, she lost all desire to go on living and threw herself into the sea, managing to swim over to his body and embrace it. Thus she perished from having loved too much."

59. About Ghismonda, daughter of the prince of Salerno.

"In his *Decameron*, Boccaccio recounts the story of a prince of Salerno by the name of Tancredi, who had a beautiful daughter called Ghismonda.[46] She was very gracious, educated, and well mannered, and her father adored her so much that he could not bear to be separated from her. It was with the greatest reluctance and under extreme pressure that he gave permission for her to marry, but in the end she was given to the count of Campania. Since the count died shortly thereafter, however, she did not stay married for long.

---

46. See Boccaccio, *Decameron* IV.1.

Her father took her back and resolved to never let her remarry. Ghismonda, who was the apple of her father's eye in his old age, was in the prime of her youth, well looked after, and conscious of her own beauty. I'm sure she was less than happy to be spending her youth without a husband, but she did not dare oppose her father's will.

"Ghismonda often sat beside her father as he held court. One day, she noticed a certain squire among the court's noblemen. Seeing him among the large crowd of knights and aristocrats, she thought he looked more handsome and more refined than all the others, and in every respect more than worthy of her love. To make a long story short, she closely watched his conduct and decided to bring some joy into her youth and satisfy the passion in her heart by taking him as her lover. She took a long time before revealing her love, however; every day, she took her seat beside her father and watched the behavior and attitude of this man by the name of Guiscardo. The longer she observed him, the more perfect he seemed to her in all respects.

"When she had watched him long enough, she summoned him one day and said: 'Guiscardo, my dear friend, the trust I have in your kindness, loyalty, and integrity makes me want to disclose to you several things that are close to my heart: confidential things that I would not tell anyone else. But before I do so, I want you to swear that you will never reveal these things to anyone.' Guiscardo replied: 'My lady, on my word of honor, you may rest assured that I will never disclose anything you tell me.' Then Ghismonda said: 'Guiscardo, I want you to know that I have set my heart on a nobleman I want to take as a lover. And since I cannot speak to him and don't have anyone to act as my intermediary, I want you to be our messenger. You see, Guiscardo, that I trust you so much more than anyone else that I'm willing to place my honor in your hands.' He fell to his knees and said: 'My lady, I know that you have too much sense and virtue to do anything that would dishonor you. I humbly thank you for trusting me more than anyone else and being willing to disclose your secret thoughts to me. My dear lady, you can safely confide in me all your desires. I offer you my body and soul to obey all your commands to the best of my ability, and I will be happy to be the humble servant of the man who is lucky enough to be loved by a lady as worthy as you are. Because one thing is certain: he will be part of a beautiful and noble love.' Ghismonda had wanted to put Guiscardo to the test, and when she heard him speak such pleasing words, she took him by the hand and said: 'Guiscardo, my dear friend, you should know that you are the one I have chosen to be my one and only love with whom to take my pleasure, because it seems to me that your noble character and your moral excellence make you worthy of my love.' The young man was overjoyed at this and thanked her humbly.

"To make a long story short, their love flourished for a long time without anyone being the wiser. Then Fortune became envious of their happiness and could no longer bear seeing the two lovers so happy, so she changed their joy in bitter sorrow in a most extraordinary way. One summer day, Ghismonda happened to be strolling through a garden, accompanied by her ladies. Her father, who was only happy in her presence, went into her bedchamber by himself to talk to her and divert himself. Finding the windows closed, the bed-curtains drawn, and no one about, he thought she was taking a nap. He did not want to wake her, so he lay down on a couch and fell fast asleep. When Ghismonda decided she had spent enough time in the garden, she went up to her bedchamber and lay down on her bed as if to have a nap, telling all her ladies to leave and shut the door behind themselves. Neither she nor her ladies noticed her father's presence. When she saw she was alone, she got up from her bed and went to find Guiscardo, who was hiding in one of her dressing rooms, and led him into her chamber. As they were chatting together behind the bed-curtains, believing themselves alone, the prince woke up and heard a man speaking to his daughter. He was so upset about this that the thought of bringing dishonor upon his daughter barely stopped him from assaulting the intruder. He managed to keep himself under control and carefully listened to the voice so he could identify it, then slipped out of the bedchamber without anyone noticing. When the two lovers had finished their assignation, Guiscardo took his leave. The prince had had him watched, however, and he was taken prisoner. Then he went to see his daughter, alone. With tears in his eyes and his face showing his grief, he said: 'Ghismonda, I thought that in you, I had the most beautiful, chaste, and sensible daughter in the world, but now I'm convinced the opposite is true, and I'm torn between anger and my reluctance to believe it. If I had not seen it with my own eyes, nothing would have made me believe that you could be seduced by a man who is not your husband. Now that I know how things stand, I'm sure I will spend my few remaining years tormented by grief. What makes me even angrier is that I thought you had a nobler character than any woman ever born. Now I see that the opposite is true, because you got involved with one of the lowliest members of my household. If you were set on doing this, you could have found in my court any number of nobles without getting involved with Guiscardo. Rest assured that he will pay dearly for the heartache he has caused me. I want you to know that I will have him executed, and I would do the same to you if I could only get rid of this foolish love I have for you, deeper than any father ever felt for a daughter. That is what keeps me from putting you to death.'

"As you can imagine, Ghismonda was grief-stricken when she found out her father knew what she had wanted to keep secret above all else. But what upset her most of all was that he threatened to kill the lover she adored. She wanted to die on the spot. But in spite of this, she controlled her feelings, put on a brave face, and without shedding a tear replied: 'Father, since it has pleased Fortune to have you find out about what I had so wanted to keep secret, there is no point in asking you for anything, except that if I thought I could obtain a pardon from you to spare the life of the one you are threatening to kill by offering myself in his place, I would beg you to take my life and spare his. As for asking your pardon, if you do with him as you say, I don't want your forgiveness because I have no desire to go on with my life in that case. I assure you that by killing him, you will also put an end to my life. And as for your getting so furious with us, you have only yourself to blame. You are a creature of flesh and blood, yet did you ever stop to think that you fathered a daughter who is also made of flesh and blood, not of stone or iron? Even though you are old, you should remember the sort of torment that afflicts young people living a life of luxury and comfort, and the temptations they face. I saw that you had decided to never let me marry again and so, still feeling young and full of life, I fell in love with this man. But I did not give my heart what it desired without good reason and careful deliberation. On the contrary: I spent a long time observing Guiscardo's behavior, and found him to be the most perfect and virtuous of all the members of your court. You should know this, because you raised him yourself. What is nobility after all if not virtue? It has nothing to do with flesh or blood. So you have no right to say that I picked the lowliest member of your court, and you have no reason to be so angry with us, given that you yourself are to blame. But if you are determined to carry out this cruel punishment, it is wrong and sinful to take it out on him. The punishment should be directed at me, because I am the one who instigated this, not the other way around. What choice did he have? It would certainly have been ill-bred to refuse a lady of my rank. So you must forgive him this misdeed, not me!'

"The marquis then left Ghismonda, but his anger with Guiscardo had not abated in the least, so he had him killed the next day and ordered his heart to be torn from his chest. He put the heart in a golden goblet and sent it to his daughter through a secret messenger, telling her that he was sending her this present to give her joy from what she loved most, just as she had given him joy from what he cherished most.

"When the messenger reached Ghismonda, he handed her the present and told her what he had been ordered to say. She took the goblet, lifted the lid, and immediately recognized its contents. Although she was torn by anguish, her courage did not fail her, and without moving a muscle, she replied: 'My friend, tell the marquis that he has acted wisely in one respect: he has given such a noble heart a fitting resting place, because only gold and precious stones would do it justice.' Then she bent down to the goblet and kissed the heart, lamenting: 'Oh, my sweet heart! Source of all my joy! Cursed be the cruelty of the one who forced me to see you like this, you who were always in my mind's eye! Now your noble life has come to an end through a tragic twist of fate, but in spite of this misfortune, your very enemy has given you the sepulchre that you so richly deserve. It is truly fitting, my dearest heart, that the last rites be performed by the one you loved so much and that you be washed and bathed by her tears. I'll not fail you in this. And your soul will not be denied the company of hers, because that would not be right. It will soon join yours. And yet, despite the harm treacherous Fortune has caused you, it is a blessing that my cruel father sent you to me, so I can honor you and talk to you before I leave this world and my soul joins yours; I crave its company, because I know that your spirit calls and desires mine.' Those were Ghismonda's words, and she said many other things that were so heartrending that anyone listening would have dissolved into tears. She wept so copiously that it was as if her eyes were two perpetual fountains pouring tears into the goblet. She made no sound and did not cry out but spoke softly, kissing the heart.

"The ladies and maidens who were with her were astonished at this because they knew nothing of what had happened and had no idea why she was in such anguish. Nevertheless, they all wept with her out of compassion for their mistress, and although they did their best to comfort her, they did not succeed. Those closest to her tried to find out the reason for her grief but in vain. When at last the brokenhearted Ghismonda could weep no more, she said: 'Oh, beloved heart, I have done all I could for you; all that is left now is to send my soul to keep yours company.' With these words, she rose and opened a chest, removing a small bottle in which she had dissolved poisonous herbs in water in case she ever needed them. She poured the liquid into the goblet containing the heart and drank it all, without the slightest fear. Then she lay down on her bed to await death, clutching the goblet to her chest. When her ladies saw her body change color, indicating that she was near death, they were horrified and summoned her father, who had gone out to try to forget his grief for a while. He arrived when the poison had already spread through his daughter's veins. Filled with anguish for what had happened and bitterly regretting what he had done, he spoke tender words to her in his grief, hoping to comfort her. His daughter, barely able to speak, replied: 'Tancredi, save your tears for someone else, because they have no business here, nor do I want them. You are like a snake that bites a man and then cries over him. Would it not have been better if your poor daughter had been allowed to enjoy her life, discreetly conducting a love affair with a worthy man, rather than you having to watch her tragic death as a result of your own cruelty and suffering great anguish even as you make a secret public knowledge?' Those were her last words. Her heart stopped while she clutched the goblet. The wretched old father died of grief, and so it was that Ghismonda, daughter of the prince of Salerno, ended her days."

60. Here she talks about Lisabetta and other lovers.

"Another story in Boccaccio's *Decameron* is about a young girl called Lisabetta, who lived in the city of Messina in Italy.[47] She had three brothers who were so miserly that they kept postponing her marriage. They had an assistant who managed all their affairs, a handsome and pleasant young man who had been raised by their father from birth. He and Lisabetta spent so much time together that they fell in love. They thoroughly enjoyed their love for some time but in the end, her brothers found out and took it as a terrible insult. They were not keen on making a great outcry about it, wanting to avoid bringing dishonor on their sister, so they decided to kill the young man. Accordingly, they took their assistant, whose name was Lorenzo, along to visit one of their estates one day. Upon their arrival there, they killed him in the garden and buried him among some trees. Then they went back to Messina and told their people that Lorenzo had been sent off on a faraway business trip.

"Lisabetta, who passionately loved the young man, was unhappy with his absence and her heart told her that something was amiss. One day, driven by the strength of her love, she couldn't stop herself from asking one of her brothers where they had sent Lorenzo. The brother arrogantly replied: 'What business is that of yours? If you keep talking about him, you will be in trouble!' That told Lisabetta that her brothers had discovered their affair, and she

47. Boccaccio, *Decameron* IV.5.

became convinced that Lorenzo had been murdered. When she was alone again, she was overwhelmed with grief. She never got any rest at night but cried so much, mourning the one she loved, that she fell ill. Using her illness as a pretext, she asked her brothers for permission to spend some time recovering on their estate outside the city. After receiving their permission and since she instinctively knew what had happened, she found herself alone in the garden where Lorenzo lay buried. Looking all over, she found a place where the soil had recently been disturbed to make a grave for Lorenzo. Using a spade she had brought, she dug through the soil until she found his body. Overcome by grief, she embraced his body, but realizing that she couldn't remain there too long for fear of being discovered, she reburied the body but took the head, which her brothers had cut off. She covered it with kisses, then wrapped it in a beautiful scarf and buried it in one of those big pots used for planting violets. On top of it, she planted some beautiful and sweet-smelling herbs called basil. Then she returned to the city, taking the pot with her. She was so attached to the pot that she couldn't bring herself, day or night, to leave the pot she had placed on the windowsill, and she watered it with nothing but her tears. While some men say that women have short memories, her grief did not abate after a few days but seemed to grow day by day. The basil grew thick and tall in the rich soil, and to cut a long story short, she lavished so much attention on the pot that some neighbors noticed how she kept weeping over it at the window. They told her brothers, who spied on her and saw the depth of her grief. Completely baffled by her behavior, they went in at night and stole the pot. The next morning, she was grief-stricken to find the pot missing. She implored them to give it back to her, promising them that she would turn over her share in the family property if they would return the pot. In her distress, she lamented: 'Alas! Under what evil star did my mother give birth to me, with such cruel brothers who so hate to see me enjoying a small pleasure that they won't let me have or give me back my poor pot of basil that cost them nothing! It is all I ask by way of a dowry. Alas! They won't give me anything!' The poor woman fell into such a state of anguish that she took to her bed and became very sick. As she lay ill, the only thing she asked for was her basil pot, refusing everything else that was offered to her. In the end, she died a miserable death. I don't think this story is made up, because people over there composed a song about this woman and her pot and they still sing it.

"What more can I tell you? I could quote you an endless number of stories about women overwhelmed by mad passion whose constancy in love is beyond doubt. Boccaccio tells a story about a woman whose husband made her eat the heart of her lover. She never ate again. The Dame de Fayel, who loved the Châtelain de Coucy, shared her fate. The Châtelaine de Vergy also died tormented by love, as did Isolde, besotted with Tristan. Deianira, in love with Hercules, also killed herself when he died. So you see, there is no doubt whatsoever that a strong woman who gives her heart is utterly faithful, although there are some women who do lack constancy.

"But these sad examples and many others I could quote you are not intended to encourage women to venture out into the perilous, damnable sea of mad passion, because that always ends in disaster and heartbreak, harming their body, their possessions, their honor, and above all, their soul. Sensible women have the wisdom to avoid this sort of passion and don't listen to men who keep trying to deceive them."

61. Here she talks about Juno and several other famous ladies.

"I have now told you about a great many ladies who are mentioned in history books. I don't propose to discuss them all, however, because that would be an endless task. So I see no need to present additional evidence to refute the opinions of the men you have quoted. I'll conclude by telling you about a few women who became more famous in the world as a result of things that happened to them by chance than for their great virtue.

"According to the poets and a misapprehension on the part of the pagans, Juno was the daughter of Saturn and Ops. She was more famous than any other woman of her faith, but this was due more to her good fortune than her outstanding qualities. She was both the sister and the wife of Jupiter, who was considered the leader of the gods. Given the opulent and prosperous life she shared with her husband, she was called the goddess of wealth. The inhabitants of Samos attributed their good fortune to a statue of this goddess that had come into their possession after her death, and considered her the patroness of the institution of marriage. Women prayed to her for help, and temples, altars, priests, games, and sacrifices were dedicated to her everywhere. The Greeks and Carthaginians venerated her for a long time. Her statue was later taken to Rome and placed in the Capitol in the temple of Jupiter, side by side with her husband. The Romans, rulers of the world, worshipped her for a long time in many different ceremonies.

"The story of Europa, the daughter of Agenor of Phoenicia, is a similar one: she became very famous because Jupiter was in love with her and gave her name to a third of the world. In fact, there are various cities and towns that have been named after women, such as England, named after a woman called Angela.

"Jocasta, the queen of Thebes, gained her fame through the dreadful misfortunes she suffered. In a tragic accident of fate, she married her son after he had killed his father. Neither she nor her son was aware of this, but when he discovered the truth, she witnessed his despair. She was also fated to see the two sons she had by him kill each other.

"Medusa, or the Gorgon, was famous for her outstanding beauty. She was the daughter of the very wealthy King Phorcys, whose prosperous kingdom was surrounded by the sea. As the ancient stories have it, this Medusa was so strikingly beautiful that she surpassed all other women. She had a lovely body and face and long, blond, curly hair like spun gold, but what is even more amazing and even supernatural is that she had such a bewitching gaze that she attracted and completely mesmerized all mortal creatures she looked at. That gave rise to the myth claiming that she turned people to stone.

"Helen, the wife of Menelaus, king of Lacedaemonia, and the daughter of Tyndareos, king of Sparta and Leda, his wife, was renowned for her great beauty. And because Troy was destroyed as a result of her abduction by Paris, the history books claim that she was the most beautiful woman who ever lived, regardless of what has been said about other beautiful women. It was for that reason that the poets claim she was the daughter of Jupiter himself.

"Then there was Polyxena, the youngest daughter of King Priam, who is also mentioned in historical accounts as a most beautiful maiden. She was also very steadfast and composed, as she proved when she was beheaded on the tomb of Achilles, her face expressionless, after she had declared that she preferred to die rather than be sent into slavery.

"I could give you many other examples, but I will stop here for the sake of brevity."

62. Here Christine talks about the claim that women entice men by being flirtatious and Lady Rectitude refutes it.

I, Christine, then said: "With respect to what you said before, my lady, I clearly see that sensible women should avoid the pitfalls of passion since they are likely to get hurt. But women who love wearing pretty clothes and accessories receive a great deal of criticism because people say they do this to seduce men."

Lady Rectitude replied: "My dear friend, it is not up to me to find excuses for women who are obsessed with dressing elaborately or elegantly because that is certainly a flaw and not a small one: outfits that are too elaborate to suit one's rank are objectionable. Nevertheless—and I say this not to excuse this flaw but to make sure that women who look pretty are not excessively criticized—I assure you that not all women do this to seduce men. Some people, both men and women, are just naturally inclined to enjoy elegance and attractive, rich clothing, cleanliness, and the finer things in life. If that is their nature, they will have great difficulty doing without them, although it would be to their credit if they did. Has it not been written about the apostle Bartholomew, who was a man of noble rank, that he wore robes of fringed silk decorated with precious stones all his life, despite the fact that our Lord preached poverty and austerity in all things? Bartholomew was naturally inclined to dress richly, and this may be seen as vain and ostentatious in other people. In him, however, this was not a sin, although some people say that this was the reason why Our Lord allowed Bartholomew to be flayed alive in his martyrdom.

"I tell you these things to show you that mortal creatures should not judge another's character based on his or her dress, because God alone has the right to judge us. Let me illustrate this with a few examples."

63. About Claudine from Rome.

"Both Boccaccio and Valerius recount that Claudine, a noble lady from Rome, loved beautiful clothes and extravagant, pretty accessories. Because she was more sophisticated in this respect than the other Roman ladies, some people spoke ill of her and her chastity, which harmed her reputation. It so happened that in the fifteenth year of the Second Punic War, the statue of Pessinus had to be transported to Rome. Pessinus was considered the mother of the gods. All the noble ladies of Rome assembled to greet her. The statue was loaded on a boat to sail up the Tiber, but the sailors were unable to reach the port despite their best efforts. Then Claudia, well aware of the unfair damage to her reputation caused by her appearance, knelt before the statue and prayed out loud, saying that the goddess knew that her chastity was intact and that she remained pure, and that she should therefore grant her the privilege of pulling the boat into port by herself. Confident in her purity, she took her belt, tied it to the boat's gunwales, and to everyone's amazement, pulled it to shore as easily as if all the sailors in the world had been there to help her.

"I did not give you this example because I believe that the statue, which the foolish pagans called a goddess, had the power to answer her prayers, but to show you that such a pretty woman could still be chaste. What she proved was her conviction that the truth about her chastity would come to her aid, not the goddess."

64. Lady Rectitude explains that some women are loved more for their virtue than other women are for their pretty looks.

"If we were to suppose that the reason why women put so much effort in making themselves look pretty and seductive is that they want to be loved, I'll prove to you that this does not necessarily mean that sensible and respectable men will fall in love with them more quickly and deeply. In fact, men who care about honor will be more readily and deeply attracted to women who are virtuous, honest, and humble, even if they are less attractive than the most fashionable females. Now you could counter that if women attract men through their virtue and honesty and it's a bad thing to attract them in the first place, it would be better if women were less virtuous. But that is not a valid argument, because it is wrong to stop cultivating good and useful things merely because fools abuse them. We must all do our best to devote ourselves to doing the right things, regardless of the outcome. And I'll give you some examples to prove to you that many women are loved for their virtues and integrity. I'll start out by telling you about several saints from Paradise who were desired by men because of their integrity.

"Take Lucretia, whose rape I have mentioned to you before.[48] It was her great integrity that caused Tarquin to fall in love with her, more than her beauty. One night, her husband was having supper with a group of knights that included Tarquin, the man who subsequently raped Lucretia. During the meal, they started talking about their wives, each claiming that his was the most virtuous of all. To determine the truth and prove which one was the most praiseworthy, they mounted their horses and rode home. Those wives found occupied with the most honest tasks were held in the greatest esteem. Among all the wives, it was Lucretia who was judged to be the most virtuous. A wise and sensible woman dressed in a simple gown, she was sitting with the other ladies of her household, working with wool and discussing uplifting subjects. Tarquin, the king's son, had accompanied her husband, and when

---

48. See II.44.

he saw her integrity, her simple, pleasant bearing, and her modesty, he fell so acutely in love with her that he started planning the outrage he was to commit later on."

65. Here she talks about Queen Blanche, the mother of Saint Louis, and other good and wise ladies who were loved for their virtue.

"Similarly, the most noble Blanche, queen of France and mother of Saint Louis, was loved by the count of Champagne for her great wisdom, prudence, virtue, and kindness even though she had already passed the flower of her youth.[49] The noble count paid close attention to the queen's wise words and listened to her sensible comments when he had gone to war against the king, Saint Louis. The wise queen expressed her disapproval, telling him he should not have done so, considering all the favors her son had done him. The count looked at her intently, amazed at her kindness and virtue, and felt so much love for her well up in him that he did not know what to do. He felt he would rather die than voice his feelings, aware that her sense of propriety would never allow her to love him back. From that time onward, he suffered terribly on account of the mad passion that ruled him. Nevertheless, he replied that she should not worry about him waging war on the king but that he would always be his loyal subject, adding that he would always remain at her command, body and soul and with everything he possessed.[50] He loved her all his life even though he had faint hope of ever seeing his love returned. He composed poems, addressing his laments to Love, singing the lady's praise. These lovely poems were set to delightful music, and he had them inscribed on the walls of his great halls both in Provins and Troyes, where they can still be seen today. I could give you many more similar examples."

Then I, Christine, replied: "You are right, my lady. I myself have seen cases such as you describe. I know some virtuous and wise women who have confessed to me their displeasure at finding themselves courted more now that their beauty and youth have faded than when they were in their prime. They complained, saying: 'My God! What can this mean? Do these men see some

---

49. Queen Blanche de Castille (1188–1252) acted as regent after the death of her husband Louis VIII. In 1234 she passed on power to her son Louis IX (i.e., Saint Louis).

50. Queen Blanche will also be important for Christine's *Treasure of the City of Ladies*. See I.9, where the queen is praised for her peacemaking ability, and I.23, where she is praised for her charity and generosity.

strange impropriety in my behavior that gives them reason to think I would agree to commit such foolishness?' Thanks to what you have told me, I now see that it was their great virtue that caused them to be loved. That is completely contrary to the views of many people who say that modest women wishing to remain chaste will never be courted or desired unless they want to be."

66. Christine addresses Lady Rectitude on the topic of those who claim that women are naturally greedy, and Lady Rectitude refutes that claim.

"I don't know what else to ask you, my dear lady, because all my questions have been answered. It seems to me that you have completely refuted the slanderous things so many men say about women. Even the oft-repeated claim that greed is a natural trait among female vices does not appear to be true.

Reply: "My dear friend, let me assure you that greed does not come any more naturally to women than to men. In fact, women are probably less greedy, as God knows and you can see for yourself, because greedy men inflict far more evil upon the world than women. But as I told you before, a fool is all too ready to see the mote in his neighbor's eye but fails to see the beam is his own.

"Just because women commonly take pleasure in collecting fabrics, thread, and other things that are useful in a household, they are called greedy. But I promise you, there are many, even a great many women who, if they had any money, would not be greedy or parsimonious in doing honorable things and giving generously to the needy. But what can a poor person do if she has nothing to give? Women are generally kept so short of money that they zealously guard the little they have, because they know how difficult it is to acquire more.

"Some people even accuse women of avarice because they have wayward husbands who waste large amounts of money on goods and food. Their poor wives, knowing the money their husbands spend so foolishly is needed to run the household and aware that they and their poor children will wind up paying the price, have no choice but to bring this matter up to their husbands and urge them to curb their spending. That is not a matter of greed or parsimony but a sign of great prudence. I am, of course, referring only to those who do this discreetly. One sees so many marital arguments because husbands don't like being admonished and wind up criticizing their wives when they should actually be praising them.

"Proof that the vice of greed is not as common to women as some claim it is can be found in the fact that they generously give alms. God knows how many prisoners, even in the lands of the Saracens, how many poor, how many needy noblemen and others in this world have been comforted and still are being supported by women and their money and goods."

I, Christine, said: "Indeed, my lady, what you are telling me reminds me of honorable women I have seen discreetly giving what they could spare. I know some today who take more pleasure in saying: 'Here, take this!' to someone in need than a greedy man in hoarding money in a coffer. I don't know why so many men say that women are greedy. They say that Alexander the Great was generous, but I can tell you that I have never seen any men who were."

Then Lady Rectitude started to laugh and said: "My dear, the Roman ladies certainly weren't greedy when their city was ruined by the war and the city's entire treasury had been spent on soldiers' pay. So the men were distraught and had a terrible time finding a way to raise money for the army they had to mount. But the ladies, even the widows, proved their generosity by collecting all their jewelry and everything they owned without keeping anything back and freely donating it to the princes of Rome. They were highly praised for their action and their jewelry was returned to them later on. Rightly so, because it was thanks to them that Rome was saved."

67. Here she talks about the generosity of a rich lady called Busa.

"Women's generosity is also referred to in the *Faits des Romains*.[51] It mentions a rich, virtuous lady called Busa or Paulina. She lived in the land of Apulia at the time when Hannibal was waging war on the Romans by fire and sword, pillaging almost all of Italy and massacring its men. After the terrible defeat at Cannae, where Hannibal won a great victory, many wounded Romans who had survived the battle escaped and fled. The valiant and very wealthy lady Busa took in as many men as she could, providing shelter to some ten thousand of them on her various properties. She had them recover at her expense

51. The *Acts of the Romans* was a popular medieval vernacular compilation of various extant Roman sources depicting the life of Caesar dated to ca. 1213. Boccaccio's praise of Busa is notable in chap. 69 of *Famous Women*. According to Christine, Busa's generosity is one example among many more possible stories.

and supported them financially until, thanks to her help and comfort, they were able to return to Rome and put the army back on its feet. She was highly praised for her actions. My dear friend, I could tell you numerous other stories about women's largesse, kindness, and generosity.

"Even without going back into the past, I could quote you many other examples of women's generosity today. Take, for instance, the amazing largesse of Lady Marguerite de la Rivière, who is still alive today. She was the wife of the late Lord Bureau de la Rivière, first chamberlain to King Charles the Wise, and she has always been known as a wise, courteous, and well-bred lady. One day, she attended a big party being held in Paris by the duke of Anjou who would eventually become the king of Sicily. There was a large crowd of noble ladies, knights, and gentlemen, all richly dressed. As this lady, young and pretty, watched all the knights assembled there, she noticed the absence of a famous knight with a great reputation by the name of Sir Amanieu de Pommiers. He was quite old then and has since died, and although she didn't think he would remember her, she remembered him for his kindness and merit. Feeling that there could be no greater jewel in such a gathering than the presence of noteworthy and famous men, even if they were old, she asked around to discover why this knight was missing from the assembly. She learned that he was imprisoned in the Châtelet in Paris because of a debt of five hundred francs that he had incurred during his frequent travel to attend tournaments. 'Oh no!' said the noble lady, 'what a disgrace for this kingdom to tolerate having a man of this caliber imprisoned for even a single hour!' Then she removed the splendid gold diadem from her head and put a wreath of periwinkle in her blond hair. She gave the diadem to a messenger and told him: 'Go and hand over this diadem as a pledge for what this gentleman owes and see to it that he is released immediately.' This was no sooner said than done, and she was greatly praised for her action."

68. Here she talks about princesses and great ladies from France.

Then I, Christine, spoke up again: "My lady, since you recalled this lady who is still alive today and are now discussing the history of ladies from France or those who live there, could you please tell me what you think of them and if it would be a good idea if some of them were to be lodged in our city? Why should they be overlooked in favor of foreign women?"

Lady Rectitude replied: "Certainly, Christine, let me assure you that there are many virtuous ladies among them, and it would please me to see them included as citizens. First of all, there is Isabeau of Bavaria, the noble queen of France now reigning over us by the grace of God, who will certainly not be refused entry.[52] She has not a hint of cruelty, greed, or any sort of vice in her body and is always kind and benevolent toward her subjects.

"Another lady no less worthy of praise is the fair young duchess of Berry, wife of Duke John, who is a son of the late King John of France and a brother of King Charles the Wise. This wise, noble duchess conducted herself so honorably and sensibly while still in the flower of her youth that everyone praises her and talks about her great virtue.

"What about the duchess of Orléans, daughter of the late duke of Milan, wife of Duke Louis, who is the son of Charles the Wise, king of France? Could you name me anyone more sensible than she is? She is strong and steadfast in her affections and devoted to her husband, she has given her children an excellent education and conducts her affairs with competence, she is fair to all, sensible in her conduct, and virtuous in all things. She is remarkable.

"And can anyone say anything to the detriment of the duchess of Burgundy, wife of Duke John, who is the son of Philip the Bold, son of the late French king John the Good? Is she not remarkably virtuous, faithful to her husband, good-natured and well mannered, with impeccable moral values and devoid of a single vice?

"And the countess of Clermont, daughter of the aforementioned Duke John Berry and his first wife, and the wife of Count John of Clermont, son

---

52. According to Tracy Adams in *Christine de Pizan and the Fight for France* (University Park: Pennsylvania State University Press, 2014), esp. 113ff, this mention of Isabeau of Bavaria is highly significant and not only points to a key intent of Christine in this work but is also linked to an important theme running through her writing, namely, support for the Armagnacs in their long-standing struggles against the Burgundians over influence and succession in the French monarchy (although here we see Christine cautiously praise ladies from the Burgundian camp as well). Adams suggests that Christine resorts here to a rhetorical strategy to present Isabeau as the culmination of a series of ladies who all share the qualities of love, loyalty, and patience with the Virgin Mary, in order to bolster the queen's appointed role as the mediator between the feuding dukes. As wife of Charles VI, Isabeau took on increasing power in the wake of her husband's progressively worse attacks of mental illness. Still, her standing and influence in the regime did not remain uncontested. It was, most notably, challenged by the king's brother Louis of Orléans and his uncle the duke of Burgundy. Despite the attempts of the Burgundians to discount and disqualify the supporters of Louis and his descendants the Armagnacs, Adams argues that Christine saw the position of the latter as more justified.

of the duke of Bourbon and heir to the duchy: does she not embody the ideal model of what a high-born princess should be? She adores her husband, has impeccable manners at all times, and is beautiful and kind. In short, her gracious and noble conduct mirrors her virtues.

"And what about the lady of whom you are particularly fond for her great virtue and to whom you feel attached thanks to the favors she has done you out of charity and love? I am talking about the noble duchess of Holland and countess of Hainaut, daughter of the late Duke Philip of Burgundy and sister of the present duke. Shouldn't this lady be included in the ranks of perfect women? She is loyal, wise in conducting her affairs, charitable, devoted to God, in short, a paragon.

"And the countess of Bourbon, greatly honored and worthy of praise in all things: shouldn't she also be cited among the illustrious princesses I've mentioned?

"What more should I tell you? It would take forever to list the great merits of all these ladies.

"The beautiful, noble, and wise countess of Saint-Pol, daughter of the duke of Bar, full cousin to the king of France, should also be included in the ranks of the most exemplary women.

"And then there is your beloved Anne, daughter of the late count of La Marche and sister to the present count, wife of Ludwig of Bavaria who is the brother of the queen of France. She would certainly not disgrace the ranks of these noble and praiseworthy ladies, because her great virtues are acknowledged by God and the whole world.

"Despite what is being said by malicious tongues, there are so many good and noble women among the countesses, baronesses, ladies, damsels, bourgeoisies, and women of all classes that we should thank God for keeping them. May He reform those who lack virtue! You should not have any doubts on that score, because in spite of slanderous and envious men claiming the opposite, I assure you it is the truth."

And I, Christine, replied as follows: "My lady, hearing this from you is pure joy." And she replied: "My dear friend, it seems to me that I have now adequately acquitted myself of the task I set myself for the City of Ladies. I have built splendid palaces and many nice inns and mansions, and I have populated the city for you with so many noble ladies of all ranks that it is now completely filled. Now it is time for my sister Justice to complete the task, and that should suffice."

69. Christine addresses herself to princesses and all other women.

"Most excellent, revered, and honored princesses of France and all other countries, all you ladies and maidens and, indeed, all of you who have ever cared about virtue and morality, including the generations to come, all of you from the past, present, and future: rejoice and be jubilant about our new City. With God's help, its construction is now almost finished, its dwellings completed, and its population nearly all present. Render thanks to God who has guided me in my great labor and my studies, undertaken in my desire to provide you with worthy lodgings where you will be able to reside for all eternity within the walls of a city. I have come this far and hope to go on and finish my task with the help of Lady Justice, who has promised that she will do all she can to help me complete and perfect the City. My distinguished ladies: I ask you to pray for me."

Here ends the second part of The Book of the City of Ladies.

Here begins the third part of The Book of the City of Ladies, *which explains
who completed the tall roofs of the towers, how this was done, and which
noble ladies were chosen to reside in the great palaces and soaring towers.*[1]

1. The first chapter tells how Lady Justice led the Queen of Heaven into the City of Ladies to take up residence there.

Then Lady Justice turned to me in her distinguished fashion and said: "Christine, to tell you the truth, I think you have worked hard and done your very best, with the help of my sisters, to finish the construction of the City of Ladies. Now it is time that I, too, honor my promise to help you with what remains to be done, to wit, bringing the most excellent Queen, blessed among women, to take up residence here with her noble retinue so she can govern and manage the city. Many of the distinguished ladies from her court and household can move here with her, because I see that the palaces and imposing mansions are prepared and all the streets covered with flowers, ready to receive her and her retinue of honored, distinguished ladies.

"Now I invite them to come forward, the princesses, ladies, and all the other women, to bid a reverent welcome to the lady who is not only their Queen but who also controls and governs all powers ever created thanks to

---

1. The third part of the *City of Ladies* is where Christine most radically departs from Boccaccio, who insisted that it was inappropriate to discuss pagan and Christian women side by side within the same book, partially because these "two groups do not harmonize very well with each other, and they appear to proceed in different ways" (see the Preface of his *Famous Women*). For a helpful general treatment of medieval hagiography and its evolution, see the introduction of Thomas Head, *Medieval Hagiography: An Anthology* (New York: Garland, 2000); Renate Blumenfeld-Kosinski and Timea Szell, ed., *Images of Sainthood in Medieval Europe* (Ithaca, N.Y.: Cornell University Press, 1991); Peter Brown, *The Cult of the Saints: Its Rise and Function in Latin Christianity*, 2nd ed. (Chicago: University of Chicago Press, 2015).

the only Son, whom she carried and conceived from the Holy Spirit and who is the Son of God the Father.[2] All women gathered here should pray that this most excellent, sovereign princess sees fit to humbly reside among them in their city and community here below without disdain for their insignificance compared to her exaltedness. But you can be sure that her incomparable humility and angelic benevolence will not let her refuse to take up residence in the City of Ladies and occupy the highest position in the building my sister Rectitude has prepared for her: a palace entirely constructed of glory and praise. Let all the women accompany me and say to her:

"'We greet you, Queen of the Heavens, with the salutation the angel addressed to you when he said *Hail Mary*, which pleases you above all. We, the devout female sex, beg you not to feel loath to live among us but to have the grace and compassion to be our defender, patroness, and guard against all attacks by our enemies and the world at large. May they drink from the fountain of virtues that flows from you and quench their thirst so completely that they abhor all sins and vices. Come to us, Celestial Queen, Temple of God, Cell and Cloister of the Holy Spirit, Vessel of the Trinity, Joy of the Angels, Star and Guide to those who have lost their way, Hope of the True Believers! Oh my lady, who could ever have the audacity to revile the female sex considering your splendor? Even if all other women were wicked, the light of your virtue shines so brightly that it would eclipse all evil. And since God chose his bride from among our sex, most excellent Lady, men should not only refrain from criticizing women but revere them in honor of you.'

"The Virgin replied: 'Oh Justice, my son's precious friend, it would give me great pleasure to dwell among you women, my sisters and friends, for Reason, Rectitude, you, and even Nature prompt me to do so. You serve, revere, and honor me and I am and always will be the head of the female sex. That is what God the Father had in mind from the beginning, foreseen and ordained by the Holy Trinity.'"

Then Lady Justice and all the women knelt and bowed their heads as she replied: "My Lady, may praise and gratitude be rendered to you for all eternity. Save us, my Lady, and pray for us to your son, who refuses you nothing."

---

2. That the Virgin Mary should be queen of the city is not that odd given how strong the cult of Mary had become by the fourteenth century. In France, this cult was nourished by Gautier de Coinci's popular *Miracles of the Virgin Mary*—with which Christine was familiar (see II.51). Interested readers can consult Head, *Medieval Hagiography*, chap. 28.

2. About Our Lady's sisters and Mary Magdalene.

"Now the incomparable Empress resides among us, whether this pleases the malicious slanderers or not. Her blessed sisters and Mary Magdalene, who faithfully kept her company by the Cross throughout the Passion of her son, should also accompany her here. Oh! What strong faith and deep love women displayed by always standing by the Son of God in life and in death, He who had been abandoned and renounced by all His apostles. That certainly made it clear that God did not scorn women's love as if it were something weak, as some men contend. On the contrary: by lighting a flame of such great love in the hearts of the blessed Mary Magdalene and the other women, He showed His approval."

3. About Saint Catherine.[3]

"To keep the blessed Queen of the Heavens, our empress and princess of the City of Ladies company, we should also provide lodgings for the blessed virgins and holy ladies. To show how much God approved of the female sex, He gave young, delicate women the constancy and strength to tolerate dreadful torment for the sake of His holy faith, just as He gave this to men. These women are crowned with glory and the stories of their lives, beautiful to hear, are more edifying to all other women than anything else. That is why they will be the most highly revered women in our city.[4]

"Let us start with the most excellent and blessed Catherine, daughter of King Costus of Alexandria. This holy virgin became her father's sole heir at the age of eighteen. She admirably governed herself and her inheritance, but being a Christian and having dedicated her life to God, she refused to marry. One day, Emperor Maxentius[5] came to the city of Alexandria on the occasion

---

3. This fourth-century martyr was the patron saint of young girls. In Christine's *Treasure of the City of Ladies* (III.5), Saint Catherine's life is singled out as particularly worthy of study for the cultivation of virtue in young women.

4. The chief source used by Christine in Part III is Jean de Vignay's French translation of Vincent de Beauvais' *Speculum historiale* [Mirror of history], a very lengthy history of the world (up to the 1240s). Another source used is Jean Le Fèvre de Ressons' *Livre de Leesce* (a late fourteenth-century text lauding women, whose chief purpose was to respond to Matheolus' *Lamentations*). See Renate Blumenfeld-Kosinski, "'Femme de corps et femme de sens': Christine de Pizan's saintly women," *Romantic Review* 87, no. 2 (1996): 157–75; cf. Quilligan, *Allegory of Female Authority*, esp. 189–244.

5. Roman emperor from 306 until 312 CE.

of an important celebration of their gods. He had made elaborate arrangements for the great sacrifice. Catherine was in her palace when she heard the blare of musical instruments and the bellowing of the animals being prepared for the sacrifice, so she sent someone over to find out what was going on. When she learned that the emperor was already in the temple making sacrifices to the gods, she rushed over there. Using all the eloquence at her disposal, she tried to convince him that he was doing the wrong thing. Since she was highly educated in theology and well versed in the sciences, she used philosophical arguments to prove that there is but one God, the Creator of all things, and that He alone should be worshipped and no one else. Hearing this beautiful, noble maiden speak with such authority, the emperor was astounded and did not know what to say, but he watched her intently. Then he sent for the wisest philosophers of all of Egypt, which was famous in the field of philosophy at that time. When they discovered why they had been summoned, they were displeased and said it had been foolish to cause them to travel from faraway places merely to have a debate with a maiden.

"To make a long story short, the blessed Catherine threw so many arguments at them on the day of the debate that they didn't know how to counter them and became completely convinced. The emperor was greatly vexed by this but to no avail: by the grace of God, the virgin's holy words convinced them all to convert and profess the name of Jesus Christ. The emperor punished them by having them burnt at the stake, but the holy virgin comforted them in their martyrdom, assuring them they would be received in eternal glory, praying to God to sustain them in their true faith. Thanks to her, they joined the ranks of the holy martyrs. Then God made a great miracle happen: the fire did not destroy either their bodies or their clothing. When the fire had gone out, the men had lost not a single hair; they remained whole and their faces looked as if they were still alive.

"Then the tyrannical Maxentius, who lusted after the blessed Catherine for her beauty, began an assiduous courtship in an attempt to bend her to his will, but when he realized that this had no effect, he tried threats and then torture. He had her severely beaten and thrown into jail in solitary confinement for twelve days, thinking he would weaken her with hunger, but our Lord's angels were with her and comforted her. When she was brought before the emperor at the end of the twelve days, he saw that she looked fitter and healthier than before. Convinced that she must have had visitors, he gave orders for the prison guards to be tortured, but Catherine felt sorry for them and assured him that the only comfort she had received came from

Heaven. The emperor, at his wit's end, tried to think of an even harsher form of torture. He consulted his prefect, who suggested he should have wheels built that were covered with razors. With the wheels turning against each other, anything between them would be cut to pieces. He had Catherine tied between these wheels, naked. She continued to worship God, her hands folded in prayer. Then the angels descended and broke the wheels apart with such force that those administering the torture were killed.

"When the emperor's wife heard of the miracles God had performed, she converted and condemned her husband's cruelty. She went to visit the holy virgin in prison and asked her to pray to God on her behalf. The emperor found out and had her tortured as well, ordering her breasts torn off. The virgin told her: 'Do not fear torture, noble queen, for today you will be blessed with eternal joy.' Thereupon the tyrant had his wife beheaded, along with a large number of other people who had also converted. He asked Catherine to be his wife, and when he saw that she continued to reject his entreaties, he decided to have her beheaded as well. She said her final prayers, begging for God's grace for all those who would remember her suffering and call upon her in their trials and tribulations. Then a voice came from Heaven, announcing that her prayer had been granted. Thus she was martyred and milk flowed from her body instead of blood. The angels took her holy body and carried it to Mount Sinai, some twenty days' travel away, and buried it there. God has performed many miracles at her tomb, which I will not describe for the sake of brevity, but I will say that the oil that flows from this tomb cures many diseases. As to Emperor Maxentius, God inflicted a horrible punishment on him."

4. About Saint Margaret.

"Let us also remember the blessed virgin Saint Margaret, whose story is well known.[6] Born in Antioch[7] of noble parents, she was introduced to the true faith at an early age by her nurse, whose sheep she humbly tended every day. One day, Olybrius, the emperor's prefect, saw her as he was passing and fell in love with her. He had her summoned, and to make a long story short, he wound up having her severely beaten and thrown into jail because she would not submit to his will and confessed to being a Christian. While in jail, she

6. Indeed it was: the story of Saint Margaret was one of the most popular in medieval times. Miniatures of her torture and death were widely used in medieval manuscripts.

7. An important city for the birth of Christianity, Antioch was located in what is today Turkey.

felt she was being put to the test and prayed God to give form to whoever was seeking to do her so much harm. Then a horrible dragon appeared that scared her out of her wits and devoured her, but she made the Sign of the Cross and split open its stomach. Thereupon, in a corner of her cell, she saw a figure as black as an Ethiopian. Margaret bravely advanced on him, threw him down on the floor, and put her foot on his throat while he uttered loud cries for mercy. The prison filled with light and Margaret was comforted by the angels.

"She was brought back before the judge, who saw that his threats were having no effect and had her tortured worse than before. But God's Angel appeared and delivered her from her torment. The virgin escaped completely unscathed, and many people converted to the faith. Seeing this, the cruel tyrant ordered her beheaded. She first said her prayers, begging for God's grace for all those who would remember her suffering and call upon her in their trials and tribulations, and for pregnant women and their babies. Then the Angel of God appeared, telling her that her prayer had been heard and that she would receive her palm of victory in the name of God. Then she stretched her neck and was beheaded. The angels carried away her soul.

"The evil Olybrius also had the holy virgin Regina, a young girl of fifteen, tortured and beheaded because she would not submit to his will and had converted many people with her sermons."

5. Here she talks about Saint Lucy.

"We should also include in our list the blessed Saint Lucy, a virgin born in Rome. She was kidnapped and taken away by King Aucejas of Barbary. On his return to his country, he decided to rape her, but she started to preach so eloquently that, with God's help, he forgot his evil intentions. He was astonished at her wisdom and said she must be a goddess. He installed her in his palace with great honor and reverence, provided her and her retinue with glorious apartments, and issued orders that no man enter them to disturb her.

"She spent all her time fasting and praying, leading a holy life and begging God to enlighten her host. Aucejas consulted her about all his affairs and followed all her advice. When he went to war, he asked her to pray to her god on his behalf. She blessed him and when he returned victorious, he wanted to worship her as a goddess and erect temples in her honor. She told him to desist, explaining that there was but one God to worship and that she was only a simple sinner.

"After she had led this holy life for twenty years, Our Lord told her to return to Rome, revealing that she would finish her life there in martyrdom.

She informed the king, who was deeply saddened and said: 'Alas! If you leave me, my enemies will attack me, and I will lose my good fortune if you're no longer with me.' She replied: 'Sire, come with me and leave your earthly kingdom behind. God has chosen you to acquire a much nobler kingdom that will last for eternity.' At these words, he abandoned everything and accompanied the holy virgin, not as her lord but as her servant. When they arrived in Rome and she proclaimed herself a Christian, she was arrested and taken away to be martyred. Mad with grief, King Aucejas ran after her. He would have gladly killed her tormenters, but she told him to refrain. He wept bitter tears, shouting that those who wanted to harm God's holy virgin were evil people. When the time came to behead her, the king went and placed his head next to hers, crying: 'I am a Christian and offer my head to Jesus Christ, the living God worshipped by Lucy!' Thereupon they were both beheaded together and crowned with glory, along with twelve others who had been converted by the blessed Lucy. They are celebrated together seven days after the calends of July."

6. Here she talks about the blessed virgin Martina.

"We should also be sure to include the blessed virgin Martina. This saint, a great beauty, was born in Rome of noble parents. When the emperor wanted to force her to become his wife, she replied: 'I am a Christian and devoted to the living God, who treasures a chaste body and a pure heart. I consecrate myself to Him and entrust myself to His care.' Enraged by these words, the emperor had her taken to a temple to force her to worship the idols. Once there, she fell to her knees, her eyes fixed on the Heavens, her hands clasped together, and prayed to God. At once, the idols started to crack and fall, the temple collapsed, and the priests serving the idols were killed. The devil residing in the chief idol cried out and proclaimed that Martina was the servant of God. The tyrannical emperor had Martina subjected to a cruel torment in order to avenge his gods, but God appeared to her and comforted her.[8] She prayed for her tormentors, who were converted through her efforts, along with many other people. The emperor became even more determined than before, giving orders for her to undergo still more cruel tortures, but those who tortured her exclaimed that they were seeing God and His saints standing before her. They begged for mercy and were converted. As she continued to pray to God for

---

8. Tradition suggests that Martina was tortured and beheaded during the reign of Emperor Alexander Severus (222–235 CE).

her torturers, a light shone upon them and a voice was heard from Heaven, proclaiming: 'I grant you mercy for the love of my cherished Martina.' Seeing them converted, the prefect shouted: 'You fools! This enchantress Martina has cast a spell on you!' But they were unafraid and replied: 'It is you who have been bewitched by the devil that dwells in you, because you do not recognize your Creator!' Enraged, the emperor ordered them hanged and quartered, but they received their martyrdom with joy, praising God.

"Then the emperor had Martina stripped naked. The spectators were enchanted with the beauty of her lily-white body. The emperor, who still lusted after her, spent a long time trying to convince her, but when he realized that she would not obey him, he ordered her body slashed. What poured from her wounds, however, was not blood but milk, and she exuded a sweet scent. Even more enraged, he had her body stretched and attached to stakes to break every bone in her body. But those charged with carrying out this torture became exhausted, because God was making sure Martina lived long enough to convince them and the spectators to be converted. The torturers exclaimed: 'Emperor, we cannot carry on because the angels are beating us with chains!' Fresh torturers arrived but they died on the spot. The emperor, shaken, was at his wit's end. He had her body stretched and covered with burning oil, but she never stopped glorifying God and a sweet scent emanated from her mouth. When the torturers became exhausted, they threw her into a dark dungeon. Aemilius, the emperor's cousin, went to keep an eye on her in prison and saw Martina seated on a beautifully adorned throne, surrounded by angels. Her cell was filled with light and the sound of mellifluous music. She was holding a golden tablet upon which she had written: 'Sweet Lord Jesus Christ, your work is lauded through your blessed saints.' Astounded by this sight, Aemilius went to tell the emperor, who replied that he had been tricked by Martina's spells. The next day, the emperor had her brought out, and everyone was amazed at seeing her completely healed. This caused many more people to convert.

"The emperor had her taken back to the temple to force her once again to worship the false gods. Then the devil, residing in the idol, began to moan. 'Alas! Alas! I admit defeat!' The virgin ordered him to come out and show himself in all his hideousness. Then a loud thunderclap sounded and a bolt of lightning struck from above, overturning the idol and burning the priests to death.

"The emperor, out of his mind with rage, had her stretched out and flayed by iron hooks. Martina continued to pray to God, and when he saw that she was still alive and still worshipping God, he had her thrown to wild beasts to have them devour her. A huge lion that had not eaten for three days approached her and bowed down before her. Then it lay down as if it were a pet dog and started licking her wounds. Martina blessed our Lord, saying: 'May You be praised, oh Lord, who tames the ferocity of these savage beasts through Your virtue alone!' Infuriated at these words, the emperor ordered the lion to be taken back to its pit, but the lion reared up in a great fury and leapt at the emperor's cousin, killing him on the spot. The emperor, deeply upset by his cousin's death, ordered Martina to be thrown into a blazing fire. As Martina stood there surrounded by flames and filled with joy, God sent a great wind that moved the fire away from her but burned her tormentors.

"Now the emperor ordered her beautiful long hair to be cut, declaring that her power of enchantment came from her hair. The virgin replied: 'If you cut off my hair, which the Apostle called a woman's glory, so the Lord will take away your empire and persecute you until you die a most painful death.' The emperor reacted by ordering her locked up in a temple dedicated to his gods. He himself locked and nailed the door shut and affixed his own seal. When he returned three days later, he found his idols knocked down and the virgin playing with the angels, safe and sound. The emperor demanded to know what she had done with his gods. She replied: 'The power of Jesus Christ has destroyed them.' The emperor ordered her throat cut, but then a voice was heard from Heaven, saying: 'Martina, oh noble virgin, you have fought in my name and shall therefore enter My Kingdom with the saints and rejoice with me for all eternity.' And this is how the blessed Martina reached the end of her life. The bishop of Rome, accompanied by all his clergy, came and gave the body an honorable burial in the church. That same day, the emperor, whose name was Alexander, was stricken with such unbearable pain that he devoured his own flesh."

7. Here she talks about a virgin named Saint Lucy and some other virgins who were also martyred.[9]

"There was a second Saint Lucy, who came from the city of Syracuse. As she was praying one day for her ailing mother at the tomb of Saint Agatha, she

---

9. On the significance of virginity in Christine's defense of the female sex, see Christine Reno, "Virginity as an Ideal in Christine de Pizan's *Cité des Dames*," in *Ideals for Women in the Works of Christine de Pizan*, ed. Diane Bornstein (Detroit: Michigan Consortium for Medieval and Early Modern Studies, 1981), 69–90. For more general treatments of virginity and chastity in the Middle Ages, see Ruth M. Karras, *Sexuality in Medieval Europe*, 2nd ed. (New York: Routledge, 2012); Ruth Evans, Sara Salih, and Anke Bernau, *Medieval Virginities* (Toronto: University of Toronto Press, 2003).

had a vision. She beheld Saint Agatha surrounded by angels, adorned with precious jewels, saying: 'Lucy, my sister, virgin devoted to God, why are you asking me for what you can give your mother yourself? Let me tell you that just as the city of Catania became exalted through me, you can do the same for Syracuse, because you have given Jesus Christ the priceless gift of your purity.' Lucy arose and her mother was healed. Then she gave away everything she had for the love of God and ended her life in martyrdom. Among the many tribulations she endured, a judge threatened to send her to a house of prostitution where she would be raped despite her vows to her heavenly bridegroom. She replied: 'The soul can never be tainted unless the mind consents. If you have my virginity taken from me by force, my chastity and victory will be twice as strong.' When they tried to take her to the brothel, she grew so heavy that neither oxen nor any other animals to which they tied her were able to move her. They tied ropes to her feet to drag her there, but she was as immovable as a mountain. As she lay dying, she prophesied the future of the empire.

"Another virgin worthy of great reverence is the glorious Saint Benedicta, born in Rome. She was accompanied by twelve virgins who had been converted by her sermons. Anxious to spread the Christian faith through her preaching, she and her companions set out on a journey. The blessed virgins traveled far and wide without any fear, for God was with them. It was Our Lord's wish, however, that they separate from each other and spread out over different countries so each one could make herself useful. When the holy virgin Benedicta had converted several countries to the faith of Jesus Christ, she received the palm of martyrdom, as did her blessed companions.

"Another virgin, the fourteen-year-old Saint Fausta, was no less righteous. Emperor Maximianus[10] had her cut up with an iron saw because she refused to make sacrifices to the idols. The men in charge of the cutting worked from the hour of terce to none[11] and still hadn't even managed to scratch her, so they asked: 'How do you do it? Are you using your spells, since we haven't managed to accomplish anything after all this time?' Then Fausta started to preach about Jesus Christ and his faith and she converted them. The emperor was furious about this and ordered her tortured by various means, such as having a thousand nails hammered into her head that made her look as if she

---

10. Famous for his persecution of Christians, Marcus Aurelius Valerius Maximianus was emperor from ca. 286 to 305 CE. See also III.9 and III.16.

11. These terms refer to Christian divisions of the day for prayer. We are told here that Saint Fausta was tortured roughly from 9:00 am (terce) until 3:00 pm (none).

were wearing a knight's helmet. Fausta kept on praying for her persecutors and even the prefect was converted when he saw the heavens open up and God sitting among his angels. When Fausta was submerged in a cauldron of boiling water, the prefect cried out: 'Holy servant of God, do not go without me!" and jumped into the cauldron. When the two other people she had converted saw this, they also leapt into the cauldron. Fausta touched them in the rapidly boiling water and they felt no pain. She said to them: 'I am in your midst like a vine bearing fruit, because our Lord has said that when several people are gathered in His name, He is in their midst.' Then a voice was heard, saying: 'Come, blessed souls, your Father is calling you.' When they heard this, they joyfully rendered their souls."

8. Here she talks about Saint Justine and some other virgins.

"Justine was a very young and beautiful holy virgin born in Antioch who vanquished the Devil. He had been invoked one day by a necromancer, who had bragged that he could make Justine submit to the will of a man who was desperately in love with her and would not leave her alone. The man realized that neither entreaties nor promises were having any effect, so he decided to call on the Devil. But his plan didn't work because the glorious Justine kept chasing the Devil away, regardless of the different shapes he assumed to tempt her. Vanquished, the Devil left in shame. Then she preached to both the man who was besotted with her and Cyprian, the necromancer, and converted both. Cyprian had led a wicked life, but Justine led him back to the path of virtue. Many other people were converted by the power Our Lord revealed through her. She left this world as a martyr.

"Another saint we should mention is the blessed virgin Eulalia, born in Spain. She was only twelve years old when she fled from her parents, who were keeping her locked up because she would not stop talking about Jesus Christ. She stole away by night and went off to knock the temple's idols to the ground. She cried out to the judges persecuting the martyrs that they were mistaken and that she, too, wished to die in the martyrs' Faith. That is how she was placed among the ranks of the soldiers of Jesus Christ. She suffered numerous torments and many people were converted by the power that Our Lord revealed through her.

"Another holy virgin by the name of Macra was also cruelly tortured for her faith in God. One of the torments she endured was having her breasts cut off. Afterward, as she lay in prison, God sent her His angel, who restored her to health. The next day, the prefect was dumbfounded to see her fit and well, but he continued to subject her to various forms of dreadful torture until she finally surrendered her soul to God. Her body lies buried near the city of Reims.

"The glorious virgin Saint Faith was also martyred in her childhood and suffered many torments. In the end, Our Lord publicly crowned her by sending His angel to bring her a crown of precious stones. God revealed His power through her on many occasions, prompting scores of people to convert.

"Another blessed virgin was called Marciana. When she saw that people were worshipping a false idol, she took the statue and threw it to the ground, breaking it in pieces. She was so badly beaten for this that she almost died. Then she was thrown in jail, where a corrupt priest tried to rape her during the night. But by the grace of God, a wall appeared between him and Marciana, so tall that he couldn't reach her. The next morning, everyone saw the wall, which caused many people to convert. Marciana suffered numerous dreadful tortures but never stopped preaching in the name of Jesus Christ. Finally, she prayed to God to take her and so her torment came to an end.

"Saint Euphemia was another martyr who endured great suffering in the name of Jesus. She came from a noble lineage and was very beautiful. Prefect Priscus put great pressure on her to worship the idols and renounce Jesus Christ, but she offered such convincing arguments in reply that he did not know how to answer. Enraged at the thought of having been defeated by a woman, he had her subjected to various dreadful torments, but the more her body was broken and tortured, the clearer her mind became, and she continued to speak eloquently about the Holy Spirit.[12] At some point during the torture, the angel of God descended, destroyed the instruments of torture, and attacked those wielding them. Euphemia emerged unscathed, her face shining with joy. Then the ungodly judge had a furnace lit, with flames leaping forty cubits into the air, and ordered her thrown in. Surrounded by flames, she sang sweet-sounding hymns to God that were so clearly audible that everyone heard them. When the fire died down, she emerged safe and sound. The judge was beside himself and ordered red-hot pincers to tear off her limbs, but those charged with this task were so frightened that none dared touch her, and the torture instruments broke into pieces. Then the ungodly tyrant had four lions and two other ferocious wild animals brought in, but

12. Note the significance of Christine stressing the eloquence of many of these saints—which has to be read within the context of her rehabilitation of weeping, talking, and weaving (the trilogy first discussed by Christine in I.10).

they sat down and worshipped her. The blessed virgin, anxious to be with God, finally prayed to Him to take her, and she died untouched by a single one of the animals."

9. Here she talks about the virgins Theodosia, Saint Barbara, and Saint Dorothy.

"We should also remember the steadfastness shown by the blessed Theodosia in her martyrdom. At the age of eighteen, this noble, beautiful virgin, blessed with a keen intelligence, engaged in a debate with a judge who threatened to martyr her if she did not renounce Jesus Christ. When she replied with divinely inspired arguments, he had her hung by her hair and severely beaten. She told him: 'Wretched are they who seek to rule others but are unable to rule themselves. Woe unto those who only think of filling themselves with food without sparing a thought for those who are hungry! Woe unto those who only warm themselves without warming or clothing those dying of cold! Woe unto those who only seek to rest and make others do the work! Woe unto those who claim all things as their own when they have received them from God! Woe unto those who want to be treated well when they themselves treat everyone badly!' Theodosia kept uttering venerable sentences of that sort throughout her torture, but because she felt ashamed at having her naked body on display in front of everyone, God sent a white cloud that covered her completely. To Urban, who continued to threaten her, she said: 'You shall not remove a single dish from the feast that has been prepared for me.' The tyrant threatened to have her robbed of her virginity, to which she replied: 'Your threat to corrupt my body is useless, for God dwells in the hearts of the pure.' The prefect, ever angrier, had her thrown into the sea with a heavy rock tied around her neck, but she was kept afloat by the angels and sang as she was brought back to shore, carrying the rock that weighed more than she did. Then the tyrant set two leopards loose on her, but they just danced around her in joy. In the end, the tyrant ran out of ideas and had her beheaded. Her soul rose from her body for all to see in the shape of a magnificent white dove. That same night, she appeared to her parents more radiant than the sun, wearing a precious crown and accompanied by virgins bearing a golden cross. She told her parents: 'Behold the glory you tried to take away from me,' and they converted that very night.

"Then there was the blessed Barbara, an exceptionally beautiful virgin of noble birth whose virtue shone in the time of Emperor Maximianus. Her

great beauty caused her father to keep her locked in a tower, and that is where
Barbara became inspired by the Christian faith. In the absence of anyone
who could baptize her, she took some water and baptized herself in the name
of the Father, the Son, and the Holy Ghost. Although her father sought a
noble marriage for her, she refused all offers for as long as she could. Eventually she declared herself a Christian and announced that she had dedicated
her virginity to God. When her father heard this, he wanted to kill her, but
she fled and escaped. Her father pursued her, still intent on killing her, and
eventually managed to track her down with the help of a shepherd, who was
immediately turned to stone, together with his animals. The father brought
her before the prefect, who gave orders that because she had disobeyed all his
orders, she should be subjected to various forms of excruciating torture, such
as being hung upside down by her feet. At that point she told him: 'Wretched
man! Do you not see that torture doesn't hurt me?' Enraged, he ordered her
breasts torn off and had her mutilated body paraded through the city. And
still she glorified God, although she felt ashamed of having her naked body
exposed to the public eye. Then our Lord sent his angel to heal her wounds
and cover her body in a white robe. After she had been promenaded around
long enough, she was brought back before the prefect, who exploded in anger
when he saw her completely healed, her face as radiant as a star. He had
her tortured anew until even her torturers tired of their task. Finally, in a
great rage, he ordered her taken out of his sight and beheaded. She began to
pray, beseeching God to protect those who would call on Him in memory
of her and her martyrdom. When she finished her prayer, a voice was heard,
saying: 'My beloved daughter, come and rest in your Father's kingdom and
receive your crown, and all things you have asked for will be granted to you.'
She climbed the mountain where she was to be executed and there she was
beheaded by her evil father himself. As he came down the mountain afterward,
he was struck by fire from heaven and reduced to ashes.

"We should also mention the blessed Dorothy, a virgin who suffered many
tortures in Cappadocia. Because she refused to marry and was always talking about her bridegroom Jesus Christ, the professor of law called Theophilus
mocked her when she was being taken away to be beheaded, saying that when
she reached her bridegroom, the least she could do was to send him, Theophilus, some roses and apples from his orchard. Dorothy replied that she would,
and following her martyrdom, a beautiful child some four years of age came
to see Theophilus, bringing a little basket filled with exquisite roses and gor-
geous, sweet-smelling apples. He told him that the basket came from the virgin

Dorothy. The professor was astounded because it was the month of February, so he converted and was subsequently martyred for the sake of Jesus Christ.

"It would take a very long time to tell you about all the other holy virgins who were admitted to Heaven thanks to their steadfastness during torture, including Saint Cecilia, Saint Agnes, Saint Agatha, and countless others. If you want to know more, you only have to look in the *Miroir histoirial* [Mirror of History] of Vincent of Beauvais and you will find many of them.[13] But let me just tell you about Saint Christine, because she is your patron saint and a most meritorious virgin.[14] Let me tell you more about her beautiful life full of devotion."

10. Here she talks about the holy virgin Saint Christine.

"The blessed virgin Saint Christine came from the city of Tyre and was the daughter of Urban, governor of that city. Worried about her great beauty, her father kept her locked up in a tower with twelve maidens for company. He also had a small but handsome pagan temple built next to Christine's room so she could worship the idols. But even though she was still a child of around twelve, she had already been inspired by the faith of Jesus Christ, and she ignored the idols. Her companions were astounded and frequently urged her to make a sacrifice. But when she took incense as though to make sacrifices to the idols, she knelt down in front of an east-facing window and looked up to Heaven, paying homage to the immortal God. She stayed by that window most of the night, watching the stars and sighing, calling upon God and entreating Him to help her against her enemies. Her companions, well aware that her heart was given to Jesus Christ, often knelt before her, their hands folded, pleading with her to not put all her trust in a foreign god but to worship the gods of her own people. If her actions became known, they said, they would all be killed. Christine replied that they had been led astray by the devil urging them to worship so many gods when, in fact, there was only one God.

"Eventually, her father discovered that his daughter refused to worship the idols, and he was deeply upset. He gave her a severe scolding and she told him she would be happy to make an offering to the Heavenly God. Thinking

13. See note above in III.3 about Christine's sources.

14. Note the unsurprisingly long treatment this saint receives here. For a detailed discussion of Saint Christine (Christine's patron saint), see Kevin Brownlee, "Martyrdom and the Female Voice: Saint Christine in the *Cité des dames*," in *Images of Sainthood in Medieval Europe*, ed. Renate Blumenfeld-Kosinski and Timea Szell (Ithaca, N.Y.: Cornell University Press, 1991).

that she was referring to Jupiter, her father was delighted and wanted to kiss her, but she cried out: 'Don't touch my mouth! I want to be perfectly pure when I make my sacrifice to the Heavenly God.' That statement pleased her father. Christine went to her room, locked herself in, and knelt down in tears to offer a holy prayer to God. Then the Lord's angel descended and comforted her, bringing white bread and other food. Christine ate some of this because she had not had anything to eat for three days. Then she looked out of her window and saw many poor Christians begging at the foot of her tower. Having nothing to offer them, she went to fetch her father's idols. They were made of silver and gold, so she smashed them and distributed pieces to all the poor. When her father found out about this, he gave her a savage beating. Christine told him candidly that his worship of false idols was based on a misconception because there is but one God in the form of a Holy Trinity. Her father should worship the one to whom she confessed, she said. She herself would rather die than worship any other god. Enraged, her father had her chained up and dragged through the streets while he beat her. Finally, she was thrown into jail. Wanting to judge her himself, her father had her brought before him the next day and threatened her with all sorts of tortures if she did not agree to worship the idols. When he saw that neither pleas nor threats would change her mind, he had her stretched out naked, tied by her arms and legs, and beaten so savagely that twelve grown men became completely exhausted. Her father kept asking her if she was ready to change her mind, saying: 'My daughter, having you tortured is a terrible affront to the natural affection I feel for you, flesh of my flesh. It is the reverence I feel for my gods that forces me to take this action, because you insult them.' The holy virgin replied: 'Tyrant! I should not call you father but enemy of my happiness! Go ahead and torture the flesh you engendered, because you have the power to do so. As for my soul, which was created by my Father who is in Heaven, you have no power whatsoever to subject it to temptation, for Jesus Christ my Savior protects it.' Her cruel father, more furious than ever, had a specially designed wheel brought in and had her tied to it. Then he ordered a fire lit beneath the sweet young girl and as the wheel turned, a river of boiling oil poured over her body, breaking all her bones. But God, the merciful Father, took pity on His servant, sending His angel to destroy all the instruments of torture, extinguish the fire, and deliver the virgin safe and sound while killing more than a thousand treacherous spectators who had been watching her without any compassion, blaspheming God's name. Christine's father asked her: 'Tell me: who taught you this devilry?' and Christine replied: 'You merciless tyrant, did

I not tell you that it is my Father, Jesus Christ, who taught me this steadfastness and the way to practice my faith in the Living God? That is why I have nothing but contempt for all your torments and how, with God's help, I will vanquish all the devil's assaults.'

"At his wit's end, her father had her thrown into a horrible, dark dungeon. As Christine lay there, reflecting upon God's great miracles, three angels came to her in a great flash of light and brought her food and comfort. Urban did not know what to do with her but went on devising new types of torture. In the end, he became fed up, and in order to get rid of her, he had a heavy rock tied around her neck and ordered her thrown into the sea. As she hit the water, however, the angels came and took her away along the waves. Christine prayed to Jesus Christ, lifting her eyes to the Heavens, asking Him if He would be gracious enough to give her the much-desired holy sacrament of baptism, using the water she was in. Then Jesus Christ incarnate, accompanied by a host of angels, descended and baptized her, naming her Christine. Before putting her back on shore, he crowned her and placed a shining star on her forehead. That same night, Urban was tortured by the devil and died.

"The blessed Christine, whom God wished to receive as a martyr as much as she did herself, was taken back to prison by her torturers. Then she was brought before a new judge, called Dion, who knew what had already been done to her. Seeing her beauty, he lusted after her, but when he saw that nice words had no effect, he had her subjected to more torture. He ordered a great cauldron filled with oil and pitch and a roaring fire lit beneath it. Then he had her thrown into the cauldron, head first, with four men turning her, using iron hooks. But the holy virgin sang sweet hymns to God, mocking her torturers and threatening them with the torments of Hell. When the vile judge realized that the torture was not having any effect, he was enraged and had her hung by her long, golden-blond hair in the public square where everyone could see her. The women ran over to her, crying with compassion that such a sweet young girl should be tormented in that way. They cried out to the judge, shouting: 'You cruel villain, worse than a savage beast! How can any man conceive of so much cruelty against such a lovely young maiden!' When the judge saw that they all wanted to charge him, he took fright and said to her: 'Christine, my dear, don't allow yourself to be tortured like that! Come with me and we will worship together the supreme God who has given you so much succor.' He was referring to Jupiter, whom they considered their supreme god, but she completely misunderstood and replied: 'Well said. I consent.' The judge had her cut down and took her to the temple, followed by a large crowd. When he brought her before the idols in the belief that she would worship them, she fell to her knees, looking up toward Heaven, and prayed to God. Then she got to her feet and turned to the idol, saying: 'Evil spirit that dwells in this idol, I command you in the name of Jesus Christ to show yourself!' The Devil materialized at once, with such a dreadful pandemonium that everyone fell to the ground in terror. When the judge regained his feet, he said: 'Christine, you have roused our almighty god, but because he feels sorry for you, he has shown himself so he can see his creature.' Angered by these words, Christine severely took the judge to task for being too blind to recognize divine virtue. Then she prayed, asking God to topple the idol and reduce it to dust. When her prayer was granted, more than three thousand men and women were converted, as much by the virgin's words as the miracles she had caused to happen. The judge was enraged and said: 'If the king found out what this Christine has done to humiliate our god, he would have me die a most horrible death.' And then, filled with anguish, he lost his reason and died.

"A third judge, called Julian, arrived and seized Christine, boasting that he would succeed in forcing her to worship the idols. Despite all his efforts, however, he was unable to physically move her from where she was standing. He ordered a large fire built around her that burned for three days. All that time, sweet melodies were heard from inside the fire, and the tormentors became so frightened of these miraculous sounds that they reported them to Julian. It nearly drove him mad. When the fire had burned out, Christine emerged unharmed, so the judge had snakes brought in and ordered two asps and two enormous grass snakes thrown at her. The bite of an asp is deadly poisonous, but the four snakes lowered their heads and lay down at her feet without harming her. Then two more horrible snakes were released, known as vipers. They hung from her breasts and licked her. Christine looked up toward Heaven and said: 'Thank you, Lord Jesus Christ, for having the grace to protect me through Your holy virtue, so even these horrible snakes recognize Your dignity through me.' Watching these miracles, Julian still did not give up but snarled at the snake keeper: 'Have you, too, been bewitched by Christine so you can't get your snakes to attack her!' Frightened of the judge, the snake keeper tried to force his snakes to bite Christine, but they turned on their keeper and killed him instead. Everyone was so afraid of the snakes that they dared not go near them, but Christine commanded the snakes in the name of God to return to their shelter without harming anyone, and they obeyed her. She resuscitated the dead man, who immediately prostrated himself at her feet and converted.

"The judge was so blinded by the Devil that he was unable to recognize the divine intervention. He told Christine: 'I've now seen enough evidence of your witchcraft.' Infuriated, she replied: 'If your eyes would see God's miracles, you would believe them.' Mad with rage, the judge had her breasts torn off, but instead of blood, milk flowed from her wounds. Because she kept repeating the name of Jesus, he had her tongue cut out, but this caused her to speak even better and more clearly than before, evoking divine revelations and blessing God, thanking him for all the favors he had bestowed on her. Then she began to pray, pleading with God to take her into His realm and grant her the crown of martyrdom.

"Then a voice was heard from Heaven, saying: 'Christine, the heavens are open to you who are pure and unblemished, the eternal kingdom awaits you, and the entire company of saints blesses God for you, because you have defended the name of your Christ since you were a child.' Christine glorified God, her eyes raised to Heaven. And then the voice was heard again, saying: 'Come, Christine, my beloved and chosen daughter, receive the everlasting palm and crown, the reward for a life full of suffering upholding My name.' Hearing this voice, the villainous Julian reprimanded the torturers and told them they hadn't cut off enough of Christine's tongue. They should cut it so close, he said, that she could no longer speak to her Christ. So they tore out the rest of her tongue, cutting it off at the root. Christine spat out what was left into the despot's face, piercing one of his eyes. Speaking as clearly as ever, she said to him: 'Do you really think, you tyrant, that cutting out my tongue will stop me from blessing God when my soul will eternally bless Him and yours will be damned forever? You failed to heed my words so it is only fair that my tongue has blinded you.'[15]

"Then she saw Jesus Christ sitting to the right of his Father, and her martyrdom ended when two arrows hit her, one in her side and the other in her heart. Her saintly body was buried by one of the relatives she had converted, and it was he who wrote down her glorious legend."

"Oh, blessed Christine, worthy virgin blessed by God, most excellent and glorious martyr! Since God has granted you sainthood, please pray for me, poor sinner who bears your name, and be my benevolent and compassionate patroness. Behold my joy at being able to include your holy legend in my book! I have recounted it in great detail to show my reverence for you and

---

15. Maureen Quilligan underscores the politically charged character of Christine de Pizan's recounting of the story in *Allegory of Female Authority*, esp. 221–34.

I hope it pleases you. Please pray for all women, who should be inspired by your holy life to spend their own lives in piety. Amen."

"What else can I tell you, my sweet friend, to fill our city with other ladies of the same quality? May Saint Ursula join us with all her eleven thousand blessed virgins, martyred for the name of Jesus Christ, all of them beheaded after they were sent off to be married. They wound up in a country of pagans who tried to force them to renounce their faith in God. They chose to die rather than renounce Jesus Christ their Savior."

11. About several female saints who saw their children martyred before their eyes.

"Oh! What is more precious in this world than the bond between a mother and her child? And what greater pain than that of a mother seeing her child suffer?[16] And yet, I think faith is even more powerful, as many brave women have demonstrated by offering up their own children to be tortured for the love of Jesus Christ. That happened to the blessed Felicity, for example, who saw all seven of her handsome young sons martyred before her very eyes. The devoted mother comforted them and told them to be patient and find strength in their faith. For the love of God she had renounced the maternal love that every mother feels for the flesh of her flesh. When she had sacrificed the last one, she asked to be sacrificed to God herself and died a martyr's death.

"Another example is the blessed Julitta, who had a son named Quriaqos. She nourished her son both physically and spiritually, insisting that he learn the Faith. That way, even though he was only a child, he could never be vanquished by anyone seeking to martyr him nor forced to renounce the name of Jesus Christ by threats of torture. Thus, when he wound up being tortured, he cried out as loudly as he could in his small, clear voice: 'I am a Christian! I am a Christian and give thanks to our Lord God!' He spoke as boldly as a forty-year-old man. His devoted mother, also subjected to cruel

---

16. Notwithstanding this passage, the figure of the mother and the virtues of maternal love are relatively discreet in the *City* (notable exceptions include II.34, II.50). Bernard Ribémont discusses this issue in "Christine de Pizan et la figure de la mère," in *Christine de Pizan 2000* (Amsterdam: Rodopi, 2000). Cf. Heather Arden, "Her Mother's Daughter: Empowerment and Maternity in the Works of Christine de Pizan," in *Contexts and Continuities: Proceedings of the IVth International Colloquium on Christine de Pizan,* vol. 1, ed. Angus Kennedy, Rosalind Brown-Grant, James Laidlaw, and Catherine Müller (Glasgow: University of Glasgow Press, 2002), 31–42.

torture, comforted him. She never stopped praising God and comforting the other martyrs, speaking of the divine joy that awaited them and telling them to have no fear.

"Similarly, what about the marvelous steadfastness and strength of the blessed Blandina? Seeing her beloved fourteen-year-old daughter tortured and martyred before her eyes, she comforted her with joy. After her daughter died, she herself submitted to torture as joyfully as a bride going to meet her groom. She was subjected to such excruciating torments that even her torturers became exhausted. She was placed on a grill and roasted, cut up with iron hooks, and still she glorified God, persevering to the end."

12. Here she talks about the holy virgin Saint Marina.

"We could recount many more stories about martyred virgins and other women who led a religious and holy life in various forms. But I will tell you about two in particular, whose legends are very uplifting and illustrate the concept of women's steadfastness.

"There was a layman whose only daughter, named Marina, was still quite young. He placed her in the care of a relative before entering a monastery and leading an exemplary life. Yet Nature drew him to his daughter, and her absence caused him much grief. The abbot, seeing him so pensive, asked him what made him so despondent. The monk eventually admitted that his mind was taken up with the little son he had left behind in the world and could not forget. The abbot told him to go and fetch the boy and bring him to the monastery. That is how the virgin came to live with her father, dressed like a little monk. She was adept at concealing her real identity and behaved impeccably. She was still striving to perfect herself when she turned eighteen and the father who had raised her so devoutly passed away. She remained alone in the cell she had shared with him, leading such a saintly life that the abbot and all the monks, still under the impression that she was a man, praised her devotion to God.

"The abbey was three miles away from a market town the monks had to visit from time to time to do their shopping. In the winter, when night fell before they had concluded their business, they sometimes stayed overnight in the town. When it was her turn to spend the night in town, Marina, known as Brother Marinus, stayed at the same inn where the monks always lodged. It so happened that the innkeeper's daughter became pregnant and when her parents forced her to reveal the identity of the father, she blamed Brother

Marinus. The parents went to the abbot to complain, and the abbot, deeply disturbed, summoned Marina. The holy virgin preferred to take the blame rather than prove her innocence by revealing that she was a woman. She fell to her knees in tears, saying: 'Father, I have sinned. Pray for me and I will do penance.' The furious abbot had her severely beaten and threw her out of the monastery, forbidding her to ever enter it again. She lay down in front of the gate, doing penance, only begging the monks for a morsel of bread. When the innkeeper's daughter gave birth to a son, her mother took the infant to Marina in front of the monastery and left it there. Marina took it and fed it as if it were her own with the morsels of bread she received from visitors to the monastery. After a while, the monks were moved by compassion and asked the abbot to show mercy and take Brother Marinus back. They barely managed to convince the abbot, a full five years after she had begun her penance. When Marina reentered the monastery, the abbot ordered her to do all the dirty work, making her carry water to clean the sanitary facilities and wait on everyone. The holy virgin carried out her duties with humility and joy.

"A short time later, she died and rested in our Lord. When the brothers informed the abbot, he said: 'Even though his sin does not deserve to be pardoned, wash him all the same but bury him far from the monastery.' When they undressed the corpse, they saw the body of a woman and started to beat themselves and wail with distress, ashamed of the wrong they had done to such a holy creature and marveling at the saintly life she had led. They reported the news to the abbot, who rushed over and prostrated himself at the holy body, weeping copiously and beating his breast, crying out for mercy and asking forgiveness. He ordered her buried in one of the monastery's chapels. All the monks assembled there, including one who was blind in one eye. He bent down, kissing the body with great devotion, and immediately recovered the sight in his blind eye. That same day, the woman who had given birth to the child lost her reason and loudly confessed the sin she had committed. She was brought before the holy body and recovered her senses. Many other miracles took place on this spot, and they still do."

13. Here she talks about the blessed virgin Euphrosyne.

"Another case in point is that of Euphrosyne, a virgin from Alexandria. Thanks to the prayers of a holy abbot and the monks from a nearby monastery, God had granted her to her father Paphnutius, who was a very rich man. When Euphrosyne became an adult, her father wanted her to marry, but since she had given herself to God, she was determined to keep her virginity and fled, dressed in a man's clothing. She asked to be allowed to enter the monastery, giving the abbot to believe that she was a devout young man from the emperor's court who yearned to take his vow. Seeing her devotion, the abbot was happy to receive her. But her father was terribly upset when he could not find his beloved daughter anywhere. He went to tell the abbot about his great sorrow, hoping to be comforted, and to ask him and his monks to pray for some news. The abbot comforted him and said that he could not believe that this young woman, who had been granted by God in answer to their prayers, might have perished. The abbot and his monks spent a long time in prayer, asking God to intercede.

"No news was received, and since the father kept returning to the abbot for comfort in his grief, the abbot told him one day: 'I don't believe anything bad has happened to your daughter because if it had, I'm sure God would have revealed that to us. But we have someone here at the monastery, a deeply pious monk who came to us from the emperor's court, to whom God gave so much grace that everyone who speaks to him finds comfort. You could speak to him if you like.' Paphnutius immediately asked for permission to speak to him by the grace of God, and the abbot had the father taken to see his daughter. He didn't recognize her but she recognized him, and her eyes instantly filled with tears, causing her to turn away as if to finish a prayer. Her beauty and fresh complexion had badly suffered from the strict abstention she had imposed on herself. She spoke to her father and gave him much comfort, assuring him that his daughter was in a safe place serving God. He would see her again before he died, she said, and she would still be a source of great joy to him. In the belief that all this was being revealed to him through divine inspiration, the father derived much comfort from these words and left to report to the abbot that he had not known such peace since the day his daughter had disappeared. 'I feel as much joy in God's grace,' he said, 'as if I had actually found my daughter.' Commending himself to the abbot and the monks' prayers, he left the monastery, but did not hesitate to pay frequent visits to the holy brother and only felt at peace in his company.

"This situation continued for a long time. His daughter, who had taken on the name of Brother Smaragdus, had already spent thirty-eight years in her cell at that point. Then God chose to call her to Him, so she fell ill. Her father was very upset by this, and when he went to visit her and saw that she was dying, he started to lament. 'Alas! What has become of your sweet words and the promises you made me that I would see my daughter again?' Then

Smaragdus died and rested in God, but the father wasn't there when this happened. There was a letter in the dead body's hand but no one was able to remove it. The abbot and his monks all tried but without success. Then the father approached, weeping and lamenting for his good friend who had been his sole comfort and who was lying there dead. As soon as he came close enough to the body to embrace it, everyone saw the hand open and give him the letter. He took it and read her words, explaining that she was his daughter and that no one should touch her body for burial except for him. He was stunned to read this, as were the abbot and all his monks, who praised her saintly steadfastness and virtue. The father shed even more tears, moved and consoled by the sanctity of her life. He sold everything he owned and entered the monastery, where he spent the rest of his life.

"Now that I have told you about a number of virgins, I will continue with stories about other women who were martyred."

14. About the blessed Lady Anastasia.

"At the time of the great persecution under Emperor Diocletian,[17] there was a most noble lady who lived in Rome. She was very rich and one of the city's most respected ladies. Anastasia, as she was called, felt deep compassion for the blessed Christian martyrs she saw being tortured on a daily basis. She dressed up as a poor woman every day to visit and console them, going with her maid into the jails where they were kept to comfort them with fine wines, food, and anything else she could come up with. She washed and treated their wounds, applying precious ointments, and continued doing this until she was denounced to Publius, a Roman nobleman eager to marry her. He was very annoyed at this news and put guards at her house to prevent her from going out.

"Among the martyrs in prison was Saint Chrysogonus, a man of great virtue who had suffered many excruciating tortures. He had been comforted by the holy Anastasia's visits and good deeds and had secretly sent her a number of letters through the intermediary of a good Christian lady, urging her to remain patient. She replied using the same intermediary. Eventually, it was God's wish that the man who had put Anastasia under such close guard should die. She then sold all her possessions and used the proceeds to visit and support the martyrs.

17. He was emperor from 284 to 305 CE.

"Anastasia had a large entourage of Christian girls and ladies, including three virgins, sisters from a noble family, who were very close to her. They were called Agape, Chionia, and Irene. It came to the emperor's attention that these three noble sisters were Christians, so he sent for them, promising them great gifts and noble marriages if they renounced Jesus Christ. When they ignored him, he had them beaten and thrown into a gloomy dungeon, where they were visited by their beloved, saintly Anastasia. She stayed with them day and night, praying to God to keep her alive long enough to use all the means she had at her disposal for this blessed work. The emperor ordered Dulcitius, his steward, to use torture on all the Christians in jail to force them into worshipping the idols. Dulcitius had them all brought before him, including the three blessed sisters.

"When the unprincipled steward saw how beautiful they were, he lusted after them and spoke to them in private, using sweet words to urge them to submit to his will and promising them freedom. They flatly refused, so he ordered one of his retainers to take them to his house under guard, thinking he would bed them whether they liked it or not. When night fell, he set out for the house where he had ordered them sent, alone and without a light. The virgins were spending the whole night praising God, and so he headed for the sound of their voices, passing by the place where the kitchen pots were stored. And then, possessed by the Devil and blinded by lust as God had decreed, he started to embrace and kiss one pot after another, thinking he was fondling the virgins. This went on until he was exhausted. He emerged at daybreak to meet his people waiting outside, looking like the Devil incarnate, covered in grease and soot, his robe torn and dragging behind him in tatters. Seeing this apparition, they took fright and fled. Dulcitius was astounded to see them go, having not the faintest idea why they would scorn him that way. He set off down the street and saw that all the passers-by were laughing at him, so he decided to go straight to the emperor to complain about being ridiculed by everyone he encountered. When he entered the palace, he came upon a large number of people waiting there that morning and pandemonium broke out. Some people hit him with sticks, and others pushed him back, shouting: 'Get out, you miserable scoundrel, you stink!' Others spat into his face and everyone made fun of him. He was so baffled about the reason for all this that he nearly lost his mind. The Devil had so blinded him that he was unable to see himself as he was, so he returned home in a huff.

"Another judge took his place and had the three blessed virgins brought before him. He was determined to make them worship the idols, but since they would not obey, he ordered them stripped naked and beaten. But his men, despite all their power, were unable to strip the virgins. Their robes clung to them so tightly that no one could remove them. Then he had them thrown into a raging fire, but they were immune to the heat, praying that it would please God to end their lives. So they ended their lives in a blaze of glory, but to demonstrate that they had died of their own free will, the fire did not consume a single hair or item of clothing. When the flames had died down, their bodies were found whole, their hands folded in prayer, their faces as fresh as if they were asleep. The blessed Anastasia took care of them and looked after the funeral."

15. About the blessed Theodota.

"Anastasia had another noble companion, by the name of Theodota, who had three young sons. This lady, having refused to marry Count Leucatius and to sacrifice to the idols, was subjected to many torments. To put even more pressure on her by appealing to her maternal instincts, they had one of her sons tortured, but since the strength of one's faith transcends one's natural instincts, she comforted her son, saying: 'Son, do not fear this torment, for it will bring you great glory.' While she was in jail, a son of the Devil tried to violate her, but he immediately suffered a severe nosebleed. He cried out that a young boy who was with Theodota had struck him on the nose. She was tortured anew and finally died, along with her three sons, rendering their blessed souls to God to glorify Him. The glorious Anastasia buried them, too.

"She had paid so many visits to the martyrs that she was finally arrested and thrown into jail, so she was no longer able to visit God's saints. She had nothing to drink or eat, but God did not want this woman, who had so diligently comforted and nourished His blessed martyrs, to suffer, so He sent her the spirit of her blessed companion Theodota, who appeared in a cloud of light and set the table, serving her a host of delectable dishes. She stayed with Anastasia for thirty days, during which time no one brought her anything to eat. People believed she must have died of starvation, but they found her alive and well. She was brought before the steward, who was enraged. He noted that this miracle caused many people to convert, so he had her put on board a ship in the company of a large group of criminals who had been condemned to death. When they reached the high sea, the sailors carried out the orders they had been given, scuttling the ship and transferring to another vessel. Then the blessed Theodota appeared and guided the passengers across the sea for twenty-four hours, as surely as if they had been traveling on level ground. Finally they reached the island of Palmaria, where many bishops and holy men had been sent into exile, and they were welcomed with joy and everyone praised God. Those who had escaped with Anastasia were baptized and became Christians.

"When this news reached the emperor's ears, he had them all sent for, more than three hundred men, women, and children, and had them tortured to death. The blessed Anastasia engaged in a number of heated arguments with the emperor and suffered many more torments, but she finally received the martyr's crown."

16. About the noble and holy Natalia.

"Natalia, the noble wife of Adrian, Emperor Maximianus' army commander, had secretly become a Christian at a time when many Christians were being martyred. One day she heard that her husband, for whom she been praying day and night, had suddenly converted while watching some martyrs being tortured and had acknowledged the name of Jesus Christ. This had so angered the emperor that he had ordered him thrown into a gloomy dungeon. The blessed lady was overjoyed at her husband's conversion and left at once for the prison to comfort him, begging him not to give up what he had started. She kissed the chains that bound him, weeping with compassion and joy, and urged him to concentrate on the great glory that awaited him instead of bemoaning the transitory earthly pleasures. The saintly lady stayed with him for a long time, comforting him and all the other martyrs, praying to God that she could soon join their number. She also begged them to encourage her husband, fearing that the impact of the torture might weaken his faith. She visited him every day, comforting him with soft words, continually urging him to remain steadfast. When the emperor saw how often she and many other ladies were visiting the holy martyrs, he issued an order banning all women from entering the prison, but Natalia disguised herself as a man. She was there on the day of his final martyrdom. She cleaned and kissed his bleeding wounds, weeping with compassion and begging him to pray to God on her behalf. And so the blessed Adrian passed away and she buried him with great devotion. One of his hands had been chopped off and she kept it, wrapping it with great care as befits a holy relic.

"After her husband's death, this holy lady came under pressure to remarry since she came from a noble family and was rich and beautiful. She never

stopped praying to God to deliver her from the hands of those who were trying to force her to remarry. Then her husband appeared to her in her sleep
and comforted her, saying she should go to Constantinople to bury the bodies of the many martyrs there. She was happy to do as he said. When she had
spent some time in God's service visiting the imprisoned holy martyrs, her
husband appeared to her a second time and told her: 'Sweet sister and friend,
handmaiden of Jesus Christ, come with me into eternal glory, for our Lord is
calling you.' Then she awoke and almost immediately passed away."

17. About Saint Afra, a prostitute who converted to Christianity.[18]

"Afra was a prostitute who converted to the faith of Jesus Christ. She was
denounced by a judge, who told her: 'As if your body's depravity isn't enough!
Now you also have to go and commit the sin of worshipping a foreign god!
Go and make sacrifices to our gods so they may forgive you.' Afra replied: 'I
will only sacrifice to my God, He who came down from Heaven to save the
sinners. His Gospel records that a sinful woman came to wash his feet with
her tears and was forgiven. He never scorned prostitutes or sinful tax collec-
tors but invited them instead to His table to share His food.' The judge said:
'If you don't make a sacrifice, your clients will no longer like you or give you
presents.' Afra replied: 'I will never again accept a sinful gift. I have asked the
poor to take the gifts I have wrongfully received, and I will ask them to pray
for me.' The judge sentenced Afra to be burned at the stake because she still
refused to make sacrifices. When she was led to the fire, she prayed, saying:
'Lord God, almighty Jesus Christ, You who call upon the sinners to repent,
please accept my sacrifice at the hour of my martyrdom and deliver me from
eternal fire through this earthly fire being prepared for my body.' When she
was engulfed by flames, she prayed: 'Lord Jesus Christ, please receive me,
poor sinner, martyred for Your holy name, You who have sacrificed Yourself
for humankind, innocent but crucified for the guilty, You who were good for
the wicked, blessed for the damned, sweet for the bitter, pure and without

---

18. Note that in the sequel to this book (*The Treasure of the City of Ladies*) Christine offers
some advice to prostitutes, inviting them to follow the path of Saint Afra, who gave up on her
"disreputable" occupation and repented. Noting the various difficulties of getting out of the
circuits of prostitution (ostracism in the community; increased poverty; male customers who
would bring them back into the circuits, etc.), Christine nevertheless insists that "there is a
solution to every problem" (III.10).

blemish for the sinners. I offer You my body in sacrifice, You who live and reign with the Father and the Holy Spirit for ever and ever.' Thus died the blessed Afra, through whom Our Lord later manifested many more miracles."

18. Here Lady Justice talks about a number of noble ladies who served and housed the Apostles and other saints.

"What more can I tell you, my dear friend Christine? I could go on endlessly, recalling similar examples, but since you told me earlier how surprised you are that so many authors subject women to such severe criticism, let me tell you that despite all you have read in the works of pagan authors, I believe you will find little criticism of women in the hagiographies, the stories about Jesus Christ and His Apostles, and the lives of the saints, as you can see for yourself. Instead, you will find many examples of women blessed by God with marvelous steadfastness and endless virtue. Oh! What unstinting kindness and charity did they lavish on the servants of God, tending to them with consideration and courage! And all the hospitality and service: are they worthless? If some foolish men consider them frivolous, no one can deny that our faith teaches us that such good works make the ladders that lead to Heaven. Take Drusiana, for instance, an honest widow who lodged Saint John the Baptist at her home, waiting on him and serving him meals. The day Saint John returned from his exile, his festive welcome by the city's inhabitants coincided with Drusiana's funeral. She had died of grief over his long absence. Her neighbors said: 'John, behold Drusiana, your kindhearted hostess, who died of sorrow waiting for you to return. She will never serve you again.' And Saint John turned to her and said: 'Drusiana, rise up! Go home and prepare me a meal!' And she came back to life.

"Another example is Susanna, a brave, noble lady from the city of Limoges. She was the first to offer lodging to Saint Martial, who had been sent there by Saint Peter to convert the pagans. She did him many favors.

"Then there is the noble Maximilla, who took Saint Andrew down from the cross at the risk of her own life.

"The holy virgin Ephigenia devotedly followed Saint Matthew and waited on him. After his death, she had a church built in his honor.

"Another noble lady was so filled with saintly love for Saint Paul that she followed him everywhere and served him zealously.

"Likewise, in the time of the Apostles, there was a noble queen called Helena (not Constantin's mother but the queen of Adiabene) who went to

Jerusalem when food was extremely expensive due to a famine. When she learned that our Lord's holy people, who were in the city to preach to the people and convert them, were dying of hunger, she had enough food purchased so they could feed themselves for the duration of the famine.

"Another example is Plautilla, a noble lady who tended to Saint Paul. When he was taken to be beheaded as ordered by Nero, Plautilla went up to Saint Paul weeping copious tears. He asked her for the veil she was wearing around her head, and she gave it to him. The wicked people who witnessed this event made fun of this, saying it was foolish to give away such a beautiful veil. Saint Paul used it to bind his eyes. After his death, the angels gave the bloodstained veil back to Plautilla and she kept it as a precious relic. Then Saint Paul appeared to her and said that because she had served him on earth, he would serve her in Heaven, praying for her. I could tell you many more similar stories.

"The noble Basilissa was especially noted for her charity. She was married to Saint Julian and both of them took a vow of chastity on their wedding night. This virgin's holy way of life and the vast number of women and virgins who were saved by her saintly preaching and inspired to lead a devout life defy the imagination. In short, she performed so many acts of charity that our Lord graced her by appearing at her deathbed.

"I don't know what else to tell you, Christine. I could tell you innumerable stories of women from various walks of life, be they virgins, widows, or married women,[19] in whom God demonstrated His omnipotence through their marvelous strength and constancy. What I have said so far should suffice. I think I have acquitted myself well of my task to complete the tall roofs of your City and populate it with illustrious ladies, as I promised you. They will serve our City as doors and portcullises, and although I have not cited and could not possibly cite all the sainted ladies of the past, present, and future, they all have a place in this City of Ladies. One might well say *Gloriosa dicta sunt de te, civitas Dei* [Glorious are the things that are said of you, city of God]. Now I turn it over to you, enclosed, completed, and well fortified as promised. Farewell, and may the Lord's peace be with you always."

19. In many medieval theological sources, while it was understood that all of these women could be chaste, the hierarchy of moral merit among them was typically understood as follows: married women, widows, and then—highest of all—virgins. See Jean Gerson's reflections on chastity in Hult, *Debate of the "Romance of the Rose,"* 217–18. For some, widows could even (through piety and doing penance) become akin to virgins again. See, e.g., Ruth M. Karras, *Sexuality in Medieval Europe: Doing unto Others*, 2nd ed. (New York: Routledge, 2012), 58–62.

19. The final chapter: Christine addresses womankind.

Most honored ladies, let us praise the Lord, because our City is now fully built and complete. All of you who love glory, virtue, and respect may reside here in great honor. Ladies from the past, the present, and the future: you may all live here, because the City has been established and built for all ladies of honor. My dear ladies, it is natural for human beings to rejoice when they find they have triumphed in any sort of enterprise and know that their enemies have been vanquished. So you have good reason, ladies, to rejoice in God and virtuousness at seeing this new city completed. It will not only serve as a refuge for all of you virtuous women but also as a bastion from which to defend yourself against your enemies and assailants, provided you guard it well. You can see that the material used in its construction is pure virtue, shining so brightly that you may see your reflection in it, especially the roofs constructed in this last part of the book, but not forgetting the sections that are relevant to you in the first two parts.

My dear ladies, please do not abuse this new legacy in the way of arrogant people who swell with pride when their prosperity increases and their wealth grows. No: you should follow the example of your queen, the Sovereign Virgin. When she learned the extraordinary news that she was to become the mother of God, she proved herself even humbler by calling herself God's handmaiden.

Since it is true that as a woman's virtue increases, she grows humbler and more gracious, this City should inspire you to live honorable, virtuous, and humble lives.

And you ladies who are married, do not be indignant about having to submit to your husbands, because it is not always in a person's interest to be free. That is proven by what the angel of God told Ezra: "Those who depended on using their free will fell into sin, held our Lord in contempt, and abused the just. That is why they perished." Those who married peaceable, kind, and reasonable husbands who are devoted to them should thank God for this not inconsiderable blessing, because they could not be given a greater boon in this world. Be sure to tend to them as best you can, love them, and cherish them with a loyal heart as you should, keeping the peace and praying to God to keep and safeguard them.

Those who have husbands who are neither good nor bad should also thank God for not giving them a worse husband. They should strive to moderate their excesses and keep the peace, depending on their social situation.

Those who married hostile, cruel, and surly husbands should tolerate them while doing their best to overcome their depravity, making every effort to convince them to lead a reasonable and respectable life. If they are so obstinate that this proves impossible, at least their souls will reap the benefits through the virtue of patience and everyone will bless them and take their side.

So, my ladies, be humble and patient and God's grace will grow in you. You will receive great praise and the Kingdom of Heaven will be open to you. Saint Gregory has said that patience is the key to Paradise and the way of Jesus Christ. May none of you acquire and stubbornly cling to frivolous opinions lacking all reason or become jealous or harbor evil thoughts or use contemptuous language or commit outrageous acts, because these are things that will make you lose your head and lead to madness. That type of conduct is extremely unbecoming and improper in women.

And you, young virgins, be pure, sober, and tranquil, but do not lack confidence, because evil men will spread their nets to catch you. Keep your eyes lowered, listen rather than speak, and exercise restraint in all your actions. Be armed with the strength of virtue against the tricks of those seeking to seduce you and avoid their company.

And you, widows, be modest in your dress, conduct, and speech, pious in your actions and way of life, prudent in managing your affairs, and especially patient and resilient when faced with tribulations and difficult situations. Be humble in your emotions, attitude, and words, and charitable in your actions.

In short, may all you women, whether aristocrat, bourgeois, or lower class,[20] be on your guard at all times and ably defend yourselves against those who threaten your honor and chastity. See, my ladies, how these men accuse you of the worst vices everywhere. Prove them all wrong by showing your virtue. Show those who criticize you that they are liars by doing the right things, so you can say with the Psalmist: "The vices of the evil will fall on their own heads." Repel those treacherous cajolers who use various tricks and cunning methods to try to take from you your most precious possessions, namely, your honor and your glorious reputation. Oh, my ladies, run! Flee from this mad passion they will urge on you! Flee, for God's sake, flee! No good can come

---

20. Many Christine scholars have emphasized this fairly unusual effort on the part of a medieval writer to address all classes—or at least, to have matters of concern for all estates discussed. In *The Treasure of the City of Ladies* Christine will also address women of different social conditions. In this volume see also Part III of *The Book of the Body Politic*, where Christine discusses the challenges and duties of "the common people."

from it. On the contrary! You may be sure that no matter how much their deceptions tempt you, they will always end up to your disadvantage. Do not believe that the opposite is true, because it cannot be any other way. Remember, my dear ladies, how these men call you weak, shallow, and docile and yet how they try their best to come up with all sorts of strange and deceptive tricks to catch you, as if they were laying traps to catch animals. Flee! Flee, ladies, and avoid their company, because their smiles hide painful and deadly poison.

Most honored ladies, may it please you to cultivate virtue and run away from vice, increasing and multiplying our City's inhabitants. May you rejoice in doing good and may I, your servant, commend myself to you in your prayers to God that He grant me the grace to live on in this world and carry on in His holy service. May He, at the time of my death, forgive me my great flaws and grant me eternal joy, and may He do likewise unto you.

Amen.

Here ends the third and final part of The Book of the City of Ladies.

The Book of the Body Politic

[*Le Livre du corps de policie*][1]

Written sometime between 1404 and 1407 (as France was facing increasing political instability), The Book of the Body Politic *is yet another text of Christine de Pizan's in the mirror-for-princes genre, one dedicated to the young Dauphin, Louis of Guyenne. But Christine's deployment of exempla here is evidently addressed to all social classes, which she, following in the footsteps of Livy, Plutarch, and John of Salisbury, conceives as interdependent parts of a body: the head (princes, addressed in Part I), the arms and the hands (knights and nobles, addressed in Part II), and the belly, the legs, and the feet (the common people, addressed in Part III).[2] If Christine again builds on the authority of countless authors here (most notably Aristotle, Valerius Maximus, Brunetto Latini, Giles of Rome, Boethius),* The Book of the Body Politic *is nevertheless a text where her own distinctive voice as a politically engaged author resonates clearly. This work is, indeed, no mere compilation. Her reflections on justice, flattery, the problems tied to excessive taxation of the poor, the importance of having experienced and honest counselors, the utility of fear in politics, and the interconnectedness of all parts of society (to name just a few of the themes touched on below) all put Christine de Pizan squarely in conversation with key interlocutors within the tradition of political theory and underscore her deep concern over the fate of France.*

---

1. Ms. F, critical edition by Angus J. Kennedy (Chantilly, Bibliothèque et Archives du Château, 294). Control: Ms. A (BN f.fr. 12439) at http://gallica.bnf.fr/ark:/12148/btv1b84497115/f98.vertical.

2. For insightful scholarly discussions of Christine's conception of the body politic, see Karen Green and Constant J. Mews, ed., *Healing the Body Politic: The Political Thought of Christine de Pizan* (Turnhout: Brepols, 2005); Kate L. Forhan, "Polycracy, Obligation, and Revolt: The Body Politic in John of Salisbury and Christine de Pizan," in *Politics, Gender and Genre: The Political Thought of Christine de Pisan*, ed. M. Brabant (Boulder, Colo.: Westview, 1992); Stephen Rigby, "The Body Politic in the Social and Political Thought of Christine de Pizan," *Cahiers de recherches médiévales et humanistes* (2013), http://crm.revues.org/12965; Anne Coldiron, "The Mediated 'Medieval' and Shakespeare," in *Medieval Shakespeare: Pasts and Presents*, ed. Ruth Moore, Helen Cooper, and Peter Holland (Cambridge: Cambridge University Press, 2013), 55–77. The analogy between the political community and the body can be traced back (if not to Plato) to the work of Plutarch and Livy. Even if Plutarch was not directly known to Christine except via John of Salisbury in his *Policraticus* (1159), John's reference to Plutarch in the development of this analogy was not without foundation in Plutarch's work, especially as noted in his "Life of Coriolanus." The *Policraticus* further developed this notion and adapted it in the form of an advice book written for princes and their counselors. For a broader history of the idea of the body politic, see David G. Hale, *The Body Politic* (The Hague: Mouton, 1971).

Here begins The Book of the Body Politic, *which deals with virtue and morals. It is divided into three parts: the first part is addressed to princes, the second to knights and noblemen, and the third to all other people. The first chapter describes the Body Politic.*

Part I

Chapter 1.

If it is possible for vice to give birth to virtue, then in this part I am happy to be as impassioned as only a woman can be. Many men believe, in any case, that women are incapable of holding their tongue and keeping strong feelings to themselves, so let the inexhaustible source and fountain of my feelings, which cannot be kept from spouting the desire for virtue, boldly reveal itself and pour out its essence through many clear streams. Oh virtue, worthy and divine concept, how dare I be vain enough to talk about you, knowing that my brain is not capable of fully understanding you and putting you into words? But I console myself and draw courage from the sense that you are too kind to be displeased if I talk about you, not about the most subtle aspects but only about what I can conceive and understand.

I will search my mind, then, for what it knows of good morals, talking first about the deeds and rules of conduct of our superiors, that is, the princes, humbly asking their majesties not to take this the wrong way or have contempt for the inferior intelligence in such a humble creature as I am for daring to speak about the principles of such exalted ranks. May it please them to remember the lesson of the philosopher who said: "However exalted your position, do not disdain or belittle the one who speaks words of wisdom to you." After that, by the grace of God, I hope to talk about the way of life that befits the nobles and knights, and third, about all the other people. These three types of estate must reside in one polity, akin to a real, living body in line with the words of Plutarch who, in a letter to the emperor Trajan, compared the Republic to a living body in which the prince or princes hold the place of the head because they are or should be sovereign.[3] From them ought to issue the individual ordinances, just as the physical actions executed by the limbs spring from a person's brain. The knights and the noblemen hold the place of the hands and the arms, because just as a person's arms have the strength to endure sweat and toil, so they must defend the rights of the prince and the state. They are also comparable to the hands, because just as the hands repel harmful things, so they must reject and cast aside all wicked, useless things. The rest of the people are like the belly, the feet, and the legs, because just as the belly receives everything that is prepared by the head and the limbs, so the actions of the prince and the nobles must be directed to the good and the benefit of the public, as will be explained more fully later on. And just as the legs and the feet support the actions of the human body, so the laborers support all the other estates.

Chapter 2. On the portrayal of righteous happiness

We must discuss virtue, then, in the interest of the way of life in the three different estates. This is the virtue that must rule human life in all its activities, and no one can attain honor without it. It should be the right degree of honor. As Valerius puts it, honor is the richest sustenance of virtue. And Aristotle says on this topic that honor should be revered as a testimony of virtue, which means that honor must only be attributed to the virtuous, because he does not mention the powerful and the rich, only the virtuous. According to him, only the good are honored. And nothing is more precious to noble hearts than honor. As he says in the fourth book of his *Ethics*, neither power nor wealth is desirable, only honor. It is good, then, that honor, and thereby virtue, is a quality that is particularly suited to kings and powerful rulers.

Now we should distinguish the three elements of what we understand as virtue. In chapter 20 of his book *The City of God*, Saint Augustine expresses it as follows: "The philosophers say that virtue is the end of human good and evil, which means that human felicity lies in being virtuous." It is appropriate

---

3. This is not the only place in her oeuvre where Christine de Pizan has recourse to this analogy: see most notably her *Long Path of Learning* (e.g., lines 5476–516). The letter to Trajan is often regarded as apocryphal and most likely something devised by John of Salisbury himself for his *Policraticus*. See Forhan, "Polycracy," but also Mark Beck, "Plutarch to Trajan: The Dedicatory Letter and the Apophthegmata Collection," in *Sage and Emperor: Plutarch, Greek Intellectuals and Roman Power in the Time of Trajan (98–117 AD)*, ed. P. A. Stadter and L. Van der Stockt (Leuven: Leuven University Press, 2002), 163–73. It was largely through this letter that Plutarch's name came to be widely known in medieval thought.

that there be great joy in felicity, otherwise it would not be felicity. The ancient philosophers portrayed this joy and felicity in the shape of a beautiful, lovely queen seated on a royal throne, surrounded by the virtues. They watch her face, waiting for her commands, ready to serve and obey her. She commands Prudence to make diligent inquiries about how she can be sure of a long reign in good health and safety. She commands Justice to do what she must to safeguard the laws so there will be peace. She commands Fortitude that if her body should suffer pain, she should moderate it by defying it and thinking virtuous thoughts. She commands Temperance to ensure that she takes wine, food, and other tasty things in moderation so that no harm will befall her by taking more than is reasonable.

From this description, one can understand that being virtuous is nothing more than having in oneself all the things that attract good and turn away evil and vice. For the body politic to function properly, therefore, it is necessary that the head be healthy, in other words, virtuous. For if it fell ill, the entire body would feel it. We will begin, then, by discussing things that benefit the head, that is, the king or the princes, and because our work begins with the head, we will first turn to age, that is, the childhood of the prince who is brought up under the guardianship of his parents.

Chapter 9. How a good prince should resemble a good shepherd

Having discussed the first point, about what should be the primary basis of a prince's virtue, we must go on to the second point, which is that he must be more singularly devoted to the public good and its advancement than to his own, according to the teaching of Aristotle's *Politics*.[4] That says that we speak of tyranny when a prince pursues his own good over the public good and that this is contrary to royal stewardship, which must be more concerned with the interests of the people than its own. What follows is advice about how that devotion should extend and demonstrate itself.

A good prince who loves his country will carefully guard his people the way a good shepherd guards his sheep. He makes every effort to defend them against wolves and savage animals and keeps them clean and in good health so they can increase, be fruitful, and produce lovely, dense fleece full of lanolin from the land that nourishes and keeps them, and so the shepherd is well paid

---

4. Aristotle distinguishes between correct and deviant regimes on the basis of whether they are geared toward the rulers' interest or the interest of all (this is central to his distinction between tyranny and kingship). See his *Politics*, most notably Book III, 1279a15–20.

for the fleece that is properly shorn in season. But a rich shepherd, who has to look after a great deal of property because he can't look after all his flocks all by himself, makes sure that he has good, competent help. He takes on skilled, careful servants who are capable, diligent, and good at their job and whom he knows to be loyal and devoted to his interest. He arranges for them to be provided with good, strong dogs with ironclad collars, well trained by frequent trips to the fields to chase off wolves. They untie them at night in the pen so that if thieves creep in to steal the sheep, the dogs will attack them. By day, they keep them tied to their belts and close by while the sheep peacefully graze the fields. But if the servants happen to hear noises from wolves or savage animals leaping from the woods or the mountains, they unleash them and let them run free. They often track those animals, and to make the dogs bolder, they run after them with strong, ironclad staffs, attacking the wolf or beast of prey. And if a sheep happens to stray and wander away from the flock, the clever dogs, which are trained for that purpose, chase it without hurting it. They bark at it and lead it back to the flock. And in that way, the capable servants defend and guard them so well that they provide excellent returns for the head shepherd, who keeps a close eye on things.

Continuing with the analogy, a good prince is vigilant about the defense and care of his country and people, and although it would be impossible for him to be everywhere at once and look after everything that needs to be done, he appoints experienced aides to take care of military matters and other affairs. They are the bravest of leaders whom he knows to be capable, loyal men who hold him in affection, such as the constable, marshals, the admiral, and others. He makes them responsible for engaging good, well-trained soldiers with battle experience. They bind them to themselves by oath and don't allow them to move without permission. They stay close by so that whatever happens, they are able to move against the enemy at once with all their men, and the country is never trampled or the people killed or subjected to plunder.

That is not to say that the military themselves make a habit of trampling, looting, and pillaging the country as they are currently doing in France. They would not dare do that anywhere else, and it is a great tragedy and a perverse practice that those who are assigned to defend the people wind up pillaging, robbing, and devastating them. There are some, in fact, who commit such cruelties that short of killing the people or setting fire to their property, any enemy could not do worse. That is not the proper way of conducting a war, which should be fought justly and without abuse. If not, the soldiers and the princes who send them off to war are in great danger of incurring the wrath of God and being severely punished, for the people's imprecations, a justifiable result of too much oppression, can undoubtedly provoke a great deal of ill fortune from God. There are many examples of that in the Holy Scripture and elsewhere, for everyone must know that God is just. All this aberration stems from bad organization, because if the soldiers were well paid, they could be ordered on pain of punishment not to take anything without paying for it. That way, they could buy as many provisions as they require and anything else at a good price. It is truly amazing how people can live under such rules and without any compassion for their lives. May they be visited by the Holy Spirit, father of the poor.

Going back to what I said before, if a shepherd had a dog that chased his sheep, he would soon let him have the stick. That is not something a good, God-fearing prince who loves his people should tolerate. And just as the dogs are unleashed at night in the pen to guard against thieves, so, too, should the chieftains deploy sentinels and spies on distant borders so the country and the people are not caught off guard at night by any ruses and can discover the enemy's tricks.

The soldiers should have yet another duty. Just as a good dog brings back a sheep that has strayed from the flock, they must shepherd any common people who are found to be eager to rebel or join the enemy, driven by fear or ill will. They must put them back on the right path, either by threat or by taking good care of them. And although it may displease and surprise some that I compare the noble office of warrior to the nature of a dog, a dog truly has many natural characteristics that a good man-at-arms should aim at and emulate. A dog is devoted to its master and extremely loyal, just as a good man-at-arms should be. It is brave and will risk death to defend its master, and when it has been told to guard a place, it listens very carefully and is highly alert so it can run after villains or thieves. It doesn't bite its master's friends but instinctively knows them, nor does it bite the neighbors or the members of the household where it is fed. Instead, it will guard them as best it can. It is very brave and fights with all its strength, it is intelligent and knowledgeable and very affectionate toward anyone who befriends it. All these traits are characteristics a good soldier should possess.

Chapter 10. On the same topic

To return to our first topic, just as a good shepherd takes care that his sheep are well kept and in good health, a good prince will not rely on his ministers for everything but will show himself to be compassionate enough toward his subjects that he wants to hear as many cases as he can. He will not dismiss or scorn the pitiful supplications of his people but will graciously agree to their requests based on mercy and justice. He will ensure that they are not unnecessarily distressed or ruined by bad ministers and officials.

To speak clearly on this topic would take a great deal of time and space, and stating the truth about many things may displease some. But it is surely a great pity that such truth must be kept hidden out of fear or favoritism. Seneca discusses this in the sixth book of his *De Beneficiis,*[5] in chapter 21. "I will show you," he says, "what those who are of high rank lack and what those who are believed to have everything need: someone to tell them the truth." That opinion is correct, because the servants close to the princes are not concerned with the well-being of their employers but with their own gain. For that reason, they tend to flatter and say things that will please their masters, thus blinding them with their cajolery. As is written in the third book, chapter 10, of the *Policraticus*, the flatterer is the enemy of all virtues and a thorn in the side of anyone he befriends.[6] As to those officials, both good and bad, and without going into great detail about them and their actions, may it please God that the princes know them well, are aware of their actions, and know the people around them and the way they administer their affairs. For I believe that there is nothing more vile or corrupt than the conscience of some of those men in all their perversities.

There are many who are so malicious that they cunningly hide their vices through deceitful trickery, casting them in the shadow and color of virtue. Yet they cannot hide the fact that their deeds and words, as charming as they seem, contain no truth, and they reveal their perversity to those who fall into their power and their hands. But this is not at all clear to the lords before whom they dissemble, and no one dares tell them for fear of displeasing them by criticizing their people. There is a common saying going around

---

5. Roman philosopher Seneca's *On Benefits* (first-century CE) is a treatise that chiefly deals with how to give and receive benefits. For the passage singled out here by Christine in a modern edition, see Book Six, chap. 30 of *On Benefits*, trans. by Miriam Griffin and ed. Brad Inwood (Chicago: University of Chicago Press, 2011).

6. The challenge posed by flattery for rulers is a common topos in classical and medieval political texts. In addition to John of Salisbury's *Policraticus* (book III), see Aristotle's *Politics*, 1313b35–1314a10. In Dante's epic poem *Inferno* (with which Christine was familiar), flatterers are immersed in feces (18.113–17). The issue of flattery and honest counsel would also be important in Renaissance political thought—e.g., Erasmus' 1516 *The Education of a Christian Prince* (see chap. 2) and Machiavelli's 1513 *The Prince* (see chap. 23).

among the people of the court these days: "My lord has such a generous spirit, because he never likes to hear ill spoken of his people." Alas! Having a generous spirit should include a willingness to hear the truth. But if someone were falsely accused through envy, as could happen, they would have just cause to mete out proper punishment after conducting an inquiry and to remove the accuser as a vicious slanderer. That way, their people would be afraid to misbehave and would stop doing many of the nefarious things that are going on. A good prince should not allow these things: he should expect every one of his subjects to peacefully perform whatever duties God has placed before him. The nobles should attend to their duties, the clergy to the sciences and the divine service, the merchants to their merchandise, the artisans to their crafts, and the laborers to the cultivation of the soil. And so everyone, whatever their rank, should live in a well-organized fashion without being exposed to extortion or unseemly charges, so they can earn a proper livelihood and live under their prince loving him as he should be loved by his people. That way, the prince is able to receive the legitimate revenues to which he is entitled and collect them from his country without sucking the blood of his poor commoners.[7] Valerius[8] recounts that when Emperor Tiberius was asked why he didn't collect more taxes from his people as he certainly could, he replied: "A good shepherd should shear his sheep once a year rather than fleece them all the time or pull off their skin and cause them to bleed."

---

7. Christine underscores the importance of not taxing commoners excessively in other works as well (e.g., *The Book of Peace*). Cary Nederman argues that Christine contributed significantly to the development of a political economy discourse in late medieval times—chiefly via her reflections on taxes and the need to feed the poor, and her discussion of the value of commerce, agriculture, and material well-being more generally. See his *Lineages of European Political Thought: Explorations along the Medieval/Modern Divide from John of Salisbury to Hegel* (Washington: Catholic University of America Press, 2009), 248–58.

8. Valerius Maximus (ca. first century CE) was a Roman historian and the author of *Factorum et dictorum memorabilium libri novem* [*Books of Memorable Deeds and Sayings*]—a key source of information about Roman history that was widely used by medieval authors. Christine had access to a French translation of that work, which is the chief source on which she relies for the exempla offered in her *The Book of the Body Politic*. But as far as the overall structure and spirit of the latter are concerned, her main inspiration is John of Salisbury's *Policraticus*. For discussions of the differences between Christine's and John's respective accounts of the corporate metaphor, see Forhan, "Polycracy"; Nederman, *Lineages of European Political Thought*, esp. 250–55.

Chapter 11. The love a good prince should have for his subjects

Now we should take a look at the legal rights of a prince to know whether a good prince can demand new taxes or financial support from the people under his rule when circumstances warrant it. It seems to me that the laws provide enough license and allow him to do this on certain occasions, as much as he can and wants to, to defend his territory from the enemy if they are waging war on him. In that case, he must remunerate men-at-arms to defend the country. Another reason is to marry off his children or to get them out of jail if they have been captured. In those special cases, a prince can impose new taxes on his subjects beyond his natural demesne without breaking the law. But that must be done with compassion and discretion to ensure that the poor are charged as little as possible and without taking more than what is necessary for purposes other than war and the reason for which it was levied.

And in that case, the rich must support the poor, instead of exempting the rich and placing a heavier burden on the poor the way it is done these days. At the risk of incurring displeasure and with respect, I dare say that it is a strange right to stipulate that the rich and the high officials of the king or princes, who have received their high and powerful rank from the king and the lords and can well afford the charges, should be exempt from paying while the poor, who have no emoluments from the king, are forced to pay. If I had given a large gift to one of my servants and greatly contributed to his way of life, estate, and prosperity and I happened to be in a predicament, would it not be reasonable to think that he would be under a greater obligation to help me out than others who never received compensation from me? It is a strange practice that is followed these days in this kingdom in deciding the amount of taxes. But if one wanted to change that, one would have to make them equal instead of making some rich people pay and exempt others, because that would bring envy: those being made to pay would see it as a humiliation and a form of servitude. If they were all charged equally, however, there would be no criticism.

But I do not mean to say that those engaged in wars for the defense of the country should not be exempt, and in what I say about the poor, I am moved to compassion by their bitter tears and laments. In raising the money to pay what has been imposed on them, some people and their households can no longer afford to eat and are forced to sell their bed or other poor possessions for next to nothing. May it please God to see that the king and the noble

princes of France are informed about this. There is no doubt at all that there
is so much kindness in their noble blood that they would not be able to bear
such hardship. But it often happens that some of those who collect the pay-
ments grow fat and rich, and God knows, as do others, whether everything
goes to the cause for which the tax was imposed. And if such a sum of money
is collected to be used for another purpose or something other than pure
necessity, it is a sin on the part of those who levied it and utterly disgraceful.

As for what was previously said about the noble Romans, who were unbe-
lievers and pagans and yet governed themselves so well that they should serve
us as an example, Valerius recounts that the law of Rome decreed that the
revenues collected for the wars could only be used for that specific purpose.
The law protected not only against excesses on the part of the state but also
against excess consumption of wine and meat because they, more than military activity and mental effort, cause the body to require rest. I will say no
more on this topic, although I could say a great deal, but while my opinion
of such things does not please the malicious ministers who have grown rich
on them and would reprimand me, I can tell them without insolence what
the great poet Euripides replied to the Athenians who asked him to remove a
sentence from a tragedy he had written. "Tragedy," said Valerius, "is a way of
writing that portrays misdeeds committed by the state and the community
or the princes." He said that he did not write in order to be criticized or to
criticize, but to teach people how to live well. Valerius also said that this poet
did not want to dishonor himself by submitting to other people's judgment
and abandoning his own opinion. Valerius further said that fealty is certainly
laudable when born from reason, which means that someone who is emi-
nently reasonable is able to judge the truth of his own good work and support
it with just cause, not out of pride or arrogance but in support of the merit of
the thing he deems worthy and laudable. For, he said, praising someone who
is clearly virtuous, and wanting to be praised for the same thing, stem from
the same mindset and a similar wisdom.

Chapter 19. How a good prince should cherish justice

I think we have now sufficiently discussed the subject matter of the first two
points and the branches that descend from them, as proposed earlier: how a
good, compassionate, nontyrannical prince should rely on the performance
of his government. To wit, he must first of all place the love and fear of God
above all else. In the second place, he should protect and cherish the public

good of his territory and country more than his own. Now we still have to talk about the third point, which is that he must protect and maintain justice. On that topic, we should first define justice and then discuss the way a good prince should protect it, what things are necessary for its protection, and how it was protected by the ancients who were well instructed in morals. We will use relevant examples, as we have been doing all along.

"Justice," said Aristotle, "is a measure that renders to each his due." Much more could be said about his words in describing this virtue. But since I have touched on this subject elsewhere, especially in my *Livre de la Prod'hommie de l'homme* [*Book of Man's Integrity*], I will only briefly touch on it at this point and then go on to the examples. A good prince should protect justice in such a way that no favoritism will lead him to violate and destroy it. The ancients loved it so much that they did not spare even their own children. This is evident from the actions of an emperor who proclaimed an edict stipulating that anyone who violated a certain rule would lose both eyes. When his own son violated this edict, he did not want to spare him the punishment. His son was supposed to succeed him, however, and someone who has lost his sight in both eyes is not suited to govern the republic, so the emperor found a remedy to carry out the punishment without preventing his son from being able to properly govern one day. This remedy was truly touching: he had one of his son's eyes removed and one of his own. My point is that while they rigorously protected justice in those days, it has certainly been renounced today. I have talked about this before and about evil ministers, so I will say no more about it.

But on the subject of rigorous justice, the valiant Roman prince by the name of Aulus Postumius did no less. Thanks to his wisdom and great boldness and bravery, he defeated a group of people called the Volsci. Before the battle began, he ordered an announcement made to the effect that no one, no matter how bold or brave, was to go into battle or leave the camp without his permission, under pain of death. Then this Aulus Postumius distanced himself from his army a little way to take care of something he had to do. He had a son who happened to discover a great crowd of enemies approaching on horseback, so the son rushed off with a large number of soldiers, engaged the enemy in battle, and defeated them. When his father returned and found out about this, he judged that despite the victory, the harm that would be caused by saving from death one who had broken the prince's law would be greater than the benefit gained from the victory over a group of enemies, because the others would follow his son's example. And so he had him beheaded.

But to go beyond such extreme examples, we will discuss how a good prince must protect justice and what he needs to accomplish that. He should, first and above all, be supplied with highly skilled, wise, worthy men and loyal counselors who care more about his life and honor and the good of the country than their own profit. I fear that they are hard to find these days! With such loyal, wise counselors, a prince can be well prepared in his country in terms of the application of justice and other specific rules while increasing and multiplying his power and wealth. Oh, what prince can ever sufficiently reward a wise, loyal, good counselor for all the great good he may derive from following his advice if he is willing to believe it? Is it not said in *The History of the Romans*[9] of the wise Scipio Nasica, who belonged to the family of the other noble Scipios who were such valiant warriors, that despite not being a warrior like the others, he was so wise and prudent in the republic's council and government that he accomplished as much through his wisdom as the others did with their weapons? And how, using his keen intellect, he fought some powerful Romans who wanted to gain control of both the Senate and the public good? Valerius says about him that he deserved no less praise in his role as peacemaker than the other warriors with their weapons, because he protected the city from many serious problems and many good things came about thanks to him.

Chapter 20. What sort of counselors a prince should take on

Now we should consider from among what sort of people a prince should select his counselors to ensure himself of good advice. Should they be young? No, because they gave King Jeroboam[10] bad advice, long ago, as they did to many others. A prince should choose the wisest and most experienced from among the old, for they are more capable and suitable to give good advice than the young. A loyal counselor needs to be well informed about matters before he gives advice and should not readily believe something based on appearances alone without first proving the truth and comparing and examining it, because at first glance, many things often appear to be something they are not.

Aristotle said in his *Rhetoric* that the old and the elderly do not easily believe things because they have been cheated in their lives on many

---

9. The author of this work is the Roman historian Lucius Florus (ca. 74–130 CE).

10. See I Kings 12.

occasions. They are not quick to decide about dubious things but look at them many times to envision the worst-case scenario, because they have seen things turn out that way numerous times before and so do not give advice in haste. They do not base high hopes on a shaky foundation and little evidence, because they have often seen things turn out differently from what was expected and thus do not encourage important undertakings without serious discussion and reflection. In the young, these things are generally the opposite; the elderly are more levelheaded by nature in everything they do. I do not say, however, that they are all wise and prudent, because, to quote Aristotle again, he says that there are two types of old age. One follows a well-ordered, temperate youth, as commended by Tully in his book *On Old Age*.[11] The other is the sort of old age that follows a dissolute and idle youth, subject to much misery and not worth recommending. And that is why I have said that a prince must select his counselors from the old and wise.

As a further comment, they may not have the same physical strength as the young, but there is greater virtue and discernment in the advice they give, and that is more useful and profitable than physical strength and deserves greater praise. The power of intelligence, discernment, and knowledge is nobler than physical power. For royal majesties, cities, polities, and public affairs are well supported and governed by the prudent advice of wise old men but are often brought down by the young, as Tully says and as is clearly spelled out in many chronicles. Thus, while old age lacks physical strength, it is generously endowed with intellectual and incisive strength, which is far more commendable. And as for those who lament their youth in old age, that is a sign that they are neither wise nor virtuous, because anyone who fails to choose the most profitable thing is certainly not wise. And some despise old age because it is deprived of physical pleasures and delights, but age is not to blame for that. In fact, it is greatly to be praised for it because it removes the root of all evil. As the great philosopher Archytas of Tarentum puts it, nature gave humans no greater pestilence than physical desire, which gives birth to treachery, subversion of cities and people, violence, and all sorts of evil. There is no evil that physical desire does not at some point tempt the human mind to commit. It stifles rational judgment and extinguishes the human spirit and thus has no affinity or connection with virtue. Thus, old age is more laudable and desirable because it offers intellectual delights that are commonly lacking

---

11. Treatise written by Roman orator and philosopher Marcus Tullius Cicero (106–43 BCE), whose *On Moral Obligations* informed many of Christine's works. But note that Cicero's good sense is called into question by Christine in *The Book of the City of Ladies*, I.9.

in youth. The elderly are nobler and without contradiction and inconsistency, as Aristotle says in book 8 of his *Ethics*. Tully says on this topic that old age is stronger and more courageous than youth. That is why the great sage Solon of Athens, when asked by the tyrant Peisistratus where he got the confidence that made him speak so boldly, replied that it was the strength of old age. These things are contained in the translation by Valerius, and I have collected a few of them in my preface about justice, to define the type of counselors who will benefit a good prince.

Chapter 21. How a good prince, even if gentle and kind, must inspire fear

Justice, how it is used, and to whom it applies are things that are well known: a good prince should punish criminals or have them punished. I will say no more about this because, as mentioned, I have dealt with it elsewhere. I now go on to the other things that befit a good prince: he should give each one his due according to the ability of justice.[12] By following that rule, which is just, he will not fail to be equitable in all things, and he will also render to himself what is due to him. For it is reasonable that the law he applies to others also applies to him. In other words, he will want to be obeyed and feared by law and by reason, as is appropriate for the majesty of a prince. Wherever a prince is not feared, there can be no proper justice.[13]

That a prince should be feared is demonstrated by the valiant Clearcus, who was duke of Lacedaemonia (a large part of Greece that used to be inhabited by amazingly brave people).[14] This duke was very chivalrous and a great warrior. To convince his people to fear fleeing more than dying, he told them that soldiers should fear their prince more than death or the enemy. As a result of these words and the punishment he set out for those who disobeyed

---

12. See also I.19 right above, where Christine invoked Aristotle's definition of justice.

13. Christine also underscores the importance of fear in *The Book of the Deeds and Good Morals of King Charles V*, III.9–10. In these chapters, she borrows from Giles of Rome's *The Governance of Kings and Princes*. Surely many other medieval writers also tackled the question of the relative importance of love and fear in politics (often inspired by Cicero's treatment of this subject). See John of Salisbury, *Policraticus*; Brunetto Latini, *The Book of Treasure*; Marsiglio of Padua, *The Defender of The Peace*. Looking forward in time, readers could compare Christine's account with Machiavelli's *The Prince*, chap. 17. For whether Machiavelli might have read Christine, see K. Forhan, *The Political Theory of Christine de Pizan* (Burlington, Vt.: Ashgate, 2002), 165–67.

14. Lacedaemonia is a part of Greece commonly associated with the Spartan city-state.

or failed, the soldiers fought without sparing themselves and achieved marvelous things. There is no doubt, then, that a prince must inspire fear even if he is gentle and kind. But this kindness should be considered as a matter of grace that should be carefully protected and kept from being scorned. That is why the ancients depicted the goddess of sovereignty in the form of a lady seated in great style on a royal throne, holding an olive branch in one hand and a naked sword in the other, signifying that sovereignty must incorporate kindness and mercy as well as justice and might.

A good prince, then, must be guided by wise elders and will render to each his due to the best of his ability, as stated. He will want those good men and all those who assist them to be honored for the merits of their abilities, according to the wise maxim that says: "Rise before a greybeard." In ancient times, people used to greatly honor worthy men of advanced age and they had an especially great respect for those from Lacedaemonia, who were very honorable Greeks. This began with the laws of Lycurgus, presented by their valiant and wise king. There were many fine laws that they maintained for a long time. One time, a very old man went to the stadium in Athens to see the games. The stadium was a special place where young men assembled to engage in a trial of physical strength against each other, with weapons or in jousts, wrestling matches, and other things. But none of the citizens of Athens offered this elderly man a seat, so he went away and happened to come upon the place where the Lacedaemonian legates, whom we would call ambassadors, were seated. They were young men, but they immediately showed the old man respect, as was their custom. They all rose and offered him an honorable place among them. When the people saw this, they greatly approved of the fine custom of this foreign city and said to each other: "We know what is right, but we must pay attention to the foreigners."

Part III

Chapter 1. The first chapter talks about how all the estates must unite and work together

In the first part of this book we presented our ideas about how a prince should be instructed, depicting the prince or princes as head of the body politic, as explained before. This was followed by the second part, in which we talked about the education of the nobles and the knights, whom we portrayed as the arms and the hands. Now in this third part, with God's help, we will talk about what we can gather from the judgment of the ancients in terms of good suggestions applicable to the remainder of this body politic, that is, the community of the common people, whom we depict as the belly, legs, and feet, so they can all be related and conjoined in a single living body, perfect and healthy. For just as the human body is not whole but defective and malformed when it lacks any of its members, so the body politic cannot be perfect, whole, and healthy if all the estates under discussion are not properly conjoined and connected together so they can support and help each other, each performing the task it is assigned. These various tasks should only be assigned and be performed for the conservation of the whole together, just as the members of a human body help guide and nourish the whole body. And as soon as one of them fails to serve, it follows that the whole body feels the effect and suffers deprivation.

We should, therefore, discuss the way these last parts of the body should be maintained in good health, because it seems to me that they support and carry the burden of all the rest of the body, thus needing the strength and power to carry the weight of the other parts. That is why just as we have spoken before about the love and care a good prince must have for his subjects and people and how the office of the nobles is established to guard and defend the people, we should discuss the love, reverence, and obedience good people should show their prince. Let us make the following broad statement on this topic: all estates owe the prince the same love, reverence, and obedience. After making a few points about ways to increase the virtue in their way of life, I may touch on three different types of estates that are a special part of this community. And because the three estates, that is, the princes, the knights, and the people, sometimes complain about each other in the belief that the others don't carry out their duties and offices as they should (leading to discord between them, which is a very harmful thing), here is a relevant moral tale in the guise of a fable:[15]

---

15. Christine de Pizan is obviously not the first to tell this story generally called the "fable of the belly": versions of it can be found in the Greek fabulist Aesop, in Livy's *History of Rome*, in Plutarch's *Life of Coriolanus*, in Valerius Maximus' *Memorable Deeds and Sayings*, in John of Salisbury's *Policraticus*, and in Marie de France (whose account of the story can be found in Nederman and Forhan, *Readings in Medieval Political Theory*, 25). See also Forhan, *Political Theory*, 50–54; Rigby, "Body Politic."

Once upon a time, there was a serious disagreement between the belly of a human body and its limbs. The belly bitterly complained about the limbs, saying that they held it in contempt and did not care for its comfort or provide it with sufficient nourishment. The limbs, on the other hand, bitterly complained about the belly, saying that they were exhausted from their work and that no matter how much they labored, coming and going and toiling, the belly wanted to have everything and was never satisfied. So they no longer wanted to suffer such pain and labor because they never managed to satisfy the belly anyway. They would all stop working and the belly could do what it wanted. The limbs stopped working accordingly and the belly was no longer sustained. It started to lose weight and the limbs began to fail and weaken. And so, to spite each other, all parts of the body died together.

In the same way, when a prince asks his people for more than they can provide and the people complain against the prince and become rebellious and disobedient, the resulting discord causes them to all perish together.

I conclude, then, that agreement preserves the entire body politic. And so attests Sallust, who says that small things grow through concord and big things wither through discord.

Chapter 2. On the differences between various nations

When writing a book, especially one that deals with customs and doctrines, one should keep it general and make it applicable to the inhabitants of countries everywhere, because books are dispersed and carried to various places and regions. The place where we live is part of France, however, and even though our words and thoughts can be useful in any other region in a general sense, we will content ourselves with addressing them to the French people. But anyone with a decent, proper intelligence will want to take them as a good example.

Lands governed by people throughout the world are ruled by various forms of government according to the ancient customs of those lands. Some are governed by elected emperors, others by hereditary kings, and so on. There are also cities and countries that have seigneuries and are governed by princes they elect among themselves. Those who vote often make their choices more by whim than based on reason, and that means that having elected them by whim, they depose them in the same manner. Such a government is not beneficial wherever it is practiced, such as in many places in Italy. Others are governed by certain families from the city called nobles, and they would never allow anyone other than members of those noble families to be part of their councils or deliberations. That is the case in the ancient city of Venice, for example, which has governed itself that way since its foundation. Others are governed by their elders, whom they call aldermen. Yet other places are governed by the common people, with a number of people from each trade being elected once a year. I think that such a government is very ineffective, and thus one rarely sees it last wherever it is introduced or any such country grow or live in peace, and for good reason. But I will say no more about that for the sake of brevity. Bologna *la grassa* was governed that way for a very short time, but it would take me too long to talk about each nation separately.

When it comes to choosing the most suitable form of government to administer the polity and community of people, says Aristotle in the third book of his *Politics*, the polity of one is best, meaning the governance and rule by a single person. Governance by a few is still good, he says, but governance by many is too difficult to succeed because of the diversity of opinions and desires.

Back to our topic, I consider the people of France very lucky. Ever since its foundation by the descendants of the Trojans, it has never been governed by foreign princes but always by the direct descendants of those who have always ruled it, as attested by the old history books and chronicles.[16] The governance by noble French princes has become natural to the people. For that reason and by the grace of God, the people of France have the most natural and sincere love and obedience for their leader of all countries and realms in the world. That is a singular and very special blessing, and they deserve great praise and merit for it.

. . .

---

16. The idea that the French state was founded by descendants of the Trojans was a popular one in late medieval France. Although its origin remains unclear, this old story often served to generate a political identity in France that stressed the community's distinctiveness from their Italian neighbors.

Chapter 6. About the second estate of people, that is, the burghers and merchants

I have said before that the second estate of the people is composed of the burghers and the merchants.[17] The burghers come from old families in the city. They have a proper surname and an ancient coat of arms. They are the most important inhabitants of the cities, and landlords and inheritors of houses and manors that provide their income. The books that mention them refer to them as citizens. Such people should be honorable, wise, and of good appearance, dressed in decent clothing without disguises or affectation. It behooves them to be true gentlemen, of good faith, and discreet. It is the good, honorable estate of the citizens. In some places, some of those old families are called nobility, when they have been people of good standing and reputation for a long time. Thus, the good burghers or citizens of the cities should be held in high esteem everywhere. It is an excellent, honorable thing for a city to have a prominent bourgeoisie, a great honor for the country, and a valuable treasure for the prince.

These people should conduct the affairs of the city of which they are part in such a way that all things related to commerce and community affairs are well governed. And since the common people generally are not very sensible in word or even deeds related to matters of public administration, they should not get involved in the regulations established by the princes. The burghers and those of high rank must take care that whatever happens, the common people must not impede matters or enter into evil conspiracies against the prince or the council. That is because such conspiracies or plots by the common people always come back to hurt those who have something to lose. It never is or has been to their benefit but always leads to an ugly, detrimental end. Thus, if there happens to be a case where the common people seem perturbed by some burden, the bourgeoisie should call together those of their members who are the wisest and most discreet in word and action. They should go before the princes or the council and humbly present the complaint. They should meekly state the case and not allow the common people

---

17. The three estates of the people discussed in Part III of *The Book of the Body Politic* are (1) the clerks (clergy; scholars; students); (2) the burghers and merchants; (3) the common people (craftsmen, laborers). For a helpful discussion of the significance of Christine's inclusion of clerks in the class of the *"menu peuple,"* see Tracy Adams, "The Political Significance of Christine de Pizan's Third Estate in the *Livre du corps de policie," Journal of Medieval History* 35 (2009): 385–98. See also Susan J. Dudash, "Christine de Pizan and the 'menu peuple,'" *Speculum* 78, no. 3 (July 2003): 788–831.

to become involved, because that will lead to the destruction of cities and countries. And so they should, as best they can, settle the common people's complaints to prevent the evil that may result from it in all places. They should protect themselves better than the others, and although the decisions of princes and their council may at times, in their judgment, seem somewhat unjust, they must not interpret everything as a defeat but say to themselves that what they did, they did with good intentions and that the reasons are not apparent to everyone. Making foolish complaints can be dangerous.

Speaking of knowing when to keep quiet, Valerius refers to Socrates in that respect, praising the wisdom of that philosopher's words. One time he was in a place where several people were talking about the princes' decrees, criticizing them. One of them asked him why he alone kept quiet when everyone else was talking. "Because," he said, "I have sometimes regretted speaking, but I have never regretted holding my tongue."

Thus it is a very good thing to hold one's tongue, because speaking may have dire consequences and lead to no good, while keeping quiet shows wisdom. Cato said the following on this topic: "The first virtue is to hold one's tongue. Someone who knows how to keep quiet, guided by reason, is close to God." And Seneca, in the fifth book of his last work, said that whoever wished to be a disciple of Pythagoras must be silent for five years. He told them that they should first learn what to say before they spoke.

Chapter 7. How wise burghers should counsel the ordinary people on their actions

As mentioned, the wise should instruct the ordinary people and the ignorant to keep quiet about things they ought not to talk about, because if they did speak, it could have dire consequences and lead to no good. Chapter 22 of the Book of Exodus testifies to this: "The law forbids such complaints." It also says: "You shall not complain about great lords, and you shall not curse those who rule the people." This is further confirmed by Solomon in the tenth chapter of the Book of Ecclesiastes, where he says: "Curse not the king, no not in thy thought," which means that a subject must not conspire against his lord.

The idea that complaining about and balking at princes' laws is perilous is confirmed by Justin in Book XII. He says that because of Alexander's many great victories when he had taken power in Persia, he wished to be greeted according to a local custom that expressed adoration (what we would refer to as kneeling or speaking while on one's knees). This was not customary in Macedonia or other regions, and there were complaints. Aristotle, no longer able to bear the hardship of traveling with Alexander, sent Alexander the philosopher Callisthenes in his place. Callisthenes harshly reproved Alexander and had much to say about this practice of adoration, so Alexander had him killed. Valerius says, indeed, that when Aristotle left Alexander, he left Callisthenes in his place. Callisthenes was Aristotle's disciple and a very wise man. Aristotle instructed him to avoid talking about the ruler's defects behind his back, telling him that this should not be done for two reasons. First, it is unbecoming for a subject to criticize his lord. Secondly, the moment such words leave one's mouth, they will instantly be reported by the sycophants. Aristotle also instructed him to restrict his conversations with Alexander, and when he did speak to him, to do so cheerfully. This was so that by keeping his words to a minimum, he would not say something that would put him in danger. Nor should he flatter him, but cheerful phrasing would make what he said more acceptable to him. But his disciple did not adhere to his master's teaching and repented too late.

Still on the topic of how one should not balk at a prince's laws and related to Alexander's killing of the philosopher for criticizing his law, Valerius recounts what the philosopher Demades told the people of Athens. When Alexander wanted to be greeted with adoration, as mentioned above, he sent word to the people of Athens to tell them that this was his wish. The Athenians, who were more accustomed than other people to respect ceremonies and legal rules, held a council to discuss this, and they were all of the opinion that they would not do him an honor that was only appropriate for the gods. Then the wise Demades, who knew quite well what could happen if they disobeyed their princes, told them: "Be careful not to lose the earth in your concern for heaven."

The above can serve as an example in any country, but thank God we do not have cruel princes in France with their hands covered in the blood of their people. I can say without flattery, because it is true, that France has more kindhearted, humane princes than any other country in the world. That is all the more reason why they should be readily obeyed. And although the people may think at times that their burdens are heavy, they do not believe that people elsewhere, in other kingdoms or countries, are less troubled than they are in France. Even if those people are not affected by certain things because of the privileges they enjoy, they are afflicted by other harmful forms of subjection, such as great cruelty committed against them or among themselves in the form of massacres. There is no justice or other system that protects them from that. And although, without disrespect to those who contradict this, no one says that there are no bad things in France or that there are no complaints about them, I hold that of all the countries in Christendom, France is the one where people generally enjoy a better life, as much because of the benevolence and lack of cruelty on the part of the princes as the courtesy and amiability of the people of this nation. And it is not favoritism that makes me say this, because I was not born here.[18] But may God be my witness in His retribution: I believe that I am telling the truth as I see it. Based on what I have learned about other countries, it is not paradise on earth, but then everyone should know that every country has its tribulations.

If I wanted to speak about cruel princes in ancient history and even in more recent times, I would find enough to say. But since that would not provide any good examples, I will not dwell on it for long. Since we have been discussing people being burdened by their lords, let me mention the tyrant Dionysius, who invented a shockingly false and dishonest trick to play on his people. Having been defeated in battle, this Dionysius conceived of a most wicked and malicious plan to recover his financial losses. He had a public announcement made to convince his people and citizens that the defeat he had suffered was caused by the sin of not having kept a vow he had made to the goddess Venus. He had vowed that if she helped him and granted him the privilege of gaining victory in the battle he was about to fight, all the country's ladies and virgins would honor this goddess by giving pleasure to any man who asked for it on the day of the festival dedicated to her. Since he had not fulfilled his vow after gaining victory in the battle, the goddess Venus, seeking revenge for his betrayal in not having kept his vow, had turned against him in his most recent battle, which is why he had been defeated. For that reason, to fulfill his vow and satisfy the goddess, he ordered that on the day of the festival devoted to the goddess, all ladies and maidens should wear the most elegant and the richest clothes they could find, and that those who did not have enough jewels should borrow them. They should go to the temple, from where they would be accompanied to the public square. The men would be made to swear that they would not touch any of them. Because of that promise, the foolish, deluded people in that lawless country took what the king led them to believe as the truth. They agreed to have their wives and daughters taken there, thinking that this would settle the matter of the vow

---

18. Recall that Christine was born in Venice (but moved to France as a child).

to the goddess Venus without causing harm to the honor and chastity of their wives and daughters. And so it was decreed. All the ladies went to the temple, dressed as elegantly and richly as they could manage. But Dionysius, their king, had other ideas. He had lied and pretended, and having discovered the wealth of his people and burghers by observing their clothes and jewels, he concluded that he could well afford to levy more taxes. He immediately sent some people to the temple to rob them of their rich robes and jewels, and the wealthiest matrons were beaten and tortured to force them to reveal their husbands' treasures.

This Dionysius, who was king of Sicily, deserves to be called an evil prince. But so that no one will feel the desire to emulate him, it should be pointed out that an evil life usually attracts an evil end. His end was certainly bad: after committing many evil deeds, he was villainously slain by his own people. He was succeeded by his son, who was also called Dionysius. He came to a bad end as well, because he was deposed and wound up teaching children in a Corinthian school to gain a living. That is how the misdeeds and sins of the father were visited upon the child. When that happens, says the Holy Scripture, "The fathers eat sour grapes and their children's teeth are set on edge." Elsewhere it is written: "Our fathers have sinned and we will bear the iniquity."

Still on the subject of bad princes, and God keep us from them, there was once a king in Egypt named Ptolemaeus Phiton, who counted debauchery and lechery among his many vices. Valerius says that he was called Phiton because the name has been interpreted as synonymous with proliferation and increase of vice. His lechery caused him to commit many crimes and infinite evil, which is why he wound up dying an infamous death. He has left an ignominious memory.

Chapter 10. On simple laborers

As for the estate of simple laborers of the earth, what should I say about them? Although despised and oppressed by many, they comprise the most necessary estate of all. They are the cultivators of what feeds and nourishes human beings, and without them, the world would come to an end in no time at all. Those who do them so much harm really do not pay attention to what they do, because if any reasonable creature did think about it, he would consider himself in their debt. It is a sin to be ungrateful for all the services they render us. And they truly are the feet that support the body politic, for they support every person's body with their labor. That they do nothing ignoble and that God respects their office is evident because in the first place, the world's two chief patriarchs from whom all life is descended were both laborers of the earth. The first one was Adam, the first father, about whom the second chapter of Genesis says: "God took the first man and put him in a paradise of pleasure to cultivate, foster, and protect it." We can draw two arguments from this scripture to prove the honesty of labor. The first is that God commanded it, which made it the first of all crafts. The second argument is that this craft was created during the state of innocence. The second patriarch was Noah, from whom everyone descended after the flood. The ninth chapter of Genesis says: "Noah was a man of the soil and after the flood he set out to work the land, and he planted a vineyard." And so our other ancient patriarchs were all cultivators of the earth and shepherds of animals. I will not tell their stories for the sake of brevity, but in the ancient past, the occupation was certainly neither ignoble nor despised.

In his *History of the Romans*, Florus relates how after winning many battles, the Roman emperor Diocletian voluntarily abdicated and spent the rest of his life in a village called Sallon working as a man of the soil. A long time later, when the princes of Rome had great need of the good governing skills of such a valiant man, Lentulus and Galerius sent for him, asking him to return to Rome and take over the empire, to which he replied: "Ah! If you had seen the beautiful cabbages I planted with my own hands, you would not ask me to return to the empire." This was to say that he had more peace of mind in his humble position and greatly preferred it to taking on a heavy and perilous responsibility such as the empire.

On this subject, Valerius tells us in the third chapter of his fourth book about the most valiant, noble Roman Atilius, who was taken from his work as a laborer to be the emperor. As he worked his plow in the fields, the knights came to find him and made him chief and leader of the entire Roman army. And after he left his post as leader of the army, this man whose hands had been hardened by his labor at the plow reestablished the Republic through the strength of his noble spirit and his own hands. Without him, the Republic would have gone into a decline. Valerius says this about him: "The hands that had led a team of oxen before the plow wound up leading battle chariots." And having gained great and noble victories, he was not ashamed to give up the honor of being emperor and return to the work he had left behind.

These stories help us understand that the estate of simple laborers or others of low rank is not to be scorned, as some would have it. When those of the highest rank choose a humble and simple life for their retirement years as being the most beneficial for the body and the soul, those who voluntarily elect to live in poverty are surely rich. They have no fear of being betrayed, poisoned, robbed, or envied, and their wealth lies in sufficiency.

To confirm this, let me tell you what Valerius said about sufficiency in relation to a very rich man. Once upon a time, he said, there was a king in Lydia by the name of Gyges. He considered himself so grand that he went to ask the god Apollo if there was anyone else happier than he was. The god Apollo replied that Aglaus Sophidius was happier than he. This Aglaus was the poorest man in Arcadia and very old, yet he had never left his small field and was content with the small yield on which he lived and with what he owned. That shows how Apollo interpreted happiness as sufficiency and not wealth, because wealth does not bring sufficiency, repose, or security. Instead, it brings great worry and much fear and anxiety. And so King Gyges, who believed that the god should confirm that no one was happier than he, was mistaken in his vain opinion and learned where to find pure, sound wealth and happiness.

That happiness, that is, sufficiency, is acknowledged by both Anaxagoras and Ptolemy in the prologue of the *Almagest*: "He who cares not in whose hands the world lies, is happy." And that this saying is true is proven by all the sages and poets and especially all the saints who chose a pure and humble life as their greatest means of salvation, which is how one can save oneself in any estate. At the same time, it is a very powerful feat to pass through flames without burning oneself. There is no doubt whatsoever that the estate of the poor, despised by all, comprises many good and worthy people leading a pure life.

Chapter 11. Christine concludes her book

I have, God be praised, come to the point where I was headed, namely, to bring to an end this book that I started with the head of the body as described by Plutarch, with the body being the polity and the head portraying the princes. I humbly beg first the king of France, supreme head, and then the princes and all others of their noble blood to take some pleasure in the diligent labor of writing by their humble creature Christine, both in this work and her other books, present and future. And since she is a woman of humble knowledge, may she be forgiven for any mistakes and her good intentions be taken into account, for her sole aim was to achieve a good result through the effect of her work. As a reward, I beg those living and their noble successors, kings and other French princes, to pray to God for indulgence and remission of my sins, in remembrance of my words in times to come, when my soul will have left my body.

Likewise, I ask those French knights and nobles and anyone else no matter their origin who think of me by reading my humble writings or hearing about them, to say the Lord's Prayer in recognition. And in the same way, may God through His holy mercy protect all people, that is, the three estates and the whole together, and ever increase their perfection of body and soul. Amen.

The end.

from Christine de Pizan's
Lamentation on France's Ills

[La Lamentacion sur les maux de la France de Christine de Pizan][1]

What in all likelihood prompted the writing of this brief and passionate text is the prospect of a true civil war taking place in France—culmination of the bitter, ongoing rivalries that had been taking place between the House of Burgundy and the House of Orléans since the death of Philippe le Hardi in 1404. Having just made an alliance with several dukes and counts (the League of Gien), the Orleanists appeared to be willing to enter Paris to confront John the Fearless, Duke of Burgundy, and his own troops and supporters. In what follows, Christine is hoping to convince the Duke of Berry, brother of the late Charles V (1338–1380), to intervene briskly to avoid an excessively bloody military confrontation between the princes. Indeed, the Duke of Berry is asked to "firmly seize the bridle." But Christine is also inviting Queen Isabeau of Bavaria (wife of the king whose bouts of insanity had been increasingly debilitating) to take up her rightful role in this turmoil. Written on August 23, 1410, this Lamentation *is striking not only for its decisive tone and its repeated invocation of a very common Christinian topos, the value of tears, but also for the hopeful note it strikes toward the end, in the midst of Christine's despondency.*

Anyone who has any compassion should bring it to bear,
For now is the time that it is needed.

Feeling alone and on the outside looking in,[2] barely able to hold back the tears that blur my vision and stream down my face like a fountain, I try to compose this sad lament even as bitter tears of sorrow for the monumental calamity keep blotting out my writing. I am terrified, and in my lament, I

---

1. Source: Ms. fr. 24864 (http://gallica.bnf.fr/ark:/12148/btv1b8451465g/f33).

2. This evocation of being on the margins and alone ("seulette") comes back repeatedly in Christine's oeuvre. See Mary McKinley, "The Subversive Seulette: Christine de Pisan's Lamentacion," in *Politics, Gender and Genre: The Political Thought of Christine de Pisan,* ed. M. Brabant (Boulder, Colo.: Westview, 1992): 157–69; Lori Walters, "The Figure of the Seulette," in *Desireuse de plus avant enquerre . . .* (Paris: Honoré Champion, 2008): 119–40.

have this to say: "Oh! How is it possible that the human heart can turn man into a rapacious, cruel beast, even at the whim of Fortune? What became of the reasons for giving him the title of 'rational animal'? How can it be in Fortune's power to change a man to the point where he is transformed into a serpent, the enemy of human nature? Alas! This is how that can happen, you noble French princes! And do not be angry if I ask you what has become of that sweet, natural blood you have shared since time immemorial. It used to be the pinnacle of benevolence in this world, recorded in bona fide, ancient history books and sung by Fame in her songs throughout the world. What has become of the clear-eyed, noble understanding that, by nature and through long habit, made you heed the advice of wise men endowed with just, moral principles? Are they now blind? So it would seem, you fathers of French society, whose ancestors used to guard, defend, and feed the many children of this once-blessed land that is now transformed into desolation unless Mercy intervenes. Those who show you divine adoration, who bring honor upon you in lands everywhere: what harm have they done you? Today you do not treat them like your children but like mortal enemies, for the discords among you cause them nothing but grief, war, and battle.

"For God's sake! For God's sake! You noble princes, open your eyes for a vision of what will happen when you take up arms! You will see cities in ruin, towns and castles destroyed, fortresses razed to the ground! And where? In France's navel! The noble knights and youth of France, who used to be united like body and soul, ready to defend the crown and the public interest, have now assembled in a shameful battle, one against the other, father against son, brother against brother, relatives against each other, engaging in deadly violence to cover the pitiful fields with blood, corpses, and severed limbs. Oh! What a dishonorable victory for whoever gains it! What sort of glory will he be able to boast of? Will it be crowned with laurels? Alas, no. It will be wrapped in shame in pitch-black thorns, considering itself not a victory but the murderer of its own blood, for which it ought to cover itself in black clothing of the sort one wears at the death of a relative.

"Oh, you knight who returns from such a battle, please tell me what honor you derive from it! Will the records of your heroic deeds add to your honor by reporting that you were on the side of the winners that day? But even though you survived that peril, it should be weighed against your other heroic deeds, because such a disgraceful day does not deserve praise. Oh, if men would only agree—because God certainly would!—not to take up arms, either for one side or the other.

"And what in the name of God will be the consequences? Famine, because of the plundering and destruction of goods that will take place and the failure to cultivate the fields, which will lead to rebellion by the people who are brutalized and robbed by the military, who are severely oppressed, ruined, and pillaged from all directions. There will be revolts in the cities because of the outrageous taxes that will be levied on the citizens and inhabitants to raise the necessary funds.[3] Above all, the English, who are waiting in the wings, will checkmate us if Fortune lets them. Finally, the dissension and lethal hatred will lead to betrayals that will take root in numerous hearts. Was that the objective? It certainly seems so!

"Weep, therefore, weep, you ladies, maidens, and women of the kingdom of France! Cry out and beat your palms together as did the disconsolate Argia with the ladies of Argos long ago in similar circumstances. For the swords that will make you widows and rob you of your children and relatives have already been sharpened. Oh, you Sabine women, we would have need of you in this predicament, because the peril and strife between your relatives was no greater than what we are facing here, when you so wisely intervened to make peace, when a great crowd of you planted yourselves on the battlefield, disheveled, with your small children in your arms, crying: 'Have mercy on our loved ones and family! Make peace!'[4]

"Oh, crowned queen of France, are you asleep?[5] Who prevents you from taking control of this side of your kin and stopping this deadly enterprise? Don't you see that your noble children's heritage hangs in the balance? You who are the mother of France's noble heirs, you respected princess, who else

---

3. See also Christine's indignation about burdening taxes in *The Book of the Body Politic* I.11 (in this volume).

4. Recall Christine's defense of the value of tears against a misogynist tradition in *The Book of the City of Ladies*, e.g., II.5, 33, 59, 60. On the Sabine women, cf. *The Book of the City of Ladies*, II.33; for Argia, see II.17. For discussions of the value of crying as at once a morally legitimate response to war and an active (rather than passive) political gesture, see Louise D'Arcens, "*Petit estat vesval :* Christine de Pizan's Grieving Body Politic," in *Healing the Body Politic: The Political Thought of Christine de Pizan*, ed. Karen Green and Constant J. Mews (Turnhout: Brepols, 2005) : 201–26; and Linda Lippig, "The Political Rhetoric of Christine de Pizan," in Brabant, *Politics, Gender and Genre*, 141–56.

5. Isabeau of Bavaria (wife of King Charles VI), whom Christine also urged in 1405 to play a more active, mediating role in her *Epistle to Isabeau of Bavaria, Queen of France*.

can take action but you? Who would dare disobey your power and authority[6] if you justly wish to impose peace?

"Come! All you wise men of this realm, unite with your queen! What purpose do you serve even as members of the king's council? Let everyone go to work! You used to intervene in even the most minor affairs! How can France take pride in so many wise heads if they don't find a way to protect her, to prevent the fountain of knowledge from being destroyed? Where are your initiatives and your wise arguments? Ah, clergy of France, will you let Fortune have her way like this? Why do you not organize processions with devout prayers? Do you not see the need? For our case already seems similar to that of Nineveh, which had attracted divine wrath through its excess of grievous sins and had thus been condemned by God to perish.[7] Our situation is extremely uncertain if the sentence is not revoked through the intercession of devout prayers.

"Make that happen, you people! You devout women, weep with compassion for this grievous tempest! Ah, France. France, a once glorious kingdom! Alas, what more can I say? Bitter tears flow like an endless stream upon my paper, leaving no dry space upon which to go on writing the excruciating lament that springs from my heart, inspired by the great compassion it feels for you. When I think about what will become of your reputation, my weary hands keep putting down the pen I use to write to clear the sight of my troubled eyes, touching the flow of tears that soaks my bosom and lap. For will you not be compared, from now on, to the cruel nations where brothers, cousins, and relatives kill each other, driven by envy and greed? Will they not say in reproach: 'Come on, you French, you boast of the sweet blood of your nontyrannical princes, and yet you revile us Guelfs and Ghibellines for our customs![8] Those have now been adopted in your own country! The seed has germinated and will not fail, and your lands have changed accordingly. Lower your horns, for your glory has been destroyed.'

6. See note for *The Book of the City of Ladies* II.68. On Christine's defense of the authority of Isabeau, see Tracy Adams, *Christine de Pizan and the Fight for France* (University Park: Pennsylvania State University Press, 2014). See also Karen Green, "Isabeau de Bavière and the Political Philosophy of Christine de Pizan," *Historical Reflections* 32, no. 2 (2006): 247–72.

7. Nineveh was a great city of the ancient world (seventh century BCE) located in Mesopotamia across the river from current-day Mosul. Civil war in Assyria due to dynastic challenges led to its sacking and decline.

8. The Guelfs and Ghibellines refer to rival political factions in the context of medieval states in Italy, the Guelfs supporting the claims of the pope to rule over contested lands, and the Ghibellines supporting the claims of the Holy Roman Emperor.

"Alas, my sweetest France! Is it true, then, that you are in such peril? Yes, absolutely! But something can still be done. God is merciful. Everything is not yet lost, however long it has been in peril.

"Oh, Duke of Berry, noble prince, most excellent ancestor and father of royal children, son of a King of France, brother and uncle, patriarch of the entire fleur-de-lis! How can your tender heart possibly bear to see you on that day, assembled in deadly battle array to raise wretched arms against your nephews? I do not believe that the memory of your natural, great love for their fathers and mothers, your beloved late brothers and sisters, could fail to make tears stream down your face like a fountain and make your heart feel as if it were breaking with such pity that you could hardly bear it. Alas! How painful to see the noblest uncle alive, uncle of three kings, six dukes, and a host of counts, in deadly battle against his own flesh with his nephews, who owe such a noble uncle as much reverence as they owe a father, ranged against him in battle! Oh, irreproachable, noble blood of France! How could you, noble Nature, endure that such shame should befall us (may that day never come!), that those who used to be the pillars of faith, supporters of the Church who always peacefully upheld the faith through their virtue, strength, and knowledge and who are called the most Christian peacemakers in all nations, devoted to concord, could find themselves in such a troubled situation?

"So come on now, noble Duke of Berry, most excellent prince, follow the divine law that commands peace. Firmly seize the bridle and stop this dishonorable army, at least until you have spoken with all parties. Go to Paris, the city of your father where you were born, which cries out for you with tears, sighs, and laments, demanding your presence and asking for your help. Go there without delay and console that city in distress. Approach your children and speak to them as a good father should, with words of correction if you see them doing wrong. Soothe them even as you reprove them, as your duty and responsibility require, bringing reason to both sides and explaining that whatever their discord, they must be the pillars, defenders, and supporters of the noble crown and protectors of the kingdom that never did them any harm. Tell them that this is more important than anything they may want from each other, and that they must not destroy the kingdom.

"For God's sake, noble Duke! Warn them that although each side is holding various talks to discuss their hope for victory in battle, saying such things as: 'We will be victorious and this is how we will do it,' this is just foolish boasting. We should not ignore that the outcome of every battle is different and cannot be known in advance. For man may propose, but Fortune disposes. What kind of victory was it for the king of Thebes, long ago, when he emerged from battle with only three knights, leaving all his other men dead on the field among all his enemies, decimated by the swords of his relatives and princes? God! What a tragic victory! And the king of Athens, mortally wounded in battle, what was his victory worth? Does anyone profit from such an outcome? Was Xerxes not crushed, he who had so many men that they covered valleys and mountains?[9]

"Is a rightful, just dispute worth pursuing? If it were, then King Saint Louis, who had won so many great victories, would not have been defeated at Tunis by the infidels. What better example is there to recognize God's marvelous disposition in letting a battle run its course when it is clearly evil and the chance that any good might come of it is highly doubtful. And above all, taking into account that wars and battles are always very dangerous and difficult to wage, fighting between such close relatives, conjoined by nature by a common bond of love, is without doubt truly perverse, dishonorable, and reprehensible, and can never achieve a good purpose. Alas, and if that is so—which it is—even if wars and battles are often waged over different causes and conflicts, there are more powerful and better reasons to avoid and end them and seek peace instead.

"May virtue vanquish victory! May a way be found to bring peace to those who are friends by nature but enemies by accident! Alas, may it please God that the effort and expenditure being made at present be used to promote peace rather than the opposite! I believe that this could be accomplished at a lesser cost and that, given a common resolve and true unanimity, this army could be converted into one that combats those who are natural enemies, employing good, loyal Frenchmen for that purpose instead of having them kill each other. God, what a joy that would be and what a tremendous and eternal honor to the kingdom!

"Oh, most honored prince, noble Duke of Berry, please hear me, for there is nothing that the human spirit cannot attain if it seeks to, especially if the purpose is just. And if you work toward this goal from now on, you will be called father of the realm, preserver of the crown and the noble lys, custodian of the noble lineage, savior of the noblemen and comforter of the people, and guardian of noble ladies, widows, and orphans. May the Holy

---

9. Xerxes was the king of Persia who led an invasion of Greece but was stopped by the much smaller allied forces of the Greek states, including Sparta and Athens.

Spirit, who brings peace to all, give you the determination and courage to bring this to a swift conclusion! Amen."

As for me, poor voice crying out in this kingdom, anxious for peace and well-being for everyone, may your servant Christine, inspired by the most just of intentions, live to see that day. Amen.

Written on the twenty-third day of August in the year of grace 1410.

INDEX